I0700888

SONG OF THE VALLEY

SONG OF THE VALLEY

A McCade Family Novel
Book One

BRITT HOWARD

Copyright © 2022 by Britt Howard.

All rights reserved. No part of this book may be used or reproduced in any form whatsoever without written permission except in the case of brief quotations in critical articles or reviews.

This book is a work of fiction. Names, characters, businesses, organizations, places, events and incidents either are the product of the author's imagination or are used fictitiously. Any resemblance to actual persons, living or dead, events, or locales is entirely coincidental.

Printed in the United States of America.

Cover design by Britt Howard

ISBN - Paperback: 979-8-218-07057-1

Library of Congress Control Number: 2022916822

First Edition: October 2022

www.britthoward.com

To the young woman searching for her place in the world—I dedicate this to you.

Mom and Gram—Thank you for helping me to find mine. I love you.

Delight yourself also in the LORD,
And He shall give you the desires of your heart.
Commit your way to the LORD,
Trust also in Him,
And He shall bring it to pass.
Psalm 37:4-5

Chapter One

MY NERVES WERE already shot by the time the plane crested to a stop on the landing strip at the Bozeman Yellowstone International Airport. It wasn't because of the flight. I wasn't afraid of flying. To be honest, I loved air travel.

Today, my typically anxious nerves were extra-jangly for a very specific reason. I lifted my hands and watched them tremble. I tried to steady them, rubbing them dry against my black joggers. Despite the icy cabin air coolers, I felt a bead of sweat roll down my spine.

After four years away, I was finally coming home. And I had no idea how to tell my three older brothers that I was planning to leave our Montana family homestead for good once the summer was over.

Only a week ago, I was walking across the stage in cap and gown, accepting my diploma at graduation. As I'd waited in the long procession to hear my name called, I'd been acutely aware of the eyes of my mother, sister, and brothers watching me from the audience. When the president of the college had paused to shake my hand as he passed me the diploma, I'd heard their shouts and whistles of joy. I remembered taking a deep breath and wondering if I could hold back the tears. The weight of the moment descended heavily upon me as I walked off the stage, my days at the University of Washington suddenly behind me. I had just completed my undergrad in nonprofit leadership and management, with a minor in marketing thrown in for good measure. All at once, the world felt like it was opening before me. Only one thing had been missing to make my day perfect.

I knew that most of my family thought it was cute, if rather strange, that I had majored in such an odd combination of subjects. As the youngest sibling, I was used to a fair amount of teasing. Anytime my education was brought up over the past few years, I had just smiled and changed the subject. But I had a plan.

If anyone was going to understand the career I was planning to pursue, it would be my older sister, Demi. She had moved away from home a few years ago to accept a modeling contract in New York City. She knew what it was like to grow up on a cattle ranch in the country and to wonder what else the world had to offer. I imagined that even my mother would understand my dreams. To all our shock, she'd turned out to be the adventurous one in our family. Over the past couple of years, she'd taken to traveling extensively, exploring all the places she and Dad had dreamed of visiting together.

The challenge would be convincing my protective brothers that I wasn't making a mistake. Like true Montana cowboys, they couldn't imagine leaving our valley home. Their idea of an adventure was riding a trail horse deep into the forest and camping next to a river.

On the holiday trips I'd taken home, my major had garnered plenty of jokes. My brothers had no inkling of the goals I'd been working toward for the last four years. They'd assumed I was planning to take a job within driving distance to our family ranch in Cascade Valley. Nothing could have been further from the truth.

This summer would change the course of my life forever and my stomach was in knots at the thought of finally voicing it aloud.

I lingered at the baggage carousel in the familiar, rustic airport, listening for the sound of Knox's rowdy laughter to announce that the McCade boys had entered the building. I kept trying to arrange my face into something less stressed-out and more *I'm-so-happy-to-be-home*. There wasn't a mirror in sight, so I couldn't be sure my efforts were working. As I walked toward the exterior sliding doors, I caught a glimpse of the mountain peaks in the distance through the floor-to-ceiling picture window. *I was home.*

Pulling two suitcases, a purse and a large duffel bag slung over my shoulder, I rehearsed my plan for the hundredth time.

Spend one last summer at home. Then apply for a job at a nonprofit organization in Europe and spend the next ten years traveling the world.

I'd saved every penny I could from working part-time jobs over the last four years. I had my passport and paperwork ready to go. My plan sounded simple enough. I had grown up in a small community in the southwestern corner of Montana, surrounded by trees, mountains, and meadows. Less than a thousand residents called our valley home. There were more cows than people. Small towns were cute, but I'd developed an itch for excitement by attending college in a large university city. It had only taken a few weeks as a wide-eyed freshman to realize that there was more to life than I'd ever imagined. Within the next few months, I would spread my wings and fly far away from Cascade Valley, Montana.

So far, I'd kept my dreams to myself. There wasn't any point in causing my brothers distress until I knew for sure where the future was taking me.

Sliding my finger across the screen of my cell phone, I refreshed my email notifications again to see if I'd received any replies to the applications that I'd submitted for administrative positions at several nonprofits across the Atlantic. So far, I'd sent applications to organizations in Spain, France, and Ukraine.

Nothing yet. I didn't care which one hired me. So long as I was out of the country by the end of the summer. The trouble with my brilliant plan was that the McCade boys would walk across hot coals before they willingly let their youngest sister go gallivanting across Europe by herself. I knew that their protectiveness toward me wasn't because they thought I couldn't take care of myself. They'd always encouraged my independent nature. But they were good men who believed it was their job to protect me.

I loved them for it. The thought of seeing them again put a genuine smile on my face. As I stepped outside into the mild, late spring heat, I finally caught sight of my tall brothers rushing across the road. My heart leaped and I ran forward, dragging my luggage awkwardly behind me as they dodged taxis and frazzled travelers in their mad dash to reach my side.

"Samantha McCade is in the building, people! Clear a path. Clear a path, please." Knox made a loudspeaker with his hands and yelled as he bounded toward me. He had turned twenty-four a few months ago. We were less than fifteen months apart in age and as he threw his arms around me in a bear hug, it hit me how much I had missed laughing with my childhood best friend every day. My luggage fell to the ground as I returned his hug.

"I didn't realize all three of you were coming to pick me up." I waved as my two remaining brothers closed the distance between us. Dean and Vincent McCade looked like they could be twins but were three years apart in age.

Vincent had opted out of college, but Dean had gone to graduate school in-state for an environmental science and ecology degree. As the head of our family's cattle ranch now, he had shifted the focus of operations to a regenerative agriculture approach. I was proud of what he was doing to restore the ecosystem in our Montana mountains. At thirty-two, Dean was the oldest McCade sibling. He nudged Knox aside to wrap me in his arms.

"Red, you're so grown up that I almost didn't recognize you." His blue eyes sparkled. The sound of my family's affectionate nickname for my bold, ginger-colored hair warmed my heart.

"Get out of here. You all saw me just a week ago."

"True. But you kids grow at an alarming rate." He winked at me, sneaking a kiss on the top of my head.

"Are you going to let me hug my little sister, or what?" Vincent moved in and I welcomed his hug. He may have resembled Dean with his dark beard and bright blue eyes, but their personalities were polar opposites. Dean had always been bold and serious, ever the wise, confident older brother. Vincent was strong and silent, but he had a wicked sense of dry humor.

People often overlooked Vincent, but I knew that nothing escaped his notice. He was my quiet, introverted brother, but he was also the one I'd always felt safest going to with my teenage-girl problems. He'd always had a listening ear and a wise answer for me.

"I missed you, little sis. I'm glad you're home," Vincent said with a smile.

"I'm glad to be home too," I replied, a sudden sharp pang of guilt hitting me. My brother's quick eyes caught my pained expression. He gave me a puzzled once-over. *Was my face really that transparent?* I flashed him a quick, reassuring smile.

"Did Mom make it to Florida ok?" I asked quickly, remembering that our mother was currently on her latest adventure. She was set to embark on a cruise to Aruba and Curacao in a few days and had informed us that she was planning to see where the summer took her next. I wondered if traveling alone had become a form of therapy to my mother. If our schedules had aligned, I would have invited myself along, just to keep her company.

"She did. And by this time, she's high on the seven seas." Knox answered my question. Hastily, he gathered my luggage and took off, running back across the street. A ride share driver honked at him in annoyance. "Last one to the truck is sitting in the back seat," he yelled over his shoulder.

We watched his tall frame move toward the parking lot. I laughed. The joke was on him. I preferred the back seat anyways.

It was going to be a couple hours' drive from Bozeman to our hometown. We lived in the country, just at the base of the mountains. My stomach was grumbling by the time I settled into the truck. There was a backpack crammed full of sandwiches on the floorboard. I wasn't shy about helping myself as we left the airport and took the streets toward home. Dean drove, as he always did. Knox had claimed the front passenger seat, so that left Vincent and I to hang out in the back.

"So, tell me all the news," I said as Dean pulled onto the highway and drove toward the range of mountain peaks that rose in the distance. The windows were down, and a breeze flirted playfully with my tousled curls. "What's everyone been up to in town since winter break?"

The five of us siblings kept up a lively group chat most of the time, but I still liked hearing about all of the goings-on of my hometown whenever I returned.

"It's been pretty quiet," Vincent replied. "A group of us took the church youth group fly fishing a few weeks ago. And a few of the guys took a camping trip to that spot we like up north."

My fingers tightened a little around the sandwich I was holding. "Oh, who went camping with you?"

"It was the three of us, Caleb, and a couple of guys from the Hobbs ranch across the valley," Knox replied.

"The weather was finally warm enough to take the herd back to the upper pastures last week," Dean spoke. "We've got the crew camping up there with them now. We're going to have to spend a lot of time away this summer, Sammie. I hope that's ok?"

I waved my hand. "Totally fine. I know this is your busiest season. There's plenty to keep myself occupied with at home."

"You could ride up there and spend a couple of weeks camping with us." Vincent's words came across as both a statement and a question.

I shook my head firmly. "No thank you. If I never ride a horse again, that's fine with me. And I can't imagine two weeks in the saddle as the herd grazes." I shuddered at the thought and pushed down the anxiety that stabbed at my insides. I had once been an avid rider, fearless on the back of a horse. Now I just did my best to avoid them whenever possible.

To my relief, Vincent didn't press the issue.

"Shelby Gentry came over to help us plant the garden," Knox interjected. "Pretty sure it was just to get Dean to ask her out though. Which he did."

"What?" I yelped. Shelby was a young military widow a few years older than Dean. Her husband had been killed in action two years ago. His loss had rocked Cascade Valley. Shelby had been transplanted into the community by marriage. While most of the younger singles seemed to avoid dating within the same circle they'd socialized in most of their lives, she wasn't a valley original, so it didn't surprise me that she was interested in my brother. "Are you dating the Cascade Valley Widow now?"

Dean winked at me in the rear-view mirror. "It's unofficial, but yes, we've gone out on a few dates. She's really nice. I'm sure you'll be seeing her a lot this summer. You'll like her, Sammie."

"I'm sure I will," I replied, deciding to keep my thoughts about my brother and Shelby dating to myself. I wasn't sure if I could see the two as a match. "What about you?" I nodded toward Vincent and Knox. "What surprises do you have for me? Do you have girlfriends you've been hiding too?"

"Oh, I get plenty of dates. But I'm still single and ready to mingle," Knox said, grinning back at me. "I'm just kidding," he continued without pause. "Brianna and I are still seeing each other. But Vincent's too shy to ever ask a woman out."

I cast my fellow introverted brother a commiserating look. He chuckled and shook his head.

Knox turned to me with an exaggerated wink. "We'll probably have a lot of new people coming through town this summer. Maybe ol' Vinnie will find love soon."

"Seriously though," Dean interjected. "Tourism has really gone up around here over the past couple of years. People come for the hiking, the fishing, and the lakes. Oh, and Caleb decided to open his ranch for that teen summer program again. So, we'll probably be working with him when we can."

"Oh, you guys are part of that?" I replied casually. My heart rate jumped, but I tried to keep my voice nonchalant. A stray butterfly fluttered through my stomach. A memory of the dark and serious cowboy jumped into my head.

Caleb Kane. Dean's childhood best friend and the man I'd publicly declared my mortal enemy four years ago. Unfortunately, he also happened to be one of the most attractive men I'd ever seen. It was too bad good looks didn't make up for horrible personalities and questionable character.

"Your favorite person," Dean joked. Knox chuckled and grinned at me.

I rolled my eyes in case Dean was watching. Caleb had been Dean's best friend since I was twelve, but our horse-ranching neighbor was now friends with all three of my brothers. There was a seven-year age gap between Caleb and I. He'd just been entering adulthood when I first met him and I'd endured a lot of teasing from him as a result. I didn't blame him for tormenting his friend's annoying kid sister though. I despised him for an entirely different reason. I still thought of Caleb as the man responsible for the darkest day of my life. He'd betrayed my trust and I'd never been able to forgive him. He probably still hated me too. After what I'd done....

And now we were going to be next door neighbors again. Silently, I resolved to hurry up and move to Europe, so that I never had to think of him again.

"What exactly is that summer camp thing about?" I asked, curiosity getting the better of me.

Dean took up the explanation. "Caleb opens his ranch to teens who have been having trouble in school or who are serving community service. They learn to take care of the horses. Everybody camps under the stars. He gives them riding lessons. It's mostly local kids from the state, but anyone is welcome. Just his way of giving back and trying to help kids who are struggling and need a reset. Almost all of the business owners around town pitch in with donations or volunteer their time. It's a community effort, really."

Cue the awwwws. Inwardly, I rolled my eyes. Of course, Caleb Kane would turn into a total do-gooder while I was away at college. It was just like the jerk to try to ruin my horrible opinion of him by doing something nice. He probably felt guilty for what he had done and was trying to make up for it. Well, it wasn't going to work on me. I knew that under the calm, cool exterior he presented to the world was a man who put profits first and people last. I just wished my brothers could see what a jerk he really was.

I turned to stare through the window as we left the city limits. Stubbornly, my nerves began to get the better of me. I may have thought Caleb rated next to pond scum, but it didn't help that I still thought he was the best-looking man I'd ever seen. At least,

I'd thought so the last time that I caught a glimpse of him months ago. He carried himself with a serious, unruffled demeanor that I'd always found mysterious and irresistible. Ever since the funeral, I'd gone out of my way to avoid him, but I still seemed to catch sight of him at least once every visit home. I'd see his dark brown hair or those broad, sculpted shoulders of his at church or in town and recognize him immediately. Sometimes, I'd catch him staring back at me with a scowl across his face. Our eyes would connect for a split second before we both looked away.

I was always left with a funny feeling in the pit of my stomach. Caleb was handsome, his shoulders and arms chiseled from chopping wood and slinging hay. His hair was always a touch too unruly and his skin was bronzed from years on the back of a horse under the broad Montana sky.

I totally hated him for what he had done, but I had to admit that it would be easier to forget about him if my insides didn't do a summersault every time I caught sight of his face. I just hoped that I could avoid him this summer.

Just over two hours away from Bozeman, Cascade Valley sat nestled at the foot of the mountains. Good summer weather, rolling meadows, and soft, fluffy grass made it the perfect place for ranchers to graze their stock.

Waves of sweet, fresh air hit me as we came over the final hill crest. I sucked in a deep breath, my auburn hair taking that as its cue to whip wildly in the wind. Swiftly, the truck ate up the straight road into town.

"So how are you feeling? Glad to be back, sis?" Knox grinned at me from the front seat.

I hesitated. "Oh yeah. Totally." I smiled and hoped that he couldn't see the uncertainty in my face. *Was I glad?* I wasn't entirely sure. Still, I found it a comfort to see the familiar shops and eateries of our quaint small town as we passed through Main Street. In the distance, I spotted the steeple of the white wooden church we'd attended since my childhood. The pretty country chapel was homebase for most of our activities as a community. The sight of it all was nostalgic and familiar, but my heart was ready to explore the village markets and rich cultures on the European continent.

The cattle ranch I'd grown up on was familiar and safe. But I couldn't wait to escape my tiny town again. Living in the city took some getting used to, but I loved it now. The country life was fine. Fresh air and all. *But,* I reminded myself firmly as we turned onto the road that would lead us home. *I am a college graduate and it's time to spread my wings and fly to places exciting and unknown. As safe as my home feels, I can't stay in my nest forever.*

Our land sat against the base of the farthest mountain in the valley, just before the road led up and into the forest. Eagerly, I breathed in the clear air. It smelled of hay and grass and pine. Though I did so grudgingly, I had to admit that I would miss this place. But city life had shown me that there was more to life than ranching. And that's what I wanted.

But am I on the right track, Lord? My mind wondered again to the prayer that always seemed to linger foremost in my mind. My brothers' chatter carried throughout the truck, but I only half-listened. I'd kept up my daily Bible study habit throughout college and I was glad I had. Scripture had sustained me throughout the long four years. The verses from Psalm 37 I'd been studying on the plane just that morning floated through my mind. *'Commit your way to the Lord, Trust also in Him, And He shall bring it to pass.' I want to do something great for You, Lord. This is a good plan. Right?*

My thoughts were pulled away by the sight of a black metal gate looming up on the left. The tall, wrought-iron gate led down a long, pine-lined path to the stables and charming white farmhouse that I knew sat at the end. Discretely, I eyed the sign hanging above it.

Kane Arabian Ranch: Breeders of Champions.

Caleb's family owned a few hundred acres of pasture, their land bordering the edge of the Montana forest. The Kane's horses were highly sought after all over the world. His father had been raising the prize-winning Arabians for twenty years and the rolling waves of light green grass, perfectly maintained fences, red stables, and all-weather arena were a testament to how successful and prosperous his careful cultivation had been.

Our own pine-lined driveway came into view as I was still mulling over how I was going to manage to avoid Caleb while I was in town for the summer. So far, I'd only been home for short visits since moving to Seattle for college. I'd spent most of my summers and holidays working a part-time job to pad my savings account. So there had been little opportunity to run into each other. It was going to take some effort to stay out of each other's way. Dean turned off the road toward our property and we jostled over a dip in the dirt. Hopefully, Caleb was just as eager to avoid me when he learned that I was back home. I doubted that either of us wanted to stir that pot again. He knew what had happened the last time that I got angry with him. A wave of satisfaction came over my heart as I considered that he was just as motivated to avoid me as I was to avoid him.

It was a satisfaction that was rudely interrupted by the sight of a conspicuous black Ford F150 parked at the end of our driveway, right next to our butter yellow farmhouse. My brothers all drove Chevys.

"Um, who's truck is that?" I pointed a finger accusingly at the vehicle.

"Uh, Caleb's truck," Knox said, enunciating each word like he was talking to a five-year old.

"What is it doing here?" I muttered through gritted teeth.

Knox jumped out as soon as Dean hit the brake. "Charlie couldn't make it today. So, Caleb offered to come over to check on the animals. You didn't think they could just be alone all day, did you?"

Charlie was the older man who came to check on Mom and the animals when my brothers were away. He was retired and lived in a cabin in the forest a few miles north. I would have much preferred to see his round welcoming face to the reality I now faced. I hadn't even stepped out of the truck, and already, I felt like sinking through the floorboard and disappearing into the ground. Knox jogged toward the Ford just as a tall man came into view.

Caleb Kane walked out of our barn with all the leisure and grace of a tomcat out for a stroll. Frozen, I sat on my hands, watching him through the bug-spattered windshield. Should I be furious that our arrival home had placed us here at the exact time my sworn enemy was sashaying out of our barn? Or should I think it ironic that here I was, fresh from college, and the first person I saw back home was the one person I never wanted to see again?

I knew I would look like an idiot if I just sat there until he left though. Shoving open the door, I jumped to the ground. Grabbing my duffel bag, I swung the straps over my shoulder, straightened my posture, and lifted my chin. He was probably just as surprised as I was that our presence had overlapped. Dean, Vincent, and Knox were gathered around him now, the four men slapping each other's backs and leaning against the Ford's tailgate. Their friendship irritated me. My brothers were too forgiving. Hopefully, I could just slip past them and disappear into the house before he noticed me.

On the off chance that Caleb was watching though, I kept my gaze fixed firmly on the porch. I speed-walked up the steps, the safety of my front door nearly within my grasp. I was so focused on getting indoors that it was little wonder that I nearly tripped and dropped my bag when a deep, familiar voice suddenly called my name.

"Samantha."

Slowly, I stopped mid-step. The moment seemed to slow. I froze, wondering if I'd heard correctly.

"Samantha." His voice would forever be etched into my memory. A shiver ran across my skin. I swallowed, trying to fix my face into a nonchalant expression, and slowly spun to face him. The sight of Caleb at the base of the porch nearly made me jump out of my skin. All six feet of him stared up at me. He'd grown a beard since I'd seen him last.

That beard suits him. The thought popped unbidden into my brain. I frowned to cover my reaction. In response, his mouth tightened into a straight line under the beard. His whiskey brown eyes flashed with what I assumed was a strong mutual bitterness.

"I'm surprised to see you here," I said stiffly, crossing my arms across my chest. I kept my gaze narrowed in on his face. I would have been better off looking anywhere but at Caleb. Instantly, my mouth went dry. It was just the two of us in the yard. My brothers had moved toward the barn to check on the animals. Caleb had always made me feel so young and awkward around him. Our seven-year age gap had always meant that I was the annoying kid sister, always underfoot and begging my brothers to let me join on the adventures they always seemed to be having.

Things had changed between Caleb and I after I'd turned eighteen. Our age gap had felt different back then....

But now I was a college graduate. A twenty-three-year-old woman with a degree and the plans to match. I wasn't going to let my brothers' older friend intimidate me. Even if his husky voice did sound like the rumbling of thunder on a stormy night.

"I'm surprised to see you back in Cascade Valley," he replied.

"I'll bet you are," I said, a sarcastic edge to my voice. My eyes narrowed. I was shocked that he'd even spoken to me. We hadn't spoken in years, and I would have been perfectly fine if we hadn't exchanged words for twenty more. I tossed my long hair back over my shoulder, hoping that I looked like a well-educated Seattle woman just passing through countryville.

"Are you planning to stick around?"

"Maybe," I said curtly. "Please try to stay out of my way while I'm here. I'll give you the same courtesy."

A harsh sound came out of his throat. "Or what? You'll get mad and call the sheriff on me again?" Caleb's words were thrown down like a gauntlet between us.

I stiffened, drawing myself up to my full height. We stared each other down in hostile silence. With an exasperated sound, Caleb was the first to break eye contact. He turned away and walked quickly toward his truck.

I stared after him for a moment, then hurried into the house, yanking open the creaking screen door, resisting the urge to turn around and watch him walk away. My hands shook as a dozen sharp-tongued comebacks popped into my brain. But I couldn't resist glancing back over my shoulder as the truck's engine roared to life.

I caught sight of my reflection in the entryway mirror as I turned. Horrified, I stared at my disheveled, frizzy, wind-blown hair and resisted the urge to scream.

"And that's what you get, Sammie," I whispered to my reflection. "So much for being the cool, mysterious woman of the world you were pretending to be a minute ago. Next time, check a mirror. Or just keep walking."

. . .

The first time I had really noticed Caleb as more than just my older brother's best friend was about a year before I graduated from high school. He was a frequent visitor at our house before that, but I hadn't given him much thought. Looking back, I knew I had annoyed him by constantly pestering my brothers to go riding or to practice shooting with me. Dean and Vincent tried to be kind and included Knox and I when they could, but I often caught Caleb rolling his eyes and spurring his horse on faster to outpace me.

As I'd moved through high school, he was usually the one planning some activity that I couldn't be part of, citing the danger as a reason I couldn't tag along. Sometimes though, I would find him in a good mood, and when that happened, I often tried to convince him to give me pointers on riding horses through the untamed Montana wilderness. I went to his family's ranch and rode their Arabians whenever I could. Those were the days. When we ran wild and free across the mountains. Before our family changed forever.

I became aware of just how tall and awkward I was as junior year ended. Suddenly, I was all legs and arms and freckles and frizzy hair. I grew to hate all my clothes, and I began to beg my poised and beautiful sister, Demi, to give me makeup lessons. Back then, it had been hard to imagine that I would ever be anything more than the ugly duckling of the family.

During planting season of my senior year, my dad had hired Caleb to help get the crops into the ground. The future hay harvest would feed our cattle during the long winter. As I passed my eighteenth birthday and blossomed into womanhood, all at once, Caleb put himself on my radar in a big way. He was older, he knew everything there was to know about horses, and those ranch-formed muscles seemed to grow bigger and harder every year.

Suddenly, I hadn't been able to keep my eyes off him. My palms would sweat, and my cheeks would turn red anytime he so much as looked toward or spoke to me. I tried to work as hard as the others that spring to prove that I wasn't just an awkward kid, but an adult to be taken seriously.

It was a slow shift but Caleb finally stopped treating me as if I was an adolescent nuisance. Slowly, I felt something change. We weren't exactly friends. But something felt different between us after my birthday. His customary brusqueness abated. If our paths crossed, he would step out of my way and raise his hand to tip the brim of his hat in my direction. He began to tease me about my wild red hair, my height, and my love for the outdoors, but I hadn't minded. As that spring had progressed, I found us sitting and talking more and more. I picked his brain about horsemanship and running a top tier breeding program. And he began to seem genuinely interested in my future plans. I perked up every time his old Ford pickup truck came rumbling up our driveway. I was basking in the heady thrill of my crush.

But my secret, adolescent crush on Caleb took a hard blow that spring. For years, it had been tradition for Dad to take my brothers and I on a camping trip to the mountains beyond the national forest. Mom always stayed behind with my older sister and did girly things. I preferred hanging out with the boys.

It was our tradition to hike to a remote, glacial lake on top of the mountain, pitch our tents, and spend the first week after school ended feasting on the fresh trout we caught in the lake. Dean, Vincent, and Knox always laughed at me because I would stick four or five books into my backpack and then grumble about how heavy they were as we hiked. But sprawling on the lake shore, the cool breeze and warm sun playing across my skin as I read, was always heaven. I hadn't told anyone, but that year was going to be extra special for me. I had just graduated from high school. It would be the last summer that I spent at home before I left for college, and I wanted to make as many memories with my family as I could.

But that was the summer that everything changed.

The morning we were scheduled to leave, I ran downstairs with my hiking gear already on, backpack packed and ready to go. A cacophony of male voices met my ears as I descended the stairs. I walked into the kitchen to find my dad, brothers, and Caleb standing around the island, a map spread on the counter in front of them. Demi lounged at the table, her head bent over a fashion magazine. She'd been in New

York for the past year, working a modeling contract, but was with us for a summer visit.

Caleb was speaking, his pointer finger stabbing at a spot on the map. The corded muscles flexed on his bronzed forearms. His hair had been shaggy and long then, grazing the collar of his usual faded blue t-shirt. He'd been more animated than usual, his face lit up as he talked to my dad.

My heart had done the little flip-flop thing that it usually did when he was in the room. I straightened my posture, wondering suddenly if my hiking pants were unflattering.

"It's the coolest spot, Dad," I heard Dean say. "The salmon in the river are at least this big." He held up his hands as a measurement.

"I love the sound of that." My dad had grinned in response. "I'm game if you boys are? Let's do it."

"Do what?" I asked, speaking for the first time.

"The only thing is, it's an expert level hike. There are some treacherous spots where the trail gets dangerous," Caleb interjected, ignoring my question.

"I think we can handle it," Dad said. I saw him glance in my direction and a sinking feeling immediately entered the pit of my stomach.

"What are you guys talking about?" I tried again.

Dad came over to me, his burly hands settling gently on my shoulders. "We're thinking of changing up our camping trip destination this year. Caleb is coming with us, and he and Dean just told us about a new fishing spot along the river."

"Ok? And?" My heart had bubbled over at the thought that Caleb was coming with us. I could hardly hold myself still. Obviously,

I knew that he was twenty-five and my girlish crush was immature and impossible. But maybe on this trip, he would see that I wasn't just a little kid anymore. I was eighteen and I could hold my own in the forest.

"It's treacherous in some spots, Mr. McCade. I'm honestly not sure if it would be a good idea for Samantha to come along."

I looked at Caleb in shock and caught him staring straight at me. His expression had shuttered and was completely unreadable. *Was he seriously hijacking our summer tradition and cutting me out of it?*

"Dad," I protested, already on the defensive.

"Honey," Dad replied, his brow furrowing the way it did when he was about to deliver some bad news. "We really want to try this fishing spot. We can do a camping trip around here later this summer, can't we? And besides, I think your mom would love to take you and Demi to Bozeman so she can pamper both of you girls." He had whispered the last bit conspiratorially in my ear.

My mouth had opened, ready to protest. I wasn't a child anymore. I could handle a tough hike just as well as the men. The forest was my second home. But from the corner of my eye, I watched Mom step toward me. Instantly, my heart sank into my boots. The look on her face said it all. I wasn't going on the camping trip this year and it wouldn't do any good to argue.

Mom's word was final and there was no point in arguing.

That hadn't stopped me from whipping my head around Dad's arm to glare bitterly at Caleb. I blamed him. No one had raised an objection to me going until Caleb brought it up and I wanted to know why.

Unperturbed, Caleb had stared back at me. I scowled at him.

"This is your fault." I'd hissed under my breath at him on my way out of the room a few minutes later. My brothers and dad were bent over the map again, eagerly discussing the extra supplies they'd need to take.

Caleb had simply shrugged, his hair brushing his collar as he bent his head to look down at me. "Enjoy your girls' weekend. Maybe you'll get a manicure and a haircut." I'd realized later he was only teasing, but in the moment, I had been instantly enraged.

"You're nothing but a jerk, Caleb." I'd tossed my head and struggled to hold back the fury. I hadn't meant it, but I was mad. The only thing preventing me from yelling the words at him was the presence of my mother packing sandwiches for the trip on the other side of the room.

Caleb's hand had shot out then and he'd caught my wrist between strong fingers. My skin had burned where he touched me. His head inclined lower toward mine. His voice grew husky. "I'm sorry, Red. I'm just trying to protect you. I promise. It can be dangerous. If you fell...."

Immediately, my anger had cooled. My brain tried to understand his quiet tone even as I searched for a retort.

"I just don't want you to get hurt up there. There will be another camping trip this summer with your family. Don't be mad at me, ok?" The corners of Caleb's mouth had turned up in his rare, but unforgettable smile.

It was the way his whiskey-colored eyes had looked at me. Like he genuinely didn't want me to get hurt. Like he was genuinely sorry he had ruined my trip. My insides had turned to mush, and I'd simply nodded. If Caleb didn't want me to get hurt on the mountain, I decided to let go of my anger and trust him. I was still disappointed, but in the moment, the fact that he'd thought of my safety had made me melt.

Little did I know that trusting Caleb would soon be the worst mistake of my life.

Chapter Two

DAD HAD PASSED away two-and-a-half months later, three weeks before college classes began in the fall. It happened while he was out checking the fence line alone. That morning, he had risen early like he usually did and saddled his newest colt to ride. The animal was a sleek, white, almost four-year-old Arabian who had just joined our ranch that spring. Lithe, yet muscular, with lustrous eyes and a proud, scooped nose, all of us had been eager to welcome the handsome horse.

Later, after it happened, we speculated that Dad had planned to use an easy day in the pasture as a teaching moment for the colt, who had already gone through nearly a year of saddle training. Dad had fallen in love with the young horse and had purchased him for recreational riding only. Though he had never been intended to work with the stock, we all knew that an essential part of the colt's training was exposure to various settings. No one wanted a horse that was easy to spook on an unpredictable Montana range. Dad had ridden one of the stock horses to work in the pasture a thousand times. It had been a small job and a beautiful morning.

The first hint we'd had that something was wrong was when the colt came thundering into the yard, riderless, his mouth foaming, the sweat slick and dirty on his hindquarters. I'd run up to him to grab the dangling loop of his bridle, my palm smoothing over the frightened animal's muzzle to calm him.

The wild, crazed look in his eyes would never leave my memory.

Dean, Vincent, and Knox had taken off running for the quads, gunning them to roar toward the dusty direction that the colt had come.

They'd found Dad in the east pasture. He was already gone. The coroner's report said that he'd hit the back of his head on a rock during the fall. He had speculated that something had spooked the colt. A rattlesnake or small animal darting across the path may have been enough to cause the inexperienced horse to buck, catching Dad off guard.

One minute he was with us. The next he was gone.

A few days later, when we all filed into the church for the funeral, I'd caught sight of Caleb, standing with his parents in the second row of pews. Most of the town had gathered to remember my father. We'd lived in the valley for all my life and our community church had rallied around us. I hadn't left my room for days and though Caleb had been at our house almost constantly, it was the first time I'd seen him since Dad's accident. His deep brown eyes had caught mine as I glared in his direction. His hands were holding a black cowboy hat, which he twisted around and around. Nervously, his eyes flashed up at me. And in that moment something had snapped in my head.

My mother had asked me to read my dad's favorite passage of Scripture during the memorial service. He'd read it aloud to us after dinner the night before he'd passed, and she didn't think that she would be able to get out the words. I didn't think I could either, but I'd wanted to honor my dad's memory somehow.

But when I'd climbed the steps to the podium of our old, childhood church and turned to face the crowd, all I could focus on was Caleb's grim face in the second row.

Carefully, I'd set my dad's Bible on the podium and straightened my shoulders. My arm had raised, and my finger extended in an accusing point. I'd looked Caleb straight in the eye.

"This is your fault," I'd screamed at him. "You sold him that horse. You knew that horse was bad. And you sold it to him anyway. You're the reason my dad is dead. You should be in jail, Caleb Kane. I will never forgive you. I *hate* you."

My voice had died away. You could have heard a pin drop in the church after that.

Vincent had hurried up the steps to my side, turning my face into his chest, *ssshhhing* me like I was a little girl. I had sobbed then, holding onto my calm, quiet brother for dear life. Beside me, I heard my mother and sister crying. A moment later, there was a loud commotion.

"Please move." Caleb's deep voice had shattered the stunned room. My head lifted in time to see him pushing his way past the other people in the pew. His mouth was set into a tight line and his eyes were fixed on the floor. Taking long strides, he'd slammed into the church doors, the bright summer sun immediately enveloping his retreating form. His parents had flashed me a stricken look and hurried after him. They hadn't attended the graveside service and I'd learned later that the sheriff had asked Caleb and his dad to come to the station for a talk.

I had vowed that day to hate Caleb Kane forever.

.   .   .

"Seriously, you should consider finding some kind of summer volunteer program to get involved in." Amanda's girlish voice filtered through the phone.

I had put my friend's call on speaker while I unpacked my luggage. It felt strange to carefully lay all my Seattle clothes into my oak childhood dresser. Unpacking was only reminding me how useless most of these clothes would be for a summer on the ranch. They were far too flimsy and pretty for cleaning the chicken coop and weeding the garden.

Sighing, I walked to my closet and slid open the door. Worn in jeans and flannel shirts hung in a lonely group to one side. My old work boots were tossed on the floor. My hiking gear was shoved in the corner. Forget looking cute; these items would be much more practical for the Montana summer. I wouldn't have many occasions to get dressed up out here.

"I'm out here in the middle of nowhere, Amanda." I yanked a pair of Levi's from their hanger. "Where am I supposed to volunteer? Should I offer to read stories to the cows?"

She laughed. "I'm just saying, when you start reaching out to Europe, they will love that you kept yourself busy this summer doing something good. It takes your reputation from *I'm a nice girl with a degree* to *I'm so passionate about this that I spent my whole summer volunteering.* Make sense?"

"Yes." I sighed again, pulling a hunter green t-shirt over my head. "It makes sense. Your student advisor side just can't help butting into every conversation, can it?"

Amanda clicked her tongue. "Nope. It's just who I am."

Knox's loud voice echoed through the house. "Dinner's ready."

"I've got to go," I said to Amanda. "Keep in touch?"

"Always, babe. Besides, I need you to send me pictures of that hot cowboy."

"Who? You mean Caleb?" I rolled my eyes. I'd mentioned him to her one time and she'd been bugging me for a photo ever since. "Yeah, I despise him, so I'm probably not going to be having him pose for photos for me anytime soon."

"Awww," Amanda laughed. "Just one. For me. You may despise him, but that doesn't erase the fact that you said he's gorgeous. Don't deny other people their dreams just because you hold a grudge."

"You're impossible. I should never have mentioned him to you." I laughed and rolled my eyes. "Goodbye."

Hanging up, I took an extra minute to run a brush through my hair. It fell down my back in gingered curls that knotted easily. I used a silk scrunchie to pull the mane up into a high ponytail. My eyes scrutinized my face, eyeballing every one of the freckles that lay scattered across my nose and cheeks with disapproval. Apple green eyes stared back at my reflection. I was every bit a ginger and there was no way around that fact.

Ruefully, I wished for the thousandth time that I had my brothers' dark, moody complexions. Even our sister, Demi, had silky brown hair, paired with creamy skin, high cheekbones, and stunning emerald eyes. All my siblings had inherited their looks from our mom. The only ginger in our family had been Dad and apparently, I was his twin, manifested in the flesh.

My heart stabbed me at the memory of his jovial, twinkling face. I wished he was here so that I could seek his guidance for my future. Blinking back sudden tears, I turned away from the mirror and headed downstairs.

"Samantha," Knox's voice boomed just as I entered the kitchen.

"Hold your horses. I'm here," I said. I eyed the table with mistrust. A serving platter piled high with spaghetti sat in the middle of the table. A green salad had been tucked to the side. I smelled the fragrant scent of garlic and toasted bread wafting from the oven. "Who prepared this food? Am I going to get poisoned by your atrocious cooking?"

"I'll have you know that we have become excellent cooks," Vincent spoke up, his hands full of icy water glasses that he distributed around the table. "For three lonely bachelors. Mom felt bad for leaving us alone when she takes her trips, so we made her teach us how to cook. But if anyone gets poisoned tonight, it's totally Dean's fault."

My bare feet padded toward the refrigerator to see if my favorite salad dressing was in stock. Donning a pair of oven mitts, Dean leaned over the oven and pulled out a baking sheet of garlic bread.

"Oh, I put something extra special in your portion," he growled menacingly in Vincent's direction. But I caught the wink that he threw my way.

Some things never changed. I shook my head and turned back to the refrigerator, my fingers closing around the handle. My eyes caught sight of a flyer attached to the metal door with a magnet. Two rows of smiling teens stared back at me from a slightly blurry photo.

Kane Arabian Summer Camp for Teens. Horseback riding lessons, educational activities, and character-building challenges.

The words were printed in a standard block font. It wasn't fancy or eye-catching in any way. If this was Caleb's doing, he really needed some help in the marketing department. But I got the gist. Briefly, I wondered how much he had paid these kids to pretend to be having fun.

Carrying the flyer back to the table with me, I laid it next to my plate, continuing to stare at it thoughtfully. It pained me to see his name in print, but the concept was interesting, and my marketing minor couldn't help but kick in. At this point, it was instinct to dissect the flyer and analyze how I could improve it. And there were a lot of improvements that could be made. To begin with, that atrocious font.

I set the flyer aside as we joined hands and prayed over our meal. But when we all raised our heads, I picked up the flyer again to study it. Knox caught sight of the flyer as he piled spaghetti onto his plate. "It's a really cool program," he said, nodding toward the paper.

"Oh yeah? What does Caleb do? Make the kids muck out the stalls for him all summer and call it 'character building?'" I joked, using my fingers to make air quotes above my head.

"It's a lot more than that. But you can ask him about it yourself." Dean handed me the salad bowl. "He's coming over tonight."

My horror must have manifested itself on my face because all three of my brothers exchanged amused looks. "What do you mean? He's coming over here?"

"It's Sunday night. He always comes over to drink a soda and hang out for a while. The girls usually come over too since we don't always get to see them during the week."

"Ok, your girlfriends coming over is fine. But Caleb?" I sputtered.

"I'm here."

Dean looked at me with confusion, one eyebrow lifted higher than the other. "And? What difference does that make, Sammie? Wait, this isn't still about that grudge you've been holding all these years? I thought you had moved past that and forgiven the Kane family. They really don't deserve your resentment."

"You've got to squash that," Knox said. "Caleb is good people. Dad's accident wasn't the Kane family's fault. Whatever grudge you're still holding is misplaced."

"We dealt with that long ago," Vincent added.

I rolled my eyes and busied myself tearing my garlic bread into tiny, inedible pieces. The sharp prick of tears threatened to spill over my eyelids. Resolutely, I blinked them back and tossed my head.

No. Mr. Kane and Caleb might not have spooked Dad's horse, causing his accident and tearing apart our lives forever. But they were the ones who had sold the horse to him. I blamed them for selling my dad an unruly colt and no one would convince me otherwise. Just because my brothers had never blamed Caleb or his family didn't mean that I would let go of the grudge that I held.

I distinctly remembered being at the Kane's house for dinner one late spring weekend, a short time before the camping fiasco. My eighteenth birthday had passed a few months before. The spring air had been balmy, and I'd kept sneaking looks toward Caleb from across the outdoor table. It had been piled high with succulent barbeque and platters of sides that my mother and Mrs. Kane had prepared.

Caleb was his usual gorgeous self, his jaw chiseled and strong, and his voice firm as he assessed the value of this year's herd with my dad. Caleb hadn't spoken to me much that night, but he'd caught my eye several times and sent a smile my direction. Each smile had sent a thrill down my spine.

After dinner, I was supposed to be helping my mom and Mrs. Kane clean up. But halfway through the dishes, I had slipped away to sneak a peek at the horses tucked into their stalls for the night. I loved the Arabians that the Kane family bred and raised. They were different than the quarter horses we kept for work on the ranch. More elegant and refined than the sturdy horses I was used to. Over the years, I'd been over many times to ride the sweet mares around the pasture whenever I could. They were sleek horses, with smart, inquisitive personalities. I loved their proud, wedge-shaped heads and long, arching necks.

It was silly, but I'd always thought that Caleb resembled one of his Arabians. They moved through life with the same striking style of energy, intelligence, and courage. His father had developed an exquisite line and Caleb was carrying on his father's passion for the breed.

Voices had filtered from the stable as I approached. Rather than announce my presence, I'd poked my head in to see who it was. The light was dim, the hay-scented interior lit by a row of lightbulbs suspended from the ceiling. Caleb was standing with Dad and my brothers at the far end of the stable. Dad was running his hand up and down the dished nose of a handsome white colt.

"He's a beauty, Caleb. Shoot, what a stunner of a horse," I'd overheard Dad say.

"My dad's planning to put him up for sale," Caleb replied, his voice rueful as he smoothed a hand over the colt's hindquarters.

"Why?" Dad and Dean said simultaneously.

In the dim light of the barn, I watched Caleb shrug. "He has a few defects that disqualify him for shows or stud services. Hate to see this guy leave the ranch though. Something so special about him."

My eyes had caught the look that Dad and Dean exchanged. Dad threw a glance back to see if the boys were watching.

"Well, son. It seems a shame to let this boy out of the family. Why don't I talk to your dad about buying him? I've been thinking about getting a horse just to ride."

Caleb's enthusiasm had radiated through the stable. "Seriously, Mr. McCade? I would love to see him go to your ranch. He is still in training though. He's probably going to need another year."

"We can continue his training just as well at our place. I'm going to go talk to your dad right now," Dad said. My brothers trailed after him as he strode from the stable in search of Mr. Kane. Caleb had stayed behind, his hands gently stroking the white horse's mane. I waited until they left, then slipped into the dimly lit space.

"He's beautiful." I'd gathered my courage and spoken in the quiet stable. Caleb straightened and glanced over his shoulder toward me.

"He is," he replied.

Boldly, I'd approached the stall. My hand came up to stroke the colt's muzzle, lingering at the soft velvet on his nose. I was acutely aware of the tall man leaning against the stall wall next to me. My heart beat an erratic rhythm against my chest, but I managed to hold my voice steady. "Is my dad going to buy him?"

Caleb nodded. "Looks that way."

"Will you teach me to ride him?"

He had laughed then. "He's feisty. There aren't many girls who could handle this much horse."

"Oh, I'm feisty too. I think I could handle him," I replied, my temper flashing instantly. "I'm eighteen now, you know? And I've been riding since I was a child."

"You certainly are a feisty one," Caleb had looked at me, amusement simmering in his eyes. "But eighteen or not, I think I'd rather you stay off this horse. Young colts can be unpredictable, you know. I wouldn't want to see you getting hurt."

"Why would you care if I got hurt?" I was still annoyed with him.

"Oh, I would care," he said gruffly. His gaze rested on me thoughtfully. "You know, you're sure going to keep your future husband on his toes someday. I like that about you though. You're rather fun." His words made me blush.

Unexpectedly, his hand reached toward me. Instinctively, I'd jumped back. The white colt jerked, his hooves restless in the straw bedding. "Hold still, Samantha," Caleb said. "You've got something in your hair."

"Oh." I made myself hold still while Caleb plucked a small beetle from my locks.

"You have pretty hair," he said, running one of my curls through his fingers.

"Um, thanks." Instantly, I felt myself flush from head to toe.

"And really pretty eyes," he had continued.

"Thanks," I replied shyly again, inwardly thrilling with the compliments. "Are you saying you think I'm pretty?"

"Yeah, I guess that's what I'm saying." He let out an awkward chuckle. Suddenly, Caleb's eyes had focused intensely on my face. He'd opened his mouth to speak, then closed it again. I had a flash of wondering if it were possible that Caleb was just as shy and awkward around me as I felt around him. Could it be that all of his teasing secretly meant that Caleb liked me? The thought made me go still. The stable became eerily quiet, the only sound the soft rustling of the horses in their stalls. We didn't break eye contact until the sound of excited, male voices approached the barn.

I had slipped away then, running back to the house before Mom discovered that I was missing. But my heart felt like it was floating on a cloud the rest of the night.

Later that evening, I'd been curled up on the back porch with my dessert. Everyone else was inside, but I preferred to watch the soft fading of the twilight as the sun dipped behind the mountains. I had so much on my mind and I wanted to be alone to think. A pair of masculine voices just around the corner of the house had broken my reverie. I'd shrunk back into the wicker chair, not wanting to disrupt the snippets of their conversation that I could hear.

"A great opportunity…." Broken snatches of Caleb's voice was the first I'd recognized. "…and we won't get top dollar anywhere else."

"I don't know." I recognized Mr. Kane's voice. "Seems like taking advantage."

"They are insisting, Dad," Caleb said.

"…not sure I'm ready to see the horse go." Mr. Kane's voice had faded as they turned and walked away from the house.

"I say we sell," Caleb had replied. And then their voices had disappeared into the night. I'd sat until the darkness descended, daydreaming of a future that was suddenly blossoming in my imagination.

• • •

"Earth to Samantha," Knox waved his hand in front of my face.

"Oh, sorry. I was thinking," I started, accepting the platter of spaghetti from him.

As I twirled the noodles on my fork, I remembered why Dad had wanted the colt. Even in the dimness of the painful memories I'd pushed away, he had been a handsome animal. But it was clear now that he'd needed more time and training before he was rider-ready. My dad had been riding for many years, but he'd been too excited to take him out. The Kane's should have warned him about the spirited animal's lack of range training. To me, that meant that Caleb was responsible, at least indirectly, for my dad's accident. The memory of overhearing that broken conversation on the porch filled my mind. Long ago, I'd convinced myself that Caleb had deliberately sold my dad an unruly, wild colt and I despised him for it. Nothing had ever come of my angry funeral declaration that Caleb was responsible, but that didn't let him off the hook.

No matter how many excuses my brothers tried to make, my opinion of Caleb wasn't going to change.

Chapter Three

DESPITE THE FACT that I thought Caleb Kane rated next to the scum on the bottom of the old pond out back, I decided not to let his presence run me out of my own house. This was my first night back in my childhood home. And my last summer on the ranch. I would do whatever I pleased, even if that meant being uncomfortable but keeping my dignity.

When I heard the roar of his Ford coming down the driveway, my instinct was to escape to my own room. But I resisted, like a well-educated college graduate, who didn't let cowboys dictate her actions. The thought of seeing him face-to-face for the second time that day was about as appealing as picking up a rattlesnake by the tail. But I took the steaming mug of peppermint tea that I had just prepared and a romance novel that I'd purchased in the airport book shop and flounced myself to the porch swing where I pointedly ignored him as he climbed the steps and entered the house.

He might have caught me off guard before, with my hair wind-blown and my composure flustered, but this time Caleb would see who I actually was: A woman with a plan who had no time for the likes of a country cowboy like himself. No matter how hard he tried to pick a fight, he wasn't going to intimidate me.

Ignoring him was easier said than done though when I realized that the men were planning to file back onto the porch one by one. Shelby and Brianna had already arrived. They both greeted me with affectionate hugs and immediately began plying me with questions about Seattle. Now, cold bottles of soda in hand, the group threw themselves down on the opposite side of the porch. Their laughter bounced against the planked ceiling, Knox's teasing tones echoing loudly above the rest per usual.

It took me about ten seconds to realize that Caleb was directly in my line of sight. All I had to do was subtly turn my head and look out of the corner of my eye to see him. He had taken a seat facing me on an old wicker chair. The chair had once been white but had long been whittled down by the heat and cold to a bone gray. His long legs stretched out on the porch, and he held the soda in his large hand. He looked every bit the true, Montana-bred country boy, down to his worn-in Wranglers and dusty boots.

Rebelliously, my stomach flip-flopped with sudden awareness of him. We were twenty feet apart and all I could feel was his presence sizzling in the air between us. His hair was a little shorter and neater than I remembered it, but it still swept back from his rugged face in dark waves. His body, which used to be lanky and thin, had filled out over the years. He was all man now, all broad shoulders and the thick, toned muscles of a rancher. None of the boyishness of years ago was left. And his fine-boned, chiseled face was even more handsome than I'd remembered. The glances I snuck toward his relaxed form made my mouth go dry.

Maybe I should sneak a photo for Amanda sometime after all? She would drool over the sight of him.

Thinking of Amanda, I reached into my jeans pocket and pulled out my phone to reread the flurry of texts she had sent me during dinner.

AMANDA: Seriously, girl, think about finding a summer program.

AMANDA: You're going to have to stand out from the crowd and prove that you are dedicated to this field of work.

AMANDA: I say this not as your friend, but as your life coach and advisor!

AMANDA: I need you to get hired by an organization in Europe so that I can come over and visit you and get swept up in a whirlwind romance. Swoon!

My smirk quickly turned into a frown as I processed her advice. I had no idea where she thought I was going to find some ultra-impressive place to show off my non-profit street cred in a place like Cascade Valley.

Um, Lord, did I make a total mistake coming back home for the summer? Should I have stayed in Seattle and found a volunteer program there for the season?

I stared at the book in my lap, twirling a strand of hair between my fingers. If I'd been smarter, I would have considered cutting my visit out here down to a couple of weeks, rather than the whole summer. The real problem was that I still wasn't ready to tell my family that I wasn't moving home permanently. How did I tell them that I was planning to pack all my things and move to Europe? *For good?*

The news wasn't going to go over well, and I'd planned to have all summer to prepare them. But it felt like coming home was quickly turning into the wrong choice.

A troubled frown settled itself between my eyes. I tried opening the novel on my lap, but the words just floated in front of me, none of them making any sense to my distracted brain. Frustrated, I snapped it closed and tossed the paperback onto the seat next to me.

They weren't joking when they said that adulting was hard. Graduation was only a week ago and I already felt stressed.

The peppermint tea had cooled in the soft evening air, but I lifted the mug to my lips to take another sip. I picked the wrong moment to take a drink because at that second my eyes aimlessly drifted toward the group lounging on the other end of the porch and caught Caleb looking straight at me. As if his bold stare wasn't rude enough, the man had the audacity to wink at me when he realized that I'd caught him staring. A very long, slow wink to accompany the smirk on his smug face.

The peppermint tea slid down the wrong pipe and I choked mid-swallow. My sudden violent coughing fit was enough to pull my brothers' attention away from their own conversation and turn in unison to stare at me like a concerned pack of mother hens.

"You ok, Sammie?" Knox rose from his seat and started toward me.

I waved him off, already embarrassed at the spectacle I was making of myself. Pounding my chest with my hand, I croaked out an unsteady, "I'm fine. Just swallowed wrong."

"Are you ok, Samantha?" Caleb's deep voice rang out in a mocking echo. If looks could kill, the glance I sent his way would have struck him dead then and there. Or tried to send his way, through the red haze of my tear-stung eyes.

It was by sheer force of will that I managed to force my coughing fit to quiet down as Knox's lanky form slunk back to the seat he had just vacated. The porch swing swung in rhythm with my cackling.

Geez, Sammie, get a grip. I could feel the waves of embarrassment burning my cheeks. Caleb probably thought I'd choked on my tea because of him. He probably thought that he'd intimidated me earlier this afternoon or that I was that same stupid little high school girl who had always blushed every time he'd looked my direction. My crush had been so obvious years ago. At least it had been before Caleb became enemy number one.

The thought that Caleb would just assume he could wink at me filled me with a tiny tornado of rage. My chest constricted and I almost choked again as I cut my eyes toward the group at the other end of the porch.

I dare him to be looking at me again, I seethed inwardly. This time he would get a piece of my mind.

I needn't have wasted my anger. Caleb was sitting forward on the wicker chair now, his gaze fixed on Vincent's face as they debated the likelihood of the stock market dipping again before the fall. The neck of the dark amber soda bottle that he gripped between his fingers looked tiny. Suddenly, a cold, refreshing soft drink sounded a whole heck of a lot more appealing than the peppermint tea I'd clearly not had much success with tonight.

I scooted forward and pulled myself out of the porch swing. It creaked as I stood. The crickets whistled in the flower bed off the porch. It was a peaceful night and I was determined to enjoy it.

Holding my head high and making sure not to glance anywhere but straight in front of me, I walked toward the front door.

It was late May. The nights still had the soft cooling-off of spring, but the day had been hot. A cold, crisp root beer would soothe my parched, coughed-out throat. It was my first official night as a college graduate and I was already stressed. And Caleb wasn't helping. I wanted him to realize that I was an adult now and not a teenager that he could tease and mock.

Caleb's presence in my home was a little too much for me to process considering everything else that I had to deal with. My temples began to throb as I reached for the refrigerator. The flyer proudly announcing '*Kane Arabian Summer Camp for Teens*' caught my eyes again from its position on the door.

Why did Caleb have to show up tonight of all nights? Just as I was getting acclimated to being back at home and gathering the courage to test the waters with my brothers regarding my future. I'd secretly hoped to be able to casually broach the subject tonight. If I could get my brothers on board with my plan, it would make it so much easier to convince my mother.

I certainly wasn't going to approach the subject with my mortal enemy around. Just my luck, he would interject all kinds of logical objections that would sway my brothers against my plans.

My family would quickly learn that there wasn't anything they could do to change my mind. And realistically nothing they could do to stop me. Thoughtfully, I bit down on my lower lip and reached to pull Caleb's flyer from under its magnet. I held it gingerly, not really wanting to touch it, but suddenly fascinated by all the obvious flaws it presented.

My family would probably never trust me enough to send me packing off to Europe to pursue my dreams. *Unless they saw for themselves just how good I was at my job.*

I continued to study the flyer, simultaneously pulling open the refrigerator with my free hand. Glancing up, I grabbed one of the frosty amber bottles that lined the lower shelf, already imagining the sweet flavor on my tongue. At least my brothers had the good sense to prefer craft soda. So much better than the artificial flavor of the sugarless varieties my college friends had preferred.

Still staring at Caleb's flyer, I swung the refrigerator shut and nearly had a conniption when I saw a figure standing behind the door.

"Caleb!" I almost shouted, nearly dropping the soda bottle in my surprise. "What are you doing? Trying to scare me half to death?"

His eyes were cold as they looked down at me. "Don't get too excited," he said, his tone gruff. "It's just me." He held his palms up at chest level.

"Like I would ever get excited by the sight of you." The words snapped out with a sharp bite before I could stop myself. They fell with an ugly thud in the empty kitchen.

His eyebrows rose. "Well, I just came in to grab refills anyway." He eyed the bottle in my hands. "Seems like you had the same idea."

I blushed for no good reason.

Cocking his head slightly to the side, he looked at the flyer in my hands. "Are you interested in riding lessons?"

The paper suddenly burned into my hand like a hot piece of coal. I looked at it, kicking myself for getting caught with something of his. I turned and slapped it on the countertop with a sharp smack.

"No, I'm not. I hate horses."

"Since when do you hate horses?" He frowned at me. "You always loved them before."

"Well, people change," I snapped at him. "Things happen. You of all people should know how quickly life can take a turn."

A dark shadow flashed across his face, and he took a step back as if I'd physically punched him in the chest. I turned on my heel and left the kitchen. Outside, I ignored the concerned look my brothers threw each other. I plopped down on the porch steps, leaning against the handrail. I called Shadow, the ranch's border collie, over to me and rubbed his soft, silky ears, sipping my cool drink as the sun began to dip in the horizon.

When Caleb stepped onto the porch, I instinctively glanced back at him, wondering if I should apologize for my sharp-tongued comment a moment ago. I was already starting to feel guilty about it. Our eyes met. But, instead of remorse, I felt a fresh flash of annoyance, so I just frowned and turned away.

"Are you two fighting already?" Vincent spoke behind me, his tone amused. "We heard raised voices in there."

"What?" I spun around. "I most certainly did not raise my voice."

The grin on my brother's face told me that he was just teasing, but I blushed anyway. Shelby laughed and Brianna looked amused. I looked at Caleb again. He had taken a seat in the wicker lounge chair next to Dean and he did not look as amused as the rest of the group. My sharp gaze darted between my brothers, practically daring one of them to say anything else. Caleb was staring at me thoughtfully, his eyes locked on mine. A deep scowl had overtaken his rugged face and his fist clenched the sweating amber bottle in his hand.

I returned his frown, then turned my back to the group and resumed running my hands across Shadow's soft fur. The dog leaned back on me, his tongue out, loving the attention.

"So, Sammie, do you have any big plans for the summer? Or are you planning to let us men do all the hard work while you sleep in and loll about?" Knox called to me.

"Oh, like you every chance you get?" The words came out far sharper than I intended.

Normally, I could handle the incessant teasing of my brothers. I knew it came with the territory of being the youngest sibling. Tonight though, I had zero patience for their good-natured barbs and jabs. But I had no right to take out my animosity toward Caleb on them or to make their evening with their girlfriends unpleasant.

Quickly, I gathered my thoughts. "Sorry." I tried to soften my tone. "I do have plans. I'm looking for a volunteer program to put my two degrees to good use while I hunt for a job. I have a few prospective employers in mind who like to see charitable applicants."

That was close enough to the truth that I didn't feel like I was lying to my family.

"That's incredible, Red!" Knox shouted as if I hadn't just snapped at him. His voice was at its usual deafening decibel. "Our little sister, boys. Destined to do great things in the world."

The girls made sounds of soft, warm approval.

Vincent's steady gaze caught mine and I felt an instant wave of guilt. I was certain that they wouldn't be so positive if they knew what I was really trying to accomplish by the end of the summer. I had put it out there though. It was something, a stand of some kind. The fact that I was a real adult, with real-world plans. Knowing that I had goals, maybe they wouldn't be so surprised when I took a job in Europe.

While the boys and their girlfriends were still carrying on with their praise, I made a snap decision. Even before I spoke, I knew there was a good chance that I'd regret what I was about to do.

"Caleb." I rose, brushing Shadow's fur off my legs. "May I speak to you for a moment?" I motioned to the lawn.

To his credit and my surprise, he was polite enough to stand right away and follow me off the porch. I headed toward the pasture next to the barn, where we would be out of earshot of the porch. A sorrel quarter horse lingered near the fence, and I deliberately steered us away from the large animal's direction. Caleb's long stride fell into step with me as we walked across the grass. He was silent and I was intensely aware of his imposing presence. I hoped that I didn't stumble over my words now.

With Caleb, I knew better than to beat around the bush. *Here goes nothing.*

"Look." I leaned against the fence and turned to face him. "I'm just going to say it. I know that you and I don't really get along."

A dark shadow passed over his face again. He nodded but remained silent.

"But the truth is, your summer program at the ranch really needs some work in the marketing department. It's deplorable, honestly. I don't know how you've gotten anyone to agree to participate." I winced at my own bluntness. I was probably going too far.

"Glad to know your real opinion." His tone matched the scowl across his forehead. "I'm sorry that my design skills don't match up to your exacting standards."

I ignored his sharp reply. "Here's the thing. I need to use this summer to work on my volunteer resume. If you were interested, I would be willing to trade in some help on the marketing and fundraising aspect of your program for a good letter of recommendation."

"You must be joking." Caleb's voice came out graveled and thick. "Why would you even propose this?"

"Because you really need help. I thought you wanted to expand the program this summer?"

"You tried to get me thrown in jail, Samantha." Caleb's words came out fast and hot. His skin flushed a bright red and his eyes flashed at me dangerously.

"That was a long time ago," I said.

"Not long enough. You accused me of negligence in front of our entire town. The sheriff questioned us." His broad chest rose and fell rapidly. "Do you know how long it took for the locals to look my dad and I in the eye again? People thought your family was going to sue mine. Why would I let you anywhere near my ranch ever again?"

That day in the church flashed in my memory. Accusing Caleb and his dad of deliberately selling a horse that was unruly may not have been my best moment. We lived in a small community. Accusations and rumors could ruin a person's standing here forever.

I still blamed him though. And I wasn't ready to let it go. I squared my stance and lifted my chin. "Are you really going to pick a fight with me over this? You know why I thought what I thought."

My arrows had struck a nerve. Caleb's fist came down heavily on the top rung of the fence. It shuddered under the force. Inwardly, I jumped a little, but I was determined to hold my ground. "I still have no idea why you thought we were responsible. And whatever you thought, you were wrong. You blasted me in front of everyone. But you never apologized or tried to clear my name."

I threw up my hands. My voice rose. "Well, what do you want me to do now, Caleb? My dad is gone, and your reputation eventually got restored. Doesn't seem like any lasting harm came to you. At least your dad is still here."

He glared at me, jaw clenched angrily. "That's a dirty blow, even for you. You know I loved your dad."

My heart constricted at the memory of the two of them laughing together. For years Caleb had been a part of our family and like a typical young girl, I'd often daydreamed about a future with my older brothers' mysterious, handsome friend. That was long in the past though. I shook myself and hardened my heart against the memories.

"Look," I held up my hands to signal a truce. "You and I can spend all summer fighting every time that we're in the same room. Or we can work together, and both get something out of it that furthers our goals. It's your choice. I'm not going to force you." I took a step backward and waited.

"You're just going to pick fights with me all the time," he retorted.

"No. I'm not. I am willing to call a truce with you for the summer. No fighting. I promise."

"And why should I believe that you have that kind of self-control?"

"Oh, believe me. It will be hard," I snapped. "I can't promise to hold myself back every time you irritate me. But it will make my family happy to see us getting along. And helping you with your charity will help me further my career. It sounds like a worthy cause anyway."

Caleb leaned against the fence. He bobbed his head thoughtfully and I snuck a glance back at the house. As I'd suspected, the group on the porch was not-so-subtly staring in our direction.

"This is against my better judgment, but the kids who come out here for the camp deserve the best. If you can really help make it better, have at it." His tone was terse when he finally spoke.

"Good," I responded promptly. I stuck out my right hand. "Shall we shake on a truce then?"

He stared at my hand for a moment, then slowly turned toward me and covered it with his own. His callused palm brushed mine. Despite myself, I couldn't help the tiny shiver that ran over my skin at the contact. I used to daydream about the day that Caleb would hold my hand.

"Truce?" I repeated.

"Truce," he nodded. The stormy flash of temper he'd shown seemed to be calming already. It wasn't like Caleb to reveal his inner emotions. He was quickly reclaiming his usual composure. I expected him to drop my hand immediately, but instead, he held it. I felt his thumb brush the skin across my knuckles and I shivered again. His face darkened. "You have to make me a promise though," he said.

"Promise you what?"

Caleb leaned forward, pulling me close enough to whisper. "Stay out of my way and I'll stay out of yours? Deal?"

"Deal," I murmured.

"And don't go around flashing those green eyes of yours at me either."

"And what's wrong with my eyes?" I replied with an instant flare of temper.

His voice became husky and deep, his lips full and soft. "Nothing at all. They just always look like two emerald flames. A man could burn up in eyes like yours and I'd prefer to stay clear of their fire."

Heat licked at my core and a flush whipped like wildfire across my skin at his unexpected words. Caleb dropped my hand and turned away, moving toward the porch with a heavy stride. I watched his retreating form, speechless for once. My heart pounded in my chest, his words replaying in my mind. I had to linger an extra minute at the fence to let my fiery cheeks cool before I went to tell my brothers of my new summer plans.

Chapter Four

"WHAT IN THE world are you going to do with a bunch of kids and horses all summer?" Amanda's energy level was as intense at midnight as it was when she woke up in the morning. "You do not belong on a ranch."

"Well, that's not exactly true," I reminded her, amused. "I did grow up here, you know. I spent most of my life riding horses all over these hills. I'm sure I can fit in again."

A memory of riding our trail horses through the forest surfaced in my mind. Once upon a time, I'd felt the most at home in the country, surrounded by the forest, the pastures, and the silence that often stretched for miles. I had been raised on the mountains and hidden lakes that abounded around the region. That had been the old me though. The teenager who thought she would end up spending her whole life surrounded by horses and cattle. Once I'd arrived in Seattle, I'd realized how limited my thinking had been.

"I'm being serious?" Amanda said. "What could a little country kids' summer program possibly have for you to do?"

"I dunno," I replied, pulling my notebook toward me to look at the list I had jotted down earlier. "I can build them a website, take new promotional photos, redesign their marketing campaign, give them an actual marketing campaign, connect with other organizations? You know how hard I work, Amanda. I'll earn that recommendation."

"I have no doubt of that," she assured me. "But how do you feel about working with old what's-his-name all summer? It just sucks that it is his charity."

"Yes, it is unfortunate that it couldn't be someone else," I replied. Then, before I could second-guess myself, I continued. "Caleb said something really weird when we had finished making our arrangement for me to help him out."

"Yes?" I could hear Amanda rummaging in a cupboard while she listened to me on speaker.

I bit my lip. "He said that my eyes look like emerald flames."

"What?" A crash clattered on the other end of the phone, then Amanda's voice came in loud and clear. "He said what now? What is going on over there?"

"You heard me," I laughed, my face heating up again, even though I was alone in my room at the end of the hall. The boys had gone to bed a couple hours ago. I was still on big-city time and wouldn't fall asleep for a few hours yet.

"You didn't tell me he had a thing for you," she accused.

"He doesn't." I hastened to assure her. "Believe me, Caleb Kane despises me just as much as I despise him. But don't you think that was an odd thing to say?"

"Honey, that was a very odd thing to say, coming from a man who supposedly despises you. You are gorgeous though, so at least I can give him credit for acknowledging that," she admitted grudgingly. "You used to have a crush on each other, right?" she continued without a beat.

A smack came through the speaker. I took a guess that she was eating gummy worms, a late-night habit she'd had through college. I pictured Caleb's face, his dark, appealing beard, his tall, broad-shouldered figure, those intense brown eyes. He had that quintessential cowboy vibe and it worked for him.

I wasn't going to admit that to Amanda though. "I think we liked each other. Who knows what would have happened if my dad hadn't passed away. But that's all in the past and I fully intend to use his charity to propel my career forward."

"You don't think that being around him will retrigger those feelings?" she asked.

"Not if I can help it," I said determinedly. "Looks don't make up for character, you know. Remember Jonas?"

"Oh, don't even get me started." That sent Amanda into a spiral of chatter about her ex-boyfriend like I'd known it would. Meanwhile, I was just glad that she couldn't see the rough sketch of Caleb's face that was somehow materializing in my notebook as we spoke.

Had I really offered a truce to my arch enemy? What was I doing? What had I been thinking? This arrangement was going to end up being a huge mistake. I'd only been home one day and already I'd gone a little nuts. It would be so much smarter to spend the summer avoiding the one person I truly disliked—the man I had literally blamed for my father's accident in front of an entire church full of people.

Good going, Sammie, I frowned, pushing my pencil deeper into the sketch paper. *Now, I'm stuck seeing his smug, know-it-all face all the time.* As if him hanging out with my brothers wasn't bad enough. Now I was going to be working for the man.

"Hello? Sammie, are you still there?" Amanda said.

"Yes, I'm still here," I replied with a sigh. For three-and-a half long summer months.

. . .

When you grow up in the wide-open spaces of a Montana cattle ranch, adjusting to city life is hard. Early in my first semester of freshman year, I'd developed the habit of going for a run every morning. I'd dodge the raindrops and just let my legs eat up the pavement, my lungs bursting with the fresh air. I'd run until I'd forgotten how cooped-up I felt, how homesick I was, and until I didn't want to cry about my dad anymore.

Then I'd shower in the dorms and wait in the study hall until Amanda had dragged herself out of bed in search of coffee and breakfast. It was a good habit and one that I intended to keep up this summer. When I slipped onto the porch a few mornings after my arrival home, dressed in running shorts, a t-shirt, and running shoes, Dean, Vincent, and Knox were already long gone. They had headed up the mountain earlier in the week to relieve our range crew from their duties of protecting the cattle on the mountain for a few days.

The teams took turns, and my brothers would be gone for the rest of the week. They'd asked me a dozen times if I could handle everything on my own. I'd shooed them out the door and assured them that I was fine. Handling the chores this morning had been a flashback to my childhood. The house now to myself, I'd cooked myself a leisurely breakfast and savored my coffee outside until I couldn't sit still anymore.

This morning, I'd lingered in bed until the sun was higher in the sky, chatting via text with my mother, admiring the photos accompanying her messages. After Dad's accident, traveling had become the way my mother chose to spread her wings. I couldn't help but wish that she had stayed home this summer though. But her wanderlust was a feeling I shared so I couldn't begrudge her the time away.

MOM: Miss you, darling. Wish you were here to soak in the ocean breezes with me. Maybe you should think about meeting me in Florida when the boat docks? Demi can join us and we'll make a girls vacation of it. Tour the coast and then end up back in New York. What do you think?

Seeing the photos of her tropical vacation made my muscles ache for movement. I stepped onto the porch and stretched my hamstrings, pulling one heel up to the back of my leg at a time.

I took the driveway at a light jog, warming up slowly. The sun was chasing away the coolness of the morning and after the cloudy and gloomy years of Washington weather, my skin drank it in. If I stayed in the sun too long, I'd end up with a million freckles, but the warmth was worth it.

My speed increased as I neared the end of our tree-lined driveway and I barely hesitated as I made a right curve onto the road. I could have gone left and probably should have. Caleb's ranch lay to the right. Avoiding a run-in with him was priority number one. But the road to the left of our land was typically rough and less well-maintained than the main road as it led toward the ski lodge on the mountain. I didn't want to break an ankle.

The start of Caleb's horse ranch was several miles ahead though. I figured I would be safe for a good run. I would turn back before I reached his gate.

Fresh, sweet air had filled my lungs for four miles of straight road before I felt the need to slow down. Pretty fields of green grass followed me on either side. The year was still early enough that they hadn't yet turned the golden color they would become later in the summer. I spotted the Kane's driveway looming a quarter mile in the distance. Pausing, I lingered on the side of the road, taking in the view that stretched for miles around me, not a building or a sidewalk in sight. Far ahead, the figures of several horses caught my eye, four-legged figures nibbling grass in the distance.

Though I'd turned myself into a city-girl over the past few years, I had to admit that the view out here was beautiful. It showed off how big and grand the world really was, something that was quickly lost in the concrete and metal jungle of the city. My running shoes kicked up a cloud of dust as I made the loop across the road to go back the other direction.

Consistent training over the past four years had given me enough stamina to go another three miles in the opposite direction before I decided to slow down to a walk. I loved running and could have gone further. My lungs burned, but in that good way that says you just accomplished something. Relaxing the last mile home and just taking in the sound of the birds singing and the warmth of the sun was a welcome reward.

"Thanks for making my return home so pretty, Lord," I said aloud on the empty road. "It's actually nice not running in a rain shower for once."

I'd walked a ways farther when the rumble of a truck approached me from behind. Immediately, my shoulders tensed. I'd banked on Caleb avoiding our ranch because my brothers were away. This was ridiculous. If I couldn't even go for a run without running into that cowboy….

My head swung over my shoulder to look at the offending truck. A blue Dodge roared toward me, its custom tires bigger than any self-respecting rancher around here would have deemed acceptable. The windows were tinted, and I couldn't identify the driver at first.

But my tense shoulders relaxed when I realized it wasn't Caleb after all. At least I'd be spared that awkward encounter.

"Well, I'll be darned." A loud, masculine voice boomed as the truck slowed parallel to me. The window rolled down and a man's grinning face peered at me from the driver's seat. "Aren't you a sight for sore eyes?"

I tensed again, instinctively backing up a couple of steps at the unexpected greeting. Panic spiked my heart rate again. His familiarity was off-putting, and I was determined not to become another human trafficking statistic. City-living had taught me a lot. Too much. I probably couldn't outrun his truck, but he was going to have a heck of a time catching me.

The sandy-haired man lowered his sunglasses to look at me. "Samantha? Don't you recognize me?"

"I'm sorry. I don't," I replied stiffly, mentally calculating just how long it would take me to sprint the quarter mile left to our driveway and how long it would take me to reach the shotgun that we kept loaded above the front door.

"Samantha, it's me. Damon? From senior year."

The man's face clicked in my memory and my mouth fell open in pleased surprise. "Damon? Oh my gosh, I didn't recognize you."

Suddenly at ease that this man wasn't a human trafficker out prowling the back roads of Montana for his next victim, I stepped closer to the window. "How are you?"

He grinned back at me. "I'm good," he said. "I heard you were back in town. I was just headed up to see your brothers. Want a ride the rest of the way?"

"Sure. But my brothers have gone up to the high pastures. They won't be back for a couple of days." Everyone knew that my brothers had an arrangement with the forestry service to graze our cattle on the mountain.

"Oh, that's ok. I can wait. I'll still give you a ride though."

Nodding, I jogged around the front of the truck to the passenger side and opened the door when I heard the lock click. "I was just out for a run. Sorry I'm a sweaty mess," I apologized as I climbed in. If I'd been any shorter, the lifted truck would have been a feat to get into.

"Don't apologize," he said, revving the engine and pulling onto the road again. "You look good. The big city didn't totally ruin you."

I laughed, feeling my eyes crinkle in genuine amusement. "Thanks. I'm glad I meet with your judgmental country-boy approval."

He chuckled and I saw my driveway looming ahead.

"Just kidding," I continued. "You look good too though. Looks like life has treated you well the past few years?"

"Oh yeah," he said. "I'm a foreman at the mill. Working on buying a house in town next."

"That's amazing. I always knew you would do well when we were back in school."

"Oh yeah?" He glanced at me, his eyes hidden behind dark sunglasses. "And how did you know that?"

I flashed him a smile. "You were always a good guy."

He pulled to a stop in front of my house.

"Well thanks for the ride." I opened the door, prepared to hop out. Damon's hand fell on my arm, stopping me. He'd taken off the sunglasses, exposing bright blue eyes.

"Since you're back for a while, I'd love to catch up. Maybe grab a bite sometime soon?"

My heart dropped a little. "Yes, sure," I said aloud. "I'm pretty busy the next few weeks with a project, but maybe soon?"

He grinned. "Sounds great." His rough fingers squeezed my arm warmly.

I made my escape to the porch as he revved the engine and sped away. From the corner of my eye, I saw a gray-haired man pause at the edge of the porch to watch Damon's retreating truck. "Hi Charlie," I called, lifting my hand to wave.

"Hey, Miss Samantha," he called in reply.

He lifted his hand to wave before continuing toward the chicken coop. Since Dean had redesigned our ranch's herd management philosophy to a regenerative approach, my brothers were often away from the ranch for weeks at a time. Charlie was a quiet, retired man who lived a few miles down the road and came over almost daily to help my mother take care of the animals who were left behind. Out of practice as I was, I was glad that I hadn't been left to manage the chickens, geese, goats, and milk cow all on my own.

• • •

My brothers returned just before dinner on Sunday. I heard the steady clip of their horses' hoofs as they rode into the yard. The trails to the mountain pastures could be treacherous and were best accessed by horseback. They were bone-tired as they piled into the house an hour later, voices loud and appreciative of the meal I had just slipped into the oven. Knox announced that Caleb was on his way over for dinner.

"You ok with that, Sammie?" he teased.

"Fine by me." I tossed my red mane back over my shoulder and straightened my posture. "Go shower and get changed for dinner. You three smell like a horse dragged through the campfire," I teased, shooing them toward the stairs. Knowing that Caleb's appearance on Sunday night was a regular thing that I would just have to accept, I had been mentally preparing myself all week.

We'd called a truce on our feud for the summer, but I wasn't sure what that would look like in practice. I may or may not have pulled my hair from its customary ponytail and fluffed my curls for good measure. I also may or may not have added a little lip gloss when I ran upstairs to change out of my work clothes for dinner. Nothing too dramatic. But I wanted to feel my best.

As the week had passed, I found myself wondering if Caleb would change his mind on our arrangement. I wasn't sure which scenario made me more nervous. Working with Caleb or not taking advantage of the chance to build my resume over the summer.

"This mac n' cheese smells so good." Vincent stood over the casserole dish I pulled from the oven a short while later. He breathed deeply, inhaling the steam rising from the top.

I laughed and shooed him away. "You'd better go help Dean with those steaks. And watch mine, please. I prefer it medium rare."

"You know that cowboy only knows how to cook it rare or charred to a crisp," Vincent winked at me.

Shaking my head, I pushed him toward the back door and watched as he headed toward the barbeque pit set up on the grass. Dean and Knox were already outside, fresh from their showers. Their girlfriends had already arrived and quickly made themselves at home on the lawn chairs. Knox threw a tennis ball for Shadow across the yard. Smoke rose from the charcoal barbeque, the scent making my mouth water, reminding me of how much I valued my brothers' commitment to their work. They were stewarding the land in a way that few ranchers did. And there was nothing like one of our own grass-fed steaks hot from the grill on a summer night.

I'd forgotten how much I enjoyed cooking. Since I'd been alone most of the past week, I'd survived off salads and sandwiches. But I had wanted to make sure my hard-working brothers had a good meal to restore their energy when they arrived back home. The kitchen was the place that reminded me most of my mom. I'd pulled her ancient cookbooks from the cupboards and dug through them for our favorite recipes during the week. Suddenly, I'd found myself craving her meatloaf, her Thanksgiving dinners, and her homemade cookies that were always just a tiny bit too crisp on the bottom.

Tonight's dinner was a collection of favorites. Mom's gooey mac n' cheese, her Caesar salad, the special garlic green beans she'd always made during the summer. She'd be proud that I had followed her recipes. The boys were in charge of the protein tonight. I'd tried to do our mother's recipes justice with everything else.

To top our dinner off, I'd made her apple pie, which was the best pie I'd ever tasted. As I bent over to peek at the dessert, still bubbling away in the oven, I chuckled aloud at the thought that here I was with a college degree and I'd been spending my days cooking, mucking stalls, and digging weeds from the garden like a housewife.

"Did that pie say something funny?" A deep voice rumbled behind me. I jumped and yelped, dropping the oven mitts I was holding and spinning around to face the intruder.

Caleb stood next to the island. He leaned his hip against the edge and stared at me with an expression I couldn't read. I eyed him skeptically, wondering if the hot-tempered man I'd gotten a glimpse of the other night had shown up today. He appeared to be his usual calm and collected self though.

I grabbed the oven mitts off the floor, turning away from him to pull the salad from the refrigerator. "No. Just me laughing to myself, as usual," I said primly. I brushed my hair back over my shoulder. "I didn't hear you knock."

"Oh, I'm sorry." He sounded genuinely apologetic, so I threw a glance at him. "The guys have always told me just to let myself in the front door. I should have knocked."

"No, that's ok," I said. A lot had changed since I'd been away, and it wasn't my place to demand that the routine change just for me. I was mature enough to admit that.

Silence lingered in the air between us. Briefly, I wondered if a truce meant that I suddenly had to make small talk with the man. *Surely, it was enough for us to just ignore each other and avoid full-blown fights?* My strategy to get through the summer was to speak to the man in front of me as little as possible. I snuck a glance in Caleb's direction. Our eyes met awkwardly.

"The guys are outside if you want to grab a drink and join them?" I motioned to the refrigerator. "I think we're eating on the back porch tonight."

"Thanks." He pulled a can from the fridge, and I noticed that he'd chosen my favorite flavor of carbonated water.

"Sammie." Knox stuck his head through the back door. "Two minutes on the steaks. Hey, Caleb. Didn't know you were here."

"Just walked in the door," he replied hastily.

"K. I'll put the food out," I called back as Knox let the screen door swing shut.

Caleb lingered. "Do you need help?"

I shooed him away, trying to hide my surprise. "No, not at all. Go join the guys. I'm good."

He gave me a snappy salute with his free hand and pushed through the screen door to the back yard.

Our back porch dinner on the large handmade wooden table brought back so many memories of growing up and spending summer nights laughing and eating in this exact spot. Long, leisurely dinners after a hot day spent working on the ranch. Dad would come in, sweaty and dusty. He'd run inside and plant a kiss on Mom, before running upstairs for a shower. When he came back, we would dive into platters full of food. Dad and the boys were always ravenous, and we'd often invite the ranch hands to supper with us. Dad would laugh his big, wide-open laugh, telling the most outrageous stories that left us begging for more and Mom shaking her head in amusement.

It didn't escape me that Dean had seemed to slip unconsciously into this role of gracious, funny, entertaining host. I snuck a glance at Caleb. He was extra quiet tonight, only occasionally interjecting a few sentences. He seemed a lifetime away from the young man that I remembered growing up.

The truth was, I realized, that Caleb was a stranger to me now. A stranger who was now seated at my family table, looking like he belonged there more than I did.

Yet, as uncomfortable as I still was with his presence around the house, I couldn't help but laugh as Dean told us yet another story of the antics of one particularly feisty calf who had been born in the east pasture this spring.

I laughed until my stomach ached, and my heart hurt for the family that we used to be.

As the evening light went deep and mute, even the familiar sound of the cicadas sparked secret tears in my eyes. I turned away so the others couldn't see them and headed back inside to grab the apple pie that sat, still warm, on the countertop.

"Sammie, where are you going?" Knox called after me.

"Just slicing up the pie," I glanced back. "Does everyone want ice cream?"

A loud yes went up in unison as I opened the screen door.

I had run into town yesterday and I'd made sure to grab several cartons of vanilla ice cream for the freezer. The sweet, cold, creamy dessert was just what I craved these warm summer nights.

I was slipping generous slices of apple pie onto dessert plates and adding a melty scoop of the ice cream on top when I heard the screen door slam again.

"Thank you for dinner, Samantha." Caleb's sun-bronzed face greeted me when I glanced up. "It's been a while since I've had a home-cooked meal that could top that."

"Your mom was always an excellent cook," I replied automatically. I bit my lip, reminding myself to avoid familiarity with him. I'd known him half my life though and I was finding it hard not to slip into old habits.

Caleb had grabbed a handful of dinner plates from the outdoor table. He carried them to the sink now. His worn-in jeans and faded t-shirt sat easily upon his muscular frame. "Yes, she is," he nodded. "But since she and Dad moved to Helena to help my sister, it's been a lot of T.V. dinners and sandwiches for me."

"Oh, I forgot that your sister had moved away." Caleb's sister was older than Dean and I barely remembered her. I blushed as I realized how nonchalantly I was falling into conversation with Caleb. "Well, I'm happy to provide a cowboy with a hot meal," I mumbled awkwardly.

Was that too much? Inwardly, I groaned. A softening scoop of ice cream plopped to the side of the dessert plate in front of me. *That'll be a sticky puddle to clean when it melts.* I tried to focus on my task before I created more of a mess.

"Uh, Samantha?" Caleb's hesitant voice broke my concentration.

"It's Sammie," I corrected without thinking, then looked up, startled at my own words. He was watching my hands with a strange expression, his eyes soft pools of amber. When he realized that I was looking at him, he straightened and his eyes went cool and indifferent again.

"Sammie?" He tried out the name, clearly uncomfortable.

Did he not want to use my nickname? Was it better that we stay formal with each other, to keep this weird truce on a level playing field? I'd begun to doubt my spontaneous offer to help with his summer program. Working together would probably turn out to be a mistake. I watched him shuffle from foot to foot.

Maybe Caleb, this big, bold cowboy, was already as uncomfortable with our foolhardy arrangement as I was. Maybe we should just call off the whole thing.

"Uh, so I was thinking," he continued after a pause. "If you'd like to come by the ranch tomorrow, you can take a look around the place and tell me your plan to fix our marketing."

It was my turn to blink uncomfortably. "Tomorrow? Ok, I, um...."

"Does tomorrow not work?" His deep voice rumbled through the kitchen. I could hear my brothers talking through the open window.

I shook myself, my hair brushing across my lower back. "No, tomorrow is great," I spoke firmly. "I should get to work as soon as possible. Lot's to be done."

His gaze fell on me, and a flush settled over my skin. We paused, the silence thick and heavy between us. He bobbed his head. "Ok, then. Come by at nine?"

My nod was curt and sharp. "I'll be there. Here's your pie." I pushed a plate toward him and grabbed two more, making my escape back onto the porch before we could be forced into any more of this painful small talk.

Chapter Five

IT HAD SEEMED like a good choice to opt for a pair of designer jeans and a silk button-down blouse the next morning. A pretty ensemble, but still practical. As I stepped down from Vincent's truck onto the driveway of Caleb's ranch though, I immediately realized that I had still overdressed. The few ranch hands that I could see were sporting loose, broken-in jeans and comfortable t-shirts. The late spring morning was already growing warm. And my jeans had been designed for fashion, not for comfort. At least I'd had the sense to wear my old, comfortable work boots. In case a horse stepped on my foot. Not that I had any intention of getting that close to the animals.

I shivered, pushing down the anxious nerves that nagged at me just at the thought of being near them. So far, I had told almost no one how nervous being around horses now made me. It hadn't always been this way. I'd once been a country girl through-and-through, a girl who felt more at home in the saddle than anywhere else. And I'd been a good rider. My dad had often said that my equestrian skills could rival those of someone with more experience. I still remembered countless daydreams I'd had of running my own horse ranch. A setup like Caleb's had been my goal.

It hadn't been until a few months after Dad's accident that horses began to scare me. Even after his funeral, it hadn't occurred to me to be afraid of them. Then, I'd come home during the Thanksgiving break of my first year of college. One late fall morning, I decided to take one of our stocky quarter horses riding for some exercise. A few inches of snow had already covered the ground, but my brothers always kept the trails around our ranch well-groomed. The day had been serene, the only sounds the occasional bird call and the clip of my ride's hooves as we meandered down the trail. Everything had gone well until a jackrabbit darted across the path. Without warning, the normally calm mare I was riding got spooked by the small, quick animal. In her fright, she had been determined to shake me and bolt toward home. The mare began to jump and thrash.

Thankfully, my experience had kicked in and I was able to cling to her and soothe her until she'd settled enough for me to dismount. I walked her the rest of the way home. But the damage had been done. Her unexpected rebellion had shaken me to my core. All I could think about was my dad in his final moments. I had been alone on a trail I'd ridden hundreds of times, but familiarity didn't equate safety anymore. After that incident, horseback riding was a risk I was no longer willing to take, and I'd avoided horses ever since.

At least my only purpose at Caleb's ranch was to get what I needed to revise the marketing for the program. Still, I grumbled to myself as I grabbed my camera bag from the floorboard, questioning for the hundredth time why I had volunteered for this. But I'd received an email from one of the organizations I'd sent an application to that morning. They wanted to schedule an interview.

The experience I would gain by managing Caleb's charity would pad my resume nicely. I needed to keep my eye on the prize. By the end of summer, I'd be happily on my way to Europe. I'd known for years that I was called to be more than just a rancher's daughter. This was my opportunity to prove it.

"This is just a stepping-stone to get where I need to go," I whispered to myself as I headed toward one of the red stables that stood on opposite sides of the path. I couldn't see Caleb anywhere in sight, but I kept my eyes carefully turned away from his house as I walked.

I pushed away the pang of guilt that always accompanied my daydreams of the future. Telling my family that I was counting down the days to start my exciting, new life on another continent hadn't exactly happened yet. They were going to be disappointed that I'd chosen to break up our close-knit unit to move away by myself to a foreign country.

I wanted to tell them that it was my calling to serve others. I wanted to explain that the thought of moving overseas alone was both exciting and terrifying. But every time I thought about bringing it up, I was hit with a crushing sensation of guilt. My plan wasn't the same as taking extended trips to see the world like my mother. It was permanent.

I shook away the feeling as I walked toward the outbuildings, pulling my shoulders back and trying to look like I knew what I was doing here.

The stable doors stood open on either end. Light streamed through the doorway, the dim stalls shadowed on both sides of the aisle. A large, fenced arena occupied the middle of the space. The smell of hay and horses greeted me as I approached. Ahead, the sound of voices echoed.

"Hello?" I called, my voice cracking.

Get a grip, Sammie.

"Hello?" I yelled louder into the stable.

A figure popped around the corner at the far end. "Hello?".

I didn't recognize the older man walking toward me, his step brisk along the straw-strewn corridor.

"Can I help you?" he said. At this distance, I could see the soft gray handlebars that hung down from either side of his mouth. He had the ease and grace of walking that came from many hours on horseback.

"I'm Samantha McCade." I walked forward, my right hand extended. "I'm helping Caleb with the marketing for the youth camp. He's supposed to show me around today."

His weathered face lit up with a smile. "Samantha, of course. I'm Griff, Caleb's ranch foreman." Griff reached out to grab my hand and I found my palm engulfed by a surprisingly gentle grip.

Of course. His hands must be strong but light-touched to handle the horses.

I returned his handshake firmly, determined to show that I was confident and sure of myself.

"It's great to meet you, Griff."

"He asked me to show you around today. I hope you're ok with spending a couple of hours with an old guy like me?" The sparkle in his eye welcomed me.

"Oh," I said, hiding my surprise. "Of course."

Griff turned to lead the way through the stable. I saw him glance at my boots and nod in approval.

"He was planning on seeing you around himself, but one of the horses needed immediate attention. You know Caleb. Ever the perfectionist. He's the kind of boss who would rather get in there himself to handle his horses."

I wasn't aware of Caleb's work ethic, but I filed the information away in my brain.

"So, what's your plan for this camp of ours?" Griff spoke. I heard the curiosity in his tone.

I hurried to keep up with his brisk, long stride. "Well, I thought I would take fresh photos of the farm, the stables, and some of the horses?" I patted the camera bag swinging on my shoulder. "Now do you use all the horses for the summer program or just specific ones? I'd love to jot their names down and maybe get some facts about them from you."

A few horses who were still lingering in their stalls poked their heads over the gates, watching us curiously. Once we'd reached the other side of the stable's corridor, Griff paused and stroked his mustache. He nodded and I got the sense that he approved of my ideas so far.

"We only use a specific group. Older geldings and mares that we know are going to be gentle with the kids. It gives them opportunities to get up close and personal with the animals and the horses love the extra attention." He lifted a hand to indicate that I should follow him outside.

Behind the stable lay a lush, green pasture. The expanse was separated into sections by the same white fence that ran across the front of the property. I watched as several fine-boned horses spotted Griff and came ambling over to the rails. Their eager press against the fencing sent a nervous spike through my stomach again.

Why did I volunteer to help out here again?

Griff pulled a handful of sugar cubes from his pocket. "Shhh." He grinned at me. I swallowed the look of panic on my face and let my lips tremble into a smile. "Don't tell anyone. Caleb doesn't approve of feeding them straight sugar. But we all deserve a little treat now and again." He rubbed the curved muzzle of the chestnut mare who had extended her head over the fencing toward him. "Don't we now, girl?"

"So, these are all the horses you use in the program?"

"Not all of them," Griff said. "This is Ginger." He rubbed the chestnut horse's muzzle again. "She's our oldest broodmare, now retired. Then the lighter black bay over there is Ben. He's our oldest gelding." He gestured toward the horse, who was separated from the group by a fence. "We do use most of these horses for the summer camp."

He pointed toward a petite horse with a dark gray coat. "And then this young lady is Sandy. She's new to this group. One of our younger mares." He reached toward the horse, but she bobbed her head up and out of his reach. He laughed, digging in his pockets for another sugar cube. This time, when he held it out to her, she took it from his open hand carefully, her lips angling gently around the cube.

"She's a bit sassy, but the others keep her in line. Hey..." He paused, looking from me to the horses. "You and Ginger have about the same hair color. Well, I'll be."

Instinctively, I reached up to touch my hair, which I'd opted to put into a thick braid this morning. He wasn't wrong, but the comment irritated me. I didn't want anything in common with these animals.

"Do you want to feed her some sugar?" Griff offered. "I won't tell if you won't."

"No, thank you. I'm ok," I replied stiffly. To keep my hands looking busy, I reached into my bag and pulled out the notebook and pen I'd stashed there.

"I'm just going to jot down their names and then I'll take some photographs. OK?"

Griff nodded and kept stroking the horses as I wrote my notes. They were obviously comfortable with him, bumping his shoulder and pushing their muzzles under his hand as he tried to give them all attention. He stepped back when I pulled out my camera. I walked back and forth, snapping a few photos of the group for the portfolio I was putting together. I calmed myself enough to admit that they were beautiful animals, their lithe but muscular bodies rippling in the sunlight. I'd always thought Arabians were a special breed of horse.

"Ready?" he said, as I snapped the lens cover on the camera and swung the strap around my neck.

"Ready."

"Follow me. I'll continue the tour and then there's someone else I want you to meet."

I followed him around the stable and toward a mud-spattered golf cart that was parked under a tree.

Griff gestured to it. "I know it's probably ridiculous to run around a ranch in a golf cart, but I figured you would prefer this to the quad?"

He had figured right, as straddling the back of a quad with a strange man wasn't my idea of a good time. Still, I smiled as I pictured us bumping over the ground looking like we were headed to tee off.

We climbed aboard and Griff turned the tiny key in the ignition. The golf cart started with a jolt. I had expected a bumpy ride, but the sandy path that ran along the white fence was well-kept. He drove us past the white farmhouse, past the vegetable garden, and toward the far pastures that stretched toward the west. I expected Griff to drive toward the back of the property, but instead he angled the cart toward a nearby corral.

"One of our trainers." He bobbed his head in the direction of a figure in the distance.

I squinted against the sunlight. I could see someone standing a short distance away from an elegant white horse. The horse was on a long lead and was prancing in a jerky circle around the corral. The figure held a small flag in her hand.

The trainer was a woman. I processed the surprising fact as Griff braked the golf cart near the enclosure. She was a petite woman, her silky black hair pulled into a ponytail that resembled the full, rich tail of a horse. Jeans that had to be work jeans but that still somehow managed to look cute sat on her pert frame. I squelched back the surprised expression on my face.

It wasn't just that I was surprised to see a female trainer working with what was obviously a young, spirited horse. The colt bucked as we approached, fighting the lead. Yet, the young woman held her ground, handling the rope with a firmness and skill that could only come from hours of experience. What did surprise me was to see a young woman working for Caleb.

"Jenna," Griff called as the horse finally settled for her. We approached the enclosure, leaning up against the fence. Jenna turned to glance over her shoulder at us and waved with her free hand. She was pretty, with petite olive features, and a wide smile. If I'd had to guess, I would have put her age between three to five years older than me.

"This is Samantha McCade," Griff called. "She's the one helping us with camp this year."

"Oh yes," Jenna replied, her tone pleasant and carrying a distinct Montana twang. "It's so good to meet you, Samantha."

"Sammie," I corrected immediately, then wondered why I had volunteered the nickname. Samantha would have been perfectly fine and more professional.

Her hands were busy as she gradually reeled in the feisty colt's lead. He pranced and scurried side to side as she drew him closer. I gulped down my nerves as his sharp hooves pounded the ground again and again. Any second and he could trample her. The colt was beautiful, but it wasn't lost on me how similar he was to the horse my dad had purchased from Caleb's family. I shivered at the memory of that horse. I'd tried not to think of him and the loss he represented over the past years. The sight of the striking horse was enough to spark my grief again though.

Briefly, I wondered what had happened to the original horse my father had purchased. My brothers told me that they had sold him and that was all I knew.

Jenna said a few words to the colt in a low, calm tone. Eventually, he settled and dropped his head, sidling up to her and nudging her shoulder. She led him toward us. Her smile was bright. She stuck her free hand over the top of the fence toward me and we shook.

"How's our boy?" Griff asked, affectionately rubbing the white colt's muzzle. The horse tossed his head and shook it so that the older man couldn't reach him. I watched him out of the corner of my eye skeptically.

"Feisty and a pain," Jenna laughed. "This is Beauregard the Magnificent. Beau for short."

I murmured that he was beautiful, hoping that she wouldn't ask me to touch him.

"That he is," Jenna stroked his neck. "He might end up being one of our future stallions. He's actually from one of our own mares. We're trying to decide whether to keep him for shows or sell him to a buyer from Saudi Arabia who has purchased from us before. In the meantime, I'm working on taming some of his fiery nature to see what his temperament is like."

From the dark and wild side eye that the young horse was giving us, she had her work cut out for her. I pushed down my nerves and tried not to show my discomfort. "So, you're a trainer here?" I asked.

"Yep," she replied brightly. "For two years now. I love it. I grew up around horses and now, being out here with them, in the fresh air every day, it couldn't be better, you know?"

Sure, if you like wide open spaces with nothing but grass, cows, and horses for miles on end, it's amazing. I was already itching for city life, with the constant noise, coffee shops on every corner, and shopping malls.

A person didn't have to think so much in the city. But I wasn't petty enough to burst her bubble, so I just nodded and smiled politely.

"So do you have lots of ideas to make all the kids want to come here this summer?" She turned inquisitive hazel eyes on me.

I swallowed, trying to remember my plan.

"Caleb said you have a degree from some school out west?" she continued.

It was from the University of Washington, but I tried not to feel irritated at her lack of knowledge. She was probably just trying to be nice.

"I do," I said, trying to match her bright tone, which was beginning to sound suspiciously fake. Some people were just too chipper to be natural. And the way Jenna kept looking me up and down was doing nothing for my nerves. I shook it off and pulled back my shoulders. "I have a double degree in non-profit management and marketing. So, I've got things all worked out for this summer. It'll be the most talked about youth camp in all of Montana." I let my accent emerge a little with the last words.

Jenna pursed her lips and nodded, then that bright smile appeared again. "Well, isn't that just the best news. I'd love to stay and chat, but I'd better get back to work with this guy." She patted the horse. "Beau here isn't going to tame himself. It sure was great to meet you. Oh, Sammie," she called as she led the horse back to the center of the corral. "I just love your brothers. And your mom. What a great family you have."

I felt like an idiot as Griff and I walked away.

He showed me the location on the ranch where the kids would make camp and sleep under the stars. Camping didn't sound exciting to me anymore, but I had to admit that it was a perfect set up. If I was a teen who was struggling to find my center in life, this wouldn't be the worst place to spend a week for some horse therapy.

After another half-hour had passed, Griff asked if I would be alright on my own for a while. He said that he hated to leave me, but he needed to get back to work.

"Oh, of course." I waved my hand nonchalantly. "I'm just going to wander around for a bit, take a few pictures, and jot down some notes. If I don't see you again before I leave, it was a pleasure meeting you. Thank you for playing tour guide."

He's really a sweet man. A country boy through-and-through, but it was easy to see that he was kind and loyal. It was too bad Jenna hadn't left me with quite the same impression of her charms. If I hadn't felt that she disapproved of my presence on the ranch, I could have seen us becoming friends.

I watched Griff speed away on a quad. It felt odd wondering around Caleb's property on my own. I hadn't seen even a peek of him since I'd arrived though. It was just as well. He'd only make me nervous, and I hated feeling young and inexperienced, which I inevitably seemed to feel around him. We'd shaken on a truce and while I intended to keep my side of the agreement, I most certainly didn't trust or like the man.

Caleb had probably figured out that it was better if he stayed out of my way while I was on his property. That way neither of us could pick a fight with the other.

I snapped a photo of his house from a distance. *His home is pretty,* I admitted grudgingly to myself. Caleb's father had built a white, modest-sized, pretty-as-a-picture farmhouse when they first moved to Cascade Valley. The black metal roof sloped away from the peak on either side, allowing snow to fall during the winter.

It was similar to my own childhood home, but with white siding, a sprawling cedar porch, and a red front door, it made an even prettier picture than our canary-colored farmhouse. I snapped a few photos, making sure to get the hydrangeas that grew along the base of the porch in the shot. I stopped to inspect the shrubs. Whoever maintained the landscaping around here did a heck of a job. The plants were thriving, even though we hadn't quite reached the summer.

It's probably Jenna, I frowned. Expert horse woman and master gardener. I wondered if she and Caleb were seeing each other. *They would make a good match. A woman who is as annoying as Caleb.* Instantly, I regretted my uncharitable thought.

I decided to get a clear shot of the front of one of the stables before heading home. The sound of laughter carried to my ears as I walked under an arching willow tree. The laughter was high-toned and carried musically across the breeze.

I lingered under the willow, peeking through the drooping branches to see whose laughter I'd just heard. I watched Jenna and Caleb walking together toward the stable. Caleb's hand gripped Beau's bridle, the white colt prancing behind them. Jenna's face was turned up to Caleb, that golden smile visible even from my observation point.

The brim of Caleb's hat was pulled down over his brow. I couldn't see his expression, but his deep laugh rumbled across the yard. I recognized it from all my teen years spent listening for the sound of it to dance up the stairs back home.

They led Beau toward the stable together. Jenna moved ahead to pull open the sliding door of his stall. The horse must have been easily spooked, because as the metal scraped across the stable floor, he shook his head fiercely, refusing to step into the building. As Caleb kept a grip on his lead, Beau reared. His nose popped toward the sky. Jenna ran forward to help.

The colt's hooves flayed, striking the air with a sharpness that left me dry in the throat. Jenna jumped to the side, moving out of his range. I watched as Caleb wrestled with the suddenly unruly animal. His long arms stretched to hold the reins of his bridle. Even from my hiding spot, it was easy to see that he was handling the animal with skill.

My camera still hung around my neck. Without thinking, I grabbed it and aimed toward the stable. The lens focused on the struggle. I pressed the shutter, capturing both Beau mid-rear and the look of patient concentration of Caleb's face. The horse landed back on the ground and Caleb took the moment to reel him in, slowly and confidently shortening the lead until Beau was willing to allow him to approach.

The intensity of the moment made my breath catch in my throat.

Once the horse was still, Caleb laid a hand on the animal's neck, moving his hand in long, gentle strokes. My vision narrowed to only him and the colt, their silhouette's highlighted in the shadow of the stable corridor. I lifted the camera again and snapped a photo of the moment, thinking that it would be the perfect cover image for the website I was designing.

Jenna came forward and took the rope from Caleb. She led the colt into his stall. I slipped back the way I'd come and headed for my truck. The morning was still young, and I could download the photos and edit some of them before lunch.

I wished that I'd been able to ask Caleb to tell me more about the details of the youth camp. I was still a little sketchy on how things were going to run. It may have been petty on my part, but the thought of getting his attention with little-Miss-Jenna nearby was distasteful.

You're acting jealous, my rebellious brain told me as I opened the truck door and climbed into the driver's seat.

"No, I'm not," I replied to it aloud, dumping my bag and camera on the passenger seat and sliding the key into the ignition. I heard a *whirr-whirr* sound, then a click, and then nothing. The engine wouldn't start. It was dead. Somehow, I'd killed Vincent's truck after he'd graciously allowed me to borrow it this morning.

"Shoot." Walking back was fine with me, but that still left my brothers to come retrieve the truck. They were busy in the hay field today and I felt bad at the thought of causing them more work. I slumped into the seat, letting my head fall against the headrest as I prepped myself for the long, hot walk home.

"Samantha?"

I jumped at the unexpected sound of my name. Caleb's voice came from just outside the open truck door. My eyes popped open, and I saw him standing a few yards away, his posture stiff.

"I didn't realize you were still here until I saw Vincent's truck. I thought you would probably prefer to have someone other than me give you the tour this morning." He was eying me as warily as I eyed him.

"Oh, Griff was great. Nice man," I replied quickly.

"Uh...ok, great," he repeated, moving a step closer. "Are you leaving already? I thought you would be here all day."

"Well, I got a lot of what I needed for the moment. I do need to pick your brain about the logistics of the camp for the website and registration forms. But now, it looks like I'm walking home. The truck died." I gestured toward the engine.

"Oh." Caleb took three long strides around to the front of the truck. I slid out as he pulled up the hood. His head disappeared. I could hear him fiddling with caps and wires and all the mechanical workings of a vehicle that mystified me.

"Try it now." Head still bent over the engine block, his voice caught my ear gruffly a few minutes later. I hopped behind the wheel again and turned the key. Nothing. Just a worrisome clicking noise.

"It needs a bit more work to get started again. I don't have time right now though." Abruptly, Caleb slammed down the hood, popping into view behind the windshield. He stared at me through the glass.

"Well, that's that," I said, trying not to dread the four-mile walk home. It wasn't like I wouldn't run the same distance with ease. But walking in tight jeans and work boots on a dusty road wasn't exactly my idea of fun. I reached across the seat to grab my bag and camera, glad I hadn't taken much with me this morning.

I glanced back at Caleb. He stood watching me, shoulders noticeably stiff, a few feet away. "Tell the boys it wasn't my fault when they come back out to get it, ok?"

Quickly, I turned away to start the long walk up the driveway to the road.

"Where do you think you're going?" Caleb fell into step beside me. His hand shot out and landed on my arm.

"Home?" It was an instinctive motion to jerk my arm away from his unexpected touch. Caleb dropped his hand.

"You're just going to walk four miles back?"

"I run more than that all the time." I stopped in my tracks and shot him an exasperated look.

"Really? Dressed like that?"

My eyes shot up, ready to take quick offense at his sarcastic tone. I opened my mouth to retort, but a look that I couldn't read passed over his face. His gaze dropped to take in the length of me. He shook his head, a disapproving frown creeping across his face.

"It's too hot and dusty for you to walk back in those fancy clothes. Get in the truck. I'll drive you home," he said matter-of-factly., his tone indicating that the matter was already decided.

Annoyed, my hands flew up in immediate protest. Being alone in a truck with Caleb for any reason was not part of our truce agreement. Especially after he'd just subtly insulted my outfit. I knew I'd overdressed with my silk button-down and designer jeans. I didn't need to be reminded.

"I think I'm good," I replied with a sarcastic bite to my tone.

"Don't be ridiculous, Samantha. I know my presence horrifies you, but you can handle it for a few minutes." His tone was the equivalent of an eyeroll. "And besides, your brothers would expect me to drive you back."

"Well, see, the thing is—they actually like you."

I watched his head shake disapprovingly. He scowled. "They'll be mad at me if I just let you walk." He gestured toward his truck, which stood parked near the house. "Get in the truck, Samantha. End of discussion." Caleb turned away.

I dug my heels into the gravel. "You know you can't make me do what you say, right?"

His head swung back toward me, and my stubbornness faltered at the determined look in his eyes. His lips narrowed to a tight line under his beard. "Are you breaking our truce already?"

We squared off at each other, both waiting for the other to break eye contact.

"No," I finally admitted.

"Then prove it. Get in the truck."

I hesitated, feeling my resolve slip away. The drive back was only a few miles. I could handle that. And it would save me a sweaty walk.

"Fine." I rolled my eyes, determined not to accept his offer gracefully. Favor or no favor, this wasn't going to change anything between us.

Chapter Six

HE WALKED TOWARD the yard. I followed, wrestling with myself.

Don't do this, my brain yelled at me. *You're going to regret it. How bad can it be though?* I reasoned with myself. *We can't possibly kill each other within a few miles.*

A few steps ahead of me, I was surprised to see that Caleb went around to the passenger side and opened my door first. He held it open as I approached. I pulled back my shoulders and held my head high.

"Thanks," I said grudgingly, climbing into the work truck. It smelled of hay and gasoline and livestock and that undefinable smell that men carry in from the outdoors. I swallowed back the lump that suddenly popped into my throat. The smell reminded me of my dad. I busied myself with arranging my bags at my feet so I wouldn't have to look up.

Caleb started the truck and swung it toward the driveway. I stared straight ahead, wondering if either of us would find any motivation to break the awkward silence. From the corner of my eye, I saw Jenna's petite form emerge from the stable as we passed. She paused and watched the truck as it rolled down the driveway.

"So…." It was Caleb who broke the silence first. "I'm sure you're anxious to be rid of me, but I promised Mrs. Jensen that I would drop a load of feed off to her before eleven and I'm just about to be late. Do you mind if I take a detour before I drop you at home?"

"Uh…." I hesitated, caught off guard. I snuck a glance at his profile. He caught me and rolled his eyes.

"It'll only be a few extra minutes, Samantha. I promise I'll get you home right after."

I frowned and turned away from him to stare through the passenger window. Memories of Mrs. Jensen serving food in my high school lunch line came to me. "Fine, Caleb. Do what you have to do."

"Sorry that my lack of time management today has distressed you," he replied, his tone irritated.

I couldn't bring myself to believe that this cowboy ever managed his time poorly. The Kane ranch was pristine. Not a blade of grass appeared out of place. It was beautiful and I knew that though it took a team of people to manage that level of maintenance, there still needed to be a strong leader at the helm. We reached the end of the driveway and Caleb swung the truck to the right instead of left. I had a moment of panic at the ten extra minutes of torture I had just volunteered to endure. Mrs. Jensen's small property was only a few miles down the road, but still. My toe tapped the floorboard nervously.

I always ended up chattering when I was nervous. Despite my determination to give Caleb the cold shoulder, I heard myself speak. "Nice of you to sell her some of your feed, so she doesn't have to lug it home herself."

The woman we were going to see had to have been in her late seventies when I graduated. Not exactly in prime condition for lugging bales of hay. I glanced backward through the window, noticing the full load of crisp, yellow hay bales in the bed of the truck.

Caleb didn't reply. The sound of the tires thumping along the road echoed loudly in my ears. Trying to control my urge to fill the silence, I leaned my chin on my hand and watched the fields speed past the window. Minutes later, we pulled into Mrs. Jensen's short driveway. Caleb must have been pushing the speed limit.

The elderly woman lived in a quaint, blue, country cottage. Her few acres of land were surrounded by an aging wooden fence. I caught sight of a garden and a chicken coop as we rumbled into the yard. A chestnut horse roamed in the front pasture. At the sound of wheels on the gravel, Mrs. Jensen stepped onto her porch. She waved.

I opened the door and jumped out with Caleb.

"You're just a doll for bringing my Foxi-girl hay," Mrs. Jensen called out, gesturing toward the mare who'd raised her head and trotted toward the fence at our arrival. The elderly woman proceeded down the porch ramp with frail, careful steps.

"No problem, Mrs. Jensen," Caleb said in a tone so cheerful that I looked back at him in surprise. He smiled at her, the expression lighting up his face. The scream of the truck gate broke into the morning. "It's always my pleasure to help out a neighbor."

Despite her frail appearance, Mrs. Jensen's eyes were sharp and clear. I watched as they turned and inspected me curiously.

"Caleb, who is this beautiful young woman you've brought to see me? Is this your girlfriend?" She smiled.

"No, no, no," I replied hastily. "Mrs. Jensen, do you remember me? I'm Dan and Emma McCade's daughter, Samantha?"

A shadow passed over her face as she stared at me. She frowned and shook her head. "Dan McCade? I don't know a Dan McCade."

"My family lives about ten miles down the road from you. The cattle ranch just before the mountains begin?"

The shadow cleared. She stretched her hands toward me, and I took them. The skin on the back of her hands was impossibly soft. "You're Dan's daughter, aren't you?" she said, her tone delighted. "Demi, right?"

"Uh, no, Mrs. Jensen." I shook my decidedly auburn hair, picturing my sister's long locks of rich, dark brown waves. We would rarely be mistaken for sisters. "I'm Samantha. I was the one who always asked for extra pickled beets on my salad in the cafeteria?"

"Ah, yes," she exclaimed, but I got the feeling that I hadn't really triggered a memory. "Well, dear, why don't you come inside for some iced tea while Caleb throws around those bales of hay?" She turned and carefully began making her way up the ramp to the porch.

I glanced toward Caleb. "I'm going to go up and sit with her for a few minutes."

He was mid-heave on one of the massive bales of hay. I knew each one could weigh at least a couple hundred pounds. Caleb's shoulders and arms bulged with the weight, but he was making it look easy.

"Fine," he replied, not looking at me. I snuck another glance as he strode briskly toward the pasture, where a small, covered shed held the hay. Handfuls of it could easily be tossed over the fence to the waiting mare at feeding time.

Mrs. Jensen's kitchen was bright and cheerful when I entered. It smelled like sugar cookies and soup. Like every older person's home I had ever entered.

She'd already set out tall tumblers of amber-colored tea. A glistening pitcher filled with more iced tea and a small bowl full of sugar sat close by.

I took a sip, the sweet taste spilling over my tongue. "This is delicious, Mrs. Jensen. Thank you. I was parched." In Seattle, I never would have uttered a word like *parched*. But put me back in the country and the vernacular just seemed to settle in naturally.

She beamed at me, then turned and peeked through the window toward the pasture. Caleb's tall figure passed on the front lawn, headed toward his truck for another bale of hay. I watched him closely. He pulled another bale from the bed of the truck and lifted it onto his shoulder like it didn't weigh more than a baby.

"I surely hope Gregory doesn't overwork himself out there." Mrs. Jensen began to fret at the window.

I peered toward the yard. "Is someone else helping you here today, Mrs. Jensen?"

She turned back to look at me, her eyes filled with a glassy expression. "My husband, Gregory," she replied. "He works so hard, and I feel bad that I can't help him in the field anymore."

I looked at her, concern flooding my face. I remembered her talking about her husband in the lunch line at the cafeteria. She'd always been going on about his charms. The trouble was, I knew for a fact that he'd passed away my senior year of high school. I knew because I'd attended his funeral. The entire school had.

"He always makes sure my Foxi-girl has plenty of sweet, fresh hay. I'd be lost without him," she continued, looking toward the window again. I watched as Caleb slammed the gate of the truck bed and made his way across the lawn toward the porch. The heavy scrape of his boots could be heard as he wiped them on the door mat.

He entered the kitchen a few seconds later.

"Is something wrong?" he asked sharply, concern spreading across his face. I wiped the stricken expression from mine and managed to plaster a smile across my lips.

"Just fine," I sang out with forced cheerfulness. I held up the sweating glass of iced tea in my hand. "Mrs. Jensen makes the most delicious iced tea in the world."

"Caleb, darling, there you are. How is your grandmother?" Mrs. Jensen bustled toward us, a plate of iced oatmeal cookies in her hand.

I glanced at him, alarm spreading in my chest again. Granny Kane had been gone for years. I distinctly remembered Mrs. Jensen singing at her graveside service when I was thirteen. None of the school-aged children had known that she could sing.

Caleb lifted two cookies from the plate and saluted her with them. "She's just fine, ma'am. Heavenly, you might say." He glanced toward me, and I could have sworn that I saw him give me the faintest flicker of a wink. "She would want me to be sure to give you her warmest regards. You two always were such good friends."

Mrs. Jensen sat at the worn oak table and took a sip of tea. She smiled, a blissful look on her face. "We always have been close. I really need to get out of the house one of these days and come up to yours for a visit. Maybe I'll bring a lemon meringue pie. She's always loved that."

"Well, you do make the best lemon meringue," Caleb replied heartily. He drained the icy glass and set it in the sink. "I'm so sorry, but I must be going, Mrs. Jensen. I'm giving Samantha a ride home and just wanted to make sure Foxi had her hay."

I rose from the wooden chair. "Thank you so much for the iced tea. It was lovely to see you again."

Her clear, sparkling eyes regarded me curiously. Fragile, crepey hands stretched toward me. "It was lovely to see you too…."

I knew she was searching for my name. "Samantha McCade," I offered, with a smile and a gentle press of her hands.

She sparkled. "Ah yes, Dan and Emma McCade. Your parents are lovely people. Please give them both my regards."

I swallowed back the tears that sprang to the surface of my eyes. "I will, ma'am." I squeezed her hands again and slipped from the kitchen as Caleb said goodbye.

I was already seated in the truck when Caleb stepped into the driver's seat. My hands squeezed together in my lap, eyes focused on a mountain peak rising in the distance. I could feel his eyes lingering on me.

"Are you ok?" He broke the awkward silence, his body angled toward me as he backed out of the driveway and onto the main road. "That was probably hard for you back there."

"I'm fine," I murmured. It wasn't completely a lie.

"I should have warned you that her memory fails sometimes. It's not always that bad and I've gotten used to it. She's completely capable of caring for herself in every other way. She's just forgetful sometimes."

I nodded, still struggling to reign in the emotions that had been triggered at the mention of my dad. It wasn't Mrs. Jensen's fault that I now felt like crying.

"I'm sorry she brought up your dad." Caleb's tone was unexpectedly soft, surprising me out of my slump.

"It's fine," I snapped, straightening my posture, and staring straight through the windshield. "Let's not discuss it. Please."

Only a couple of seconds had passed before I felt guilty for my short-tempered outburst. "I'm sorry," I said. "I shouldn't have snapped at you. Hearing her talk about my dad like he was alive and just working a few miles down the road triggered me. But it's ok. It's no one's fault."

"Except for mine?"

Startled, I turned to him. His whiskey-colored eyes swept over me.

"No," I said automatically. Then, with a grudging shrug of my shoulders, "Well, you said it. Not me."

The expression on his face shifted from stoic to sad in an instant. "Well, there you have it," he said. "The one reason we'll never be friends."

The weariness in his tone was unmistakable. I shook my head. "It's crazy to think that we were almost more than good friends once." I stopped myself before I said any more. The past was the past. There was no point in bringing old, dead hopes into the future.

The truck stopped in front of my home. It idled, the rumble of the engine the only sound to break the silence. I tried to calm the hasty beat of my heart. Both of us were quiet as we stared at the yard.

"Thanks for the ride." I grabbed my bags, ready to leap from the truck and run straight to my room where I could finally let the tears go.

"Samantha." Caleb stretched a hand toward me. I stared at it, noticing a few white, fine-lined scars in the skin. Scars he'd probably obtained while working on his ranch.

"I think you should come out and spend some one-on-one time with the horses this week. Really get to know the ones we use for the program."

I pursed my lips, prepared to vehemently refuse the idea of spending one-on-one time with any horse. He continued quickly before I could protest.

"I think it'll help with the new marketing program if you really know the horses for yourself. There are some truly special ones who have a real gift for working with the kids. I'm moving a group of them to one of our rear pastures to let them graze this week. You can come along."

I cocked my head at him, my right eyebrow lifting skeptically. "Really? The horses have a gift for working with kids. Really?" I tried to keep the impatience from my voice, but it slipped through anyways.

His big shoulders moved up and down in a shrug. "You'd be surprised. Horses know more than you give them credit for. They are emotional, intelligent creatures who are sometimes stubborn, sassy, and flighty. Kind of like you in a lot of ways." I watched as he flashed a reserved grin at me. The stern expression on his handsome face softened.

That smile. Involuntarily, my heart skipped a beat. Underneath his stern, stoic exterior, I caught a glimpse of the young, confident cowboy who used to inspire my girlish daydreams of the future.

No. I'll never let myself be sucked into his orbit again. I shook my head, refusing to let myself be pulled from my bad mood. Instead, I rolled my eyes. "Fine, I'll come out again this week."

With that, I hopped from the truck and ran toward the house without glancing back.

Chapter Seven

I DECIDED TO stall for as long as I could, hoping that Caleb would forget that he'd asked me to come to the ranch again. Not only did I want to avoid the horses, but I preferred to avoid as much contact with their owner as I could. I may have volunteered to work for him, but that didn't mean I wanted to spend time in his company.

The next couple of days passed quickly as I divided my time between working in our garden and downloading and editing the photos I'd taken. I also worked on a new website for the program. I was glad I'd taken so many extra photos. The summer program was going to need its own social media account. Sitting at my bedroom desk for the second day in a row, sipping cooling tea from my mug, I almost laughed aloud at the thought of Caleb trying to navigate social media. Just the concept of hashtags and engagement, let alone the algorithm, would probably drive him batty.

Good, I thought, adding crisp, bright photos to a folder on my desktop. Eventually, I'd put the whole file onto a flash drive and help him install it onto his own computer. *Caleb deserves to be driven batty occasionally.*

My phone pinged with another message alert. Amanda and I had been chatting back and forth over the past couple of days.

AMANDA: I still can't believe that you, of all people, work at a horse ranch!

In my opinion, her over-use of emoticons nearly negated her whole college degree. I glanced at my phone, smiling with amusement at my overly dramatic friend.

ME: I don't work AT a horse ranch.

ME: Technically, I'm volunteering my services for a summer program that happens to be located on a horse ranch.

ME: There's a difference. I absolutely refuse to work with those hulking beasts.

Amanda was the only person who knew that horses made me uncomfortable.

AMANDA: Hulking beasts? Do you mean Caleb or the actual horses themselves?

The message was accompanied by a winking face.

ME: Ha! Funny. I meant Caleb for sure. Lol.

AMANDA: You still haven't sent me a photo of him.

AMANDA: I want to know what this beastly cowboy looks like.

One of the photos I'd snapped of Caleb with the colt was open on my desktop. I brought it up, studying the way the light had created a soft, pale glow all around his tall form. It was a good photo. I couldn't deny that he was an eye-catching man. Did I really want to send this one to Amanda though? I didn't trust her not to jump on the next plane to Bozeman once she caught sight of it. My phone pinged again.

AMANDA: He's probably ugly.

AMANDA: Frankly, I'm not sure I trust your taste.

AMANDA: Remember the guy in Econ that you thought was cute?

This time a series of faces conveyed Amanda's opinion of my taste in men. I sighed, studying the angles in Caleb's face.

ME: Fine. I'll send one over soon.

AMANDA: Don't take too long. I'm planning to fly out for a visit next month.

AMANDA: I want to be prepared to meet your cowboy. Wouldn't want my jaw to drop on the floor.

AMANDA: If he's as good-looking as you say....

I cringed.

ME: He's definitely not my cowboy. I can't even stand the man.

ME: He knows how I feel about him too.

ME: It's a miracle we haven't flown at each other's throats with just this amount of contact. I'm only doing this for my brothers and my career.

ME: But oh my gosh! Are you really coming to visit me?

ME: That would be amazing! I can't wait to see you.

AMANDA: Can't wait to see you too. I expect you to give me the full country welcome.

I wasn't sure what the full-country-welcome was supposed to entail, but I reassured my city-dwelling friend that we would have a wonderful time.

"Sammie?" Dean's voice called up the stairs.

I took a moment to minimize the photo of Caleb before walking to the landing.

Dean was standing at the bottom of the stairs, one dusty, boot-clad foot resting on the first step. He looked tired. The three of them had worked in the hay field all day and were preparing for another trip up the mountain. Normally, summers meant that my brothers would spend a lot more time camping on the range with our herd, working on reforestation projects, and guarding the cattle from the wild animals and treacherous mountain trails. Since Mom's trip had landed in the summer though, I suspected that they were trying to stay closer to home to keep me company.

The scent of the pot roast I'd put in the crockpot this morning wafted up to me from the kitchen. Succulent browned beef, baby potatoes, and sweet carrots. I'd make a graving from the drippings later.

I was glad I'd been able to put my mom's recipes to good use this week and have a hot meal waiting for my brothers when they returned home. It wasn't any trouble for me and from the way they raved and devoured every scrap, they certainly seemed to appreciate it. Fixing dinners for my brothers was doing a tiny bit to alleviate my guilt for planning to move overseas in a few months.

"Hi, Dean. Are you guys back for the night? I can finish dinner and have it on the table in about twenty minutes."

He smiled at me. "Thank you. That's perfect. I'm headed to take a shower to wash off all this dirt."

"Yeah, you stink," I teased. "I can smell you boys coming in the back door."

"You've got jokes," Dean teased back. "By the way, Caleb called me this afternoon. He said he can't wait any longer to take this group of horses to pasture. He wants you there tomorrow at six sharp."

"Why did he call you?" I sputtered, trying to think of some reason I could give Dean that would get me off the hook. "I don't want…."

My brother's sharp blue eyes pierced up at me. "Is there some reason you can't make it tomorrow morning? Do you have other plans?"

He was teasing, but I knew he was right. I'd signed up for this. Maybe not the full horse ranch experience, but I owed it to my commitment to make sure I wasn't missing anything important for the campaign. And Caleb must have thought it was important to enlist my brother's help.

"K." I turned away so that he couldn't see the sour expression that was imprinting itself onto my face. "Text him and tell him I'll be there. Do you think Vincent will mind if I borrow his truck tomorrow?" Caleb had discovered that one of the spark plugs needed to be replaced on the truck. He'd made the repair and dropped the truck off the same night I'd visited his property.

"That depends. Are you going to break it again?" Dean called to me. I spun toward him and rolled my eyes. He grinned. "And now I'm off to shower. We're starving, woman. Can't wait to eat your cooking."

I waited a few moments until he was out of sight before heading downstairs to the kitchen. My shoulders felt tense as I busied myself carving the roast and spooning the fall-apart potatoes and carrots into a serving dish. I ladled out spoonfuls of the drippings and made a quick savory gravy on the stove. Fresh bread warmed in the oven, and I quickly pulled a green salad from the fridge and dressed it with a vinaigrette.

I may have been away for years, but I hadn't forgotten the ravenous hunger of men fresh from the range. I'd been looking forward to the succulent beef, but my own appetite might have taken a hit.

As my brothers piled into the kitchen one-by-one, I couldn't shake the awful feeling of dread that tomorrow was going to be a complete disaster. Best case scenario: I had to face my worst fear and be face-to-face with the horses for more than a few minutes. Maybe even touch one?

Worst case scenario: One of the horses took an instant dislike to me and kicked me right in the head. My successful tour of Caleb's ranch had been a fluke. It was supposed to be a one-off. I'd never intended to have anything to do with the horses themselves. Once upon a time, riding one of Caleb's beautiful Arabians was an activity I had relished. I'd been so carefree as a teenager, trusting that my strong dad and brothers would always take care of me. I didn't want to be that girl anymore though. The one who naively thought that no harm would ever come to her loved ones.

My brothers were aware that I'd avoided horses since our quarter horse had nearly thrown me and they disapproved. Their philosophy was that if you had a bad experience with a horse, you got right back on it and rode again. I never told them the real reason that the incident had scared me so much. I didn't want to tell them the truth. They didn't know how hard I had to work to calm my racing heart when I watched them ride out of the barnyard on the backs of our range horses. Or how I prayed every night that they would return safely.

Sunrise was just beginning to tinge the sky as I drove to Caleb's ranch. I'd considered simply not showing up. But backing out of something I'd committed to doing wasn't usually my style.

Caleb seemed convinced that I needed a hands-on experience to be able to do the youth camp its full justice. As the truck rumbled down the road, I worried that he secretly wanted to watch me suffer. Maybe he wanted to watch me get stepped on by a horse just so he could pay me back for my hostility toward him.

Hands shaking, I parked the truck in the yard and walked toward one of the stables where I could see that a small group of horses had already been gathered. What did Caleb expect of me anyways? Was I supposed to brush down a horse? Give it some grain? Open a gate as the ranch hands led the groups into their new pastures? I was pointless here, a fish out of water, and I knew it. And the way Caleb eyed me as I entered the stable told me that he knew it too.

"You're late, Samantha," he called sternly. I winced. His voice was too loud for this early in the morning. I'd barely managed a sip of coffee and a bite of toast before I'd had to leave.

His long legs made quick strides toward me. To my right, Jenna was handling a speckled gray horse, its feet dancing on the hay strewn floor. I recognized the horse as one of the mares Griff had introduced me to the other day. Jenna angled her body toward me. I saw her watching Caleb's approach.

He stopped two feet away. I tilted my head to look up at him.

"You look as tired as a cowboy after a five-day ride." His tone was mocking. "What's the matter, city-girl? Too early for you?"

Irritated, I cocked an eye at him and scowled. My hand ran down the braid that I'd carefully plaited my hair into this morning. Better to have my mane safely tamed and away from the reach of large, snapping horse teeth.

"I am tired," I snapped. "Not everyone runs around at the crack of dawn doing ranch things. Watch it, Caleb Kane." I pointed a finger toward him sharply. "You're already starting on the wrong foot. I'm here doing you a favor."

"You tell him, Samantha." Jenna's smooth, even voice appeared behind Caleb. I peeked around him to see that she had led the mare toward us. She clapped a hand on Caleb's shoulder. Her even, white teeth sparkled. "This one needs a taking-down sometimes. He's a feisty one."

Her perfectly pitched voice made me want to roll my eyes. In my opinion, Jenna was a little too pretty to be running around a horse ranch. How did she make old jeans and a worn-in flannel shirt look like an influencer's fashion post? I straightened my posture as she continued, feeling like an overly tall, gangly slog in my worn-out jeans and equally worn-out t-shirt.

"And besides…" She turned to me, her eyes lit with a sus-piciously friendly sparkle. "You only look the tiniest bit tired, Sammie. You must think us ranch-people are crazy to be out on the land while most of the world is still sleeping." Her laugh carried throughout the lofty space.

I stared at her, too shocked by her passive aggressive tone to reply. Her face was beginning to annoy me as much as Caleb's. Warily, I eyed her, wondering what had caused this sudden, subtle aggression. I sensed Caleb observing our exchange quietly.

Did Jenna like Caleb and assume that I was a rival for his affections? It all began to click. *Great. Just when I hoped that I could make a friend out here.* The morning was passing, and my mood was not improving.

It got even worse when Caleb cleared his throat. "Samantha, you'll be riding Sandy today."

Jenna moved up and pressed the mare's lead into my hand. I dropped it and stepped back. The gray horse dipped her head and began to nuzzle around for stray bits of hay on the stable floor.

"What? Excuse me? What?"

Caleb looked at me and cocked his head. "You'll. Be. Riding. Sandy."

"I don't want to ride this horse." I was seconds away from stamping my boot on the floor. It was possible that I was going to have a full-on meltdown before seven in the morning.

The creases around Caleb's eyes deepened as he frowned. "I can put you with one of the other horses, but I think you'll be more comfortable on Sandy. She's very sweet and I'm assuming you haven't ridden for a while?"

"I don't ride horses anymore," I replied stiffly. Jenna was watching me from just outside the arena, staring boldly at our exchange. Tension crackled in the stable. I wondered if Caleb would ever figure out why I had stopped riding. I wondered if the guilt was consuming him the way it had been consuming me for the last four years....

He stepped toward me, grabbing Sandy's lead from the floor. "Samantha..." Unexpected kindness seeped into his tone. "We're just leading the horses to pasture and I thought that you might as well take the chance to get to know them with a short ride. I promise you'll be safe. Sandy is gentle and easy-going." He held the lead toward me on the tips of his fingers. "I would never put anyone in harm's way."

Lies, my rebellious brain seethed. I shook my head stubbornly, refusing to allow his quietly spoken words to sway me. *I know who you really are, Caleb.*

"Besides, I happen to recall many afternoons that you spent riding here," Caleb continued. "You're a really good horsewoman."

"That was before…." I started to spit out a barbed reply but forced myself to stop. My mind raced. I could curtly remind him of the colt that he and his father had sold to my dad and put a stop to the entire exchange. But if I continued to make a scene, the tension it would cause would destroy my opportunity to prove my qualifications to my family. There would be no way Caleb would want me working on his program if I said what was on my mind. If I got kicked out of the youth camp, how would I advance my career?

Picking a fresh fight with Caleb would damage my plans and I refused to do that.

I could throw a fit. Or I could grit my teeth and pray that I could get through the next few hours without having a full-blown panic attack. I eyed the mellow dappled horse. I knew I could manage her. I just didn't want to.

Please give me the strength to get through this, I prayed silently. "Fine." I rolled my eyes and grabbed Sandy's bridle.

"Do you need help getting up?" Caleb asked as I moved carefully to the horse's side. He stepped forward, hand extended. His fingertips hovered near my arm, but I shook him away.

"No. I don't need your help."

"Good." He walked outside. "Be ready to leave in five minutes."

There wasn't any point in delaying the inevitable. If I was going to do this because I was too stubborn not to, I just had to get it done. I placed my left hand on Sandy's withers, feeling her powerful, warm energy below my hand. Her body responded to my touch, a shiver rippling over her hide. She was probably a sweet horse. I just didn't want anything to do with her. Anxiety rippled through me, a gray sweeping wave.

It had caught me by surprise that Caleb remembered the days I'd spent here riding his family's elegant, poised Arabians. It was no mystery to me why my dad had wanted to purchase one for himself. Maybe—for just a few hours—I could pretend to be his fearless daughter again. Maybe I could regain some of what I'd lost if I just set aside my anxiety and rode the dang horse.

Just like riding a bicycle, I tried to convince myself.

I used my left hand to grab the saddle horn. Sliding my foot into the stirrup, in a quick, fluid motion, I lifted myself up onto Sandy's back and settled into the saddle. Involuntarily, my eyes squeezed themselves shut as I prepared for her to buck or kick. But when the seconds passed and I wasn't thrown and crushed against the stable wall, I opened my eyes and looked down. The ground was far away on the back of a horse, farther than I remembered. The world began to spin.

"Looks like you're a natural up on that horse." An unfamiliar voice spoke behind me. Whipping my head around, my eyes landed on a good-looking, brown-haired young man around my age. He was grinning at me, his wide brown eyes twinkling in my direction. The horse he rode was a pretty bay. It danced back and forth, obviously ready to go.

Instinctively, I pulled my shoulders back and assumed my best riding posture. I couldn't tell whether he was being serious or making fun of me.

"I used to ride quite a bit," I replied, trying not to let my uncertainty show. Gently, I tapped Sandy's flank with the heel of my boot, urging her forward to follow the group of horses now exiting the yard. Ahead, Caleb and Jenna rode next to each other, their heads bent together in conversation.

The stranger nudged his horse to come alongside of mine. "It shows," he said. "You can always tell a longtime rider from their posture." Sandy broke into a slow trot.

"I'm Ian, by the way," he continued. I glanced at him. A shy smile crept over my lips. I'd never admit it to anyone, but most men made me nervous. Especially brown-haired, grinning, handsome young men like Ian. *Or Caleb.* But he intimidated me for a host of other reasons.

"I'm Samantha. Sammie," I volunteered. Ian smiled at me, his expression welcoming.

"Pleased to meet you." He tipped his tan hat at me, and the old-fashioned gesture sent a tingle of appreciation down my spine. "I'm a ranch hand here. Haven't seen you around before. Did Caleb just hire you?"

I shook my head. "Oh no! I do not work here. Well, in a way that's not true. But I don't work on the ranch."

Ian gave me a puzzled look and I hastened to clarify. "I'm the new social media advisor. So yes, in a way Caleb did just hire me, but he is my client. I'm helping the ranch coordinate and market the camp while I'm here for the summer."

Had I just made my job sound way more important than it was? Social media advisor? Where had that come from? I bit my tongue before I volunteered any more information.

"Oh, you're the McCade girl?" Ian exclaimed, understanding dawning in his brown eyes.

I nodded. Curtly. *The McCade girl.* I knew Ian didn't mean anything derogatory by it. He didn't know me. But the expression made me feel like I had really become a stranger in my own hometown. As if I needed any help in remembering that Cascade Valley wasn't my home anymore.

"I've heard that you're already doing amazing things for the charity. Thanks for helping us out. It's nice of you. I'm sure you're very talented."

Slightly mollified, I glanced at him and let my smile bloom. "Thanks, Ian."

"Have you made it out of the creative cave long enough to enjoy some relaxation? A group of my friends and I hang out at the lake all the time. I'd be happy to escort you up there sometime if you'd like to go?"

Ian cleared his throat, and I gave him a sidelong glance.

Escort. Such a quaint word you'd only hear in the country. The kind of old-fashioned gentlemanliness that had gone out of style in the cities. I smiled and my eyes flickered at him shyly. He was cute and seemed sweet.

I did need a new group of friends. Most of my tiny graduating class had moved away to the bigger cities to pursue jobs and families. My return home had been quieter and lonelier than I'd anticipated, so Ian's offer of friendship was a welcome one.

"Ian." Caleb's gruff voice interrupted before I could reply. We both looked up to see him waving us over. Our horses had slowed as we'd talked and were lingering far behind the rear of the group.

Caleb nudged his mount and trotted toward us. "Samantha will be riding with me. I'd like you to go up ahead and herd the extra horses to pasture with Jenna."

"Sure thing, boss," Ian replied to Caleb's orders without hesitation. But I caught the regretful glance he threw my way. "Nice to meet you, Samantha. I'll see you around." He winked at me and let his horse break into a quick trot to the front of the line.

I was disappointed that he was leaving. Ian had taken my mind off my nerves. Looked like I'd be stuck at the back of the line by myself. My cheeks reddened as I caught Caleb watching me as I watched Ian ride away.

Caleb whistled and waved over his head. I saw Jenna wave back and the small group of horses began to move toward the gate that led to the rear of the property. I did my best to remain straight and steady in my saddle as Sandy trotted gracefully. To my surprise, Caleb kept pace with me.

His silence was unnerving. "Shouldn't you be riding at the front of the line? Boss?"

"No. Jenna and Ian can handle it. We're riding up a different way."

"Why?" I countered in alarm, my voice echoing loudly in the early morning air. Having to deal with Caleb at all was bad enough on my nerves. Having to deal with him alone was too much. Jenna turned in her saddle to look at us.

"They are taking the shortest route to the pasture." He nodded toward the small herd. "It's quite a bit steeper than the longer route.

There are a couple of hills. I figured you might want to avoid the narrow switchback, since you haven't ridden in a while."

"Uh, ok," I stammered, suddenly grateful that he'd changed the plan. I'd forgotten that Caleb's property wasn't entirely flat. It rose up, then opened to a long stretch of meadow on the backside. If I was too stubborn to refuse to ride Sandy, avoiding a narrow trail sounded like the better option. I wasn't sure that my stomach could handle the descent down a steeper path.

Jenna whirled her horse around and called to us. "Are you two going to catch up with us?" She lingered, holding her horse back from trotting after the others.

"You go on," Caleb waved at her. "I'm going to take Samantha the long way."

I wondered if Caleb caught the long, hard stare Jenna threw me. Her mouth set itself into a straight line, but with a curt nod and wave, she spurred her horse forward.

The trail branched off a few paces ahead. Caleb moved in front of me, nudging his horse into a quicker pace. I watched as Ian and Jenna steered the horses to the path toward the left. It was a narrow trail that looked rocky and climbed straight up the hill behind the property. Caleb led us toward the right, a path that was much wider with only a slight incline. A two-lane trail, with plenty of room for a truck or a couple of horses side by side.

"I thought you might like to see the view on this side anyway. It's pretty in the mornings." He broke the silence after several minutes, interrupting the steady clip of our horses' hooves along the trail. "And I want to show you an expansion idea I've been mulling over for the youth camp next year."

I was too busy trying to reaccustom my body to the jarring bounce of my ride's stride to answer. Sandy had picked up her pace to match Caleb's. By the way she kept tossing her head and snorting, she seemed to be enjoying the journey. I already knew that my backside was going to regret this decision tomorrow.

The awkward silence stretched between us as the morning opened. Despite my tension, I found myself captured by the freshness of the air, the promise of warmth entering the chilled earth as the sun rose above the eastern horizon, and the sweet, happy trill of birds chirping in the pines that bordered the trail. It wasn't surprising that my brothers always said they loved getting onto the ranch before the sun came up. This was nothing like the chaotic, hectic rush of traffic and human bodies on the streets of Seattle. This was magical. Peaceful.

Inwardly, I resolved to be better about rising early in the morning to enjoy these cool, fresh Montana summer days. Before I left my family home for good.

"So…." Caleb's voice broke into the chirping of the birds. I glanced toward him, my expression friendlier because of the beauty of the morning.

"So?"

"You and Ian made each other's acquaintance today," he said slowly. "He's a good man. Hard working. Honest."

"He seemed nice," I admitted. "He invited me to hang out at the lake with his group of friends."

I blurted the last sentence out before I could bite it back and then felt myself blush at the odd look Caleb threw my way. He cleared his throat.

"Ian's probably invited a few girls out to the lake. He's understandably popular with the young ladies in the valley."

"Oh? And what's so understandable about it?"

Caleb raised an eyebrow. "Come on, Samantha," he said with a sarcastic echo in his tone. "You can't tell me you don't appreciate the company of a good-looking guy? Ian may not be University of Washington quality, but he's top tier for Cascade Valley."

We had climbed above the ranch now, ascending a slight incline that led to a green and pretty valley. Rich and fertile grazing land stretched toward the line where the forest began in the distance. But the view was lost on me as I let my temper boil over toward the cowboy riding next to me.

"Oh, so you're saying that I'm so shallow that all I care about is the way someone looks?" My eyes shot daggers at Caleb. "That the fact that I have a college education has somehow turned me into this materialistic jerk and destroyed my ability to see good character when I find it?

"That's not what I was saying, but now that you bring it up, didn't it?" He stared at me coolly. "Are you really telling me that Seattle didn't influence the way you look at the world now?"

"Yes, it did. It taught me that there's more to life than horses and cows and Cascade Valley." Without thinking, I dug my heels into Sandy's flank. I slapped the reins against her shoulders, desperate to escape this conversation. The mare responded immediately, springing into a gallop. Suddenly, I found myself attached to the back of a horse who was flying down the gently sloping trail.

I gasped. The speed made the wind catch sharply in my throat. I'd forgotten how fast an Arabian could run and the downward slope wasn't doing anything to slow Sandy's stride. Instinctively, I pressed my knees into her side, feeling myself shake and bounce in the saddle, desperate to avoid flying off her back.

All my years of experience on the back of a horse flew out of my head. I couldn't remember what I was supposed to do to make Sandy slow her pace. Terror whipped through me. *Was I going to get thrown and strike my head on a rock just like my dad?* I heard my own scream as I tucked my face into the silky mane on Sandy's neck and hung on for dear life.

"Hold on, Samantha." Caleb's deep voice pierced my ears. "I'll slow her down."

He must have been racing after me. I opened my eyes to see his tanned hand reach out to grab the reins. The veins in his forearms flexed as he took control of the mare. I let the reins slip from my fingers, giving him complete control.

"Whoa, girl. Whoa." Caleb's voice was gentle but firm as he coaxed the galloping horse to slow down to a brisk trot. "There you go. Slow it down. Nice and easy."

Sandy responded quickly to his commands. It couldn't have been more than thirty seconds before I felt her lithe body descend into a gentle walk. I risked raising my head and saw that we'd just emerged from the trail onto level ground again. I drew the reins back through my fingers, yanking them from Caleb's hand, and steered Sandy toward a creek that ran along the valley floor.

I walked her to the edge, then stiffly dismounted. I could sense Caleb's presence behind me as he swung to the ground. Silently, he walked his horse to the water. I avoided looking in his direction. My eyes were trained on the hilltops in the far distance.

"Samantha? Are you ok?" He was standing right next to me. I felt the warmth of his fingers as they brushed over my arm. His touch made a tingle flash across my skin. Angrily, I jerked my arm away.

"I'm fine," I hissed through gritted teeth. My eyes shot daggers at him.

"Are you sure? Did Sandy scare you? She's always been fast. It takes people by surprise if they don't know her. I should have warned you, but I didn't expect you to spur her on like that."

"You know what, Caleb. Why do you even care if I'm alright? You're the reason it happened in the first place." I spun around to face him, my fury flashing as I stared into his eyes. I stretched up to wave a finger in his face. I hadn't been this close to him since….

Don't think about that. Don't think about that day. I scolded myself as I waited for him to yell back at me. I wanted him to yell. So that I could unleash the full onslaught of my grief onto him.

Caleb didn't know that I'd developed a fear of horses after my dad's death. He didn't know that I'd been terrified to ride Sandy today, but I'd done it anyway because I'd wanted him to see that I wasn't the same starry-eyed young girl who had lost her dad…because of his selfish actions. I was strong and I was resilient, and I wasn't going to let him intimidate me.

But his nearness was more disconcerting than I'd anticipated. Suddenly I found myself trapped in his warm whiskey eyes. I expected them to be filled with the same animosity that I felt. Normally, his expression was unreadable to me. But now it was filled with an unmistakable combination of uncertainty and concern.

I was crowded between Caleb and Sandy, her bulky withers pushing me toward his chest. The scent of hay and early morning dew and Caleb filled my nostrils. He'd always had a unique scent that I would recognize anywhere.

I shuddered, thinking of how fortunate it was that he'd stopped Sandy before I lost all control. My dad's broken, bruised body flashed through my head, but I hardened my heart, refusing to break down into tears in front of this man.

"Samantha, I do care," Caleb replied in a quiet voice.

"Right?" I scoffed. "Because of the insurance claim you think you'd have to pay if I got hurt? Because of the questions you know would be raised if another person from the same family got thrown from one of your horses. You know what? I'm not sure if you have any business letting a bunch of inexperienced kids come here for your summer camp."

"Sandy is a well-trained and gentle horse." Caleb's temper flashed at me, catching me off guard. His face darkened. "She did exactly what you told her to do. Then she did exactly what I told her to do. You do realize you're ok, right? Nothing happened to you."

I spun away. "Does everyone just do what you tell them to do, Caleb? Good ol' boss, Caleb. He says *jump* and everyone else says *how high?*"

"What are you talking about?"

"I resent the fact that you implied that I'm just some shallow woman who only cares about materialism and good looks." My voice inched toward a shout. Suddenly, I remembered why I had been mad in the first place. "Ian was nice to me. He actually tried to make me feel welcome here, not treat me like an inconvenient stranger. I appreciated that he tried to talk to me and make friends with me. That is more than I can say of you."

"You're actually trying to say that I'm not nice to you?" Caleb's eyes narrowed. He bent over me, his bearded face only a few inches away from mine. "And when did I call you shallow?"

"You didn't." I threw up my hands in exasperation.

"I'm not nice to you? I've welcomed you back home. I've given you an opportunity to build your resume. What am I missing here? I thought we could try to be friends. Get along for the sake of your brothers. What horrible and mean things have I done to make you resent me this badly?"

"You got my dad killed." The words flew from my mouth.

Caleb froze, the fiery expression in his face turning to ice as he watched me. He straightened to his full height and stepped backwards.

Resolutely, I lifted my chin and squared my shoulders, determined not to be intimidated by the stern expression written across his face.

"You're never going to be able to move past what happened to him." Caleb's voice was low and grim. "You're never going to be able to forgive the fact that my family sold him that horse, are you?"

"I don't think so." I shook my head, tears stinging my eyes. "I know that's wrong. I know the Bible tells us to forgive, but I just don't know how to forgive *you*. I resent you so much because you and your dad sold him the horse that ended up getting him into that accident." My voice broke and a sob came from my throat. "He wanted that horse so badly. He was so proud of him. And you knew that colt hadn't gone through enough training to be safe for a rider. That's why I can't forgive you."

"Why do you keep going around saying that?" Caleb threw up his hands. "What do you think I did? Why did you tell our entire town that I deserved to go to jail?"

It was time that I told him the truth. "Because I heard you and your dad talking the night that my dad bought the horse. Your dad said that it would be taking advantage if you sold the horse, but you insisted that it should be sold. That you wouldn't get top dollar for him anywhere else. And I was going to tell my dad what I'd overheard, but I trusted your family. I trusted you. I *liked* you. And I thought that there was no way you would do something to take advantage of us."

I stared at him bitterly. "My brothers tell me that I shouldn't blame you. And honestly, I should blame myself. Actually, I do blame myself. I betrayed my dad's safety because I had a crush on you. And I thought you liked me too."

We both froze at my frank admission. It was more than I'd ever wanted to admit, but I was too tired and annoyed to care. Caleb shook his head. "I did like you. I liked you a lot, Samantha. Until you accused me of something I hadn't done."

He stepped toward me. His hands lifted to grip my elbows and he pulled me toward his chest. I wanted to resist, wanted to pull away, wanted to yell at him again. But I was exhausted, the emotional outburst having stripped me of energy.

"I wish you had talked to me before." I felt his strong arms go around my back in a gentle hug. He drew me closer.

Despite the instinct to push him away, I leaned in and buried my face in his shirt. The buttons pressed cold and hard against my cheek. At least now I could cry without him seeing me look like a blubbering idiot. His embrace was an unexpected combination of strong and soft.

Caleb was whispering against my hair. "If I could take it all back, I would. Nothing that you heard that night had anything to do with the colt that your dad was riding that day. My dad and I were discussing a man from Texas who wanted to purchase one of our older mares for his daughter. The horse had been slightly injured and she was really only suitable for slow recreational riding. You must believe me. I loved your dad. And you must believe that I really care about your family. I've always cared for you."

The last words were whispered so softly that I wasn't sure if I'd heard him. I lifted my head, tears streaking down my face. What he'd just said echoed in my mind. "So you didn't sell him that colt knowing it was a risk?"

"I would never do that to anyone," Caleb stared at me earnestly, his head bent low over mine.

Everything that I'd believed about that day came crashing around me. Tears streaked freely down my face. My voice faltered. I felt like I was about to break. "I don't know how you think this is supposed to make it better. So I falsely accused you and you never said anything to correct me?"

"You never gave me a chance. I knew you were grieving. I thought we had time to talk after you calmed down. I didn't know you were going to leave the valley and never speak to me again," Caleb replied.

"You should have tried to talk to me," I blubbered. "But now it's too late. Maybe you didn't take advantage of my family. But don't you understand what was taken from me? Celebrations, life milestones, my wedding, future children…my dad won't be present for any of those events. I can't even ride horses anymore because I am afraid."

His face was still inches from mine, his hat pushed back on his forehead. I watched his eyes flicker down to my mouth, his gaze resting briefly on my lips before flickering up again. His lips parted, then clamped shut. As if he wanted to say something but stopped himself before he could utter the words. Warmth spread though my limbs, unfurling all the way to my fingertips.

"I do understand," he finally murmured. I realized that his arms were still wrapped around my waist. They flexed, pulling me up and into him a little more

His lips twitched and I felt a tingle of awareness flood across my skin, responding instinctively to the strong, masculine body pressed against mine. His beard looked like it would be soft if I ran my fingers through it. His nose was straight, his jaw sharp and strong. It was my turn to flicker my gaze down to the full lips hidden beneath the beard.

He could kiss me right now. Unbidden, the thought popped into my head. My stomach dropped, but to my shock, the thought sent warm shivers along my spine. If he kissed me, would I even want to stop him?

What is wrong with me? I was supposed to be giving Caleb a piece of my mind. Not imagining what it would feel like if he leaned forward and pressed his lips to mine. I couldn't let him hug me. I couldn't let him whisper words of comfort in my ear as we stood next to a babbling brook. Our life wasn't a romance novel. There was real grief and heartbreak standing between us.

Placing my hands firmly on his chest, I pushed away, breaking the hold of his arms.

"Samantha." Caleb reached for me again.

I backed away, not letting him touch me. "I'm happy to work with you on this project. I'm doing it for my brothers' sake. It makes them happy to see us getting along. You're a part of my family's life here. And what you're putting together for these kids is noble. I'll give you that. But that's as far as it goes. We can't be friends."

He took a long step toward me. His eyes flickered darkly. A tingle ran up my spine in response. "But I'd really like to be friends, Sammie. Just like before," he said quietly.

I took another step back. "No."

"Uh, Sammie?"

"No, Caleb. We're both adults. The past needs to stay in the past. Let's keep this professional and be civil for Dean, Vincent, and Knox's sake."

"Samantha!" Caleb's voice was urgent, and he lunged for me, hands outstretched. Panicking, I took one last step backward and felt a snap as my ankle twisted under me. The air behind me gave way and I scrabbled my hands, trying to keep my balance. With a splash, I slipped into the creek and was suddenly submerged under fifteen inches of icy mountain stream water.

"Are you kidding me?" I yelled, both in pain and fury. The horses danced sideways, no doubt frightened by my outburst.

Caleb came into my view, leaning over the edge of the creek bed, hands on his knees. His face was a battle between worry and amusement. "I tried to warn you," he said.

"You could have done a better job," I yelled again. "Are you going to help me up or what?"

He stretched a hand toward me, and I grabbed it, using the leverage to haul myself up.

"My ankle," I exclaimed as I put weight on it.

The pain shooting through my ankle was excruciating. And I was soaking wet and beginning to shiver.

"Have you broken it?" Caleb said, leaning me against him and bending over to look at my foot.

"I don't think so. It might just be sprained."

"Well, it looks like that's the end of your ranching adventures for a while." His voice was grim. "I need to get you home and get that ankle looked at."

"Don't worry about me. Go on ahead and take care of whatever you need to do today."

He threw me a look. "Like I'm going to put you back on a horse and let you ride by yourself after all of this. Your brothers would have my head."

"Well, what do you want me to do then?"

Instead of an answer, I found myself scooped off the ground and lifted into the air. Caleb's strong arms lifted me from the water, and he stepped up the embankment, back onto dry ground.

"What are you doing?" The instinct to protest was immediate. I kicked my feet and regretted the move instantly. A grimace flashed across my face. The sharp, shooting pain in my ankle made me bite my lower lip to keep from whimpering.

"Carrying you back to Sandy," Caleb replied. "Unless you prefer to hobble to her on your one good foot? I know you don't want to ride her, but that's the quickest way for me to get you home."

"Put me down." My dignity took a dying shot.

"Nope. You may be a perpetual thorn in my side, but you're my responsibility today."

We were at eye level for the first time ever. His face was inches from mine. I noticed the flecks of gold in his irises, the laugh lines in his bronzed skin. He was undeniably handsome, and he was now striding across the ground with me as if I was a damsel in distress. Carrying me didn't seem to be an effort for him at all.

A disapproving expression crossed my face to hide my discomfort. Caleb was holding me. A few years ago, this would have been my teenage dream. But now? Could this day get any worse? Sandy loomed in the corner of my eye. As much as I didn't want to get onto the back of a horse again, even her bulky presence would be more comforting than this.

Caleb lifted me easily onto Sandy's back. He set me on the saddle, allowing my injured leg to loop over the saddle horn. "Trust you to manage to hurt yourself out here." He shook his head in obvious exasperation. "Now let's get you home so your brothers can fuss over you."

Chapter Eight

I HADN'T REALIZED how much I enjoyed being active on our ranch—puttering around the house, working in the garden, and collecting eggs every morning—until I was stuck on my butt for the next week. It was taking everything that I had in me to allow myself to rest and recover for the week.

My ankle had been badly twisted by the fall in the creek, but it wasn't broken. *A week of taking it easy and staying off it as much as you can and you will be good to go again,* Dr. Burke had said when he came out to visit.

My brothers had been predictably fussy when I hobbled into the house after slipping into the creek. Caleb had driven me home and let me use his arm for support. I'd flat out refused to allow him to carry me again and had even used his arm begrudgingly.

Vincent and Knox had helped me to the sofa, while Dean went to call Dr. Burke. When I had looked up, Caleb was gone.

My brothers had delayed their trip to the herd for a couple of days, fussing over me and making sure that I was plentifully supplied with snacks and drinks. But after a couple days passed, I had insisted that they continue with their plans for the week. Charlie wasn't too far away if I needed any help. They left reluctantly, but the sudden quiet gave me the chance to finish Caleb's website during the day. I spent the evenings watching old movies while I sat on the sofa with my foot propped on the ottoman.

After only a few days of house arrest, I'd accomplished several key tasks, but I was bored and going stir-crazy. A person could only stare at a computer screen for so long.

I knew the boys would be back soon. For the past couple of weeks, they'd been going on and on about some deal they were putting together. They had a meeting set up with a real estate agent in town early the following week. I hadn't really listened to their chatter, but I knew it had something to do with the old ski lodge on the mountain and a renovation project.

I pushed my laptop to the other end of the sofa and stared at myself. I'd just sent out my eighth application of the summer, this one for an overseas position as a non-profit scholarship foundation facilitator. I was more than qualified for the position. It was based in France, one of my dream destinations, and I could hardly sit still with the nervous tension racing through my body.

I eyed my clothes skeptically. "Not looking like a chic French woman today," I muttered aloud in the quiet house. The three-day old sweatpants and the faded Christian band t-shirt that I'd slept in for two nights were probably due for a wash. I ran a hand over the frizzy auburn braid flung over my shoulder. My hair was probably due for a wash as well.

After a moment's consideration, I decided to forget about the shower until later and rewarm my tea instead. I'd left it on the countertop, and it had probably gone cold. Pulling myself to my feet, I hobbled the short distance to the kitchen.

"I really should shower. I'd probably feel like a new woman." I had a habit of talking to myself aloud when I was alone.

The bell on the microwave beeped. I'd just limped forward to reach for my cup of freshly warmed tea when I heard a tapping at the back door.

I froze, as if the person standing on the porch couldn't see me from their vantage point through the glass. My mind raced and for a second, I wondered if I could drop out of view below the counter. It was not a good day for me to have visitors, looking like something the cat had dragged in from the barn.

"Uh, Samantha?" A deep voice called through the door. "Are you ok? You know I can see you standing there, right?"

Too quickly, I whirled around and winced as the pain in my ankle throbbed. Caleb's face stared at me through the screen. A subtle smirk seemed to cross his mouth.

"Do you mind if I open the door and come inside? I brought something over."

I waved my hand toward him carelessly, as if I totally hadn't been caught talking to myself and trying to play possum. "Do whatever you want. My brothers aren't here, but you can leave whatever it is on the table for them."

I kept my head down, hoping he wouldn't look too closely at me. I winced again when he opened the door and stepped inside. For once he wasn't wearing his broken-in cowboy hat. His hair was swept back neatly from his forehead. His face looked like it had been chiseled by wind and the Montana sun. Despite the heat, he was wearing jeans and a black denim button down, its silver buttons polished and shiny.

Should have opted for that shower.

He came toward me, two paper bags clutched in his hands.

"I know they're not here. I came to see you. Figured you could use a lunch out, with your bum ankle and all." Caleb stopped a few feet in front of me. His scent, that outdoorsy smell that seemed unique to him, hit my nose. He smelled like a Montana sunrise, and I knew that I most certainly did not. I tried to pull myself up to my full height and look confident. The awkward way we'd left our argument the other day flitted through my memory. I was surprised to see him.

His nose wrinkled up and he tilted his head to the side. "Have you been wearing the same clothes all week?"

"No," I spat out, instantly mortified. "Why are you here, Caleb?"

"I told you. I brought you lunch." He held up the bags.

"Well thank you." I motioned toward the kitchen table. "You can just leave the bags there on your way out."

Without missing a beat, Caleb turned toward the counter. He opened each bag and reached inside, pulling out several to-go containers.

"I'll just set them out for you and set you up with a bowl. The cafe in town was serving up a couple types of soup today. So, I brought you some of each and some ice cream too."

"Do you think that I'm five years old? Or that I have a cold?" I wanted to laugh at the unexpected combination but forced myself to frown instead.

A short, barking laugh erupted from his throat. "Well neither, but who doesn't like ice cream?"

It was true. Who didn't like ice cream?

"What kind did you get?" I eyed the containers.

"Black cherry and vanilla." He shrugged. "I remembered you getting black cherry at the drugstore once but wasn't sure what other flavors you liked."

Somehow, he'd remembered. Both flavors were my favorite.

"I'll take a scoop of each right now," I replied primly. "And no need to be stingy."

That short snicker came from his throat again. "Ok, go sit on the couch and I'll bring it to you. I can see that you're still favoring that foot."

For once, I was willing to comply without fuss. "And just for the record," I called as I hobbled to the living room. "I prefer pie with my ice cream."

I limped to the sofa and sat down with a huff of air. Caleb followed a few minutes later, coming to the front of the sofa to hand me a chilly bowl. I nodded in approval. He'd been generous with his scoops.

"Drat, I forgot my tea," I exclaimed, starting to pull myself up again. I'd need it to rewarm my hands after eating the cold treat.

"I'll get it." Caleb motioned me back down, striding toward the kitchen before I could move. I heard him restart the microwave and a minute later, he emerged in the living room again.

"Just set it on the coffee table, if you don't mind," I instructed.

"I don't mind." He set down the steaming cup and I spooned a bite of the black cherry ice cream into my mouth.

"I haven't had this in forever. Good choice," I mumbled around scoops. Sweet bites of cherry burst in my mouth.

"Would you just mind handing me the T.V. remote and my book before you leave?" I asked. "Sorry for asking you for so many things. You're just already standing." I smirked, the ice cream working its magic on my mood. Maybe plying myself with sugar was the secret to being able to be nice to Caleb for once.

I filed the thought away as he grabbed the remote and the paperback I'd indicated from the sofa table.

"I'm here to serve." He extended the remote toward me. He held onto the book though, his eyes dropping to its cover. I blushed, suddenly realizing which book I'd asked him to grab.

Caleb's head bobbed slowly, eyes hidden behind lowered eyelids. He glanced up at me after a moment, then laid the book on the sofa next to my leg.

"Cowboy romance, huh?" The words were spoken in a solemn tone. His head did an odd little bob. "I would really have pegged you more for the highlander-slash-time-travel type myself."

I blushed, a fierce heat spreading over my face. I snatched up the small paperback and hid it on the other side of my leg.

"Yeah?" I retorted without thinking. "Well, that goes to show how much you know about my type, doesn't it, Caleb Kane?" Too late, I realized how my sassy response sounded.

The same unreadable expression he'd worn at the creek flashed over his face. His lips tilted up at the corners. "It really does. But if you ever want to have a conversation about your type, I'm here for it. You certainly are a mystery to me, Samantha McCade."

He lingered over my name. My chest began to thump with nervous energy. I shoved a bite of ice cream into my mouth. Caleb leaned over me and I nearly choked at his sudden nearness. My head hit the back of the sofa, full panic mode causing my mind to race. The calm steeliness of his gaze contradicted the panic that I knew showed in mine. He was too handsome, too big and too masculine. All at once, the living room felt like it was closing in. I couldn't breathe.

Just like the other day, his gaze flickered over my face, lingering briefly at my lips. His hand lifted toward my face. I braced myself to react. "What are you doing?" I whispered. *If he kisses me, I can't kiss him back. I shouldn't. I wouldn't.*

The rough pad of his thumb brushed across the corner of my mouth. Our gazes locked. Mine was wide with fright. His simmered like the sea at midnight.

Abruptly Caleb pulled away and sucked a smear of pink ice cream off his thumb. "Mm, that flavor really is delicious."

The instant blush tinged my entire body a bright pink, heating me to my very core. He seemed to be waiting for me to respond, staring at me with a quiet, intense expression. I struggled to gather a thought coherent enough to protest the liberty he'd just taken. Just as I opened my mouth, the loud jingle of his cell phone pierced the awkward silence.

Caleb answered on the third ring. "Yeah, Jenna?" He didn't break my gaze.

An unreasonable feeling of irritation surged through me at the sound of her name. He sounded so familiar and comfortable with her.

Not that I wanted him to sound that way with me, but her presence intruding on this strange moment between us instantly annoyed me. I gathered my composure swiftly, my heart slowing its erratic beating.

"Uh huh? Well, that's not good. I'll be right there. I'm just down the road." Caleb clicked off the call. "One of the foals has colic. I need to go see about him."

"Oh, of course." My tone came out a bit snarly. "Don't feel like you need to stay on my account. You'd better go. Jenna needs you."

He was already headed toward the door but stopped to give me a strange look. A crease furrowed his brow.

"It's the foal who needs me. Enjoy that ice cream. Eat some soup later. Wouldn't want you to spoil your dinner."

I considered throwing my book at his retreating head but decided against it. Getting it back would be too much trouble. When the roar of his truck had died away, I opened my novel, determined to put our awkward exchange behind me. But I was restless. Suddenly, I couldn't concentrate. Couldn't think about anything but the sight of Caleb's chiseled face and full lips leaning over me.

It meant nothing. He wasn't ever going to kiss you. He despises you as much as you despise him.

There had been a time when I'd known that things were different. Despite my determination to focus on the novel, I couldn't help but let my mind wander back to the evening that Caleb had almost kissed me for real.

The moment had happened a few weeks before Dad's accident. Caleb's sister had just gotten married and a big group from the community had piled into the old chapel to watch. We had all been invited to the reception afterward, which had been held a short drive up the mountain at the Bear Creek Lodge, a rustic ski lodge that doubled as an event center and retreat during the summer. The long, foliage-decorated tables in the dining room had been piled high with food and drinks. A local band played folk music in the corner. Everyone kept swaying toward the dance floor, celebrating the happy couple until the bright full moon began to rise in the sky.

The newlyweds had just cut the cake. I decided to sneak outside with my piece to watch the stars as they appeared in the wide night sky. I walked toward the lookout, where I could stand and get a sweeping view of nearly the entire valley. As I watched the moon as it rose, the feeling that life was moving by all too fast swept over me. The ski lift chairs hung empty to my right, softly swinging in the summer breeze. The mountain peaks rose dark and formidable in the twilight.

I couldn't stop thinking about the months to come. I'd be entering college and leaving home for the first time. It was all so new and exciting. By the time the autumn colors washed over Cascade Valley, I would be on a journey to womanhood that seemed like a river with no end, endless possibilities stretching vast and wild before me. I heaved a deep sigh, the sound echoing into the stillness.

"That's a big sigh." I looked over my shoulder to see Caleb's dim figure approaching the lookout. "I saw you out here from the balcony and thought you looked lonely." He held two flute glasses in his hands, the liquid in them a soft, sparkling amber. He handed me one of the flutes. I took it and breathed in the scent. *Sparkling apple cider.*

Surprised by his presence, I had tried not to let my expression reflect my thoughts. I'd hardly seen him since—weeks ago—he'd complimented my hair and eyes as we stood alone together in the stables. I'd wondered if he was avoiding our ranch. After seeing him around several times a week for years, I hadn't known what to think about his unusual absence.

"A toast." He'd held up his flute and we clinked the glasses together. "To new beginnings and old friends."

We sipped the sparkling drink. It was sweet and crisp against my tongue. The longer he'd lingered on the lookout with me, the more the butterflies had danced in my stomach.

"Your dad says that you are headed off to college in a few weeks?" Caleb asked.

I nodded. "Yes, I'm headed up to the University of Washington."

"That's a big city. Quite the big change from Cascade Valley."

I had only nodded in reply, not wanting to admit how much I was going to miss my childhood home.

"I'd like to come visit you up there sometime." Caleb cleared his throat. "If you aren't too busy to see me, that is?"

His softly spoken words had caught me off guard. "Oh, no. I won't be too busy," I'd stammered quickly in response. "I would love to see you there."

"We're good friends, aren't we, Samantha?" The question had come out rushed and breathless in the twilight.

I'd glanced at him from under my lashes, trying to read his face in the moonlight. Suddenly, he had seemed almost shy, nothing like the cool, confident Caleb I'd known for years. "Yes. I think we could be good friends if we wanted to be." My hand had rested on the railing. I felt his strong, callused fingers intertwine themselves with mine. He had tugged me a little closer. Our hips had brushed.

"I'd like to be good friends with you." Caleb's murmur had whispered across my skin. He reached up and tucked a stray curl back behind my ear. "I think we would get along really well if we wanted to."

My breath had hitched, frozen in my lungs as my inexperienced brain tried to process what was happening. An indescribable joy had fluttered into my heart as my girlish daydreams seemed to be manifesting before my eyes. *Could it be possible that he likes me too?*

Suddenly, Caleb had bent over me, his tall, slim frame lowering down to my height. My heart had kicked into overdrive. Instantly, I knew that the magical moment under the stars was going to be my first kiss and that it would be claimed by none other than this handsome cowboy. The future flashed before me as I felt his breath brush the corner of my mouth. His voice had been low and graveled, a whisper that caressed my face. "I really like you, Red. I want to ask your dad about—"

"Caleb?" Dean's voice had cut through the night. "Where are you?" I'd heard Malia DeWitt's soft, amused laughter. She and Dean had been dating at the time. Their voices had drawn closer as they searched the grounds, breaking the spell that had fallen over Caleb and I.

He'd dropped my hand and stepped away. "We'll finish this conversation later. Ok?"

My heart had thrilled in my chest at the sound of the familiar nickname. I'd only nodded, watching him stride in the direction of Dean's voice. I didn't even care that my brother had interrupted the moment. Caleb had almost kissed me. And he wanted to talk to me later. I could only hope what that meant for us.

But later never came. We never had the chance to continue our conversation. If Caleb had intended to ask Dad if he could take me on a date, the opportunity had been lost and with it, all my hopes of a future with my handsome neighbor. Within a couple of weeks, Dad had passed away and I'd sworn to despise my handsome neighbor forever.

Chapter Nine

"SAMMIE." KNOX SWEPT into the kitchen where I was pulling a hot lasagna from the oven a few days later. "What are you doing tonight?"

Dean and Vincent had been on the mountain with the cattle for the last few days, but had just returned. Knox had come back early to handle the chores around the farm. I'd enjoyed the chance to connect with my youngest brother before our elder siblings arrived.

"Oh, puttering around in my slippers, brushing my cats, playing solitaire, just regular recluse, stuck-at-home kind of things."

I was mostly joking, but the words came out with a little extra bite. My ankle was healing well, according to Dr. Burke. Not as quickly as I would have liked, but enough that I could get around the house well enough now. The feeling of being stir-crazy had long since set in. I wanted to be anywhere but stuck at home, but I'd resisted the thought of leaving the ranch the past few days. I felt safe here, protected from the confusing thoughts that had been keeping me up late at night.

Knox gave me an odd look. "Um, ok weirdo. You're not doing any of those things tonight. There's a bonfire happening at Smith Ferry's place. We're all going and you're coming with us."

"Oh, Knox, no." Immediately, I began to protest. "I don't feel like going somewhere with a bunch of people."

"No is not an acceptable answer." Knox snagged a cherry tomato off the cutting board. "You've been moping around this ranch for so long that people are beginning to think we've got you locked up in here. They're asking questions, Sammie." He wiggled his eyebrows at me dramatically.

"What people?" I groaned, pulling plates from the cupboard. Dean and Vincent had arrived home a couple of hours ago. After grooming and putting up the horses, they'd both crashed in their rooms for a rare mid-afternoon nap. I expected them downstairs any minute, hungry and ready to eat.

"The town's people," Knox replied gravely, as if that was all the answer I needed. "You'll see how fun it is. Cold drinks, music, toasted marshmallows. Besides, the highlight of your week has been cooking a weekend lasagna for your brothers. That is sad."

He loped out of the kitchen. It was a beautiful evening, the warmth of the day lingering as the sun began its downward descent. Knox was right, of course. It was early summer, and the weekend stretched long and lazily in front of me. I needed to do something fun before I went crazy and hightailed it back to the city, where the endless streetlights and beckoning businesses wouldn't let you get bored, not even for a second. Since returning home to the countryside, I'd realized how true it was that cities never slept.

After he disappeared, I left my crutch in the house and limped to the garden. I maneuvered between the rows of rapidly growing vines and bushes toward the greenhouse in the corner. *Mama's Herb House of Remedies and Potions.* I could remember my siblings affectionately nicknaming the glass structure the odd little name after our mother had mentioned that she'd like to add a greenhouse to the garden late one spring many years ago. The pretty building had been built and tucked into the corner of the garden within a matter of weeks.

I smiled at the memory as I stood in the doorway. Anytime my father could make my mother smile or do something sweet to surprise her, he had always jumped at the opportunity. I could only hope to someday find a man to marry who was equally as strong and gentle as my dad. The memory made a sigh escape through my lips. I wondered if Mom missed her greenhouse. I hoped she returned home before I left again.

Limping into the greenhouse, I grabbed a small, thrifted garden basket. With its hydroponic watering system and carefully maintained internal temperature, the greenhouse could produce beautiful tomatoes, peppers, and herbs, even when the growing conditions outside weren't ideal.

I went straight toward the basil which crept over the sides of a raised bed in the far corner. Plucking the leaves from their stems, I inhaled the deep, rich fragrance.

Knox's words echoed in my memory. I had to admit that my injured ankle had become an excuse to mope over the past couple of weeks. Technically, I hadn't had to stay on the ranch. I could easily have borrowed the truck, gone into town, and done some shopping. Anything to get my mind off the two things that had been bothering me.

My daydreams lately had been filled with visions of quaint Spanish villages. I could practically taste the salty spray off the coast. The director of an orphanage just outside of Madrid had returned my email a few days ago with a long list of questions for me. They were looking for an administrative director for the orphanage and I was practically hyperventilating as I waited for her reply. It was all I'd been able to think about the past few days.

I thought about Spain and the rancher who lived down the road. The look that Caleb had given me just before he'd leaned over and wiped ice cream from my face with his thumb kept popping into my memory unbidden. I didn't want him to be on my mind as often as he seemed to be.

Despite my anxiety over the future, I'd woken up in a positive mood this morning. The sun had seemed to shine a little brighter than usual as I dressed myself and sipped my first cup of coffee. Life was going to work out the way it was supposed to. I'd run across a verse in the book of Jeremiah as I was reading my Bible late last night that read *'For I know the plans I have for you,' declares the Lord, 'plans to prosper you and not to harm you, plans to give you a hope and a future.'*

I'd learned to read by memorizing Bible verses. I'd gone to Sunday school every week and listened to my dad read the Bible aloud after dinner every night. But it hadn't been until I'd entered middle school that the words I'd heard my entire life began to click. God would be an active presence in my life…if I invited Him to be. I had to choose to enter that relationship. He wasn't going to force Himself upon me.

I'd been on a journey to understand the heart of God the last few years. The Bible was clear to me. God was the same yesterday, today, and forever. He wasn't going to leave me in the dark. He wasn't going to ignore the desires of my heart. He'd placed a calling on my life and would help me fulfill it. That was a promise I had been clinging to lately, choosing to focus on it rather than the thoughts of the future that troubled me.

Rather than thoughts of Caleb.

Why had he brought me soup and ice cream the other day? Soup and ice cream, of all things. It couldn't get more random and yet I could tell that the thought had come from a good place. And he'd remembered my favorite ice cream flavors. Years later and he still remembered the flavor of ice cream I'd chosen on random trips to the drug store.

I ripped a large leaf of basil a little too aggressively from the stem and the whole plant rustled.

He probably just felt sorry that I'd injured myself while riding his horse. Well, not exactly while riding, but while on his property. Caleb was a responsible business owner. He'd probably come by to do reconnaissance and make sure I wasn't planning to sue him. After all, we still weren't friends.

Even if I was helping him to scale up his non-profit youth camp.

I groaned under my breath as I awkwardly balanced the basket of basil under my arm. I'd put it off all week while I nursed my ankle back to recovery, but I'd have to call him to schedule a meeting to go over the final edits to the website before much more time had passed. He'd need to approve the website design so that I could move forward with the ads I was planning to place in various publications across the country. Applicants for the program needed a working website to visit.

Was it too much to hope that Caleb wouldn't be at the shindig, bonfire thing tonight?

After dinner, Knox directed me upstairs. A tired Vincent and Dean lounged on the back porch, their stomachs full and content. I wondered if the three of them would be spending longer stretches of time on the mountain with our herd if they hadn't felt obligated to watch over me this summer.

We employed several cowboys who lived with the herd full time, but I knew my brothers were hands-on ranchers. Dean had arranged permission with the forestry service to graze our herd across the mountain during the summer months. It was part of the environmentally regenerative cattle ranching program he had designed. *Planned grazing, regenerative methods, and nutrient cycling.* Terms I didn't fully understand, but in only a few years, Dean had already been able to restore several of the wild landscapes on the mountain ranges. Technically, according to the terms of my dad's will, I was a partial owner of the ranch. It hadn't been a responsibility I'd given much thought while in college, but I was proud that my brothers were impassioned stewards of the land.

"Twenty minutes, Sammie," Knox called.

Upstairs, I took my hair out of its customary braid and let it fall around my shoulders and face. Taking a hard look at myself in the mirror, a whoosh of air exhaled forcefully between my lips. I couldn't explain why I felt so nervous. If the crowd at the bonfire was the same old crowd that my brothers had been friends with for years, it had been a long time since I'd socialized with many of them. As an introvert, the thought of seeing so many old, but unfamiliar faces, sent ripples of anxiety through my stomach.

At least that was the explanation I gave myself as I applied a layer of mascara and touched up my lips with a glossy tint. I didn't want to look too citified in front of the group, so I'd skipped my usual going-out makeup look, opting for simple and fresh instead. I'd tried to tame my curls, but to little success.

I pulled on a cute blue paisley maxi skirt and a fresh, white t-shirt. With my favorite brown gladiator sandals and a pair of gold studded earrings, it was about as fancy as I wanted to get for a marshmallow roast in Cascade Valley. I knew I would rather fade into the background tonight, even though I'd been part of the community my entire life.

Hoping that I didn't end up feeling like a tall, gangly, ugly duckling around my brothers' friends, I dragged my feet downstairs, where my brothers waited on the porch.

Vincent stood in the doorway and as I approached, he swept out his arm dramatically and stepped aside. "Ladies and gentlemen, presenting the honorable Miss Samantha McCade."

"You look so pretty, Red." Dean stepped forward and held out his arm for me. "May I escort you to your awaiting carriage, m' lady?"

"Ok, you boys watched way too much nineteenth century television while I was away." I rolled my eyes and laughed, but their sweet teasing abated my anxiety a little. With three brothers as protective as mine, I shouldn't have any trouble fitting in tonight.

"Samantha McCade?" The perky voice filled my ears and I found myself suddenly wrapped in a pair of lean arms. "I would recognize you anywhere, girl. That hair is just as gorgeous as it was in high school."

Laura Simpson hugged me and stepped back to look at me. I blushed under her approving nod. The young woman, who'd been a year above me in high school, had made a beeline for me when she saw Dean's truck roll up under the trees.

A bonfire had already been lit and was beginning to blaze as the sun descended. Shelby and Brianna had already arrived and quickly took their places on Dean and Knox's arms.

Laura stepped to the side and pulled my arm through hers. I caught a whiff of a rosy floral scent on her hair. "I just got back into town myself. I've been living in Bozeman, but I like to get back to see my parents whenever I can. Everyone is going to be so happy to see you. You'll recognize quite a few of the faces and maybe quite a lot you won't. A lot of our old crowd left after high school. I guess they escaped just like you?"

She squeezed my arm and I tried not to stiffen. It wasn't unusual for a young woman to leave her state to go to school. So why did I always feel like my old friends considered it a betrayal?

Probably because Laura and I hadn't exactly been friends. We'd been acquaintances, civil to each other, and had even partnered up a few times on various projects in school. But nothing like the BFFs she kept trying to depict us as while she dragged me around the bonfire, reintroducing me to this person and that.

When I caught her eye drifting over to Vincent for the fifth time in about as many minutes, it clicked. Vincent was the only one of my brothers without a date tonight and it made sense that Laura would try to buddy up with me to get to him.

"I'm going to grab something to drink." I extracted myself as quickly as I could, withdrawing my arm from Laura's and moving away from the crackling flames. I walked across the yard, smiling at the various greetings that were called out to me. My face was set in a pleasant, but preoccupied expression. I pretended like I was headed for an important destination, but all the while, I scanned the yard with my peripheral vision.

I hadn't yet caught sight of Caleb and I couldn't help but breathe a sigh of relief. If he was absent, it would be one less element to make me nervous while I navigated the social event. I beelined for the back door, making my way into the ranch style home's kitchen. Refreshments had been laid on the faded butcherblock countertop. I pulled a can of cola out of the sink that had been filled with ice and slipped from the house before anyone noticed me.

The porch was dark. Rather than rejoin the groups on the yard, I found myself settling into the shadows. In my own element, I wouldn't consider myself shy, though I could never have been termed a social butterfly. This large of a group was unnerving. I'd kept my social group small during college, preferring a few close friends to many acquaintances. Being home at the ranch or shopping in town was one thing; an entire party of people laughing and making small talk was another. I wasn't good at small talk.

What I hadn't accounted for was how edgy an entire evening spent catching up with old acquaintances would make me. I was already itching to leave, but it would be impossible to escape for another few hours.

My own discomfort puzzled me, and I tried to put my finger on what was bothering me as I sipped from the cool can. I was part of this community. I'd grown up here. Most of these names and faces were people I'd socialized with dozens of times. Why then did I feel so out of place? And what was I going to say when the inevitable questions about my future started coming? I shouldn't lie. But I also didn't think my business was the business of any of these people.

From my dim vantage point, I watched the small groups that lingered near the bonfire.

"Looks like I've found myself a wallflower." I nearly dropped my drink at the sound of Caleb's voice. "Didn't picture you as the shy type, Red."

He stepped onto the porch. The back door swung shut behind him with a whine of rusty hinges. My heart beat a little faster.

"Oh, just catching my breath for a moment." I tossed my head casually. "I didn't see you out there earlier."

"I just got here a few minutes ago." He stepped forward. A soft drink was clutched in his hand. "I wondered where you were when I didn't see you either. Dean said you were planning to come tonight."

A mental note to ask Dean why he and Caleb would be having conversations about me filed itself into the back of my brain for later. "Can I tell you a secret?" I regretted the words as they fell from my mouth.

The moon's light caught his eyes as it began its ascent in the sky. "Your secrets are safe with me," he replied solemnly, leaning forward. His voice brushed over my skin. Instant goosebumps prickled my arm.

I leaned closer conspiratorially. "I'm not a social butterfly. I'm really just a little old grandma who would rather be curled up on her sofa with tea and a book right about now."

Caleb's laughter rippled into the night. "Right. Your cowboy romances."

"Hey, I read plenty of things beside romance," I protested.

His fingertips rested briefly on my elbow as he laughed again. "I'm just teasing you, Samantha. I'm sure you read lots of Highland romance as well."

His laugh boomed out again. All at once, I found myself laughing too. Caleb had always had a nice laugh. It was contagious.

"So…." He leaned toward me and lowered his voice. "Are any of these cowboys catching your eye tonight?"

"Uh, no. I don't date." I rolled my eyes. "And my brothers would have a literal cow if you even suggested such a thing."

"You don't date cowboys? Or you don't date at all?" Caleb rested his hip against the porch railing.

Oh, now we are having conversations like friends? Where is this coming from? And why do I want to answer him?

Thoughtfully, I sipped the last of my soft drink. "Well, both, actually. I'm not interested in any of the local men, and I honestly would prefer to let God bring my future husband across my path in such a way that I totally can't miss the signs. I don't want to waste anyone's time. Hanging out with old friends is one thing. But dating without intention seems pointless."

I blushed, realizing that I'd just blurted out some of my most private thoughts about love and life. *To Caleb Kane of all people.* "How about you?" Quickly, I continued my ramble, not giving either of us the chance to dwell on what I'd just admitted. "Is there a future Mrs. Kane out there?"

He was quiet for so long that I wondered if he'd even heard me.

"Uh, yeah." I had to lean forward to catch his mumbled reply. "There's someone I've had my eye on for a long time."

"Well, who is she?" I prompted when he didn't continue.

His head swiveled toward me, but I couldn't see his expression in the shadows. "Oh, it doesn't matter. Just someone I don't even have a chance with."

My mouth dropped in surprise. I wondered if I'd heard him correctly. I may have had my issues with him—issues that I was starting to doubt I had any basis for—but even I knew that he was a catch for any woman in Cascade Valley.

Caleb pushed off the railing and turned away. "I'm going to greet a few friends. Have a good time tonight, Samantha."

A moment later, I was alone once again on the dark porch. I shivered, feeling cold as I watched him walk across the yard toward the bonfire. Reluctantly, I decided that it was time I rejoined the party too. I walked across the yard accompanied by an unexplainable heaviness.

"Hey, there you are." Vincent's eyes warmed as I approached. The group greeted me enthusiastically. "Did you get lost?"

"No. Just saying hi to everyone." I tried to keep my voice bright.

His sharp gaze examined me swiftly. "Are you ok?" He lowered his voice, turning slightly away from the group so they wouldn't overhear.

"Oh yes," I reassured him quickly. "Having a great time." To prove my statement, I jumped into the conversation, allowing my laughter to ring freely at the jokes and witty quips of his friends. A few minutes later, a voice spoke at my side.

"Is this group full?" Immediately, the group of friends parted to let Caleb enter. His sharp, humorous banter jumped right into the fray with the comfort of a long-time member of the social group. I noticed that he didn't even glance in my direction. Briefly, I wondered if I'd said something to upset him, but then reminded myself that there wasn't any reason for him to go out of his way to make me feel welcome.

"Caleb, there you are." Malia DeWitt's low, throaty voice purred in his direction. "I was planning to call you this week."

"I didn't do it," Caleb replied, throwing up his hands. The group laughed. Discretely, I eyed the young woman. *Is she his mystery crush? I could see them together.*

Malia DeWitt was the other ginger of the group. I didn't know much about her, other than the fact that we were both redheads and she had been in Vincent's grade at school, placing her quite a bit outside my social circle. She'd nodded a polite hello to me when Dean introduced me to the group. The two of them had been dating when I'd left for college. I wasn't sure what had happened to break them up, but I was surprised to observe that there was no ring visible on Malia's finger.

We may have shared our hair color, but I was quite sure that the two of us had nothing else in common. I always felt awkward, gangly, and too tall for my own comfort. Malia, on the other hand, was the picture of poise. Her luscious mahogany hair lay in waves over her shoulders, and she looked like a model in her designer jeans and white, ruffled blouse.

"Always innocent, aren't you?" she teased Caleb. "Actually, it was about the youth camp. I wondered if you had a head count for me for snacks and lunches?"

"We're a little behind on registering this year, Malia," Caleb replied. "But you and Samantha should connect. She's the one managing our marketing and rebuilding our website." Caleb motioned to me, acknowledging my presence for the first time.

"Oh?" Malia's cool, gray eyes took me in swiftly. I got the feeling that she was conducting a thorough analysis of me behind her steely gaze. "Well, isn't that wonderful? I didn't know you were in marketing, Samantha."

Subtly, I straightened my shoulders, trying to appear professional since most of the group had swung their heads toward me. "Not officially," I said. "But I do have a degree in non-profit management and a minor in marketing, so I have a few tricks up my sleeve."

"Malia runs the catering service in town," Caleb explained. "She'll be providing all the snacks and lunches we'll need this summer. Do you have an estimate for when we'll be ready to open the site for reservations, Samantha?"

"I do need to know as soon as possible so that I can make sure to order enough supplies," Malia interjected before I could reply. I tried not to squirm under her gaze.

"Within the next few days if everything meets with your approval?" I spoke firmly in Caleb's direction, determined to sound like a woman armed with confidence for once in my life. "Shall we get together sometime soon to discuss the catering portion of the brochure?" I offered to Malia. "I'll need that information for the website."

"Absolutely." She purred in my direction, but I got a sinking feeling that her politeness came with reservations.

"Excellent. And Caleb, I was also going to request a meeting to go over the final edits on the site with you. Early this week?"

"Sure," Caleb nodded.

"Ok, enough work talk," Malia interrupted again, clapping her hands together. "I brought smores kits and I think it's time to break them out. Caleb, will you walk with me to the kitchen to grab them?"

They walked toward the house together. *Why do I feel like I just got put firmly into my place?* I reflected as I watched them go.

"Well, well, well. If it isn't the city girl showing up to our little country shindig." A light-hearted voice echoed behind me a short while later. I spun to see Ian walking toward me from the shadows. I smiled at him when he stopped in front of me.

He tipped the brim of his faded cowboy hat, and I resisted a sudden urge to curtsy and giggle. "Howdy ma'am, pleased to see you here on this fine night," he continued to tease. The bonfire lit up the sparkle in his eyes.

"Howdy do, Mr. Ian?" I laughed, the grin coming easily to my lips in response to his casual, but exaggerated country-boy mannerisms.

"I'm not sure how our humble country parties will compare to your city soirees." Ian held out his arm to me. "But may I request this dance?"

Someone had brought out a banjo and I heard the first notes being strummed behind us. A harmonica jumped in and then I recognized the high tones of a fiddle. A tune I recognized from my childhood danced into the night.

Accepting Ian's offered arm, I turned toward the groups who were pairing up against the glow of the bonfire. Feet began to pound the earth in a perfectly timed, familiar dance. The energy in the air was instantly contagious.

"Let's join them," I said. Ian and I ran toward the others and timed our jump into the boot tapping rows of dancers.

I'd learned to square dance as a child. The heel-clicking, swing-your-partner-round-and-round cues came back to me in smooth, muscle-memory fashion. Ian grabbed my waist and spun me, the skirt I'd worn swirling around my ankles. Laughter caused my breath to catch. We pounded our boots and kicked our heels, in sync with the intoxicating rhythm.

Suddenly, I was a young girl again, laughing deliriously as my father danced with me to the rhythm of the fiddle, his handlebar mustache twitching as he threw back his head and chuckled along with me. My heart began to thud with an ache that wasn't induced by the dance. If only I had the chance to go back in time. How I'd treasure every moment with my dad. I wanted to talk to him again. I had so many questions about my life and future that only my wise father could answer. My throat constricted with a sudden painful lump, and I pressed back the tears.

"And pass your partner to the right." The sonorous tones of the banjo player called out the command in time to the beat. Ian twisted his lips, but he spun me as instructed. A new pair of hands reached for me, and I found myself caught in the strong arms of another man.

"Howdy," I said reflexively, trying to trick myself into feeling the exhilaration of a few moments earlier. My face lifted to see who had caught me. My heart skipped an uncomfortable beat when I caught sight of the last face I was prepared to see at the moment. Nonetheless, a tingle danced along my arm from his touch on my skin.

"Howdy," Caleb echoed, peering into my face, his eyes dark under the shadow of his hat. "I didn't know you still danced." He spun me, then pulled me close again.

Instantly, I was triggered.

"My daddy taught me to dance," I replied. My lips pressed into a thin line as I stared into his eyes, my gaze hard and unyielding. Caleb's palm was rough and warm on mine, callused from a lifetime of gripping the reins of a hundred horses. They felt just like my dad's hands. Masculine and strong. His arm slipped around my waist as we moved automatically to the call of the banjo.

"I know he did," Caleb said, his voice warm and gentle on my ear. "He was a good dad."

The unbidden memory of the last time Caleb and I had danced together surfaced in my mind. Vividly, I remembered a scene much like this one at his sister's wedding the summer before I'd left for college. I'd been lingering along the edge of the dance floor that had been set up at the lodge that night, watching as everyone whirled and swiveled to the celebratory music.

"Come on, Samantha," I'd heard Knox shout, his hands waving above his head. "Dance with us."

My inherent shyness had kept my feet glued to the edge of the dance floor, but my body couldn't help but sway to the contagious rhythm. I'd caught the second Caleb's eyes found me over the top of the crowd. He had zeroed in on my face and his eyebrows lifted as if in question. When my only reply had been to give a subtle shake of my head, a look had swept over him. He'd broken free of the crowd and made a beeline straight for me, his hand outstretched.

"Come on," he'd commanded, grabbing hold of my wrist. "You should be having fun with the rest of us."

I'd laughed and protested, but he'd pulled me into the crowd of dancers, keeping his arm twined firmly around my waist so I couldn't escape. I'd been swept into the exhilaration of the moment and when the musicians had shifted and begun to play a slow dance song, Caleb hadn't let go. He'd held me, pulling my arms up and around his neck. We'd swayed, our eyes locked as we danced together for the first time.

I felt myself soften at the memory.

"He truly was." My words thickened with the lump in my throat. I lifted my chin to Caleb's face, our eyes meeting in the fire-lit darkness. His expression was tight, a grim line across his mouth. He was watching me closely and I felt an overwhelming urge to cry. I needed to be alone before I burst into tears in front of the entire crowd. Another spin in time with the step and this time, I pulled away. He slowed and stared at me, his hands outstretched.

"I need to go." I turned on my heel and dodged the dancing couples. I ran toward the parked trucks, my boots thudding across the dirt.

"And switch partners now." The banjo player's voice called out, his words a thin echo behind me as I escaped into the safe, comforting cover of darkness.

Chapter Ten

"ALRIGHT, WHICH OF you boys would like to drive me to the airport?" I walked downstairs early the next morning, my fingers gripping the leather duffel bag I'd pulled from the closet. I'd packed a small selection of clothes for an overnight trip.

"Um, where do you think you're going, young lady?" Vincent looked up from the Bible that was open in front of him on the kitchen table. His expression was wide-eyed and alarmed.

"We didn't mean to run you off, Sammie. Please stay and make us some more of your delicious chocolate chip cookies. We promise to be good." Knox bounded over to me, his hands clasped in a dramatic pleading gesture.

I laughed and pushed him aside. "I'm not leaving you boys." The lie rolled too easily off my tongue. A sharp pang of guilt stabbed my insides. "I'm just going to run up to Seattle for a couple of days. There's something I want to arrange for the summer program, and I'd prefer to go up there and handle it in person.

Another lie, but at least this one was only a half-fib. What I wasn't going to say was that I'd come home last night and immediately begun searching for last minute flights. I needed to get away from my childhood home so that the memories and longing for days gone by didn't crush me. I needed to be reminded that there was a big, wide world out there and it was called Destination Europe. And the fastest way to get there was by route of Seattle, where I had smart, driven college friends and restaurants and a brightly lit nightlife to distract me and remind me of my goals.

"Will you be back soon?" Dean's brow was furrowed. I wondered if my big brother could see right through my shaky reasoning.

"In just a day or two. Can one of you spare the time to drive me to the city? Or can you spare one of the trucks? I'm happy to just drive myself…." I trailed off, feeling uncertain of myself.

"Vincent? You up? Knox and I can handle things around here for a few hours." Dean answered for the group, the set of his tone indicating that I wouldn't be driving the truck alone into Bozeman. "We've got a meeting in town today, but you should be back in plenty of time."

Vincent nodded and rose to grab his hat and a set of keys.

"Give me five minutes, sis," he said. Inwardly, I groaned. Of the three of my brothers, Dean was the most intimidating, Knox was the clumsy, lovable goofball, and Vincent…well, Vincent was the wise one. Deep and wise and oh-so-observant. Dean was sending him with me on purpose, I had no doubt.

Did they notice the way I disappeared last night? One minute, we had all been dancing across the grass. I'd seen my brothers there, kicking up their heels and laughing with the rest of us. And then I'd disappeared. I'd hidden in the truck until I saw the fire dying down and various groups making their way toward the cluster of parked vehicles. Then I'd slipped out and rejoined my brothers, pretending like I hadn't just spent the last hour huddled in the truck, tears slipping down my cheeks as my heart broke for all the promises of joy that had been lost to me. If my brothers had noticed my tear-streaked face last night, they hadn't said anything.

I hadn't caught sight of Caleb again after I'd run away from the dance.

I knew it was highly probable that Dean was counting on Vincent to dig the truth out of me. I bit my lip, steeling myself for the drive. I wasn't going to break. Some things were better left unsaid.

"Well," Vincent said as we settled into his truck. "Thanks for giving me an excuse to skip out on chores today." He winked in my direction.

I laughed and shook my head. "You're very welcome." Though I was well aware that he was the one doing me the favor. Managing our herd while they were on the mountain was a laborious job, even more so than regular ranch life. The past few years, my brothers had been away from the ranch for weeks at a time. I knew the fact that they'd tried to stay closer to home since I'd been back had been for my benefit.

We roared onto the road, the truck's diesel engine eating up the miles. Strategically, I turned my head when we passed the Kane's ranch, pretending to be engrossed in the distant view of the hills.

I didn't want to talk about the youth camp or the man in charge. Thankfully, Vincent didn't bring up any of it.

"So…" He broke the silence. "Any big plans for Seattle?"

"Not really," I fibbed again. "I'm just going to have dinner with a couple of friends. Will it be too much trouble to pick me up at the valley airport later this week? I'm just going to charter a flight with one of the small planes coming back to the valley."

He knew I was referring to our mini runway and airport in Cascade Valley. Flights out were few and far between, but it was easy to hop on a Cessna at the main airport in the city. I could land in my own backyard in a much shorter time than it took to drive the distance.

"Sure. Or we may just leave a truck for you there if we are gone already." I saw his blue eyes glance my way. "You sure have grown up to be quite the woman, Sammie."

They were simple words, but I heard the deep notes of approval in his voice. A lump found its way into my throat. I reached over and squeezed his hand, not trusting myself to answer him without bursting into tears.

"Maybe you could pass some of your maturity over to Knox though. That boy…." Vincent raised his hand and made a chopping motion over the top of his head. He winked at me as an exaggerated grimace spread across his face.

I burst into laughter, my tears fleeing gratefully, knowing exactly what he meant about our energetic, passionate, charming, yet totally clueless Knox. Compared to my wise and serious older brothers, he was like a floppy-tongued retriever. Loyal to the end, but a goofball getting there. Vincent began to tell me story after story of Knox's hijinks and pranks over the years I had been away at college. The miles sped by and when we rolled into Bozeman, my cheeks hurt from laughing and I had nearly forgotten why I'd felt the need to run away to Seattle in the first place.

Vincent hugged me as I prepared to go through security. I relaxed into his embrace for a moment. As always, my deep and quiet brother had known exactly what I needed. My heart felt lighter.

"If you need anything, you just call," he said to me. "If you can't handle those city boys, the calvary will be at your side in two shakes of a lamb's tail." He was teasing me. His bright eyes shone, and his lips twitched, but the promise was a comfort anyway.

I rolled my eyes. "I can most certainly handle the Seattle boys. But thanks, Vincent. And thank you for the ride."

He nodded toward TSA. "You'd better get going. Don't want you to miss your flight."

"Love you," I called after him.

"Loved you first." He threw a wink back at me and turned away. Vincent stood a head and shoulders above most of the crowd. I watched his hat weave through the passengers until it had disappeared through the sliding doors into the bright sunshine.

. . .

"Let me see your beautiful face." Amanda grabbed my shoulders and squeezed me in an embrace so tight that it took my breath away. "I cannot even begin to explain how much I've missed you." She grabbed my bag before I could reach for it and began to drag me toward the airport exit.

"I've only been gone a few weeks and we've talked nearly every day," I laughed, trying to keep up with her short, quick steps.

"It's not the same. There's no substitute for the real you." Amanda waved down a cab and we slid inside the musty interior. In typical Seattle fashion, the skies were overcast, and the smell of rain lingered in the air. The interior of the cab had seen too many wet shoes and clothes. The upholstery carried a perpetually damp scent.

How do the people in this city make it in such a gloomy atmosphere? For the hundredth time, I compared the gloomy, gray streets of this part of the Pacific Northwest to the endless blue skies and sunshine of my own Montana home. I had forced myself to get used to Seattle, but now that I'd spent some time at home again, the contrast was striking.

"I really don't know how I'm ever going to let you leave me again," Amanda prattled on after she'd given the driver an address. "I really may have to resort to kidnapping you."

"Or you can simply fly out to visit me?" I laughed again, casting a quick glance at the driver, hoping he wasn't taking my friend seriously. An unexpected flash of uncertainty made me turn back to Amanda. I studied my vivacious, blonde, blue-eyed companion. Life in the city versus life in my slow, mountain valley home were very different. I wasn't sure how my uber-sophisticated friend would view the simplicity of country life. Maybe I should work harder to keep the two worlds separate.

"Goodness, yes," she replied, clapping her perfectly manicured hands together. "I would love that."

Suddenly self-conscious, I curled my fingertips in and nestled my hands in my lap. I hadn't gone to a nail salon since I'd returned home. Somehow, painted nails just seemed silly when you were going to be collecting eggs and picking weeds in the garden most of the time.

"If I visit, I can get to know your handsome brothers better. And meet your gorgeous horse rancher-slash-neighbor that you are so determined to hate." Amanda fluttered her eyelashes at me and gave an exaggerated wink.

"I don't hate Caleb." The reflexive words surprised me as they fell from my mouth. I paused for a moment and gathered myself. "I never hated him," I corrected. "Resent and distrust? Yes. And I'm still not sure how I feel about the man." Sternly, I stared at her, suspicion growing in my expression. "And how do you even know what he looks like?"

"I looked him up." With a smirk, Amanda slid her hand through the crook of my arm. "And I'm glad I did. Any man who brings that much of a blush to your face is worth the look. Did you know that his Arabians are like *famous-famous* around the world?"

The cab rolled to a stop. We stepped onto the damp sidewalk. I was glad for the cool air to lower the heat I felt in my cheeks. "Yes, I did know that about his horses. But his looks don't have any effect on me," I protested as I pulled my bag from the trunk. "And another thing, my brothers are off-limits. Two of them have girlfriends, and I don't need you breaking Vincent's heart, city-girl."

"So Vinnie is single, huh?" She tossed her hair over her shoulder, stepping forward to lead us toward the entrance of her apartment building.

"Yes. And if you rolled into town and started flirting with him, he wouldn't have any idea what to do with you."

"That's exactly the way I like them," she laughed. I rolled my eyes and bit my tongue. Instead of answering her, I peered at the tall apartment building. A cold clash of metal and glass met my eyes.

"Is this where you moved?" I asked.

"Yep. My new home. It's the perfect location, don't you think?"

I paused for a moment before I replied.

We were just off-center from the heart of downtown. The building wasn't pretty, a combination of gray and black, the bland exterior broken up by planters of green ferns. I was sure that an apartment here came with a hearty price tag, nonetheless. It was the perfect location for a budding young professional to plant herself. Walking distance to restaurants, shopping, and work. The effect resembled living in a concrete jungle, but at least it was convenient.

I shouldered my bag and followed her into the elevator. Her apartment was small, a single bedroom that overlooked another jumble of concrete, metal, and glass next door.

"We have dinner reservations with the gang at seven. Anything you want to do between now and then? Maybe shop for an outfit that will make Jake swoon for you even more?"

Jake Anderson had been a mutual friend of a friend during college. He had been adopted into our group of friends along the way. He was fun and lively, and we had both had crushes on each other at different times. But my crush on him had passed before much could come of it. After a couple of casual dates, Jake and I had agreed that we were much better as friends, and I, for one, planned to stay that way.

"You can just stop that right now," I laughed, shaking my head. "Jake is not swooning for me. We had that conversation a couple of years ago. This is a just a friend asking an old friend to do her a favor. And what do you mean, gang? I thought this was just a quiet dinner with you, me, and Jake to discuss my plan?"

Amanda kicked off her shoes and grabbed a bottle of water from the fridge. She offered it to me. It was cold and tasteless, nothing like the fresh water from our well back home. I hid the grimace that swept across my face and set the bottle on the breakfast bar.

"Oh honey, that shows what you know." Amanda flopped on the worn-in futon couch she'd kept from our shared college apartment. A TV, a stand, and a potted plant were the only other items that decorated the sparse room. "The man positively adores you. He talks about you all the time. And when everyone heard that you were coming into town, naturally they wanted to join us for dinner."

I had no doubts that Amanda had sent out a group text as soon as she heard that I was headed her way.

"So, what do you think?" She gestured to the space. "Of my new digs?"

"I like it," I fibbed, rubbing my arms. The apartment suddenly felt cold and dark as clouds covered the sun's attempt to break free of the overcast day.

"I still need to get…well…pretty much everything," she laughed. "But it's not a bad spot for a fresh-from-college graduate."

"It's nice. I'm happy for you," I replied. "Do you want to grab coffee and get our nails done before dinner?"

•　•　•

Jake stood at the table and folded me into an awkward hug when Amanda and I entered the restaurant a few hours later. Amanda had made reservations at La Mesa, a tiny Spanish kitchen run by an even tinier abuela. I loved the food, and I loved the homey, rustic, candlelit atmosphere. It had been a favorite spot of mine to visit. I appreciated Amanda's good memory and thoughtfulness. A sharp longing for the sunny skies of Spain wedged itself deeper into my heart as I returned Jake's hug.

"What's up, stranger?" Jake drawled, squeezing me a little tighter before relaxing his hold. He had graduated two years ahead of Amanda and I, but we'd all remained friends.

"It's good to see you." I gave him a squeeze in return, then pulled away as the rest of the group began to clamor for my attention. As I settled between Max and Josie, I clutched a cold glass of lemon water and took in the familiar faces around the table.

Ten faces. Ten familiar smiles. Quick, loud laughter. Inside jokes. Gossip. Chatter. It was like I'd never left. Like I hadn't said goodbye to these people and left to begin the rest of my life. Graduation had only been a few short weeks ago, but it already felt like a lifetime. In just a few, short years, I'd created another family—a mishmash of personalities and backgrounds, but I had always known right where I fit in with them.

"So, what's this big secret project you wanted to talk to me about?" Jake switched places with Max and bent his head toward mine.

"Did Amanda already fill you in?"

"Just vaguely. Something about a cowboy, kids, horses? She was vague on the details," Jake chuckled. His laugh was light-hearted and quick.

"Ok. Well, here it is." I took a deep breath and dove straight into the plan I'd been formulating. When I finally came up for air, the group had paused their conversations to listen. I became aware of the audience and blushed.

"You have to do it, Jake," Josie quipped as I reached for my lemon water. "None of us are even going to let you consider saying no."

"How could you say no?" Carter exclaimed. He leaned across the table and caught my wrist. "This is a really amazing idea, Samantha. And think of how it will look on your resume."

A murmur ran through the group as they nodded their approval.

"Well?" I peered over the edge of my glass at Jake. Suddenly, my throat felt parched. My hand shook a little. I hadn't realized how much I wanted my idea to work.

He threw up his hands. "It looks like the group has spoken. How could I say no? When would you like me to fly out?"

The bottom of my water glass hit the table with a clink. "Do you mean you'll do it? Are you being serious, Jake? Don't tease me." Without thinking, my hand shot out and grabbed his. He squeezed my fingers, his skin smooth over mine.

"I would never tease you, Samantha. I would love to help you with this."

The table erupted into applause. I smiled at Amanda, wondering why a sudden lump had worked its way into my throat. As much as I loved my brothers and as often as I'd been homesick during my years in Seattle, the people gathered around the table also felt like a family to me. All of us had clearly defined goals and aspirations for our lives. We were a predictable and focused crew. These friends not only understood but had encouraged me to pursue my passion to work with non-profit organizations across the globe.

I couldn't have asked for a more supportive group. So it baffled me all the more to realize that I would rather be back home, sitting on the porch with my brothers, telling them what I'd arranged for Caleb's summer camp while their beaming faces reflected the pride they felt in my accomplishments.

Chapter Eleven

FOUR DAYS LATER, I leaned back in my desk chair and looked thoughtfully at the screen of my laptop. When I had returned home from Seattle, I'd gone straight into work mode. I owed Caleb a website and I needed to make a few tweaks before he could give his approval for it to go live.

If the truth was to be told, I'd spent too much time avoiding Caleb under the excuse that he made me uncomfortable. My hair-brained proposal to help with the youth camp had been impulsive and born of my own stubbornness, but I had committed, nonetheless. Fulfilling my responsibility to the teens who would benefit from the camp was priority number one.

I needed to honor the job, even if I was on the verge of moving halfway across the world.

The director of the orphanage in Spain had reached out to me again. The board wanted to schedule an online interview within a couple of weeks. I was fired up and ready to prove that I could chase my dreams and take care of myself.

"If it's ok, I'm going to borrow one of the trucks this afternoon?" I had announced over a breakfast of bacon and eggs that morning.

"Going shopping?" Knox teased. "Or are you running off to hang out with your girlfriends in Seattle again?"

"No, goofball," I teased back. "I'm going to Caleb's. I've set up an interview for him with a journalist from a paper in Seattle to feature the youth camp."

Knox's eyes widened.

"And she says it just as cool as a cucumber," Dean exclaimed. "That's going to be really awesome press for the program, Sammie."

"Yeah, great job," Vincent praised.

I hadn't expected any accolades. A self-conscious blush crept over my face. "Thanks, guys. Just doing my job."

A few hours later, I had put the finishing touches to my outfit and stepped back to look at myself in the mirror. My brothers' praise had been on my mind since the morning, and I thought of it again now. Today felt like the day my budding career might finally spread its wings and take flight. I'd made good use of my connections and sought out press that would give the youth camp brand new opportunities to connect with those in need. When I'd offered to help Caleb revamp his summer program, it hadn't been for any reason other than my selfish desire to pad my resume and look good in front of prospective employers. And to convince my family that I was cut out for the work.

But the bonfire party I'd gone to with my brothers had lit a flame under me. No pun intended.

Malia DeWitt's obvious passion for contributing her talents to the program had given me a new perspective. Caleb's horse camp was more than just a passing whim. It had taken me a while, but I finally understood why it was a worthy cause.

The day after I'd returned home from Seattle, I'd called Malia and asked if we could schedule a coffee date. She had been quick to agree and suggested that we meet at the coffee shop in town that very afternoon. I'd gulped down my nerves and met the pretty redhead at Cuppa Joe. The butter yellow walls of the rustic coffee shop mimicked the bright summer sunshine outdoors.

"So…." She had assessed me coolly once we'd sat at a table, cappuccinos in hand. "I have to admit that I was surprised to find out the other night that you are working on Caleb's pet project."

"Oh, why is that?" I'd dabbed a bit of foam off my upper lip, hoping that I hadn't just smudged the lipstick that I'd applied before I stepped out of the truck. There was something about Malia's cool, confident presence that made me want to put my best foot forward.

"He's very protective of things he cares about," Malia had replied. "And it's not like him to let a stranger get her hands on his youth camp."

I'd felt my shackles rising at the challenge in her coolly spoken words. I struggled to keep my tone friendly and neutral. "Well, I'm not really a stranger. I grew up around these parts you know."

"I remember you," Malia said softly. Her steely eyes could have frozen lava. I'd resisted the urge to squirm and instead held her gaze. "I'm so sorry about what happened to your dad."

At that moment, I did freeze. My back had straightened, and I'd clenched my jaw. Her opinion was clear to me now. Malia was skeptical of me because of the scene I'd caused at my dad's funeral, when I'd run Caleb out of the church, screaming and accusing him of being responsible. He'd told me that my accusation had haunted him until his name was cleared—and that it took a long time for the valley residents to look at him the same again. I'd certainly never publicly recanted what I'd said about him, and I wondered if I should make a greater effort to make amends. Ever since the day I'd twisted my ankle in his creek, I'd struggled with guilt over the trouble that it now seemed I had caused him unfairly. It was no wonder that my brothers had been so quick to forgive him. Caleb hadn't truly done anything wrong.

I wondered if Caleb had been complaining about me to his friends behind my back. I couldn't blame him. I deserved it.

"Thank you," I'd replied to Malia's condolences, matching her tone. "Now, if you don't mind, can we talk about the catering services for the camp."

She nodded. Her long, tapered fingers had tapped the table between us. "You have to understand what a blessing this camp has been to the whole town, Samantha. What may have originally just been a way to enrich the lives of teenagers who needed some extra encouragement inadvertently became an opportunity for the local business owners to make a little extra money during the summer. Caleb has always encouraged parents to stay in the inns close-by or to spend a few afternoons at the ranch with their child for a full-family bonding experience. Business increases for everyone during the summer months."

She'd chewed at the corner of her lip, her eyes staring at me earnestly. "We are grateful to Caleb because he found a way to bless the whole town. We are very invested, both for altruistic and personal reasons. And we don't want someone's personal feelings corrupting what Caleb has created."

As uncomfortable as I'd felt, her honesty had been appreciated. She was telling me in a roundabout way that she'd be watching to make sure I didn't sabotage the camp simply because of my feud with Caleb. I leaned forward, hoping the earnestness in my green eyes matched her own.

"Whatever happened in the past—I'm working to put it behind me. I've realized that I've made some mistakes and I'm trying to fix it. You can count on me, Malia."

She'd nodded again and straightened her shoulders, shaking out her mane of mahogany hair. She opened the folder she'd set on the table. "Well, let's discuss the menu, shall we?"

Later, I'd asked around and discovered that in just a short time, Caleb's camp had been adopted by the valley as their own special project, a way to give back to those in need. Many of the business owners contributed whatever they could, whether that be chaperones, teachers, supplies, or donations.

I wasn't surprised to discover that my own family had contributed both time and money to the program.

"Most of the kids who sign up are from one of the nearby cities and have rarely interacted with a horse, let alone spent time on a ranch," Knox had shared over after-dinner root beer floats on the front porch. I'd brought up Malia's contributions to him and asked if other county members had done anything similar.

"They don't get to experience living off the land, waking up with the sun, breathing in the fresh, clean air of the country. City life is hard on any teenager. The endless noise and activity can be draining; sometimes their neighborhoods are dangerous, or they are struggling at home. There's never any peace and quiet to help them get their perspective back. So, they get into trouble," Knox had continued.

"But these aren't bad kids," Vincent's low voice had quickly chimed into our conversation. He spread his hands on the table, leaning forward earnestly. "You should see the difference in them when they come out here for a few days, Sammie. It's like they can breathe for the first time. The horses, the land—it all brings them back to life. It gives them a reminder that life is bigger than the city. Bigger than their problems at home."

"I see." My reply had been thoughtful. I realized that I needed to step up my game to prove that I was bigger than the grief-driven disagreement that had ruined my relationship with Caleb.

·   ·   ·

The day that Jake was due to arrive in Cascade Valley was a very important day. I smoothed down the skirt I'd chosen and checked my appearance in my mirror again. I'd chosen a blue linen midi skirt to wear. To that I'd added a white sleeveless silk blouse and cork wedges. I was going for casually chic, thinking it more professional to greet Jake in something other than faded work jeans and a t-shirt. My ensemble wasn't practical for the ranch, but I needed to feel empowered for the afternoon. I'd wrangled my hair into a low chignon and added small gold hoops to my ears.

Caleb still didn't know that Jake was coming to interview him, so I wanted to feel prepared for him to put up resistance. I wasn't sure how he would feel about the plan that I had put together. I was prepared for his reaction to go either way. My clothing was my armor, and I was determined to win this battle.

For the kids.

As I drove up the lane to Caleb's ranch, I wondered if I should have given him a little more advance notice. Showing up and announcing my plan might not have been the best strategy. Jenna was carrying a saddle into the stable when I stepped from the truck.

"Hi Jenna," I called and waved. "Is Caleb around?"

"I think he's in one of the paddocks behind the far stable," she replied, her tone a little cool. She turned her back on me and continued walking. Our paths hadn't crossed since I'd twisted my ankle and I thought she looked decidedly displeased to see me this morning.

Poor Jenna, I thought. *She probably thinks I'm here to get Caleb to notice me. If only I could tell her that nothing is farther from my plans.*

I walked toward the stable that lay on the other side of the path, catching sight of Caleb and Griff working on a fence a short distance ahead. It was a hundred yard walk and I spent the distance coming up with what I wanted to say.

When Griff saw me, his face broke into a smile. He waved. "Well, as I live and breathe, if it ain't the prettiest girl this side of Yellowstone. What good deeds have we done to be graced with your presence this morning?"

I laughed, my smile emerging easily. Caleb swung his head toward me, a distinct look of distance in his eyes. It was understandable that he'd be skeptical of my visit after I'd run away from him during the bonfire dance.

"Samantha." He tipped his hat in my direction. "What brings you out this way?"

"Well, don't be mad at me," I began, glad of Griff's presence in the pasture. I propped my arms against the top rung of the fence.

Caleb's eyebrows lifted. "Uh, ok…."

"In a few minutes, a friend of mine who writes for *The Seattle Times* is going to be pulling up in the driveway. Would you be willing to give an interview and allow a few photos to be taken of the ranch for a feature article?"

"Samantha?" I had already mentally prepared for his stern reaction, so I simply leaned against the fence with a casual air. Caleb frowned darkly at me. "Why is a journalist coming to my ranch?"

"I thought that if we were really going to give the summer program a proper makeover this year, a write up in a big newspaper would be just the thing to get the public interested in it. It's a fantastic human-interest story and I believe with a write up like this, many more children who could benefit from the program will get the chance to sign up."

"And was there a reason you didn't call ahead to let me know this was happening?" Caleb's voice had gone raspy, causing Griff to chortle with a choked-back laugh.

"I didn't want you to be nervous," I replied, lifting my chin and meeting his gaze with a calm expression.

He scowled at me. "Do I seem like the nervous type to you?"

At this, Griff erupted into full-blown laughter. "No, that you sure don't," he shouted.

Caleb ignored him. He stepped up and swung his leg over the fence. He was standing in front of me before I could blink. "Griff, can you finish up here while I go handle this journalist?" Caleb stared down at me, his eyes pools of unreadable amber light.

"Sure can, boss. You go let that city reporter know that we've got everything handled just fine out here in the country," the older man chirped in reply.

Caleb and I walked in silence toward the house. A depression in the ground caught the heel of my wedge and I teetered a little. Swiftly, his hand shot out to steady me. Lightly, he touched my elbow, his fingertips warm on my arm. "Careful there. You're going to show her around a horse ranch dressed like this?" I saw his eyes appraising me skeptically.

"Him, actually. I'll be showing him around the ranch dressed like this," I replied primly. "And pardon me for dressing nicely. Sorry you don't approve of my outfit."

Caleb's hand fell from my arm. "Who said I don't approve? But how do you know this him?"

"From college," I quipped, annoyed by the intrusive line of questioning. "He's a friend that I met in college. We've kept in touch."

"Is he your boyfriend?"

"Uh, no." I rolled my eyes.

"Huh," Caleb grunted. "But he came all the way *to middle-of-no-where-Montana* from the great big city of Seattle just because you asked him to? When's he supposed to get here? It's probably hard to drive without all those street signs telling him where things are."

I glanced at him, unsure what had brought on the suddenly aggressive vibe toward my friend. "Soon. I'm here early."

"To prepare me in case I turned into a raging bull over the fact that I'm being interviewed with absolutely no time to prepare?"

"Precisely." I turned toward the sound of a car coming down the graveled drive. "So be nice to my friend. It isn't his fault that you didn't know until two minutes ago."

"Oh, I'll be nice, Samantha," Caleb growled. "Don't worry about me. I know how to mind my manners."

I frowned at him, puzzling over the dark look that had settled across his face. A door slammed and I heard my name called. Staring at Caleb, I tried to read his expression for a moment. Turning away, I waved to the medium-height, light-haired, slim man who'd just emerged from the gas-conserving sedan that was an obvious rental.

"Jake, I'm so glad you could make it," I called. "Thank you for coming on such short notice." I walked across the lawn, aware of Caleb's large presence as he kept pace just to my rear. When we reached my friend, I motioned between the two men. "Caleb, this is Jake Anderson. Jake, this is Caleb Kane, the owner of this ranch."

The two men shook hands, then Jake swept me up in an exuberant hug. He lifted me off the ground. It took a moment for my feet to hit the gravel again.

"Jake was two years ahead of me in college," I cast a glance toward Caleb when Jake finally let me go.

One bushy eyebrow lifted. "And you've already landed yourself a job at *The Seattle Times?* Excellent work."

"Well," Jake hemmed modestly. "Technically, I was already interning for them before I graduated. My dad worked for the paper for years and I'm sure some strings were pulled. Incredible place you have here." Jake did a slow three-sixty rotation to take it all in.

"Thank you," Caleb said. "Would you like the grand tour? We've bred some prize-winning Arabians that I'm very proud of. I'm not sure how much that Samantha already told you about the place?"

The two men fell into step together and I was left to pick my way across the lawn toward the stable. It wasn't as easy as I'd hoped to walk across the uneven ground in wedges. I also hadn't expected Caleb to jump into the interview so graciously. Jake already had his camera out and was snapping photos of the farm with energetic clicks.

He continued his enthusiastic photography as we walked into the stable. An elegant white head popped over a stall door. Beau nickered in our direction, his muzzle bobbing toward us.

"Who is this?" Jake exclaimed, approaching the colt with a brisk stride. He reached out a hand, trying to connect with Beau's head. But the colt kept nudging his hand out of the way, obviously annoyed that he hadn't come bearing treats.

Caleb leaned against the stable wall. "This is Beau. He's one of our colts currently in training. We're trying to decide whether to sell him or keep him as one of our future stallions."

"That would be a hard choice to make," Jake replied, stepping back to admire Beau. "He's a beauty. Samantha, I bet you're out here riding every day."

"Samantha doesn't ride horses anymore. Do you?" Caleb's amber eyes turned to me with a challenge.

"I'm not a fan," I replied firmly, trying not to allow my instant annoyance to show. "It seems that riding horses is just an injury waiting to happen for me." I gestured to my ankle and turned away, leading the men back into the soft, late spring morning.

Within a half hour of touring the property, I was regretting my shoe choice in earnest. Even Jake had thought to wear practical tennis shoes. The two men were lingering just ahead, waiting for me to catch up as we entered the east pasture. I wondered if Caleb had consciously chosen to walk us over the entire property, rather than take the golf cart that had been charging, unused, near the stable. They looked back at me as I followed them through the gate. I caught the disapproving glance Caleb threw at my feet just as one of my ankles made a painful and unexpected twist to the right.

I grimaced but lifted my chin and straightened my shoulders anyways. Hurrying forward, I caught up to the men. "It's a beautiful place, isn't it, Jake?" I said, taking my friend's arm as we walked toward the small herd of mares who were grazing with their foals a few yards away. They lifted their heads, obviously recognizing Caleb, their ears turning forward in interest.

I stiffened as several trotted toward us, the earth trembling slightly under their thundering hooves. I had done my best to put aside my nerves during the property tour and was thankful when the horses stopped short in a graceful show of agility. The mares hovered, obviously hoping one of us had hidden treats in a pocket.

"Really incredible," Jake agreed, reaching out a hand to stroke the nose of the bronze Arabian nearest to him, his eyes wide behind the glasses that he wore. She bobbed her head as his hand ran up and down her signature dished nose. I saw Caleb reach into his pocket and pull out a sugar cube for the gray mare who was nuzzling at his shoulder.

"I grew up in the country. I'd forgotten how beautiful and peaceful it is," Jake continued. "The paper is going to love the article I write up for your charity. I can see why you came home, Samantha." Jake turned to me. "I've half a mind to kidnap you and bring you back to the city with me though before we lose you to the country forever."

"Oh, I'm still a city girl," I said quickly, the urge to protest Jake's assumption washing over me. "Being back home is only temporary."

"That's a relief. We all miss our favorite Montana girl," Jake nodded.

"It sounds like you and Samantha are really close friends." Caleb looked at us. He dusted his hands on his jeans, wiping off remnants of sugar dust.

Jake snaked an arm around my shoulders, giving me a squeeze and pulling me toward his chest. We were about the same height, so my temple nearly collided with his forehead. His sudden gesture of affection caught me off guard.

"Very good friends," Jake affirmed. Then, in a half-rueful, half-teasing tone, he continued. "I was quite in love with her when she first showed up in Seattle. She eventually let me take her on a few dates."

I didn't want to make it awkward in front of Caleb, so ever-so-subtly, I tried to push myself away from Jake's embrace. "And we realized we were such good friends that we didn't want to mess that up." Involuntarily, I glanced at Caleb, uncomfortable with the topic of conversation. He was staring at me with unreadable eyes.

"Right. Too good of friends." Unexpectedly, Jake dropped the arm he'd snuck around my shoulders. I was finally free. But the sudden release caught me unawares. I took a big step to the side to catch my balance.

Immediately, I felt the distinctive, warm smoosh of fresh horse manure squelch into my shoe. The wedges were open toed, and warmth spread all the way across my foot. I looked at the men in shock, rendered speechless for one of the first times in my life.

Jake's face instantly reflected my distress. "Are you ok?"

"Of course," I said, shaking my head and trying to regain some dignity.

"You sure about that?" Caleb said. I heard the rumble of laughter enter his voice.

I scowled at him, daring him to laugh. "Completely fine," I insisted. "One of the hazards of country life, I guess." Gingerly, I pulled my foot from the still warm pile. I took a step forward toward the gate and felt an uncomfortable squelch between my toes. "Shall we go back up toward the house? I'd like to rinse this off."

"Samantha, hold still." Caleb walked up behind me. "You've been favoring that injured ankle of yours all day. Let me carry you out of this pasture so you don't hurt yourself again."

"What's wrong with your ankle?" Jake said, his tone concerned.

"Nothing. I just twisted it by falling into the creek the other day. And Caleb, I am completely capable of walking." I waved him away in protest. Too late, the big man bent toward me and swung me into his arms. I felt a *whoosh* as I left the ground and found myself for the second time in a couple of weeks pressed against Caleb's firm chest.

"Put me down this instant," I hissed under my breath.

"No," Caleb replied, holding me firmly. "Jake, would you mind getting the gate and latching it back behind us?"

I debated how badly it would reflect on the ranch if I pitched a fit and demanded that he let me go. The last thing I wanted was for

Jake to sense animosity between the two of us. My stomach fluttered at how easily Caleb strode across the ground with me in his arms. He was warm, the heat from his skin radiating into me like a sleepy summer afternoon.

How does he always smell so good? I resisted the instinct to nestle my nose into the crook of his neck and inhale.

"I'm perfectly capable of walking." Loudly, I protested one more time.

"I know you are perfectly capable. But you shouldn't be tramping around on that ankle until it's completely healed either. Just let me help." Caleb's voice was low and soft in my ear as Jake ran ahead to swing open the gate.

"But you're embarrassing me," I hissed.

"It's only embarrassing because you're letting it be embarrassing. I'm a man. I'm strong. And I can save a lady from some discomfort. Nothing embarrassing about that. Just a friend helping a friend. Unless you want Jake to know that we're not actually friends. He might think it's rather weird that you're so involved in the youth camp though?"

I scowled at his blackmail, but kept my mouth shut as he strode through the gate. "Be sure to latch it good, Jake. Those horses are escape artists," Caleb called back as he walked up the incline toward the stable.

I bit my tongue and hoped that no one else could see me in this ridiculous position. They might get the wrong idea.

To Caleb's credit, as soon as we were within a hundred feet of the driveway, he set me carefully on my feet. Briefly, my palm rested against the hard plane of his chest as I steadied myself. His skin radiated warmly against my hand. "Do you think you can walk the rest of the way?"

I glared at him. "I could have walked the whole way. But I guess I should thank you for saving me the trouble."

"Happy to save a lady from getting herself into trouble anytime." He tipped the brim of his hat toward me. I had to shake off the flutter that the gesture stirred up in me. "So, what's the deal with this guy?" Caleb turned to watch Jake huffing slightly as he walked up the incline. "Seems like he has a thing for you."

Jake had paused on the pathway. I watched as he placed his camera up to his eye and directed the lens toward us. The click of a shutter echoed across the grass.

"I don't think so," I shook my head. "We went out on a few dates, but that was a couple of years ago. We quickly realized it wasn't going anywhere. We really haven't talked about it since. I don't date, remember? Men and women can actually just be friends, you know."

Caleb threw me a skeptical look. His low voice rumbled as Jake approached. "Well, you should do a better job of telling him that profound truth before he gets his heart broken."

Annoyed, I ignored him and turned to Jake. "So, how's the article going to be? Did you get everything you need from Caleb? From me?"

"The article is practically going to write itself," he replied enthusiastically. "I can't wait to show my editor the photos I took. She loves human interest stories like this one."

Jake and I fell into step together, angling ourselves toward the driveway where his car waited. Carefully, he set his camera on the front passenger seat before pulling me into a hug. I felt Caleb's presence as he lingered nearby.

"It was so good to see you," I smiled.

"It was so good to see you too."

I expected him to let me go, but he pulled me against his chest again. "I'm planning to take the day to go hiking tomorrow. Thought I'd turn this work trip into a mini vacation." His quick laughter rumbled. "How about we catch up some more over dinner the day after tomorrow?" He released me quickly. "We can talk about the article and just hang out. What's the fanciest place in town?"

"I…um…that would be fun. Let's do it," I stuttered. "Pietra's is about as fancy as we get. Should we meet there?"

"No, no." Jake slid into the front seat of his car. The engine purred to life. "I'll pick you up. Just text me your address. How's seven?"

"Seven is good," I nodded.

"Great." Jake smiled at me through the lowered window. "And Samantha, this is my treat."

He winked at me as he pulled away, giving a final wave to Caleb as his rental car crunched over the rocks on the driveway.

"His treat, huh?"

I jumped at the sound of Caleb's graveled voice just behind me. Kneeling, I unstrapped my shoes and stepped onto the grass barefoot.

"Did you just break your own dating rule?" Caleb continued. "He must have jumped at the chance to come all the way out here to take you out and show you how much he likes you."

I told myself to ignore it, but his words pricked at my already anxious frame of mind. "Jake's just a friend, Caleb. Let it go. It's none of your business anyway." I glared at him, but suddenly I found myself also wondering what Jake's intentions were. The invitation to dinner had been unexpected.

But friends go to dinner and hang out and text and call each other all the time, I reasoned silently. *There's nothing abnormal about us catching up while he's in town. I'm reading way too much into this.*

A shadow swept across Caleb's face. He held up his hands and stepped back. "You're right. None of my business. But you might want to check with Jake on the status of your 'friendship.'" His air quotes on the last word infuriated me. And nothing about his reaction to Jake's invitation was making sense to me.

"I'm going home." Abruptly, I turned away, still carrying my manure crusted shoes. "I hate to ask this, but do you have time to come to the house tonight? I need you to go over the final edits on the website and check a few other things so I can get your site completely live and start blasting the registration dates on social media."

The brim of his hat tipped toward me in a single nod. "I can do that. I need to finish up a few things here, so will later on be ok?"

"That's fine." My posture was stiff as I clambered into the truck I'd borrowed from the ranch.

"And just so we're clear…" I looked back, catching Caleb's eyes turned on me intently. "Jake and I are not going on a date. We are just friends. And I'll be very sure to set that record straight with him."

Caleb shrugged and turned away, leaving me watching him stride back to the stable with long, measured steps.

Chapter Twelve

JAKE'S INVITATION NAGGED at me all afternoon. Not because I wasn't looking forward to having dinner with someone whom I considered a good friend. But because that friend had suddenly done something that could morph him into something more than a friend. All with three little words.

It's my treat.

Jake and I had spent time together throughout college dozens of times. Since he was Amanda's friend too, he had been a frequent figure in our group hangouts. Jake knew Amanda's brother and had merged naturally into our group of friends as all of us navigated life as fresh-faced, new adults.

My one rule with male friendships was to establish a firm independence right away. I wanted my freedom to come and go as

I pleased, so I'd always paid my own way. Whether it was coffee, snacks from the vending machine, or dinners, if I didn't want it to be a date, I stuck resolutely to this one rule. It wasn't that I didn't want to date. But I only wanted to date someone I could see myself building a future with. And so far, I hadn't found him yet.

With one sentence, Jake had upended the friendship lines I thought we'd established and moved the goal post way out of my comfort zone.

When I arrived home after leaving Caleb's, I felt restless and confused. Wandering into the kitchen, I made myself a sandwich and ate it while leaning against the counter. My toes traced the knots on the wooden planks as I stared at the floor. I was still barefoot but had taken a shower as soon as I arrived home.

The smell of hay, horses, and barnyards was hard to wash off in the country. I had to admit that I didn't think it was the worst smell. There was almost something comforting about it, but today the scent only reminded me of Caleb as he'd effortlessly carried me up the hill.

As I nibbled the second half of my sandwich, it was hard not to compare the two men. Caleb and Jake were as alike as night and day. Physically, mentally, and emotionally. Whereas Jake was close to my height and had slim, lean muscles built by runs on paved city streets and air-conditioned gyms—Caleb was tall and broad, a tightly toned body built by decades of training horses in the sun and dirt.

Jake was exuberant and lively, with a personality that was easy to like. Caleb drove me nuts in the worst way. I couldn't even count the number of times that something he had said or done had annoyed me. He was bossy and sarcastic and crossed my boundaries all the time. Yet, I had to admit that Caleb was also quick to step in to help when he saw a need. Like saving me a walk up a hill with manure-crusted shoes and a sore ankle.

Before this morning, I thought Jake and I were on the same page, but as I swallowed the last bits of my sandwich, I wondered if I'd misconstrued Jake's actions all along. His friendliness, his quick habit of touching my arm or my shoulder or pulling me into a hug. Maybe he didn't feel like staying in the platonic friend zone I'd put him in long ago?

I brushed crumbs from my shirt. "Or I could be a conceited brat who is completely misconstruing Jake's invitation to dinner?" The words fell harshly on the quiet kitchen. Maybe all my anxiety was for nothing?

The sound of a car door slamming brought me out of my reverie. I peeked around the kitchen doorway in time to catch Caleb mounting the porch steps.

"Already?" I groaned, not ready to deal with navigating another awkward encounter with this man. "That's probably not fair," I scolded myself immediately.

It had come to my attention that Caleb was funding most of the youth camp from his personal bank account. I knew that the Kane family was well-off, both as a result of the investments his father had placed years ago and from the line of Arabians they'd developed. But that didn't erase the fact that it was generous of him to use his own wealth for such a worthy cause. When I'd discovered that Caleb's generosity extended to more than just playing host of the camp, my heart had fluttered in my chest. It was so...good.

"I didn't expect you so soon," I said, swinging the door toward him. Caleb caught the edge of it between long fingers.

"I asked Griff to handle a few things so that I could get this done. I thought this should be priority today."

He followed me as I led us toward the kitchen. My laptop was sitting on the table, closed. Reaching across, I grabbed it and booted it up.

"Dean and Knox are headed up to the range," I said over my shoulder. The ingredients from my sandwich lay scattered across the countertop. "They probably won't be back for the rest of the week. Vincent went to town." Nervously, my words tumbled out as I moved to clean up my mess. "Sorry, I was just eating a sandwich. The laptop will just take a minute to get set up."

"I talked to Dean this morning." Caleb shuffled toward the counter to move out of my way. "How's the ankle feeling?"

"Fine." Casually, I waved away his inquiry. "I still keep getting painful little twinges in it sometimes, but that's probably because I overdid it too fast."

"You're a hard woman to hold down." His tone was so droll that it pulled a chuckle out of me. "You're probably always dreaming up a new scheme."

"Ok, I'm not going to argue with that," I laughed. I do tend to be a bit of an energizer bunny. But I tried to take it easy last week."

We fell into an awkward, uncomfortable silence. I could hear the chickens clucking as they hunted for insects in the yard. It occurred to me that we were very much alone in my home for one of the first times ever. Other than the day he'd brought me lunch and checked on my ankle, we had rarely ever been alone. The most alone we'd ever been was the night at his sister's wedding when I'd been convinced that he was about to kiss me.

The thought of what would have happened if that kiss had never been interrupted made my skin flush.

I grabbed the sandwich fixings off the counter and walked toward him to put them away in the refrigerator. "Did you eat yet? I can fix you something?"

"Grabbed a sandwich myself about half an hour ago."

"Iced tea or lemonade then?"

"I wouldn't turn down a lemonade."

"Lemonade it is." I grabbed the pitcher and spun on my heel. The movement caught my ankle sharply. I stumbled, letting out a sharp, involuntary gasp.

"Samantha." Caleb leaned forward to take the pitcher from my hand. He set it on the counter.

"Thanks. It was just a little pinch." I hobbled forward. "My own fault."

"I don't know," Caleb said. "It's been long enough. It seems like it should be feeling better by now."

"No, no. It's fine. Just a little sore."

"Let me take a look at it." He bent toward me before I could move. Quick as a flash, I felt myself lifted at the waist and set on the island's countertop.

"Caleb, let me down," I protested quickly, trying to scoot around him.

"No." His voice was firm. "You can get down in a second. Just let me look at it. It could be a missed fracture."

I folded my arms and narrowed my eyes at him. "And Dr. Burke would have missed that, but you'll know just by looking?" I replied, sarcasm dripping from my tone.

"No, but if there's any lingering swelling, I'll be able to check. You forget I've spent my whole life around farm animals. I've handled my fair share of injuries."

Slowly, as if giving me ample time to protest, he reached for me. When I didn't object, I felt his warm fingers clasp themselves around my ankle. He lifted my foot up a little and felt around the ankle bone.

"So now you're comparing me to a farm animal?" I broke the silence.

"Shh, I'm working."

I rolled my eyes as he continued a combination of massage and examination on my ankle. For a man that I knew to be strong, his fingers danced lightly over my skin, using just the right amount of pressure. I felt a little of the soreness in the tendon begin to fade away.

"It appears that Dr. Burke was right after all. No breaks or fractures. It's not even swollen anymore. You probably just overdid it. I prescribe an evening on the sofa and ice cream."

I laughed aloud, shaking my head. "You and ice cream."

Caleb's free hand went to his chest. He gave me an exaggerated expression of shock. "Are you honestly going to tell me that ice cream doesn't fix most things?"

"It does," I admitted. "Most things. Did I ever thank you for bringing that ice cream the other day?"

"Probably not." A hint of a smirk spread across his lips as he lowered my ankle. I felt my heel touch the cabinets. Caleb had positioned himself in front of my knees. Warmth radiated from his muscular frame. For such a quiet man, he seemed to burn with unfettered energy. Lifting my head, I looked up at him, my nerve endings firing with intense awareness of him. His hands came to rest lightly on the island, one hand on either side of my legs.

"Come to think of it, have I ever thanked you for stepping in to help with the horse camp?" Spoken in a low and husky tone, his words were barely a murmur. The flecks of gold in his eyes reflected at me. The dark stubble on his jaw looked soft and silky. Each moment under his intense gaze only increased the tempo of my heartbeat.

"Probably not," I echoed.

"I should really be the one to thank you in that case. I know it would mean a lot to the town to know how much work you've put into expanding the program's reach."

I swallowed, the sound loud in the quiet kitchen. "It's a good cause."

"It is." He nodded. My eyes studied my knees, suddenly unable to quite meet his gaze. "So, how can I thank you, Red?"

"You don't have to thank me." I shook my head.

"Look at me."

Reluctantly, I obeyed.

"But what if I want to thank you?" Caleb's hand rose to cup my face. His thumb stroked along my jaw. We weren't quite at eye level, but he only had to lower his face slightly over me before his lips touched mine. A flash of electricity surged through me the instant we connected.

Shock froze me to the counter. I couldn't move. Caleb's kiss was soft and hesitant. His lips moved against mine, uncertain and slow, as if even he was surprised by what he'd just started. The hand on my face barely grazed my jaw. Instinctively, I knew that he was giving me the freedom to pull away, to end the moment he'd initiated. The years I'd spent believing the worst of him nagged at me to shove him away.

To my surprise though, I didn't recoil from Caleb's touch. Instead, I found myself reaching for him. My arms came up to twine around his neck, and I pulled him down to me a little more. My lips came to life. I kissed him back, my heartbeat roaring in my ears. I couldn't think. Couldn't reason. Instantly, I was drowning in a moment that I thought had been lost long ago.

Caleb is kissing me. Time stood still.

Despite the fire that instantly raged in my veins, the moment was sweet and almost innocent. Two equally uncertain people exploring a brand-new sensation. When Caleb finally pulled away, I found myself left with hot cheeks and a racing heart. His face lingered inches away as we stared at each other. I felt the beat of his pulse under my hands on his neck. The hair at the back was soft and untamed.

"What is happening?" I stammered. Then, without waiting for an answer, I pulled his lips to mine again. He bent over me without resistance. The stubble on his jaw rasped my skin. Our lips merged with a little more force and heat. He took possession of my mouth as if it had always belonged to him. As if I hadn't spent years rejecting every thought of him. Throwing caution to the wind, I returned his kiss—the memory of that night under the stars when our futures could have aligned playing through my mind. His arms wrapped around my waist, and he pulled me closer.

"I have to tell you something," Caleb murmured against my lips.

"Not now," I whispered, unwilling to let him go just yet. Because I knew that when this moment ended, I was going to regret submitting so willingly to his touch. Kissing this cowboy wasn't a good idea.

The kiss could have lasted for minutes. It could have lasted for hours. I had lost all sense of time. Suddenly, a ringtone erupted loudly, disrupting the charged stillness of the kitchen. My phone buzzed on the counter beside my leg. Instantly, our lips parted. Caleb stepped back and I noticed the absence of his strong arms around my waist immediately. We stared at each other. His hand came up to brush through his hair in a quick gesture. Glancing at my cell phone, I saw my mother's photo lighting up the screen.

"I have to take this," I said, my voice a little hoarse.

He nodded without a word. Quickly, I hopped off the counter and slid my finger across the screen.

"Hi, Mom. How is your vacation?" I hoped that she couldn't hear the shake in my voice. Legs weak, I moved to the table, where my laptop had come to life. With nervous hands, I pulled it to me and typed in the password. The screen came to life, but I sat frozen, unable to remember what I'd needed to show Caleb. The nerve endings on my skin felt like they were on fire.

Externally, I tried to look calm and like I hadn't just enthusiastically kissed the man I'd promised myself I would never fall for again. But, internally, I trembled, realizing how eagerly I would repeat the moment that had just passed between us if I could. Processing what had just happened would take some effort.

•　•　•

Caleb kissed me. My heart pounded to the beat of the words as I walked around the barnyard later that evening. A quiet dinner had been eaten and the dishes put away. The light was quickly fading in the west, but I'd needed to get out of the hot, stuffy house.

I'd offered to round up the chickens for the night and managed to ignore Vincent's exaggerated eyebrow raise.

Caleb had kissed me. I stopped dead in my tracks, a fluffy rust-colored hen breaking into a run toward the coop. The truth hit me then like a ton of bricks.

I kissed Caleb.

"Samantha, what are you doing?" I groaned under my breath, clucking at a hen to get her moving away from the tall grass. She veered off the path and I followed to corral her back in.

Setting aside the fact that I still needed to process *who* I'd kissed, the whole situation had thrown me off balance. I didn't know what I was supposed to do to move forward. Dating hadn't been my focus in college. I had been known as the serious and career driven one. I'd accepted a few date invitations, from Jake and a few other guys, but they'd never achieved the instant level of intensity Caleb and I had reached this afternoon.

"So, the one man I manage to kiss in four years just happens to be the guy I swore that I would never trust again?" Another hen ran at the sound of my voice over the echo of the crickets.

Can I truly say that I feel the same negative emotions toward him that I used to feel though?

I'd come to accept his presence over the past few weeks. I no longer cringed when he was around. The sight of him didn't make me want to draw blood. After we'd yelled at each other by the creek after Sandy had nearly run away with me and I'd learned that my assumptions about his character may have been completely wrong, I knew that my animosity toward him had largely dissipated. I couldn't say that I fully trusted him, but did I despise him? Not anymore.

So, what did it mean that I'd not only let him kiss me, but that I'd kissed him back too? If I didn't trust him, there was no way that I could possibly like him. Right?

"This is not going to happen. You'd better get it together and remember what your goals are," I scolded myself. "There's nothing for you in Cascade Valley. There's no man on earth who could tempt me to give up a lifetime of adventure in Europe."

My muttering was interrupted by Vincent calling from the back porch. "Samantha, your cell phone is ringing."

I raced to the house, wincing a little as each step sent a tiny shiver of pain up my still-sore ankle. My heart began to pound. If I was getting a call from one of the organizations I'd applied to in Europe and Vincent saw the caller I.D., I wouldn't know how to explain it.

I wasn't ready to tell my family of my plans. I'd rather get the job and surprise them with the news, than watch their faces crumble before I even had a firm prospect. I tried to think of which job opening would likely be calling at this hour. They probably didn't realize that it was nearly nightfall in the States.

What time is it in Europe anyways?

I burst through the back door. "I'm here. Where's my phone?"

Vincent handed it to me. I didn't even glance at the caller I.D., but immediately slid the screen to answer the call. Turning away, I hurried into the front room. No one sat in the house during the summer. We were always outside or on the porch. I'd be alone.

"Hello?" I spoke into the receiver.

"Hey! Samantha?" a female voice replied.

"Yes, this is Samantha," I said, my heart pounding. *This is it. Is this seriously happening right now?*

"Hey, Samantha. This is Jenna." Her bright, overly peppy voice crackled in my ear like the buzzing of a mosquito.

My heart dropped into my boots. I hoped that I had simply heard her name wrong. I felt my energy sink, suddenly zapped like a faded flower in the summer heat. She was the last person I wanted to talk to tonight of all nights. "Who is this?"

"Jenna. I work at Caleb's ranch. I just called to check on you. That ankle did not seem good this afternoon."

"Um?" I pressed my fingertips to the bridge of my nose, trying to squeeze my sudden headache away. "Thanks, Jenna. That was kind of you."

"Sure, of course. Gosh, it sure seems like you have that reporter twisted around your little finger though. Is he your boyfriend?" A giggle came from the other end of the line.

Why in the world is Jenna calling me to giggle over a guy? This was too weird. "Um, no. He's not my boyfriend. I knew him in college, and we've been friends for a while. Why do you ask?"

Instead of answering me, her voice teased again, "Oh my gosh, you cannot tell me you haven't considered dating that good-looking guy? He was so nice. A city boy with good looks and good manners? Count me in."

She rambled on before I could get in a reply. "And it's so obvious he's smitten with you. Gosh, he couldn't take his eyes off you. I tried to get him to talk to me and nope, he just wanted to stare at you. You lucky girl."

I wasn't buying the fake friendship vibe I was suddenly getting from her. And to say that I was uncomfortable was an understatement. Was there a point to this call?

"You're going out on a date with him tomorrow, aren't you? I overheard him ask you," she continued. "You know, your story is going to end up a lot like mine and Caleb's probably will. Best friends who just knew they were meant for something more."

It clicked then. What I should have understood as soon as she opened her mouth. "Oh, I see. Like yours and Caleb's relationship? Wouldn't that be something?"

The truth was as clear as the night of a full moon. Jenna had called to ever-so-sweetly warn me away from Caleb. She wanted me to know she had staked a claim on him and that I'd better back off. She would probably never come right out and say it. We went to the same small-town church after all. But I had received the message, loud and clear.

And I was furious. With myself, with Caleb, and with Jenna. She probably didn't deserve my ire, but I'd throw her into the mix of my fury anyway.

How dare he kiss me when he is in a relationship with her? I'd known it. I'd sensed it the first day I had set foot on the ranch. She'd been passive aggressive, always watching me with a sour look on her face, and I'd foolishly dismissed it as petty jealousy.

For whatever reason, she and Caleb must be keeping their relationship private. I understood. Small communities were notorious for gossip that spread like wildfire. Maybe they hadn't made it official yet. But that did not give him the right to come into my house and kiss me. No matter what history we had together. Another line had just been added to my list of grievances toward the man. He had to have known that I would find out the truth eventually. Or maybe he'd just wanted to finish what we had been on the brink of starting years ago and had banked on me moving away again before I discovered his secret.

And I'd kissed him back. Eagerly. How humiliating. I could hardly breathe. My pulse beat erratically. This was almost worse than everything I'd accused him of before. And I had no one to blame but myself for falling for his good guy act.

"I seriously wish you all the best, Samantha. Jake seems like a great guy," Jenna said.

She was right. Jake was a great guy. But he wasn't for me, though it didn't really matter if she understood that. My heart began to ache. I had almost let myself.... I stopped myself before I finished the thought. But I'd see pigs fly before I fell for any of Caleb's tricks again. "Thanks, Jenna. My best to you as well. I have to go now, ok? Thanks for calling to check on me."

"Sure. I'm headed to visit my grandmother in Idaho for a couple of weeks, but I can't wait to see everything you've done for the camp when I get back. You're doing such a splendid job. At least that's what Caleb says."

If you only knew what your precious cowboy was up to this afternoon, you probably wouldn't be so enthusiastic about my presence around the ranch.

I wished that I could tell her. Warn her. But her relationship with Caleb wasn't any of my business. Telling her would only hurt her. But I would absolutely make sure he understood exactly what I thought of him.

I stormed onto the front porch when we ended the call, my mind running in a dozen different directions. This changed things. I felt like I had to honor my commitment to the youth camp for as long as I could. It was a good cause. Fortunately, the launch of the website would release me from some of my obligation. I could continue running the camp's social media from nearly anywhere. But I didn't want to work closely with Caleb anymore.

I felt almost as betrayed as I'd felt four years ago.

I stopped and stared into the darkening yard. He had to have known that his behavior was unacceptable. That I would find out. That I wasn't the kind of woman who went around kissing another woman's boyfriend.

"You ok, Red?" Vincent's soft drawl caused me to jump and whirl around. I hadn't realized that he was on the front porch. I hoped that he hadn't overheard any of my conversation.

"Just fine," I fibbed. "Do you mind if I borrow your truck keys? I need to run a quick errand."

"Uh, sure." Vincent dug in his jeans pocket and handed me the keys. "It's getting dark. Are you sure you don't want me to drive with you?"

"No, not at all. You sit out here and relax. I'll be back in a few minutes."

"I don't mind driving with you," he called after me as I hurried down the porch steps and across the yard.

My brothers. Each one my lifelong protectors. I appreciated Vincent's concern, even if his presence wasn't welcome for my present task. I waved in his direction. "Don't worry about me. I'll be fine."

The truck started with a roar, and I threw the clutch into drive. When I was on the open road, I pressed on the gas. I wanted to get in and get out, with no fuss and no drama. But what I was going to say had to be said. His ranch loomed up in the encroaching gloom of twilight. The white fence stood in contrast to the darkness. Caleb didn't close the main gate until later. Without pause, I took a sharp turn to the right and roared down the driveway.

The front porch was aglow, and I could see lights in the kitchen when I turned off the ignition. I hoped that I wasn't going to show up at his door only to find that Jenna was perched inside. That would be an awkward encounter.

My spontaneous resolution to confront him was probably a mistake. But he had to have heard the truck rumble down the driveway. These diesel models didn't make it easy to creep up on anyone. I was here and I was forced to commit, whether I was chickening out or not.

Caleb had already opened the front door and was standing on the stoop watching me by the time I exited the truck. He stood with his arms crossed over his broad chest. Slowly, I walked across the yard. His expression was unreadable when I glared up at him.

After our kiss had been interrupted this afternoon, we hadn't spoken of it again. I'd finally managed to pull up the website and shown him what I'd created. There had been an awkward tension crackling in the air between us. But it was like the kiss had existed in a temporary twilight zone, an alternate universe broken by the ringing of my cell phone. When it was over, we both seemed to want to avoid further discussion.

"Do you want to come in?" Caleb asked as I marched up the porch steps.

I thought about the offer. Despite my indignation, I knew that I wasn't ready to have this conversation on the front porch. A couple of the ranch hands lived on site in the bunkhouses and having an argument outdoors with Caleb would probably just incur a lot of gossip. "For only a minute."

He turned and led the way.

It had been ages since I'd been inside the Kane's family farm-house. I had always thought that it had a special charm when I was growing up. A charm that was surely amplified by my head-over-heels-crush for the serious young cowboy who lived there.

"Why did you kiss me this afternoon?" The words burst out before the front door had even closed behind me.

"Do you want some sweet tea?" Caleb asked, glancing over his shoulder at me without concern. I was forced to follow him deeper into the house.

"Stop ignoring me." We emerged into the brightly lit kitchen. I hadn't been in his home for years, but I could tell that he hadn't changed much. "You might be interested in knowing who just called me to chat."

"And who's that?" He turned to face me, folding his arms over his chest again and leaning against the countertop.

"Jenna decided that she needed to call to congratulate me on my good fortune."

He raised an eyebrow. "And that's made you storm over here in the middle of the night? Is there something I forgot to congratulate you for?"

"It isn't the middle of the night," I corrected petulantly. "It seems like I'm the one who should be congratulating you. According to Jenna, my friendship with Jake is shaping up to be an epic friends-to-lovers story."

I paused for dramatic effect. My heart was pounding nervously. I flexed my hands at my sides, trying to pulse away some of the frustration. "Just like hers and yours."

"So that's why you're upset?" Caleb frowned, but his hands dropped to his sides. He seemed to relax, which irritated me all the more. "Because Jenna called you to establish her territory?"

"I'm not upset." I began to pace the kitchen floor. Caleb's eyes followed my movement. "That's not true. I'm furious. You know, I've tried to give you a second chance. For my brothers' sake. For the youth camp. But you've proven to be just as much of a cad as I thought you were."

"Oh now you're calling me a cad?" he replied roughly. The instant scowl on his face matched the fury seething from mine. "Is that a word you picked up from a Victorian romance novel?"

"Regency romance actually," I retorted sarcastically. "This isn't funny. I'm not in the habit of kissing men who are in relationships with other women. And I'm angry that you put me into that position today." My voice went up an octave.

Without warning, Caleb stepped in front of me. I stopped just short of crashing into his chest. He loomed above me, tall and sturdy. I faltered as I took in his imposing presence. My pulse fluttered. My first thought was of how I was just the right height to lean against him and nestle my nose into the crook of his neck. My next thought was of how angry I felt, how betrayed yet again.

"Do I get a chance to say anything? Or are you both the victim and the judge here, Samantha McCade?"

I bit back a sharp retort at his words. He was angry. I could see a storm brewing in his eyes. My resolution faltered at the look on his face.

"Jenna was out of line," he continued. His voice had become harsh and guttural. It shivered over me. "There isn't anything going on between us. I took her out to dinner a few times late last year. And I knew she wasn't the woman for me so that was the end of that."

"Well, she certainly doesn't seem to have gotten the memo," I yelled, thrusting my chin into the air. "I don't need half the town knowing that she had to put me in my place."

His hands shot up and gripped the back of my elbows. He pulled me closer, bending over me. "Would it bother you so much to have people gossip about us?"

Our eyes met. My pulse jumped at the pressure of his fingers on my arms. His touch was electric. I could feel the heat pulsing off his skin. I swallowed, my throat instantly going dry as I prepared to protest. "There's nothing to gossip about." My voice was hoarse. "Nothing is even going on between us."

"Are you sure about that, Red?" Caleb murmured, tugging me a little closer. The charge in the room was overwhelming. "I could have sworn that something began between us this afternoon in your kitchen."

My head shook, my hair bouncing wildly around my shoulders. "No, this afternoon was a mistake. I shouldn't have let you do that."

"But you did let me," he replied, his words a whisper. "Why?"

"Something came over me."

Caleb's arms had moved to snake around my waist. He pulled me into his body, holding me still. As if by instinct, my hands moved to twine around his neck just like this afternoon. Gently, he pressed his lips to my forehead. A delicious shiver crept across my back at the touch. "If you only knew…." he whispered.

"Knew what?" I demanded, still struggling to hold onto my anger. Conflicting emotions warred for dominance in my brain.

"How could a man have eyes for any other woman when you are in his line of sight? There's just something about you, Samantha, that instantly sucks me in. For better or for worse. You know that I nearly kissed you four years ago, right?"

I nodded. "That night at your sister's wedding?"

"Even before that. The night we were alone in the stable. You were so stubbornly determined to convince me that you were all grown up. There was a fire flashing in those emerald eyes of yours that I couldn't resist. I was drawn to that untamable nature of yours. I don't think you realize that when you walk into a room, it's as if all the sunlight is instantly drawn to your beautiful face. Everything else falls into the shadows."

Caleb thinks I'm beautiful. The thought flashed through my mind as I tried to rapidly process his words. *Why is he saying this to me now?* Wasn't it too late for this? A confusing mix of frustration and delight began a chaotic dance in my chest.

His breath tickled my ear. "You're like the sun. I want to tame that fiery nature of yours, but I'm afraid I'll be left with a burn if I stay near you too long. I don't think I can help myself though."

"Caleb, we can't do this," I whispered, clinging to him.

"Why not?"

"I don't know," I murmured, suddenly unsure of why I'd been angry with him tonight in the first place. "My brothers would probably have a fit."

"You let me handle the McCade boys. And your mother. But does anyone else matter? It only matters what you and I want." Caleb's fingers stroked my jaw. He lifted my face to meet his, those amber-colored eyes smoldering as they met mine. "When you came back home, I knew you would be trouble again, just like before. But I don't care, Samantha."

He was going to kiss me again. I saw it on his face. My heart began to sing, eager for the feeling of his lips on mine. And then my eyes fell onto the mantel and a crushing wave of disappointment and regret washed over me. Roughly, I planted my hands on Caleb's chest and pushed him away. "Stop."

He let me go immediately, though I saw disappointment flash rapidly over his face.

I walked to the mantel, grabbed a frame, and spun around. I thrust the framed photograph toward Caleb. The two men in the picture were smiling broadly. My heart ached at the sight of my dad, his arm thrown around the beautiful white colt that had started all of this, the excitement evident across his face. A younger version of Caleb stood on the other side of the horse. His serious face was shadowed under the brim of his hat.

"This is why I can't let anything happen between us, Caleb. My dad was everything in the world to me. And I don't know if I can feel the way I used to feel about you ever again." I exhaled sharply, willing myself to hold it together. My eyes spiked with unshed tears, but I forced myself to stand my ground and meet his frustrated gaze.

I heard the crack in his voice when he spoke. "Your dad fell in love with that colt. What happened was a fluke accident, but if I could go back and do things differently, I would give my right arm to change the outcome of that awful day. I loved him too, you know." The last words came out as a whisper, and I almost had to strain to hear. My heart constricted at the pain so clearly evident in his voice. We had both lost something precious that day.

"I'm not saying you didn't," I admitted, my voice thick with tears. "You said that I misconstrued what I overheard between you and your dad. And I believe you. It all was just an accident. But he was my dad."

I took a deep breath, needing to make this right, to set the record straight with Caleb. "I think you are a good man. Coming home this summer has shown me that I don't have to hate you anymore to honor my dad's memory. I'm trying to fully process all of this. I want to finish out my work for the camp." A shudder ran across my shoulders. "But my heart is still broken. I can't feel the way I think you want me to feel."

"Don't do this. Talk to me."

I couldn't listen anymore. Slamming the frame on the butcher block countertop, I ran from the kitchen. Caleb's hand reached for my arm, but I brushed him away. He called after me. I refused to slow my pace. I escaped into the night, the slam of the front door a hard and final echo in my ears.

Chapter Thirteen

"I DON'T THINK that Jake has ever gotten over that crush he had on you." Amanda's eager voice echoed through the speaker. I was finishing the last touches of my makeup before Jake was due to arrive to pick me up for dinner. "And the fact that he trekked to the wilds of Montana to meet up with you. How romantic."

"It's hardly the wilds, Amanda," I laughed, weighing the pros and cons of wedges versus flats in my mind. Jake wasn't much taller than me, so I decided to opt for the flats. At five-foot-eight, I was often one of the taller women in a room. I didn't mind my height, but I also didn't want to tower above Jake, so flats it would be.

I always feel delicate and small next to Caleb. The thought hit me unbidden. An image of his ranch-hardened frame popped into my head. Resolutely, I shook off the mental picture. "Besides, this isn't a romantic date and he knows that," I continued. "He needed a story to write. I provided said story. Tonight is simply about two friends catching up with each other."

"Uh huh," she teased. "Try telling that to Jake. You haven't hung out with him and listened to him go on and on about you. The guy was smitten long ago, and he agreed to write this story to show that to you."

"Do you think I should cancel our dinner then?" I sat on my bed, suddenly filled with anxiety. "I'm not interested in him like that. I don't want to string the man along."

"Absolutely not. It sounds like you have done positively nothing exciting since you got back home. You need to get out, have fun, be young," Amanda said in a sing-song voice.

Does it count as fun to kiss a man you aren't supposed to be kissing?

"I have been working," I retorted aloud. "This is my time to get a job secured and get my career on track. There's plenty of time to have fun when I get to Europe."

"How's that going?" she asked.

"Slow," I sighed. "I have an interview scheduled next week for a position in France. I'm still talking to the organization in Spain. In the meantime, I'm just trying to build up my resume by working on the camp project."

"And how is our handsome rancher, Caleb?" she laughed. "You haven't mentioned him in awhile."

He is entirely too handsome. Too tall and masculine. Too appealing. I'm struggling to process every feeling I ever thought I had toward him. It doesn't make sense to like him, but it makes even less sense to dislike him.

"He's just fine, Amanda," I said with forced sweetness.

"You're lucky I haven't come out there and swooped him away from you. You can't have both Jake and Caleb all to yourself, Sammie."

"Believe me, you're welcome to both of them," I said, rolling my eyes. "Jake is a nice guy, but Caleb might make you want to jump off a cliff. The man could win medals for being the most exasperating human on the planet."

An exasperating man that you liked kissing. I brushed the stray, stubborn thought away.

"Don't tell me that you are passing on sweet Jake because you have a secret crush on Caleb?"

"What? No!" I yelped. "We literally just had a fight the other night and I doubt we're on speaking terms anymore."

"Sounds like love to me," she teased.

"You're crazy and I have to go."

"Sammie, your date is here." Vincent's voice drifted up the stairs just as I ended the call. I took one last look in the mirror before inhaling deeply and turning to head downstairs.

. . .

I was ready to return home halfway through dinner with Jake. The food was as delicious as I remembered and he was a nice person. But I was bored out of my mind. Spending time with a friend one-on-one was far different that hanging out in a group setting, I was quickly discovering.

Jake had chosen the best restaurant our little town had to offer—an Italian bistro on Main Street called *Pietra's*. I'd eaten here plenty of times. The food was delicious. Each dish—homey, rich, and comforting—could rival those of even Seattle's best Italian restaurants.

I was happy with the food. It was the company that had me squirming with discomfort on my chair. Jake had been rambling for fifteen minutes straight about his many grievances against his editor. I wanted to be a good friend, but his droning voice was going to put me to sleep face first into my *spaghetti aglio e olio*.

I tried to remember if Jake had always seemed this dull. He had always seemed so exciting and wise-to-the-world. Not tonight. My thoughts began to drift to the projects I still needed to finish for the website. There were a couple of minor tweaks that Caleb needed to approve so we could get the website live and open for registration.

Caleb. My stomach did a flip flop as the feeling of that kiss in my kitchen flooded my memory again. I hadn't been able to get it out of my head since it had happened. It had been warm and sweet and deep. And later that night…the things he'd murmured in my ear. And then I'd destroyed the moment with my resentment and rage.

Had I made a mistake by running away? Not that I could allow anything to happen between us. It wouldn't be fair to him. But it was too easy to imagine kissing Caleb again. And that was a problem. A problem that could ruin my plans.

"But here I am just rambling on and on about myself. Tell me about you, Samantha. How's life?" Jake's voice broke into my thoughts.

Sharply, I pulled myself back to the present moment. A shadow of Caleb's ever-serious, bearded face lingered in my imagination though.

"I'm good," I scrambled, trying to think of something to say. Jake was part of the group texts that our friends kept running. If he'd been paying attention, he already knew most of my highlights. And from the sudden pressure of his fingers laid over mine, I suspected that he had been keeping tabs on me.

"I'm just working on my next steps in life," I continued hastily. "Enjoying the summer with my family. You know I'm applying for positions overseas, right?" I wiggled my fingers, hoping I could make him let go. But the pressure of Jake's hand remained firm.

"I've really missed you," he replied in a low tone, leaning toward me in the booth. I pulled back, using the pretense of picking up my napkin off the floor to create distance between us. The owners of this bistro knew me. I didn't need a deluge of gossip once I left.

"I doubt that," I laughed. "You're off in your big, fancy, grown-up world, writing incredible stories, working for a newspaper that gets read by thousands."

"But you're all grown up too," he insisted. "And it's been lonely without you around to give me sass."

"Me, sassy?" I splayed a hand across my chest, pretending to be shocked.

"Sassy and you know it," he replied, giving me a wink. "But I love it. You're such an interesting person. When are you going to come back to Seattle and let me take you out again?"

"You want to take me out again?" The words fell out sharply before I thought better of them.

Jake spoke around a mouthful of ravioli. "I do. I'd like to take you on lots of dates, Samantha. I'd like you to move back to the city and let me see you every day. I'd like to date you for real. How do you feel about that?"

His eyes watched me closely. I felt my cheeks heat. The night was quickly shifting toward a direction I hadn't wanted. "This is unexpected, Jake. You know I'm planning to leave the country. I thought we agreed years ago that we would just be friends?"

"We did. But I've always liked you. I came all the way out here in the middle of nowhere to write a story about a horse camp for underprivileged kids. It isn't exactly ground-breaking news. My editor refused to even cover the cost of my trip."

My heart sank at his words. Amanda had suspected as much, but I hadn't believed her until now. I had to make sure that my actions didn't give Jake a reason to ditch the story. There were too many people counting on me to make sure this went smoothly. Letting Jake down was the last thing I wanted to do, but I needed to set the record straight between us. "You're a great guy, Jake, and a wonderful friend. I can't begin to thank you for agreeing to write this story. But if I'm being honest, I only think of you as a friend."

His disappointment was evident. "Can you see yourself dating me? I'm a nice guy."

I shook my head, guilt spilling into my stomach. If I'd known that this was how he felt, I wouldn't have asked him to write the article at all. I tried to choose my words carefully. "I would never want anything to ruin our friendship."

"Is there someone else? Be honest." Jake said, leaning toward me expectently.

"I'm just focused on my career right now. There isn't anyone else." It was the truth, so I wasn't sure why the words felt like a lie. Or why I also felt a flush creeping over my face. It wasn't like I was interested in anyone else.

Jake seemed to pull himself together. He gripped my hand again and squeezed. An awkward silence fell over the table.

As we ate *migliaccio* for dessert and the lemony flavor danced across my tongue, I wondered if I'd just lost a friend.

. . .

A few days later, Amanda called to tell me that Jake's story was live. Hands shaking, I rushed to my laptop, typing so hastily that I made three mistakes before I could reach the newspaper's web address. And then there it was, headlining the human-interest section, an engaging article about the charity youth horse camp hosted by Kane Arabian Ranch. Jake had written it beautifully, in a way that would make both donors and students want to get involved.

And I had to admit that the photographs he'd taken were stunning. Candid, richly colored photos of the land, the ranch hands, and the horses. My breath hitched a little as I scrolled and caught sight of Caleb in one of them. Jake had captured him in a moment with Beau. In the photograph, Caleb looked every bit the rugged Montana cowboy that he was, his hand resting lightly on the handsome white colt's shoulder. I had to admit that the contrast between his rugged manliness and the elegant horse made a striking photograph.

I laid my hands flat on my desk, pulling in one deep breath after another. I couldn't explain my nerves lately. Suddenly, I'd find myself all aflutter, heart beating fast, butterflies jumping around in my stomach. I hadn't been able to figure out why I was so nervous and edgy. *I just have the jitters about everything that I have in the works, I'm sure.*

But the story of the youth camp had officially been launched into the world. Readers would see it and pass it on, hopefully to the people who needed it the most. The website had gone live for reservations earlier in the week. Applicants would be asked to fill out a questionnaire and relay some personal information to make sure the camp was a good fit for the student in question.

I'd emailed a link for the website to Caleb so that he could look it over for final approval. Only a single word had been sent back: *Approved.* Despite the curt reply, I'd proceeded. I checked the dashboard now and saw that the web traffic had already increased exponentially. With Jake's article going live, we'd be flooded with applicants at this rate.

The single word reply to my email had been all the communication that I'd received from Caleb the entire week. Our argument still hung in my mind like the morning fog, thick and heavy. I couldn't see my way through it. I felt lost.

I wandered aimlessly into the living room, too anxious to find something constructive to do. My brothers were away. I was alone. I'd already completed all the tasks that I could think of, both at home and for the youth camp. I'd spent a large chunk of the morning marketing the camp on social media, connecting with churches and influencers who might take an interest in the camp's mission.

I flopped down on the sofa and looked over the books on the coffee table, hoping that something would spark my interest. The cover of one of the romance novels Caleb had teased me about caught my eye. Next to the paperback, a Bible lay open. Vincent had a habit of leaving his Bible open to wherever he had been reading. A highlighted verse caught my wandering gaze, and I leaned closer to read it.

'He heals the brokenhearted and binds up their wounds.' Psalm 147:3

The verse made me pause. I read it again, lingering over each word to fully absorb its meaning. Dad's accident may have been several years ago, but the wound caused by his loss still felt fresh. There were days and weeks, even months, that I could ignore it. But inevitably something would happen to tear the scab off and start the healing process all over again. At this rate, I didn't know if I'd ever be finished mourning my father's death. We'd been so close. *"Two peas in a pod,"* Mom had always said.

I curled into the comforting arm of the sofa and let fresh tears slip down my cheeks. The yellow highlighter in the Bible caught my attention again. I wiped my face.

All this grief, yet here I was with the promise of healing right in front of me. Dad's voice echoed in my mind. Growing up, he'd always whispered in my ear as he tucked me into bed, *"I may love you to the moon and back, but your Father in Heaven loves you more than a thousand trips to the moon."*

I covered my face with my hands and whispered into my fingers. "If there's healing for my broken heart, Father, please help me to receive it. Because I really don't know how. And Father, please… help me to know if Caleb is…."

The ringing of the house telephone interrupted my whispered prayer. It shocked me that in an age of instant communication and cell phones in every pocket, most of the valley still had landlines installed and used them frequently. I grabbed the cordless handheld without thinking.

"Hello?"

"Uh, hello? Samantha? This is Ian." A friendly, masculine voice greeted me on the other end of the line. I tried to connect the face with the name for a moment before it clicked.

"Oh, Ian. Hi."

"Hi. Uh, listen. Some of the gang and I are headed up to the lake tomorrow afternoon. It'll be cold as heck still, but we're going to run in for a quick dip and then roast marshmallows around a fire. Should be fun. You in?"

"You're inviting me to go with you?"

"Yeah, I am. If that's ok? We're a cool group and I know it probably gets boring up at the farmhouse by yourself all the time. Thought you'd enjoy getting out of the house and making some new friends."

"Sure, I'll go. Thanks for the invite."

"Great. I'll pick you up at two."

We signed off and I held the phone in my hand for a moment, lost in thought. Jumping up, I grabbed a set of keys and headed outdoors. I needed the sun on my skin and the wind in my hair to process all the thoughts spinning around in my head. A drive would do me good and my brothers had invited me to borrow their trucks anytime. Maybe I'd make my way into town to pick up a pie from Sherry's.

The back roads were quiet as I pressed down the gas in the truck. The roar of the engine was a comforting sound. An endless stretch of grassy landscape lay around me. Miles and miles of rugged foothills terrain stretched into the distance. I sighed. This land was deep and powerful and full of heritage. I had roots here. And so much history.

So why did I want to run away so badly?

A familiar wooden fence began on my left. *Mrs. Jensen.* I'd nearly forgotten about her in the weeks that had passed since Caleb had taken me to visit her. I'd promised her that I would return.

Spontaneously, I swung the steering wheel to the left and turned into her driveway. Her pretty mare tossed its mane and galloped alongside me on the other side of the fence as I approached the tiny cottage.

The aging woman waved happily to me from the porch.

"Well, if it isn't the youngest McCade girl. How are you doing, darlin'? Come on up and sit a spell with me."

"Hi, Mrs. Jensen." I kissed her soft, wrinkled cheek and settled into the rocker next to hers. She limped into the house and brought out a plate of still-warm oatmeal cookies and lemonade.

"I just stopped in to say hello and to see how you are," I said, savoring the sweet, crumbly cookie.

"Doing just fine." She settled back into her rocker. "The Lord's been good to me for eighty-two years. And your young man, he certainly takes good care of me too."

I nearly choked on a cookie crumb. "My young man? Who do you mean?" I stared at her in alarm, wondering if she thought I was someone else entirely.

"Well, the Kane boy, of course. Would you believe I've known that boy since he was just a baby? Babysat him many a time when his daddy was still just a ranch hand. A finer young man you couldn't meet. You hang onto that one now, you hear me?" Her gnarled hand reached out and gripped my arm lightly.

I shook my head. My heart fluttered. "Caleb and I are just neighbors. We are not going together."

Her eyes sparkled. "Well, I wouldn't believe it if you hadn't told me. The way you two looked at each other, I thought for sure he was fixin' to propose."

I stared at her in shock. She stood and motioned for me to follow her. "Now, come along with me. I want to show you the beautiful blooms that just sprang up in my garden."

I followed her down the path and around to the back flower garden, willing the butterflies in my stomach to settle, trying to push her words out of my head. I spent the next hour with her, wandering around her flower garden and admiring her chickens. Mrs. Jensen said that she was too old to manage the work of a vegetable garden, so she'd settled for flowers instead. I noticed a few repairs that needed to be made around the old house and made a mental note to ask one of my brothers to come back with me next week to fix them.

To please her, I even set aside my nerves and allowed her horse to come up to me for a petting. I stretched out my hand and stroked her soft muzzle. I had to admit that she was a pretty horse with a sweet disposition. I was trying to work through my fear of horses and Foxi's soft, warm nose made each moment easier. The mare nuzzled my hand, pushing me to stroke her long face again. I complied, running my fingers up and down the stripe on her nose.

"Pretty girl," Mrs. Jensen crooned. "She's about as old as I am, but she sure looks a sight better." She laughed at her own joke. "You know, this horse was a balm to my heart when I lost my Gregory several years ago. I'd come out here and cry into her mane, wondering how I could ever feel happy without him. She'd stand still as a statue, letting me lean on her. Every now and then, she'd turn her head and her lips would whisper at my hair, as if making sure I was alright. I think God put her in my life so she could piece me back together when I was broken."

My heart constricted in my chest, and I looked at Foxi thought-fully. The old woman stroked the mare's neck. As if on cue, the horse nudged her good-naturedly, rooting around in the pocket of her dress for treats.

"She's always wanting sugar cubes. A bad habit I should never have started her on years ago. What can I say though? I have a sweet tooth too." Mrs. Jensen chuckled, reaching into her pocket for the white cubes.

"And speaking of sweet things, here comes your young man now." She turned and waved enthusiastically in the direction of a truck that had just pulled into the driveway. I recognized it immediately. My heart dropped.

"Of all the…." I murmured under my breath as Caleb rolled to a stop next to my own vehicle. Stepping out, he grabbed a fresh bale of hay from the bed and set it on his shoulder. His long legs ate up the ground as he approached us. I sank back against the fence, wondering just how awkward this was going to be. But Caleb ignored me as Mrs. Jensen bustled about him, thanking him for thinking of her.

"Let me get you a cookie," she exclaimed.

"I'm fine, Mrs. Jensen. I just came to leave a few bales for Foxi."

"I really don't know what we would do without you, Caleb." She fluttered about until she couldn't hold herself back any longer.

"I'm surprised to see you here." Caleb turned to me as she limped back to the house, insisting that he at least drink a glass of fresh lemonade before he left. He didn't sound or look at all pleased with me.

"I'm equally surprised to see you here," I replied dryly. Then, trying to check the sarcasm in my tone, I continued. "I was out for a drive and just thought that she could use a visit." I nodded up toward the house where Mrs. Jensen had disappeared.

He nodded, his hand coming up to rub his chin. His beard looked soft and full. "She can use the company. It's easy for people to forget others once they've gotten too old to contribute to society much. But Mrs. Jensen was a good influence on a lot of people. I'm grateful to you for thinking of her."

His admission surprised me. "Well, a visit now and then from me isn't much to brag about. But you—keeping her horse fed and her pantry stocked. You're a good man."

It was evident that the unexpected compliment shocked him. He'd avoided making eye contact with me, but now his gaze darted up to mine. It was hard not to drop my eyes shyly at the intense expression on his face.

"Walk with me while I unload the rest of the hay into her shed?" He paced away.

Automatically, I jumped forward to follow. Caleb lifted another bale from the bed of his truck as if it was as light as a feather. He carried it toward the small, three-sided shed that protected the hay from the elements. My legs moved double-time to keep up with his long strides. He waited until he set the hay down, then turned to me.

"I want to apologize for how I acted the other night. You were upset and frustrated and hurting over your dad and I could have handled that better."

Guilt washed over me. I was the one who owed him the apology. I waved my hands in protest. "Please don't. I should be apologizing to you." I paced a few steps and came back to face him. "For years, I've done nothing but resent you. I know what happened to my dad was just a terrible accident, but I've unfairly blamed you. I've screamed at you. I've insulted you. I tried to damage your family's reputation in our community."

"It's natural to need someone to blame," he shrugged, the brim of his hat drawn low over his eyes.

"Natural, but not always fair," I replied. "Seeing you, being at your ranch, it brings up painful memories that I just haven't been able to put to rest. I'm not sure if the loss of my dad will ever fully heal, but I don't want to keep taking my grief out on you in the meantime."

He picked up a blade of hay and rolled it between his fingers until it crumbled. "You don't have to think of me as a friend. But I don't want to be your enemy."

"I don't want you to be my enemy either."

Caleb's head lifted and he caught my gaze. "A truce then? A real one this time? Not total enemies?"

I stepped forward and extended my right hand. "To not totally friends, but not total enemies either?"

His large hand covered mine. My fingers brushed the calluses on his palm. The warmth from his fingertips spread up my arm. "I'll shake on that."

I felt my cheeks flush at the look in his eyes, but I couldn't have explained why.

Chapter Fourteen

IAN WAS RIGHT.

Despite the warmth of the afternoon, the lake was frigid. I dragged myself through the freezing water back onto the shore, wondering if it were possible to shiver yourself right out of your own skin.

"Are you going in for a dip or will I have to carry you in?" Ian had grinned over at me mischievously when we'd arrived at the sunny lake shore.

"Well, you're definitely not carrying me in." I'd grinned back but made sure that my eyes conveyed a warning. "It's probably too cold for me though."

"Suit yourself." He shrugged good-naturedly. "Going in is tough at first, but afterward you'll feel like you've just accomplished this big,

momentous thing. It's good for your character to do tough things."
He nodded at me solemnly.

He hadn't meant anything by the words, but I felt a pang strike my heart. I wanted to feel accomplished. I wanted to feel happy and pleased with myself, like I'd done something that amounted to more than my decidedly average accomplishments. Setting my jaw, I'd kicked off my sneakers. Shimmying out of the loose dress I'd worn and revealing my one-piece and swim shorts underneath, I'd followed Ian toward the shore. I watched him bounce up and down on his heels a few times, shaking his whole body as he steeled himself for the plunge.

With a *whoop*, he'd made a sudden dash for the water. A quick dip and he plunged in, popping up a few feet farther out, water streaming off his brown hair in rivulets. "Chickens stay out on the shore."

Shrieks echoed as a few of his friends dove into the water as well. I hadn't let myself think about it any further. Bracing myself for the shock of the frigid snow melt, I'd dashed forward and plunged under the surface. The cold had hit my chest like a ton of bricks, making it hard to catch my breath as I surfaced. I'd sputtered and choked as I sucked in a mouthful of lake water. My whole body tingled. The sensation was decidedly unpleasant.

Yet, by the time I'd managed to find my footing on the rocky lake floor, something else began to set in. A sense of exhilaration washed over me. My skin had stopped tingling and a warmth flooded my insides as my body quickly regulated its temperature. I'd floated in the clear water, marveling as the sun danced along the rippled surface. The lake shimmered. Suddenly, my brain felt clearer than it had in ages. As I'd carried myself out of the water back to shore, I'd wondered if it was possible to feel this light and refreshed all the time.

The lake was hidden in a small dip between two mountains just above Cascade Valley. I'd ridden up with Ian and two of his friends, a girl named Miranda and a boy named Samuel. They were a little younger than me and I found their happy chatter refreshing. They'd plied me with questions about Seattle and the state of Washington. They both seemed convinced that I'd been living in the Emerald City, going to shows and staying out late on the town every night. They were disappointed to hear how often it rained and that the gloomy skies couldn't hold a candle to the warmth and ease of a Montana summer day.

A warm breeze brushed my skin as I walked back to our picnic blankets.

"Was that your first dip in the lake this year?" Miranda's cute, round face smiled up at me. She was stretched on the blanket, her skin, hair, and clothes still dry. I grabbed an extra towel from my bag and tried to remove some of the excess moisture from my swim shorts, wringing them out with my hands, water splashing onto the rocks.

"It was my first time jumping into a lake in years," I admitted, settling on the blanket next to her. I used the towel to squeeze out some of the moisture from my braid. It was going to dry a frizzy mess and I was going to end up covered in freckles, but I didn't care. I wanted to soak up the rays. A soft, balmy breeze sang among the trees, setting their leaves dancing and shivering across the mountains.

"I'm so proud of you, Samantha." Ian came running up from the lake, enthusiasm written across his face. "It takes guts to take a plunge like that."

"Guts that I apparently don't have," Miranda laughed, motioning down to her still dry clothes. "Impressive."

I grinned. But my exhilaration was already wearing thin. If only all of life's uncertainties could be solved by a quick plunge into the lake. I shivered, the chill of the lake clinging to me despite the heat. I pulled myself to my feet and dug around in my bag for my cell phone. I needed to move, to shake off some of my nervous energy that wouldn't seem to go away. "I want to take a picture to send to the gang back in Seattle. Everyone will wish they were here with me."

"I'll walk with you," Ian said, falling into step beside me.

"Want to come along, Miranda?" I looked over my shoulder toward the younger woman, hoping she would walk with us.

Miranda shook her head. She tilted her head up to the sun and closed her eyes. "I am more than happy to lay in the sun and just relax all afternoon. You two go explore."

Ian and I walked along the shoreline, stopping to admire the pretty view. Stepping onto a small boulder, I held up my phone and snapped a photo of the lake. The water sparkled like diamonds where the sun caught the waves.

"Makes you want to stay up here forever, doesn't it?" Ian came to stand next to me. His shoulder brushed my arm. I breathed in the fresh, forest-scented air.

"Oh, I don't know," I replied. "Don't you think you'd get lonely and bored up here?"

His eyes went wide in mock surprise. "You mean that the idea of spending your days fishing and chopping firewood and sleeping under a tent doesn't appeal to you?" He wiggled a finger at me. "You'd better stop that, or I'll take away your country-girl pass."

"But I am a country-girl," I laughed. "And a city-girl too, I guess. I get claustrophobic if I'm in the city too long, but restless if I'm in the country too long. I don't really know where I fit in, to be honest."

"Sounds like an identity crisis." He winked at me. I smiled back and shook my head. "Did your brothers tell you I'm headed up the mountain with them to manage the herd next month?"

"No, they didn't tell me. So does that mean I won't see you anymore this summer?"

"Oh, I'll be back. Probably not until September though. Sleeping under the stars, chasing off wolves, spending the day on horseback. That's the life." He interlaced his fingers behind his head.

"Well, you be careful out there," I said in a grandmotherly tone. "I'd hate for you to be eaten by a wolf while living out your cowboy dreams."

"It'll take more than a wolf to take me out," he joked back. I laughed and the sound echoed off the mountains.

Later, as we picnicked on deli meat sandwiches and greasy chips, Ian's words lingered in my mind. *Do I have an identity crisis?* Was I trying to be someone I wasn't called to be? If I wasn't going to go out to save the world, what was I supposed to do with my life?

As the crystalline lake shimmered before me, I realized the troubling truth that I couldn't begin to answer those questions.

Chapter Fifteen

A FEW DAYS later, I turned away from Dean's truck and walked toward the picnic table to set down the massive bowl of cold pasta salad that I'd made for Cascade Valley Church's summer picnic. I sighed. The sense of sadness that I'd been struggling with since the lake hadn't yet dissipated.

Sunday morning's church service had been released only ten minutes ago. I'd stowed the pasta salad in a cooler and surrounded it with ice before we left home. My brothers were still lingering on the front lawn of the chapel, chatting among a large group of men. Laughter and shouts occasionally burst from the group. Women were gathered at the picnic tables that had been assembled on the grass in a long line. Lunch would be a potluck. Children dashed backward and forward across the church grounds in an impromptu game of tag. Babies too young to walk watched their siblings' wild antics with wide eyes.

The church held a picnic one afternoon after church every year to celebrate the beginning of summer. It was a tradition our little town looked forward to, the perfect launch to the busy summer season. I'd been coming to these events since I was a child.

But today as I looked around, I realized how much had changed in my valley since I'd been gone. The realization only deepened my sense of loneliness.

As I'd listened to our pastor's sermon, I regretted avoiding my childhood church most weeks since I'd been home. I'd only made an effort to go when my brothers were around, using my shyness as an excuse to stay at the ranch. For the last few weeks, I'd been telling myself that there was no point in getting involved in church again, since I'd only be leaving at the end of summer anyway. In addition, my inherent introverted nature tended to avoid facing large groups of people on my own.

As I observed dozens of faces that I didn't recognize, understanding suddenly hit me. Children who were toddlers when I'd left had now sprouted into adolescence. The church sanctuary had been nearly overflowing. Pretty soon the fire marshal was going to insist that either the building or service options be expanded.

Cascade Valley was growing up.

Each year, new people were moving into our valley, bringing with them a fresh, unfamiliar wave of culture and history. We wouldn't just be the little, unknown Montana town much longer. The world must have discovered us sometime within the last few years. Some had already been quick to rush in to secure their little piece of paradise.

The growth spurt explained the new shops I'd seen popping up in town and the new houses under construction that could be spotted nestled throughout the valley.

Could I blame them? I lingered near the drinks station, wondering how our original townspeople truly felt about the changes. Could they accept the uncertainty of an unknown future without feeling like something precious and fundamental had been lost?

I poured a glass of fresh lemonade into a paper cup and sipped it. It was sweet and tart, a play of contrast against my tastebuds. I watched as a man in his mid thirties whom I didn't recognize approached my brothers. From his disciplined posture and muscular frame, I guessed that he was formerly in the military. The group of men parted, opening like a gate to welcome him in. Hands slapped him on the back and reached forward for a shake. They welcomed him like he was one of their own, like they'd known him all their lives.

Perhaps things don't have to stay the same forever to still feel like home? I mused as I sipped the lemonade.

"Attention, please." Pastor Miller stood at the top of the church steps and waved his hands. Everyone shifted toward him and the yard quieted. The only sounds were of laughter as the children kept up their game of tag.

"We are so happy to be hosting another summer picnic with you this year," he continued. "Mrs. Miller and I and all our church members want to welcome the new families who have joined us this past year. Your presence in this valley as we walk toward the future is something we are all glad to have." He smiled and beckoned to someone standing at the base of the steps.

"I'm sure many of you know Caleb Kane, but for those who don't, we are especially proud of him in this valley. He's going to say a few words to you before we pray. And then we can eat."

The congregation murmured approvingly. I watched as Caleb climbed the steps to join Pastor Miller. He rose a head and shoulders above the shorter man. Even at a church picnic, his idea of dressing up was a plaid button-down shirt and the same broken-in jeans he always wore. It was a sharp contrast to Pastor Miller's crisp white shirt, sports blazer and tie, but of the two, Caleb seemed relaxed and natural in the pine-dotted setting.

Caleb cleared his throat. "I'm not one for giving speeches, but I just wanted to take a few minutes to say how grateful I am for this town's support and help with this year's youth camp. Because of you, we've been able to open spots for thirty more teens to register. Whether you've made donations, offered to help with food and setup, or signed up as a chaperone, I want to thank you."

He cleared his throat again. "If you haven't been around for a while, these camps may seem like a small thing. But to the kids, it's a breath of fresh air. And for some of them, being with our horses and finally seeing that there is something different out there gets them set back onto the right track. And we owe our ability to host these camps to you. So, thank you."

He stepped to the side. I didn't have time to watch him further, because Pastor Miller called for us all to bow our heads to give thanks.

When everyone raised their heads again, Caleb was gone. He and I had only spoken briefly over text about the camp since we'd shaken on a truce at Mrs. Jensen's, and I wondered if things were still going to be just as awkward between us now. I found myself checking my phone often, wondering if we'd ever discuss what had happened between us.

I spotted his dark hair disappearing around the corner and then I lost sight of it as the congregation swept toward me. I stepped aside as fathers and mothers and children grabbed plates and began to feast on the bounty spread on the picnic tables. If there was one thing that small towns did well, it was hosting a potluck. Salads and cold cuts and finger foods and sandwiches beckoned. There was easily enough to feed a small army and that wasn't even counting the dessert table.

I waited until most of the crowd had filled their plates before I stepped in and made one for myself. My stomach growled at the sight and smell of so many familiar potluck dishes and I realized that I had missed our quaint summer tradition.

"Well, Samantha McCade, I think you've been avoiding me." An unfamiliar voice broke into my thoughts, and I looked over my shoulder to see who had called my name. Sandy-brown hair and bright blue eyes caught my attention. Damon stood just to my rear, a plate piled with sandwiches and cold cuts in his hand. He gave me a warm grin and I smiled back.

"Now why would I do a thing like that?" I said to my high school friend.

"I haven't seen you since you first got back to town. Still running?"

"Most days," I said, feeling an uncomfortable flush at the thought of him watching me run, my limbs flapping as I ran along the uneven road. It couldn't be cute to watch.

"I don't know." He pretended to think, tapping his lips with a finger. "I always look for you when I drive past, and I never see you."

I shrugged, scanning the available seating at the tables spread across the lawn. "I'm not sure what to tell you."

"I'm just kidding," Damon laughed, falling into step beside me. "I've been in Idaho for a few weeks helping at the mill I used to work at."

"Oh, that's nice."

I caught sight of my brothers sitting with Shelby and Brianna across the lawn and made a beeline in their direction. My stomach growled. It was hard to concentrate on Damon's voice when my number one thought was sitting down to eat. But he followed me to their table.

"We still need to schedule a time to catch up. Now that I'm back in town, how about dinner some night?" His voice echoed loud and clear across the grass.

All three of my brothers swung their heads toward me collectively. I watched Dean's eyebrows go up. Knox smirked. Only Vincent kept his face neutral. A fresh flush started at my hairline and worked its way to my toes. I spun to face him.

"I, uh, well…." I began to stammer. And then I saw him, standing a few yards behind Damon. Caleb's eyes were dark and hooded as he boldly stared at me. I got the feeling that he was waiting expectently to hear what my answer would be. And to my confusion, he looked angry. I could feel his displeasure burning in the grassy space between us. Everything we'd left unsaid about our unexpected kiss suddenly crackled in the air between us. We'd been acting like it had never happened.

And it never should have.

His eyes bore relentlessly into mine. He shook his head ever so slightly and my heart dropped into my stomach. Before I could gather my thoughts, I heard myself blurting out a reply. "Dinner sounds great. How about sometime this week? Why don't you call me to set something up?" I smiled brightly at my high school friend, hoping that the uncertainty swarming in my stomach wasn't painted across my features.

With Damon's pleased expression still in my eye, I turned away from Caleb's scowl before I could change my mind.

•   •   •

It turned out that I should have changed my mind. Damon had grown into a nice guy, but I couldn't remember why I'd thought him so funny and charming in high school. He was sweet, good-natured, and humorous, but just like as I'd found myself feeling with Jake, I was bored.

He hadn't wasted any time in calling to schedule dinner. His enthusiasm to reconnect was flattering. But I knew that one hang out session was going to be enough for me. It was obvious that Damon and I had nothing in common besides our valley upbringing. Dinner had been ribs and potato salad at The BBQ Shack. Entertainment was playing pool at his favorite spot. I had nothing against pool, but more conversation and less teasing would have been nice. The good-natured ribbing about my education had ceased being funny about thirty minutes into the evening.

I was sitting at a high-top table watching Damon cue up yet another game of pool and regretting my tendency toward impulsive choices. Inwardly, I was mulling over the possibility of cutting the evening short. Outwardly, I was laughing at another story that Damon was telling about our high school years.

"We really had some fun times," he said. "Too bad so many in our class have moved away to the city. It would have been nice to get us all together."

"You stayed though."

Damon shrugged. "The valley has always just been home, you know? I've gone other places, lived in them for awhile. And they are nice. Don't get me wrong. But something always brings me back to Cascade Valley. I couldn't see myself living anywhere else for very long."

"You don't want to explore the world? See things you've never seen?" I probed, curious as to his answer.

"I can travel and see whatever I want. But I want to have a place that makes me feel grounded, you know?"

"I get that," I admitted.

Damon seemed like he was about to say something, but instead he looked over my shoulder and raised his hand in a sudden wave. "Hey, Caleb. Surprised to see you here."

Instantly, my veins turned to ice. I froze, not daring to turn around. A breeze tickled my skin as a man walked up from behind me. Caleb extended his hand toward Damon. The two men shook as I glared at Caleb's back, immediately annoyed.

What in the world is he doing here?

"Care to join us in a game?" Damon asked, including me and the pool table in a general sweep of his arm. "I never see you in town anymore. We're just hanging out and having a good time tonight. You know Samantha McCade, don't you?"

"I'm just here to pick something up. And yes. Samantha and I are neighbors," Caleb replied, turning to acknowledge my presence for the first time. His dark gaze took me in. He tipped his hat in my direction and I hoped the men didn't notice my immediate flush.

Ignoring him, I hopped down from the barstool. "I need to use the ladies' room. Would you mind excusing me, Damon?"

"Don't think you're getting away before I kick your butt in pool again," Damon warned in a teasing tone. He wagged his finger at me, and I forced a smile. "You may think you're a city-slicker now, but no one plays pool like we country boys."

"Oh, don't worry. I'm sure you'll win another game when I get back." Turning on my heel, I grabbed my purse and walked toward the back of the building where I knew the restrooms were located. The room was quiet, and I was glad to be alone. I wished that I could stay there for the rest of the night. Or at least until Caleb left.

Locking myself into a stall, I sat on the closed toilet seat. It was force of habit to pull my phone from the pocket of my purse to check my messages. The screen lit up in my hand. A message was already waiting. My eyes froze on the text.

The message sender read *Caleb*. My heart skipped a beat. Sternly, I told it to calm down and slid open the message. Probably a question he'd sent earlier about the website, I was sure.

CALEB: *Had enough yet?*

I stared at the screen, the seconds lengthening into minutes. A triple set of dots bounced on the message thread, indicating that he was already sending another text from the front room.

CALEB: *Tell Damon that you just found out that a friend isn't feeling well.*

CALEB: *You need to excuse yourself to check on her.*

A third message appeared on the screen.

CALEB: Tell him that he doesn't need to drive you home. You'll just walk to meet her. Then meet me in fifteen minutes outside of Sherry's Diner.

My brain struggled to catch up. *So, this message has nothing to do with the camp or the website or marketing, but he's trying to get me away from Damon? Seriously?* First, he crashed the evening I'd set aside to spend with an old friend. Then he thought that he had the right to tell me what to do? My fingers flew across the screen.

ME: Shows how much you know. I won't be telling Damon any of that.

ME: Thanks, but no thanks.

The screen showed that he was typing.

CALEB: Ha, sure you won't. Text me when you're on your way.

Scowling, I stuffed my phone back into my purse without replying and exited the stall. I washed my hands slowly, my brain hurtling in a million different directions. As if I was going to run out on a friend and put myself into an even more awkward position with Caleb. True, I didn't have a ride to get back home tonight. I was stuck until Damon decided that he was through playing pool. But I was in the middle of spending time with a good friend from high school, for crying out loud. Did he think that I was going to rudely interrupt my night with Damon and just walk out with him?

We may have agreed to a truce, but that didn't mean he got to act jealous.

I was still annoyed as I reentered the main room, but Caleb was nowhere to be seen. *Good.* My mood lightened instantly. But it sank again when I saw how eagerly Damon watched me as I approached. I always made a point to keep my male friendships casual, but I was beginning to doubt that Damon had gotten that memo. Given the small size of Cascade Valley's dating pool in our age group, I hoped he hadn't assumed that agreeing to dinner meant I was available.

"Are you ok?" he asked as I grabbed a pool cue.

"What? Oh yes, I'm completely fine."

"So...." he said, sliding next to me. "Want to break first?"

His proximity was warm and intense. Suddenly I felt as if I was being stifled. I felt a bead of sweat trickle down my spine under the casual summer dress I'd worn. "Damon, I'm so sorry. But I just learned that I need to leave."

Instantly, his face fell. I felt a wave of guilt as I blurted out the words. He was a nice guy, but I had to get out of this stifling pool hall and away from his eager teasing before it crushed me.

"When I was in the restroom, I learned that a friend of mine needs me."

Was it an outright lie? A fib? I wasn't sure which jurisdiction this fell under. Well, the friend part was probably a lie. But the truth would just hurt his feelings.

His face lit up with sudden inspiration. "I'll drive you. Maybe I can help?"

"No," I said quickly. "I don't think so. And I'm just going a few blocks away. I'm going to walk over there and see what's going on."

"I'm leaving again. I'll be gone a few weeks. Will I see you before I leave?" Damon pouted, giving me sad, puppy dog eyes. My heart cracked a little. This was cruel of me.

"We'll probably see each other around town." It was the best that I could offer. I set the pool cue across the table. Damon stepped forward and I felt myself pulled into a firm hug before I knew what was happening.

"It's been so good to see you, Samantha," he crooned in my ear. "I didn't realize how much I'd missed seeing your pretty face every day in school." His hands slid over my back. "We should set up another dinner or a day on the lake before I leave."

Feeling like he was getting too intense, I pulled away quickly. "It was so good to see you too, Damon. Have a safe trip. I'll be leaving myself again soon. If I don't see you again this summer, I'll look for you at our high school reunion."

Maybe the six years left between now and our ten-year reunion would be enough time to bridge the awkwardness that suddenly gaped between us. Hurrying away before I could change my mind, I made the mistake of glancing back as I pushed open the door. Damon was still standing by the pool table, watching me. He lifted a single hand in farewell.

I left before he could call me back, ridden with guilt. He was a nice guy, but maybe some friendships were better left in high school. Now I was headed to fall out of the frying pan, right back into the fire. Briskly, I walked toward Sherry's Diner.

ME: I'll be there in five minutes.

I sent the text to Caleb before I could chicken out and call one of my brothers to pick me up instead. That was a scenario I wanted to avoid. Damon was part of our community. Everyone had known and liked him since high school. I really didn't want my brothers to know that I'd skipped out on the evening because I felt uncomfortable.

The diner Caleb had directed me toward was located a couple of blocks over from Main Street, on Second Street. Sherry's was an actual diner in the old-fashioned sense, but her friendly owner was also our local pie expert. On-site, she baked and sold the scrumptious pie offerings in the spinning cooler located at the front of the restaurant. Her soups, salads, dinner plates, and burgers were all delicious in the way that only country-spun food can be. But her pies were exceptional.

I had never found a duplicate for the mouthwatering, homemade goodness of an original Sherry's pie in Seattle. Flaky, buttery crust, scrumptious pastry cream, rich flavors. It was one extra perk to being home for the summer. Every week I looked forward to having a slice. Perhaps I'd pick up a pie to take home to self-soothe my own guilt for running out on Damon.

While my feet picked up their pace at the thought, I was not so enthusiastic about the person I was headed to see. Chances were good that this was going to end just as awkwardly as my spontaneous agreement to catch up with Damon. I still didn't know what had come over me when I'd seen Caleb's darkly glowering face watching the two of us talk at the church picnic. In an unexpected flash, I'd seen the invitation as an opportunity to distance myself from him, despite the memory of his kiss that seemed to have lingered all week in my mind.

We'd simply finished the kiss we nearly started years ago. Now I can move on with my life. It didn't mean anything.

I wasn't sure who I was trying to silently convince as I rounded the corner toward Sherry's. As much as I was dreading the drive home with Caleb, the familiar nerves that I felt anytime I was near him were already fluttering in my stomach again. Caleb and I hadn't seen each other since the church potluck. *How had he known when and where I'd be with Damon? And why had he offered to rescue me?*

Chapter Sixteen

WHEN I ROUNDED the corner and came within sight of the diner, I spotted Caleb immediately. He stood on the sidewalk, leaning casually against the brick wall of the restaurant. I slowed my brisk walk, suddenly unsure of myself. Letting Caleb drive me home was probably a mistake. Maybe I should turn around and go back the way I'd come? Tell Damon that I wasn't needed after all and continue our evening?

But Caleb had already seen me. I watched as he took me in. The evening was beginning to get that hazy golden glow it gets just before sunset. He was illuminated in a halo of soft light. I swallowed. The effect was just like that morning when I'd photographed him and Beau together. He took a step forward.

"You came," he said.

"I did," I replied. "Why did you ask me to meet you? Are my brothers ok?" I had the sudden alarming thought that something had happened on the mountain where they were grazing our herd and that Caleb had been sent to warn me.

"Your brothers are fine. As far as I know."

Relieved, I finally noticed the two boxes that he was holding. They were pink and square. I knew Sherry's put takeout pie into boxes just like that. "What are those?" I asked, pointing to them. "And what am I doing here?"

Caleb paused a moment, looking at me with serious eyes. "I have a special request for you."

Immediately, I was on guard.

"I want to show you something," he continued. "Will you come with me somewhere?"

"And why would I do that?" I bristled, sensing a trap. Suddenly, I wished that I was back at the pool hall with Damon.

Caleb held the pink boxes toward me. "I brought pie as a peace offering."

"What kind?" I eyed them suspiciously, eyebrows rising.

"Lemon meringue and blueberry sour cream."

He was lucky that they were both my favorites. I'd take the pie from him regardless, but I wasn't sure that I was willing to go on a mystery trip. "Where do you want me to go?"

"It's a surprise. Not too far away. I'll drive you home afterward."

At this point, I needed the ride. And there was pie. Despite the fact that I still felt awkward around him, I wasn't afraid to leave with Caleb. I just didn't want to. Finally, I rolled my eyes. "Fine. I'll go with you. But this had better be worth it."

He led the way to his truck, which was parked across the street. As I passed Sherry's window, the bluish glow of her revolving pie case reflected at me. A few late diners stared at us. Caleb opened the truck door for me, and I stepped inside. He walked to the driver's side and climbed in. He cleared his throat as he started the truck. The only other noise was a country Gospel station playing low and quiet on the radio.

When we had turned off Main Street and started down the open highway—in the opposite direction of home—I swallowed my nerves. My hands twisted in my lap.

"How was your date?" Caleb's voice rumbled into the quiet of the car.

I shifted in the passenger seat. "It wasn't a date. Just two old friends catching up."

His eyes flickered toward me with a skeptical glance, and my arms rose to cross my chest defensively.

"Ok, well, I hadn't ever intended for it to be a date," I admitted. "But I guess Damon missed that memo."

"Did he try something with you?" His low-pitched growl shot into the quiet cab of the truck. I watched Caleb's fingers tighten on the steering wheel. He swung toward me, face crossed with a dark scowl. The truck slowed in the empty road as he pressed the brake.

"What? No," I protested immediately.

"Tell me the truth, Samantha. If he touched you without your permission, so help me, I'll be having harsh words with him tonight. At the very least." The seething intensity of his words sent my brain spinning. He held himself still, tightly controlled, but I could feel the energy radiating from his body.

I raised my palms, trying to calm his unexpected reaction. My heart jumped into overdrive at the intensity of his gaze. "He didn't do anything inappropriate. I just got the feeling that he wouldn't have minded if I wanted the night to take a romantic turn." The words felt presumptuous and foolish as I said them aloud. I reached over and laid my hand on Caleb's forearm. The veins were tight and flexed under my touch. "Nothing happened. I promise."

Though I didn't think that I owed Caleb an explanation, I still felt the sudden urge to reassure him. His arm flexed in response to my words, amber eyes fluttering over me in assessment. After a moment, he nodded once and pressed the gas again. All at once, I was conscious of the heat from his skin burning my fingertips. I dropped my hand and fell silent as the truck picked up speed. My hands went back to twisting in my lap.

"Where are we going?" A moment later, I broke the charged silence.

Caleb took a right turn onto an old fire access road that I knew was hardly used. It was outside of town, where the valley began to meet the forest. I remembered hiking with my family on this side of the ridge as a young girl, but I couldn't think of what he could possibly want to show me in this out of the way place.

The sun was just beginning to tinge the sky a wash of blush and tangerine behind us. I knew one thing. I didn't relish the thought of being caught in the forest at nightfall. Bears, cougars, and wolves were not uncommon.

"There's something that I want to show you," was the only reply that Caleb would give me. We drove a few miles down the dirt road and I was just beginning to think of insisting that he turn around and take me home when he finally pulled the truck over to the side of the road. We were surrounded by lush vegetation and tall pines. He jumped out and walked to the passenger side.

He swung the door open and held out his hand for me without a word.

"What are you up to, Caleb?" I eyed him suspiciously, ignoring his hand. "I've gone along with your mysterious little adventure because I needed the ride home. But you had better not be planning to leave me out here. I will send all three of my brothers after you. And my mother too when she gets back home."

He threw his head back and laughed, the sound deep and rich in the stillness of the mountainside.

"Only you would think that I would do that to you, Samantha." His earlier intensity had dissipated. His eyes sparkled. An attractive smile peeked from under his beard. In the still, lonely surroundings, Caleb seemed even bigger and more imposing than usual. He blocked my view, hedging me into the passenger seat of the truck with his body. "I guess now you know not to give me any sass tonight, don't you? I would just hate to leave you here to teach you a lesson in manners." He leaned over me, his hands planted on either side of the truck frame above my head.

"Caleb," I warned. My hand rose to push against the hard plane of his chest, holding him back from leaning in closer.

"Like I would pull such a dirty trick on you, Red. I'm not even scared of your brothers' wrath. I'm scared of yours. And maybe your mom's." He flashed me another grin.

I shook my head disapprovingly, but my heartbeat betrayed my inner thoughts.

Caleb stepped aside and the space in front of me suddenly felt very empty. "I brought you up here because I thought you might like to watch the sunset. It's really something special from this vantage point. I come up here sometimes when I need to think."

I stared at him. He shrugged and stuck his hands into his pockets as if it was the most natural thing in the world to share his secret place with me. My jaw dropped as I took in the view behind him, trying to simultaneously process his words. So, he'd picked up my favorite pie, offered me a ride home, and brought me to his special place to watch the sunset? *Why would he plan this? What was all this about?*

The view really was spectacular. I slipped from the truck, stepping across the dirt and grass toward the edge of the embankment. Caleb moved away. I heard him rummaging in the back of the truck while I marveled at the view.

The spot he'd chosen sat along a ridge that ran above the valley. Grassy rolling hills dotted with grazing cattle were spread below us. In the distance, I could see our little town. It wasn't that far away, but above the valley, it felt like a different world. The air was so fresh and clean, and you could see for miles and miles. A person could make decisions up here. No wonder Caleb loved it.

I was still confused about the fact that he had chosen to take me here though. I swung back towards the truck with the intention of asking him what all of this was about. "Caleb, I don't…Oh wow…."

While I had been ogling the view, he'd been busy. I eyed the blanket spread on the ground skeptically. He'd added a few throw pillows, a couple of lanterns, and a thermos. The pretty pink boxes from Sherry's were sitting like the cherry on top.

"Here, you might need this. The temperature drops quickly once the sun makes its way down." His voice had dropped an octave, becoming raspy and low as he extended a flannel shirt in my direction.

Still trying to process the scene in front of me, I took it automatically from his hand. Accidentally, our fingers brushed, and I jumped as an electric thrill shot up my arm.

"Uh, thanks," I murmured, instinctively pressing the flannel to my nose. It was soft and worn in from many washes. I wasn't prepared for how good it smelled. The fabric smelled of hay and horses, of earth and wind, of musk and campfire. A comforting smell that was as familiar to me as my mother's cooking. It was the smell of my childhood, of my father and brothers.

It was Caleb's smell, I realized with a start as I inhaled again. Caleb had just handed me one of his own shirts in case I got chilled.

"Caleb, what is this about?" I gestured around me. "All of this… it's a pretty place, but I don't understand why I'm here." I'd begun to babble, but I didn't care. I didn't know what to think.

He walked to the blanket and stretched his body along the ground. I stood frozen in place, clutching his flannel between my fingers, until he looked over and patted the blanket beside him.

"It doesn't mean anything," he replied casually. "I just thought it unlikely that you saw sunsets like this in Seattle."

I felt a quick flash of sadness. Everyone seemed to bring up my choice to leave the state for college. It was as if they were implying that I'd betrayed my roots. To the residents of Cascade Valley, the state of Montana was the only place to be.

With quick steps, I walked to the blanket and plopped next to him. Caleb didn't understand. No one understood. As if I didn't love our small country town. My family's ranch. The open earth and sky. I'd been raised here. It was all I'd known until I went to college. But I'd also known that there was more out there for me to see.

Letting my heart dictate my life choices wouldn't get me anywhere. Nor would it satisfy the ache in my heart. My sister had left for New York. My mother had begun to travel, checking off all the places she and my dad had dreamed of visiting. She would be back, but her life wasn't limited to the valley anymore. My brothers were the only ones who seemed to have stayed the same. My brothers and the lifetime of memories that I carried. There had been so many good memories made here, but some that had left deep scars as well.

Then there was Caleb. I was a walking contradiction whenever he was near. One minute, he'd make my blood churn. The next minute, he would catch my eye, and my stomach would summersault. And when he'd kissed me, I'd reached out for more.

That kiss…we still hadn't discussed it. His nearness and the memory of the soft pressure of his lips on mine made my skin tingle. But every inch that I gave to our past was another inch that I could be taking from my own future. I wasn't ready to give up my dreams, but as I sat quietly next to him watching the colors of the sunset splay across the sky, I knew that if anyone could tempt me to stay, it was Caleb.

"Did I make you mad?" His throaty voice broke our silence. I felt his elbow nudge my side.

A deep sigh heaved from my chest. I felt a wave of tension float away with my breath. My shoulders dropped as I drew up my knees, tucking the hem of my dress over my legs.

"No, I'm not mad. You're right. There's no sunset like a Cascade Valley sunset. I mean, look at it." I gestured toward the apricot-tinged valley that stretched out below us. "This place is perfect. It's idyllic. But often, I just find myself—"

"Longing for something more?" Caleb finished my sentence.

"Yes." I turned to look at him. His dark eyes glimmered in the gathering dusk. "But you probably wouldn't understand that urge. You've got everything you want right here."

I heard him echo my sigh from earlier. "Not everything I want. There are a few things missing from my life. A few empty spaces in my heart that ache when I pray."

"Like what kind of empty spaces?" I asked, surprised by the candid reply. Caleb seemed so calm, so confident. I couldn't imagine what he could want that he couldn't get.

"Like a wife, children, a family of my own," he replied.

"You could easily have those things if you wanted them," I swallowed. "I'm sure there are lots of women who would jump at the chance to be Mrs. Caleb Kane."

Instead of replying, he picked up a pie box. "Which flavor of pie do you want?"

"The blueberry sour cream, please," I said promptly. He set the box next to my foot. "Are you going to answer my question? Why don't you have a wife and a family already?"

He opened the second box and deliberately took a bite before shifting his body toward mine. Following his lead, I slid a forkful of the creamy pie into my mouth and murmured in approval at the sweet, familiar taste. "Well? I'm waiting. This is delicious, by the way."

Caleb set the box on the blanket. "If I said that there was a time when I could have seen you and I getting married one day, are you going to get mad and throw something at me?" His voice had thickened again. It rasped across my skin, making me shiver with awareness. Our eyes locked.

"That was such a long time ago." I spoke hesitantly. "Things changed. It doesn't make sense to bring up the past."

"And what if it's not all in the past?" Caleb challenged me. Quickly, he rose from the blanket and began to pace along the edge of the ridge. His hand raked messily through his hair.

Carefully, I set down the pie box. All at once, the dessert seemed too cloyingly sweet.

"Samantha, you drive me absolutely nuts." Each of the roughly spoken syllables raked down my spine. "You're hostile and willful. One minute, you're melting against me as I kiss you. The next you're yelling at me and blaming me for what happened to your dad. As if I didn't blame myself enough already, you had to come back to town and rub the truth in my face every day."

"And what truth is that?" I jumped up, planting my feet.

Caleb's fists clenched at his side. A hollow expression had overtaken his face. "That I lost my chance with you before it ever began. I thought I had gotten over my attraction to you when you tried to ruin my life and then left town. But you had to come home and waltz your way right back into my life, my ranch, my charity. If you hate me so much, what are you doing here?"

"I don't hate you." My hands flew up and my voice rose, echoing among the pines. "I used to blame you for the accident, but I know

now that I was wrong to do that." My eyes locked with his across the open space. "What do you want from me, Caleb?"

"Everything." He growled the words at me, and I reeled backwards. "I know that I don't have any right to feel this way, but I want you. I want that wild hair that never seems to be tamed, those lips that mouth off more than they should, and those eyes that glare daggers at me. As crazy as it sounds, I want your heart. And I think I want it forever."

I tried to speak, but my voice hitched. I swallowed, my throat unwilling to cooperate. "What are you saying?"

Caleb faced me. "I'm saying that I liked you before and despite trying to move on, I still like you now. I thought about you often while you were away. I wanted to reach out, but after what happened, I figured you would tell me to get lost. But now you're back." He raked his fingers through his hair again and sighed. "I don't know what to do with these feelings. And what I want to do with them, you won't let me do."

Coherent thought escaped my racing mind. My chest heaved. My mouth opened and closed as I tried to speak again.

"Well, I'm in the exact same boat," I finally managed, throwing up my hands. "I had such a crush on you back then and I thought I was over it. It was so easy to hate you before...." I stopped and clenched my fists, fighting my emotions. "But now that I'm home and I've spent time with you...I've seen what you're doing for the summer camp. And the truth is...."

I inhaled deeply, the intensity of what I felt overtaking me and causing my words to catch in my throat. "The truth is that I like you, Caleb. I like the man you've become."

An expectant silence fell between us. It felt like a rope had suddenly been stretched between my heart and his. I felt it tug with an energy that I couldn't ignore. I sensed him before he even moved. Caleb started toward me, his long legs eating up the ground. I nearly jumped into his arms as he reached for me. His hands snaked around my back, drawing me up and into him. Just like before, my hands twined around his neck. With a sense of shock, I suddenly realized that I'd been waiting for this exact moment. I couldn't deny what I felt anymore.

I really like him. Despite all the resentment that I'd stubbornly held on to for years, I was drawn to the man. *Falling in love with Caleb Kane wouldn't be hard to do.* The tiny voice inside my head startled me and I gasped.

Caleb's dark gaze washed over my face with an intensity that I felt curl itself all the way into my toes. An unspoken question passed between us. It was as if we had suddenly gained the ability to communicate without words. A blush overtook my cheeks like a wildfire.

"If I try to kiss you now, are you going to throw pie in my face?" he said solemnly.

The serious-toned question caught me completely off guard. Throwing my head back, I burst into laughter. My heart felt like it could float into the sunset. I squinted at him as if sizing him up.

"Depending on what you do next, I may have to keep that in consideration," I said, pulling his head down and stretching toward him. "But in the meantime, will you just kiss me, please?"

Immediately, he bent his head toward me. I closed my eyes just as our lips collided. Sweetness filled my senses, and I temporarily lost all rational thought. He still tasted of lemon meringue. Our kiss was sweet at first, two people finding their way through still new and unfamiliar territory. My fingers twined in his hair as his arms locked me against him. We were in sync, innocently exploring.

At the same moment, our heads angled, and I felt a shift into something new. The sound of a raspy growl filled my ears as Caleb swept me into his arms. I clung to him. My feet left the ground as he lifted me. Our kiss deepened, a roller coaster of emotion coursing through me. A current of thrills sparkled up and down my spine.

I leaned into the brand-new sensation as our mouths explored each other. Suddenly, I felt a whoosh of air as he lowered me gently onto the blanket. Despite the hard forest ground beneath me, I felt like I was floating on a cloud. I reached for Caleb again, already missing the feeling of his strong arms. He knelt over me, fingers twining themselves in my hair as he kissed me again. A soft sigh escaped my lips.

I sighed again when he broke the kiss, this time with frustration. I wanted more and I wondered if Caleb felt the same.

"I'd better stop while I'm ahead," he murmured ruefully against my lips, untwining his fingers from my hair.

He was right.

"I agree," I whispered. My head was spinning, my heart pounding, my stomach tight. Our kiss had gone from sweet-and-gentle to intense-and-overwhelming in the space of a moment. I wasn't sure that I could handle more. Kissing him wasn't supposed to feel so wonderful.

"Are you ok?" He nuzzled my cheek. The sensation of his beard scratching my skin sent tingles down my spine.

"Very ok," I replied, letting my palms brush across his face and down his shoulders. "As very ok as I feel right now, you're probably right. We should slow down."

He settled onto the blanket and pulled me into his arms. We watched the sun slip into the western horizon in silence. For once, I didn't really know what to say.

As the twilight deepened, Caleb's fingers found my chin. He angled my face toward his. We stared at each other, and I felt the heat rise again in my cheeks. Never in a million years would I have guessed that I'd be in this moment right now. Or that it would feel so right.

"I have no idea how I'm going to tell your brothers that I've been kissing their sister behind their backs." Caleb broke the silence solemnly. "And that I like it and I want to keep doing it."

"They're just protective of me. They are the same with Mom and Demi."

"I understand why they would be protective of you," Caleb replied quietly. "I feel protective over you too. You're so accident prone. I find myself worrying that you'll trip and land under one of my horse's hooves."

"Hence the reason I stay as far away as possible from them," I said dryly. A sudden flash of guilt made me look away from him. I fixed my eyes on the sunset-painted hills in the distance, worry eating at me.

I was a terrible sister and daughter. I was planning to move out of the country and my family still had no idea. I had no business letting Caleb kiss me either. Leading him on was the wrong thing to do. "I think we should keep all of this between us," I said. "For everyone's sake. I'm only here for the summer and the future may hold lots of changes."

Caleb's arms tightened around me. "So, you don't want to be friends then?"

My head swiveled toward him. "Oh, I do. But maybe it's better if we are just secretly friends? Casually? While I'm still here…."

"So, you really are planning to leave Cascade Valley?"

"I am." I bit my tongue. Not telling him the truth was torture. The truth danced on the tip of my tongue. Dusk had crept over the mountainside, and I couldn't see Caleb's eyes clearly anymore. I searched his face in the gloom, wishing he would argue and demand answers. Hoping he didn't.

"Ok. If keeping our friendship casual is what you want, that's what we'll do."

I couldn't tell if his tone was one of disappointment or relief. My hand found its way to his and nestled between his fingers. He squeezed gently. We sat like that as the soft sounds of twilight began to descend around us.

"I'm sorry I was so mean to you the other night," I mumbled against his shoulder. "There's still so much grief that I don't think I've ever fully processed. I need to let it all go. But the truth is that I'm still trying to heal."

He tightened his hold on me. "It's ok to grieve and be sad, Red. It's ok to be mad even."

My spine shivered as Caleb's lips brushed the top of my hair.

"But I just want you to know that if there was ever any indication that that horse was going to be a problem, my dad would never have sold him to yours. I promise you."

My heart ached, but I let his words sink in until I believed them. It was time to let the wound of my father's loss scab over and heal. Stubbornly, I pushed away the tears that rose in my eyes. "You'd better take me home now," I said.

He slid his hand into my hair, pulling my face close to his. "Ok, but do you remember that summer night four years ago when I told you that I thought we could be really good friends if we wanted to be? I still want that. I think we should at least give it a try."

He bent forward to hear my whisper. "I'm not staying in Cascade Valley, Caleb."

His forehead touched mine. "Maybe not. But maybe God's plan for your future is different than the one you've created for yourself?"

I knew that I should end this now, before heartache and disappointment destroyed us again. I had no right to risk Caleb's heart. My secret sizzled in the air. But as his lips lowered to claim mine one last time, all the reasons that this secret romance was a bad idea slipped away with the last rays of the sunset.

Chapter Seventeen

"HOW WAS YOUR night?" Knox's voice startled me when I slipped into the house.

I jumped and swung toward him in surprise. My brother was sitting in the living room in the dark.

I'd made Caleb stop at the gate to let me out. I didn't want him to drive me all the way up to the house. Keeping Caleb at a distance felt like the safer choice at the moment. So, I'd walked our long driveway under the moonlight, my thoughts racing as I clutched the little pink Sherry's box in my hand.

I laid a hand across my collarbone. "Knox, you startled me. What are you doing here? Is everything ok?"

He stood up and yawned, his long arms stretching over his head. "I volunteered to ride back and be the one to wait up for you. Dean and Vincent are still on the mountain. I just came back a couple of days early."

I wasn't sure whether to be amused, flattered, or offended. "Bro, you know I'm literally a college graduate, right? I don't need my brothers to wait up for me until I come home. I'm a big girl."

Knox paused in front of me. The soft moonlight that filtered through the windows highlighted his puzzled face. "I don't think you understand, Sammie. You're our little sister. It's our job to protect you. Of course, we're going to wait up for you and interrogate any man you ever bring home."

He reached out and rubbed his knuckles softly across the top of my head. He chuckled. "So, get that through your stubborn, independent little noggin."

I rolled my eyes, but a smile crept on my face. Reaching out, I wrapped my arms around his waist. His arms came down around my shoulders.

"Hey, did something happen tonight?" he said. "Do I need to get Dean, Caleb, and Vincent and kick someone's butt?"

"No." My heart leaped at the sound of Caleb's name. "Everything was fine. I'm just glad you're my brother."

"Glad you're my sister." He gave me another squeeze. "Now I've got to get to bed. I'm beat."

I heard his deep yawn as he climbed the stairs. It wasn't late by city standards, but my brothers always turned in early. Making the long trek down the mountain and staying awake to make sure I got home safely was a true act of love on Knox's part.

Unlike my hard-working brothers, my day didn't usually start at the crack of dawn. The night had left me wired and restless. I knew

I wouldn't be able to sleep until I had processed everything that had happened. I grabbed a spoon from the kitchen and slipped onto the back porch with my leftover pie.

Sinking onto the worn porch swing, I stared at the yard. All the animals were tucked away for the night and their soft sounds rustled on my ear. I had grown up staring at this exact same barnyard. Every inch was familiar, but I felt disconnected from it all. Was this home anymore? Did any part of me belong here? Or had I completely severed that connection when I'd moved away to college and promised myself that I'd do something that felt more important than my life here?

"Is there a place in this great, big world for me, Lord?" I breathed the prayer onto the soft summer night air. "I feel like I'm called to serve others. But I'm also afraid that I'll give up something else if I leave the valley forever."

Like Caleb?

"I feel different when I'm with him," I whispered at the clear sky. A star winked at me. "When he kisses me, I can imagine what life would have been like if Dad's accident hadn't stopped us." I picked at the seam of my dress. "Losing Dad still hurts, but I think I'm finally ready for that wound to close."

The last bite of crust lingered on my tongue, its buttery sweetness a familiar memory.

"If I rekindle the feelings I had for Caleb, that's just going to mess up what I believe you're calling me to do, Lord. But I really like being with him. Why is all of this happening?" My prayer was a frustrated murmur under my breath.

"Are you ok out here?" Knox's voice interrupted me.

My head whipped toward him as he peeked at me from the threshold of the door. I stood hastily, brushing crumbs off my lap.

"I'm fine," I said, walking past him into the house. "I was just unwinding. I'm headed up to bed now. Thanks for waiting up for me. You're the best brother a girl could ask for."

He walked to the sink for a glass of water. I heard his voice float up the stairs after me. "Goodnight then. And you're a pretty good sister youself. But if you ever need to talk, I'm here."

I wondered what my brothers would think if they found out that I'd be daydreaming about their best friend as I fell asleep tonight.

. . .

Despite my internal confusion, I couldn't stay away from Caleb's ranch after that night. I found myself drawn there nearly every day. I'd launched a full-blown social media campaign to bring in more followers for the youth camp. The program was a chance to connect with kids who needed a reset. I was determined to make the summer a success for their sake. In the mornings, I would pop over to Caleb's to snap photos or film footage of the property and stables for future montages. In the afternoons, I'd spend time writing up blogs and captions to familiarize the public with the camp's mission.

My own life goals seemed to have moved to the back of my mind. It felt good to set aside the stress of applications and the web interviews that I'd been secretly scheduling to throw myself into all my volunteer duties instead.

Jake's article had put the youth camp into the spotlight it deserved. Caleb's phone began to ring with calls from various charity organizations who wanted to collaborate in the future. So many donation requests came in that we ended up expanding the reservation list. Each teen's travel expenses were paid for in full.

I hoped that Jake was over the disappointment that I didn't want to date him. He'd done a good thing for Cascade Valley and I was grateful.

Caleb's ranch was a flurry of preparation the last few days before camp launched. All the volunteers and ranch hands had passed their background checks, taken a CPR and first aid course, and were registered as certified in the training.

Activity hubs were planned and built. Fences were checked and reinforced. Riding trails were examined with a fine-tooth comb to make sure that they were safe for all levels of riders. Even the gentlest horses in the program were given a little extra training to make sure they would be easy-going partners for the students. We had our final inspection and the facilities passed with flying colors.

It was a rush. Even my brothers set aside a few afternoons to help finish all the projects.

Caleb and I hadn't been alone for more than a few minutes since the night on the ridge. In the flurry of checking off the to-do list before opening day, there wasn't time for much besides flirtatious glances, smiles, and late-night texts. Flirting with Caleb made me feel as if we had picked up right where we'd left off the summer before I'd left for college. Every time his handsome face swiveled my way, my heart did a flip.

Eventually, I would have to come clean about my plans. While thoughts of a long-distance relationship with him were filling my dreams at night, I knew I couldn't expect him to be happy about the prospect of dating someone who lived on an entirely different continent. The reality that I might lose Caleb for a second time made me nauseous, but every time the thought arose, I pushed it away. I was too happy basking in the heady rush of flirting with him to dwell on it for long.

One afternoon, Caleb released Beau into the arena for another training session. He'd been working with the white colt whenever time allowed between projects. Beau's sale to the Saudi Arabian buyer interested in him hadn't been finalized yet, and Caleb didn't want to waste the opportunity to gentle him at a young age. Watching from the safety of the other side of the arena fence, I admired his calm sense of authority over the colt. Beau was nearly ready for saddle training, but he was stubborn. Caleb was using the flag on the colt, working him little by little out of his comfort zone. "We've got ourselves a stubborn boy, but shoot, isn't he a beauty regardless?" he said with a proud tone in his voice.

At one point, Beau got startled and hit the end of his lead rope, his head tossing wildly as his feet bounced against the sandy earth. I felt the ground shake as he fought Caleb's control. The horse's unruly reaction made my heart race, but Caleb never broke his calm demeanor. He followed Beau, confidently reeling in the lead until the horse calmed. My pulse came down as Beau settled. When Caleb led him toward me and paused at the fence, I surprised myself by reaching out to stroke the colt's muzzle.

"He really is a pretty horse," I said.

Caleb winked in my direction. "If I decide to keep him, I'm going to get you to ride him someday."

Quickly, I shook my head, but just the thought that Caleb was thinking of me in a future sense sent my head spinning. Which was why it felt like a bucket of cold water had been dumped over my head as I watched Jenna sidle up to Caleb one afternoon.

He had just come up and asked me quietly to walk with him to plan out a spot to play outdoor games. I'd quickly agreed, even though I felt my face heat with an instant blush at the thought of walking alone together. Jenna must have overheard his murmured request because she quickly announced that she could use a walk to stretch her legs. At the last minute, my brothers decided to take a break from their task and join us as well.

So, I ended up trailing behind the group as Jenna claimed the spot next to Caleb. Her profile was all smiles as she pranced along next to him. I felt ashamed of my irritated thoughts. So what if Caleb and I were in the middle of a secret summer flirtation? She had no way of knowing that. And who was I to complain when I also knew that I had no right to lead him on? Long distance relationships usually didn't work.

"Are you ok?" Vincent's quiet voice spoke at my side. I was glad to have my brothers home. The farmhouse was lonely without their quick, loud laughter. I knew they wished that I would ride with them to see the herd's grazing spot for the summer. Though I could feel my nerves lessening around the horses, the thought of endless miles of riding in the mountains was still too nerve-wracking to consider.

Quickly shifting a smile to my face, I looked at him. "Of course. Why wouldn't I be?"

"Your mood just seemed to downshift all of a sudden."

"Just a little tired. Ready for lunch," I said aloud. Inside, my brain continued the words I hadn't said: *I'm also attracted to one of your best friends and I don't know what I'm doing. And I wish I could talk to you about everything going on in my life, but I don't want to disappoint you.*

Jenna turned to grin at me a minute later. "Oh, Samantha, I forgot to tell you. I overheard Alex telling one of the guys that he thought you are cute. You two should totally go out on a date. I can give him your number if you want?"

Alex was one of Caleb's summer stable hands. He was a sweet, cute freshman who was just working in the valley for the summer before he left again for college. A wave of annoyance washed over me. Jenna had to know what she was doing. Involuntarily, my eyes shifted to the tall, bearded cowboy striding ahead across the grass. She would probably have a conniption if she knew about us.

It was hard to keep my patience with Jenna. I reminded myself that I had no right to be rude to her, even if she always seemed to be trying to stake her claim over Caleb. He didn't even really belong to me after all.

"I'm sure you're lonely. After being surrounded by cute guys for years in Washington," Jenna continued. I did not appreciate the taunting lilt to her voice.

"I'm not lonely at all, Jenna," I replied sweetly. "Plenty to keep me occupied out here. And as for Alex, I wouldn't want to take him out of the running. He seems like a perfect match for you."

Not trusting myself to stick around, I spun on my heel. "I'm going to take one of the trucks to grab lunch," I called over my shoulder to my brothers as I walked away. I didn't dare to look in Caleb's direction.

· · ·

I rolled my eyes and checked the time. It was nearly midnight. I'd gone upstairs early tonight, claiming a headache. It wasn't a total lie. I did have a headache, but I wondered if my heart hurt more.

Things were as perfect as they could be, considering the circumstances. The summer camp was set to open tomorrow. By ten in the morning, the first group of teens would arrive.

The first day of camp was Parents Day. Together, that week's group of teens and their families would spend time touring the ranch, meeting the horses in the program, and learning what to expect of their week at the summer camp during orientation. It was going to be a whirlwind. I'd heard my brothers shuffle upstairs earlier than usual as well. In addition to regular ranch duties, they would be pitching in during the first week of camp. Morning would be here before we could blink.

So far, it seemed like opening day was going to be perfect. I should have been happy—overjoyed, full of nerves, but excited. At the very least, I should have been sleeping. As lead camp coordinator, I would be a busy bee for the next few weeks. Instead, I was moping in my room at a quarter to midnight, unable to sleep, eyes stinging with unshed tears. It was habit to glance at my phone when it buzzed. When I'd seen Caleb's first messages come through a few minutes ago, I'd automatically slid open the screen to read them.

CALEB: If I haven't said it, thank you for all you've done on this year's summer camp.

CALEB: I hate to say this about my "frenemy..."

CALEB: But we make a great team.

The tears already swelling against my eyelids had taken the opportunity to slide down my cheeks then. With a frustrated swipe of my hand, I had dashed them away. He'd used our new word for each other. *Frenemy.* Not friends, but not enemies. It was a joke. You didn't kiss your frenemy. And I'd kissed Caleb.

And I wished I could do it again.

ME: Thank you. I did it for the kids.

We may not have kissed since the night he'd taken me to the ridge to watch the sunset, but that moment had been lingering between us ever since. I'd felt it as we'd prepped the ranch. As we'd inspected camp sites and planned coordinated activities. It couldn't have been an accident that our fingers had often seemed to brush as we'd worked. An electric thrill had shot up my arm every time. Randomly, our eyes would meet, and I would instantly be flooded with awareness of him.

Not friends. Not enemies. Something else entirely.

And I couldn't let this emotion—whatever it was—develop between us any further. It would be wrong. I couldn't pretend that I was here to stay. Secrets seemed to be piling around me. The stress of keeping them was starting to get to me. I was struggling to hold myself together.

Ten more minutes. I sat up and swung my legs over the side of the bed, deliberating. I should text Caleb back and tell him that I didn't want to meet him on the dark, moonlit road. But that wasn't what

I wanted to do. The truth was that I wanted to see him. Needed to see him. Without nosy, listening ears close by.

I padded to my closet and slipped on a light rain jacket, careful not to make any noise that could wake my brothers. Our stair treads creaked as I crept downstairs, but when I paused to listen at the base, the only sound was the rhythmic chirp of crickets in the yard. Sliding my feet into rain boots, I eased open the front door. The perk of living in the middle of nowhere was no alarm system to disarm. Our doors were hardly ever locked.

Shadow slept on the front porch, faithfully keeping guard. He sat up as I stepped out of the house.

"It's ok, buddy. Go back to sleep," I whispered to him, patting his silky head until he rolled onto his side again with a sigh.

The early summer nights still brought with them a heady chill and I was glad that I'd worn a jacket. The faint glow of headlights appeared through the trees at the head of our driveway as I walked up the path. Caleb was already waiting.

"I wasn't sure if you were going to come out of the house." His greeting was quiet as I stepped into the truck and shut the passenger door. The raspy, deep tones of his voice whispered over my skin, sending tingles up my spine. "Are you ok?"

My hands fiddled in my lap, and I chose not to answer his question right away. "I'm surprised you're not sleeping. Big day tomorrow." I couldn't quite meet his gaze.

"Getting there. Hard to sleep when there's so much to think about."

I wondered if he meant the summer camp or us. "I couldn't sleep either."

"By those circles under your eyes, I'd say you've been struggling to sleep for a few nights now."

His low-spoken observation startled me. I glanced at him quickly, noting the way the disheveled locks of his dark brown hair swept back from his face. Even his beard looked a little unruly. He was watching me with a look that I couldn't interpret.

"I'm fine," I protested. "There's just been so much to do. I wanted to make sure that everything was perfect for tomorrow. It's a big day and I don't want to overlook any of the details."

His eyes didn't turn away and I felt the challenge of his gaze. "Did you know that I can see your bedroom window from mine?" To my surprise, Caleb shifted the subject.

Instinctively, I glanced up the road toward his ranch as if by sudden x-ray vision, I would be able to see his house. The thought of him looking into my window night after night made a strange feeling run over me. "No. I didn't know that. I'll be sure to keep my blinds drawn from now on though."

"No. I can't see in," he clarified with a short laugh. His body angled toward me. "But I can just make out the light in your window. When it pops on, like a little yellow beacon and then turns out a few minutes later, I've always known that you and your family were safe at home. But when that little yellow light stays on hour after hour, night after night, I wonder why you can't sleep. It's been on a lot lately."

The thought of him keeping watch over my house night after night made my heart constrict. I wanted to blurt the truth out right then. But I knew that once I told my secret, we'd go right back to being nothing to each other. Like we had been before—only the truth would make it worse, because we had *almost* had a second chance.

"I'm fine," I lied, my tone sharper than I meant it to be. "I can take care of myself."

"I know you can. I have no doubt of that." His quiet reply surprised me. I was used to the Caleb who took charge, not this intense, deep-voiced, still, midnight version of the man.

"I just feel like there are so many decisions coming at me lately." The unexpected honesty burst from my lips. "I thought life was going to get easier after college. I thought everything was just going to make sense and now I just don't know. And this all probably sounds silly to you."

He shifted. I bent my head, letting my hair fall around my face, curtaining it like a waterfall. Fresh tears spilled onto my cheeks.

"I think you and I are more alike than you think." His husky voice broke the silence. "I've discovered that just when you think you have life figured out, something or someone will come along and completely derail your perfectly laid plans. The beauty of it is though, that if you let go of the need to control and learn to trust, change won't break you. God will use the uncertainty to mold you into His vision."

"Thanks. That's a good way to think about it," I whispered. My hand slid to his and gripped his fingers. I felt his warm, strong hand wrap itself over mine. He squeezed, the movement a gentle pressure.

"Samantha, whatever you choose to do in life, I know it's going to be a success. But it's easy to get so caught up in searching for the extraordinary that you miss the beauty of the ordinary gifts right in front of you."

I gave his hand a return squeeze, unable to reply. His simple words had tapped into a longing that had been stirring restlessly deep within my soul. A soft whisper of hope began to sprout amidst my confusion.

"Come on," Caleb said. "You need to sleep. Let me walk you back to the house."

"I'm fine," I protested, but he had already leapt from the truck and headed toward the passenger side. The chill of the night struck me when he opened the door. He stood in front of me for a moment, his presence comforting. Despite the rockiness of our past that we'd just begun to clear, his calm, masculine strength called to me, and I couldn't deny that it always had.

He held out his hand. We walked up the driveway in silence, the pine boughs shivering around us. Instinctively, our fingers sought each other, interlacing in the darkness. Our footsteps crunched softly on the gravel. Crickets chirped in the fields, but everything else was quiet.

Caleb paused at the base of the porch steps, turning me to face him. His face was shadowed, but when he bent over me, I didn't hesitate to stretch upward to meet his lips. It was strange to me how warm and familiar kissing him was, as if this new sensation between us wasn't new at all. I leaned into him, my arms reaching to slip around his neck. Tears pricked at my eyes again, but not because I was sad. Because I suddenly felt both safe and afraid all at once.

Caleb pulled away just enough that our lips parted. He brushed the loose hair around my face behind my ear. His free hand slipped around my back, holding me close. "Samantha?" he whispered.

"What?" I whispered back.

"I think that I'm…."

Snap. I heard the click of the switch before the porch light bathed the steps in its yellowed glow. The old screen door creaked as it opened. I sprang back from Caleb, pushing him away as I turned to face the front door of my home.

"Samantha?" Dean's voice was tinged with confusion. "Caleb? Is that you? What's going on?" My brother stepped onto the porch, his bare feet scuffing the wooden planks.

"Nothing. Caleb and I were just talking," I protested, immediately feeling myself switch into defensive mode. A shiver of discomfort ran through me. "We were just talking," I repeated aimlessly, my voice small and swallowed quickly by the thick silence in the yard. My feet shuffled.

Dean stepped forward, his brow furrowed. Nervously, I glanced at Caleb, but he was perfectly still, his chin lifted to meet his friend's gaze. The chirp of crickets intensified. I could hear footsteps inside the house hurrying down to the first floor. Knox appeared behind Dean, his hair tousled, still rubbing the sleep from his eyes.

"What's up? Is something wrong? Why are we outside in the middle of the night? Caleb, is that you? What? Oh...." It only took a few seconds for my youngest brother to cycle through his barrage of questions. His eyes sharpened with understanding. He fell silent, stepping aside to watch the exchange between Dean and Caleb.

"Caleb, would you care to explain why you're outside in the middle of the night in the dark with my sister?" Dean's voice was deep, each word enunciated with an intensity I'd never heard him use. Vincent slid onto the porch without a word, his expression serious.

It didn't matter that Caleb was their friend. My brothers had instantly gone into protective mode. I knew that catching the two of us in the dark mid-embrace looked sketchy at best. I could imagine what was running through their minds.

"Samantha, will you give your brothers and I a chance to talk in private?" Caleb said. I glanced at him, the tingle of worry spreading throughout my limbs. No matter how this conversation went, things had just gotten more complicated. He glanced at me, a reassuring smile playing at the corners of his mouth.

"It's going to be ok." He found my hand and gave it a squeeze. "Go inside."

I tried to believe him as I walked up the steps and across the porch, my protective brothers parting to open a path for me as I approached. I crept up to the top of the steps, ears straining to hear. The murmur of deep male voices went on for a while, then I heard my brothers reenter the house. Quickly, I disappeared into my room, not ready to face them as they came up the stairs.

Chapter Eighteen

BREAKFAST WAS AWKWARD, but I had to give my brothers credit. They didn't bring up the fact that they'd caught me kissing their best friend in the middle of the night. With camp starting in just a few hours, we all knew that it wasn't the time or the place for explanations. I wondered if they would wait on me to broach the subject first.

"Good morning." I attempted to smile at Vincent when I first walked into the kitchen.

The sun had barely risen, but I hadn't been able to sleep any longer. When I heard movement downstairs, I dressed in the soft light of my bedside lamp. After weeks around the ranch, I'd learned my lesson. Worn-in jeans, a white t-shirt under an old flannel shirt, and sturdy work boots. I braided my hair and grabbed a straw hat.

Just to be on the safe side, I made sure that my curtains were securely shut until I was fully dressed.

"Good morning," Vincent replied, glancing over his shoulder at me. "There's breakfast." He tilted his head toward the stove.

"Where are Dean and Knox?" I asked, hoping they weren't avoiding me in anger.

"Finishing up the last of the chores. Figured today needed an extra early start."

"Uh huh," I murmured, finding it hard to concentrate, waiting for the deluge of questions. But they never came.

I sat at the table and picked at a bowl of oatmeal studded with brown sugar, strawberries picked from the garden, and fresh cream. The porridge felt like paste in my mouth. I wanted to ask what Caleb had said last night, but each time I opened my mouth, I stopped. If Vincent hadn't brought it up, maybe I shouldn't either?

When Dean and Knox entered the kitchen a few minutes later, their greetings were stilted but friendly. I caught Knox staring at me, but he just gave me a reassuring grin and walked over to plant a kiss on the top of my head. It was Dean who made me nervous, his stern expression a reminder of Dad's when he had been displeased. I tried to shake off the nerves and act like nothing was wrong.

What would I say when Dean wanted to talk? How could I explain?

My anxiety flared at the thought. But I pushed it away. I had enough on my plate to worry about, so I decided to focus on my last-minute preparations for opening day. I didn't have time to antic-ipate awkward future conversations again until nine o'clock when we parked the truck among the others gathered near the weathered red barn on Caleb's ranch that would serve as an activity center should we end up getting rain in the weeks to come. A small crowd of ranch hands and volunteers from town stood in a circle, Jenna at the center. Her voice rang out as we joined them.

"Ok, everyone. Within the hour, we'll have the first of our guests arriving. You all have your assignments, but the point of today is to get our young guests excited about the week. Everyone ready? Ok, three cheers for Cascade Valley and our favorite cowboy, Caleb." The small group put their hands together in a round of applause.

By the time the first families arrived, my head was spinning with last minute details, charts, registration lists, and the hundred questions I'd been asked in the last hour. I'd put myself in charge of registration, wanting to make sure every bit of information was gathered, both for the students' sake and our own. Plus, I wanted to make sure each guest's first impression of the ranch was as pleasant and welcoming as possible. I hadn't been sure if I could trust anyone else with the duty.

I needn't have worried. Not only were the ranch hands and volunteers quick to welcome each carload of newcomers, each calling out a greeting whenever they were near, but the families of our young guests were immediately taken with the charm and beauty of the ranch. With wide eyes and even wider smiles, they tumbled out of their vehicles, pointing to various spots on the ranch within their range of vision. But not everyone was in such a pleasant mood.

"Hello. Welcome." I smiled at a narrow-framed boy of about fifteen who had just exited a faded gray sedan. He glanced at me with a bored expression and tossed down a worn duffel bag. A young, tired-looking, dark-haired woman joined him at the registration table that I'd set up in the shade of a large sugar maple.

"I'm Lana Alvarez. I'm here to check in my son, Jax," she said, tossing her hair over her shoulder.

I shuffled through my paperwork, looking for the correct printout to match with the name. "Here you are." I slid it from the stack. "Would you be able to fill this out for me, sign here and here, and then you'll be all set. Orientation and a tour of the grounds is in fifteen minutes, but feel free to explore until then."

Off to the side, the boy stood silently. I smiled at him again, hoping to coax a return smile from his slightly hostile face. Dressed in dark colors and long sleeves, his attire was out of place for the season and the location. The sides of his hair were shaved close, but he'd let his bangs grow long and dyed the edges a bright green. A combination of boredom, misery, and anger was displayed across his face. He reminded me of some of the kids I'd worked with during volunteer mission trips in high school. I wondered what series of events had led him here.

"How did you two hear about our youth camp?" I pried.

Lana finished adding her signature to the page. "My pastor read an article and then saw your page on Instagram. He thought a week in the country might be something Jax enjoyed. He used to love horses when he was little." She glanced at her son, and I caught a hint of wistfulness in her expression. "Jax had some trouble at school this past year and he just got through with community service. I'm hoping the fresh air and hard work of a ranch will do him some good."

"It's hard work all right, but at the end of the day, when you've fed and bedded down the animals and you're eating food that you dug from your own garden, there isn't a better feeling in the world." I was surprised to hear the words slipping so easily from my own mouth, considering how glad I'd been to purchase produce from the supermarket when I'd moved to Seattle. "I'll see you at orientation, Jax." I flashed him a grin and got another eyeroll in return.

The pair wandered away. Lana's head bent toward her son, murmuring quietly in his ear. I wondered if this particular form of therapy was the best choice for him. Is he just going to be miserable for the entire week?

I'd caught flashes of Caleb moving around the yard and stables since I'd arrived, but we hadn't spoken yet. And he hadn't come to find me. I wasn't sure whether to be embarrassed or nonchalant about last night's situation. *Caught kissing my brothers' best friend in the dark shadows of our front porch.* It was like high school, except that I hadn't even had a boyfriend in high school and if I'd had one, I wouldn't have had the nerve to date a friend of my brothers.

"They were the last people I wanted to know about us," I mumbled under my breath as I organized the registration paperwork. Walking across the yard to the house, I opened the door and slipped inside. I would stash the paperwork in Caleb's office to file later. "They are going to be so disappointed in me."

"Talking to yourself?" My heart leaped as Caleb's amused voice stopped me in my tracks. I whirled to find him leaning against the doorframe.

"I do that sometimes," I replied, glancing shyly at him from under my lashes. "How are you?" We stared at each other, gazes locked, but neither of us moved toward the other.

"A little the worse for wear," Caleb yawned. "Barely slept a wink. But I'll live. How are you?"

"Nervous," I admitted.

"About today or…." Last night stretched between us.

"All of it," I shrugged. A figure flashed across the window. "I couldn't hear anything you said last night. What did you tell my brothers about us?"

"Caleb?" Griff peeked through the door just then. "There you are." He gave me a friendly nod, but his eyes were curious. His handlebar mustache twitched. "Everyone's assembling for orientation. We'll be waiting for you."

"I'll be right there," Caleb said. Griff's eyes shifted to me once more before he nodded and disappeared.

"Looks like duty calls, so I guess you'll just have to wait to find out if your brothers threatened to take me into the woods and bury me for dating you." Caleb spoke solemnly, but his eyes carried a sparkle. I tried not to blush.

"We're not dating though." I shook my head.

In two quick strides, Caleb stood in front of me. I peered up at him, my eyes running over each of his handsome features. The brim of his white cowboy hat was pushed back on his forehead as he bent over me. "Maybe not officially. Yet…."

My hands lifted to curl themselves into his t-shirt. The blue fabric was soft and worn in from many washes. "I just don't know, Caleb. Long distance relationships don't usually work out well."

"Who said that it had to be long distance?"

I shook my head again, guilt pushing at the back of my mind. "When I get a job, it isn't going to be around here."

"Maybe you'll change your mind?" His fingertips touched my chin, and he nudged my face upward. The tears brimming in my eyes gave me away. "Hey now. Don't worry. I'll make it work."

When his eyes glanced downward, I was ready as his lips touched mine. The kiss was sweet, but that didn't lessen the fireworks that I instantly felt.

"Gotta go." He winked at me. I nodded reluctantly, wishing that we could continue the conversation.

Instead, I laid a hand on his chest and gave him a gentle push toward the door. "Go get 'em, cowboy." I paused to regain my composure and let the flush fade from my face. When I stepped outside, the yard was empty. I joined the group gathered by the stable in time to hear Caleb's voice echo above the crowd. I took a place next to Jax and Lana and gave the pair an encouraging smile.

"This week is a reset for a lot of you," Caleb said. "Maybe you struggled in school this year. Maybe life kicked your butt. This is a safe space to leave the past behind you. We don't care why you are here, but we do care about what you take away from camp when you leave next week.

You'll each be working closely with an Arabian horse picked just for you. We're partial to our horses out here and ask that you treat them with respect and kindness. I can guarantee that you'll never meet a kinder or smarter horse." He paused to look over the group before continuing. Most of the students seemed to be watching him closely.

"Our horses are your partners this week. They will take care of you on the trails and in the arena. They will ask you questions, and they will accept whatever answer you give them. But these horses are smarter and wiser than you. If you can honor and respect their wisdom and let them lead, you'll never forget what they teach you." Caleb lifted a hand and indicated that the group was to follow him. "Now, let's go on a tour of the grounds and the stables."

"See, you're going to like it here," I overheard Lana whisper in Jax's ear. Angrily, he shrugged off the hand she'd laid on his shoulder.

"Horses are stupid. I don't even want to ride them," he grumbled sourly. I trailed behind the two as Caleb led the group through the stables, introducing the geldings and mares who stood behind their respective stalls. The horses stepped forward, eagerly waiting for muzzle rubs and the cubes of sugar that the volunteers handed to each family.

"Normally, we try not to give the horses too much sugar," Caleb said in an exaggerated drawl. "But I guess your visit is a good reason to celebrate."

The group laughed. I watched in fascination as Caleb's easy-going charm seemed to win over most of the teens. They watched as he introduced each horse and demonstrated how to slip on a bridle, his words peppered with stories about the ranch and the Arabians. Only Jax and Lana kept to themselves.

The sun was bright and warm as we proceeded from the stables and through the yard. Caleb pointed out the gardens and led the group on a tour of the sites that had been readied for camping.

"How about some lunch?" he finally concluded, pointing toward the picnic tables set up under a grove of trees. Malia had arrived while we were on the tour. She'd set up a spread that could have rivaled a buffet.

It was the perfect welcome luncheon for our first group of guests. I ran around, answering questions and talking brightly with each family. If first impressions are everything, I would have said that we were off to a good start.

"Looks like it's going to be a good week," Malia said to me when I stopped by her drink booth for a cold lemonade. "You're certainly a busy bee out there."

"Doing what I can to connect with everyone," I replied cheerfully.

"You've got a knack for this sort of thing," she said thoughtfully, topping off my lemonade glass.

"For chatting up our guests?" I smiled, glancing toward the families enjoying their lunch on the picnic tables.

"For event planning, coordination, marketing. Everything you managed for the camp really," she clarified. "Have you ever thought of becoming an event planner?"

I laughed and shook my head. "I may have a marketing degree, but my heart is in non-profit management. I'm hoping to get a job with an organization soon."

She cocked an eyebrow at me. "Isn't this a non-profit youth camp right here?"

"Somewhere bigger than this. Where I can really make a differ-ence," I replied quickly, then bit my tongue. Malia glanced at me, her gray eyes sharp. She nodded, then turned away. Internally, I kicked myself for my hasty, thoughtless comment.

By late afternoon, I knew every child's name and their story. Most of them briefly told me of the challenges they had faced that had led them to seek out the camp. School and home trouble, and minor run-ins with the law seemed to be common among the group. None of them had any violent marks on their record, but a few had gotten into fistfights at school or been caught vandalizing. Only Jax and Lana remained standoffish, and I secretly wondered if the boy would last an entire week on the ranch. He seemed miserable.

By late-afternoon, the parents had climbed into their vehicles and waved goodbye. A group of twenty teens, ranging from ages fourteen to seventeen, stood near the stables. Brushes and sponges had been pulled from the tack room. Jenna and Griff gave them a lesson in horse grooming. Most of the campers were excited to be up close and personal with the horses, but I kept finding my eyes drawn to Jax. He was going through the motions, but it was obvious that he wasn't into the activity. I caught Caleb watching him subtly as well.

"Looks like we're off to a great start." I jumped when Dean's voice spoke unexpectedly at my side. I'd stationed myself under the arms of a big sugar maple, fanning myself with my straw hat. The afternoon was the warmest we'd had so far this year, but I relished the feel of the sun on my skin.

"A great start," I repeated, glancing at him shyly. Dean and I had barely spoken during the day, which I hoped was only because we'd been going in different directions. I took the opportunity to enlist his help though. "There's a young man here…." I began, nodding toward Jax. Dean's attention shifted toward the boy. "He seems like he's struggling. I got the impression that he had gotten into quite a bit of trouble back home. Do you think you could keep an eye on him?"

Dean nodded. "Absolutely. And I'll have Vincent and Knox talk to him too when they get a chance. Maybe he just needs to be reminded that there's no judgement for his past here."

"Thank you." I angled away from the barnyard and faced Dean. "Do you want to talk about last night?" The words were abrupt, and I cringed at the blunt sound of them coming from my mouth. But I knew it was my responsibility to address the situation.

Dean glanced at me. His face was stern, but I saw with relief that his eyes were still warm. "I would like to talk about it. How long have you and Caleb been secretly dating?"

I blushed at his directness. "We're not dating. We've just been… talking. We've kind of become friends."

"I thought you despised him?"

"Before, I did." I swallowed, my throat tight. "It's hard to explain. When Dad had his accident, I was looking for someone to blame and Caleb came into my crosshairs. But since I've been volunteering for the camp, I realized that I'd never taken the time to talk with him about what happened. About what I thought had happened. Caleb isn't the man I thought he was. He didn't do what I thought he did."

"You were pretty rough on him," Dean replied, rubbing his chin with his hand.

"I'm trying to repair the damage that I did now."

"So you decided to repair your wrongs toward Caleb by kissing him under the stars?" My brother's voice was amused.

I felt my face flush with what I knew had to be a beet red. "What did Caleb say about it?"

"Well, it seems that under my very nose, you two have been flirting. Of course, I knew that you liked him years ago—"

I reached out to smack him lightly on the arm.

Dean grinned. "To be honest, I knew that Caleb liked you years ago. He talked to me about it shortly before Dad's accident. You challenge him. So seeing you two rekindle what might have been isn't a complete surprise. And honestly, it could be rather fun to see how Caleb handles your feisty nature. Honestly, I'm not sure that anyone else is man enough to take on a spitfire like you."

"He's pretty feisty himself, as much as he trys to hide it. Maybe I'll be the one to tame him?" I cocked my head and smirked, but my face quickly grew serious again. "Why didn't you ever tell me any of this before? Are we ok? You're not mad at me are you?"

"I could never be mad at you, Sammie. I'm not sure that I'm pleased at the thought of my thirty-year-old best friend dating my twenty-three-year-old sister, but if you're saying that you're just friends…?"

"I don't know what the future holds," I admitted honestly.

Dean nodded. "Just don't break his heart, ok? It's more fragile than you would think."

We were both called away at that moment, but I kept wondering what Dean had meant as the evening shifted into twilight. One of Caleb's first lessons was to teach the small troop of guests how to bed the horses down for the night. Normally, I tried to stay out of the stables, my nerves around the horses a constant nag in the back of my subconscious. But the hum of laughter and youthful voices raised in enthusiastic curiosity drew me to the entrance despite myself. Caleb, Jenna, and Griff were at the helm, instructing the campers on how to properly lay bedding in the freshly mucked stalls.

"There you go," Griff encouraged, his gruff voice softened for the moment. "Spread it across the floor in even layers. So, their hooves stay nice and comfortable through the night."

"This scratchy hay doesn't seem so comfortable to me," one of the teens scoffed.

"It probably would be if you were a horse," Jenna retorted with a hint of sharpness. She quickly followed it up with a laugh to play off her tone.

I couldn't help but laugh myself as a boy a little older than Jax tried to lift a bale of hay off the floor. The bales easily weighed two hundred pounds apiece and it didn't budge as he pulled upward. The group laughed.

"Need some help with that, son?" Caleb grabbed the strings that held the bale in place. He lifted it and carried it easily to the end of the stable, setting it in place next to the other bales stacked against the wall. It was a sight I'd seen a thousand times on my own family's ranch. Ranching developed strong men and strong women. But tonight, I felt as though I was watching it through the eyes of someone who'd never seen such powerful, masculine strength in action. My heart fluttered as I watched Caleb. The girls giggled and the boys looked on with admiration written visibly across their faces.

"Now let's get the rest of these horses settled, then we'll roast those marshmallows like I promised. You've never had a roasted marshmallow until you've had it nearly burnt over a campfire," Caleb called over his shoulder to the rest of the group. He turned then and caught sight of me in the doorway. He smiled and winked in my direction.

With a flush, I dropped my eyes. The rest of the group returned to following Griff's instructions, but when I looked up again, I caught Jenna's gaze directed toward me. *Did she catch Caleb's reaction to seeing me?*

I smiled and waved in her direction, but she turned too quickly back to the group for me to know if she'd seen my greeting and what she'd thought if she had.

Chapter Nineteen

"YOU'RE USING THE bit too much, Jax. She'll respond to a lighter touch," Caleb called to the boy.

Sandy had been assigned as Jax's ride for the week. I questioned whether she had been the right choice. She was a good-natured horse, but she knew what she wanted. And right now, she wasn't motivated to listen to the young man's cues. Her feet danced out of place, and she shook her head, chomping on her bit. I could see the frustration growing on Jax's face. He looked stressed and uncomfortable. A storm was gathering across his brow.

The group was playing red-light-green-light, ranch style. Each of the campers was mounted on the mare or gelding they'd been assigned at the beginning of the week. They had assembled in a line at the other end of the corral. On Caleb's signal, they moved the horses forward a few steps, then stopped when he called "red light." Caleb was stationed on a black gelding near Jenna and I, where we observed from the other side of the arena's fence.

We were on day three of the group's week-long stay. Over the week, I'd watched Jax relax a little. His shoulders seemed looser, and his eyes were lighter. The group had learned the basics of riding the day after they'd arrived. Most of the kids had been eager to get on the horses, but I'd noticed Jax's hesitancy right away. It took him a few minutes, but he had managed to clamber atop Sandy's back. Today, he was positioned at the far end of the corral.

Despite his progress, his stance today was stiff and unnatural. Like he was afraid the horse was going to buck him at any moment. I understood how he felt. Pushing away my anxious nerves around the horses had become a moment-by-moment habit. I'd been well-trained by my dad to read equestrian body language though. I knew that Sandy was aware of her charge. She'd keep him safe, but Jax was not currently convinced.

"Jax is struggling," I said to Jenna in a low tone. She lifted her leg onto the lower rung of the fencing and glanced toward the teen.

"He looks fine to me," she replied, her tone stiff. Ever since the night the group had arrived, her attitude toward me had taken a downturn. It was more stiff and unfriendly than it had ever been.

"He's convinced she's going to take off on him."

Jenna swiveled her head in my direction. "Well, why don't you go show him how it's done, city-girl?"

The words were said in a sing-song tone, but I caught her drift. "You know what, I think I will," I replied, hopping on the fence and swinging my leg to the other side. Her challenge had sparked a fiery retort in my chest, and I needed to step away before I said something I'd regret. "He just needs to be shown a better way of doing it."

Quickly, I skirted around Caleb. When he caught sight of me, I held up my hand as a signal for him to hold the riders in place. The group watched as I strode across the dirt-packed corral, my boots scuffing up the dust as I approached Sandy. I eyed her nervously but pushed away my anxiety for Jax's sake. Even from ten feet away I could see the death grip he had on her reins. He stared at me, a miserable expression on his face.

"I don't understand what he wants me to do," he muttered under his breath as I stopped at Sandy's shoulder. Lightly, I rested a hand on the mare's withers. Her flesh shivered under my touch, and she turned to brush my shoulder with her muzzle.

"Jax, what's wrong?" I peered up at the boy. His green edged bangs flopped over one eye. The other peered down at me.

"I don't like horses," he replied.

"Are you sure? Sandy sure seems to like you." I wasn't about to tell him that she'd nearly run away with me a few weeks ago. "You don't have to yank on her mouth like you're trying to stop a herd of bulls. The bit is hurting her. Just a tiny bit of pressure and she'll do exactly what you say." I stroked Sandy's mane, trying to convey more enthusiasm for the moment than I felt. Externally, I was calm, but I had to struggle to keep myself from shivering.

"Here, let me see the reins." Jax handed them to me promptly. I threw my arm across Sandy's withers. "Stay up there. I'll lead on the next round and show you what I mean."

I lifted my free hand to tell Caleb that we were ready to proceed. He called "green light" and the riders nudged their mounts to move them forward a few steps. My fingers gripped Sandy's reins and I tried to relax as the mare stepped forward gracefully. Watching her hooves, I kept out of her way, but stayed close to her side. Her ears flickered and she turned her head to glance at me curiously. I knew she was as aware of me as I was of her.

"There you go, girl," I murmured encouragingly to her, making sure that Jax could hear me. We moved forward in tandem another two steps, then Caleb called for the riders to halt their horses. At his signal, I eased back on Sandy's reins, giving the bit a quick, gentle tug. "Whoa, girl." Sandy's lithe body stopped immediately, as I'd known it would. She was a well-trained Arabian. Her delicate hooves planted themselves in the dusty earth. She shook her head, a gentle whooshing sound emitting from her nostrils.

"See?" I swiveled my head to smile up at Jax. He looked down and gave me a lopsided smile. "Now you try. Sit heavy in the saddle when you want her to stop."

"I don't know what that means," Jax grumbled.

"You'll figure it out. Feel the movement with your whole body. She needs to know you're steady up there." I transferred the reins back to him, then stepped toward the fence.

"You can do it, Jax." An encouraging murmur ran down the line. Caleb gave another green light signal. Jax clucked his tongue and pressed his heel lightly into Sandy's side. With her usual grace, she stepped forward a few paces.

"Talk to her," I said, keeping pace with the two. "Let her know what a great job she's doing."

The low murmur of Jax's voice fell on my ears. His hand stretched out to touch her velvety neck. Caleb called for the riders to stop. I watched as Jax tugged on the reins. He sat back on the saddle, his hands releasing the straps of the bridle quickly. "Whoa," he said. Sandy pulled up at his command. Her hooves danced for a moment, then she settled quietly.

Jax glanced over his shoulder to me, his expression uncertain. "Like that?" he said.

"Just like that," I encouraged, giving him a thumbs up. "Keep communicating with her like that and you'll be a pro in no time." I waited until I saw his body relax into the saddle, then I turned and clambered over the fence. Once I was safely on the other side, I wiped my sweaty palms on my pants while I watched the rest of the game.

Caleb caught my eye and gave me an approving nod, the tail end of a smirk playing across his lips. Watching Jax's progress through the rest of the afternoon made me glad that I'd braved my nerves and gone to help him. A weight seemed to slowly begin lifting off his shoulders after that.

"Amazing what a boost of confidence can do," I mumbled under my breath as I walked back to join Jenna. She stared as I approached.

"Jax is already riding better. Brava, Samantha. I didn't realize you were such a horsewoman."

For the first time in a long time, my smile back to her felt genuine. "It's been a long time," I replied. "But old habits die hard, I guess."

. . .

"Both a horse-whisperer and a teen-boy-whisperer. You're an impressive woman, Samantha. And a really pretty one too," Caleb murmured in my ear that evening as Jenna and Griff helped the group of teens settle the horses for the night.

I shook my head in embarrassment but let a glimmer sneak into my eyes as I glanced at him. These quiet, whispered moments had become our subtle way of flirting.

I'd fallen into a routine over the past few days. As the horses were being stabled, I'd check on the cookout for dinner. Then I'd walk back to the stable to check on the campers' progress. Jax seemed to be in a better mood than he'd been in so far. His step was brisk and his expression content. Occasionally, he would stop to smooth a hand across Sandy's muzzle. Once, I caught his eye and he nodded in my direction.

Caleb had been lingering near the stable doors when I arrived tonight. I turned my attention from watching Jax and grinned at his words. I couldn't help but be pleased that I'd conquered my nerves enough to help Jax during the game. "Sandy had it covered. Jax just needed a little encouragement. I know it's intimidating to be on top of a horse if you're not used to it. Sitting on nearly a thousand pounds of pure muscle can make anyone nervous."

He winked at me. I flushed under his clear, steady gaze. "Well, he already seems to have grown in confidence," he said. "I think we actually got a smile out of him playing follow-the-leader this afternoon. Thanks to you."

"I'm happy that I was able to help," I murmured.

"I'm happy that you're here to help," Caleb countered. The back of his hand brushed across mine as he moved to hang a bridle on its hook in the tack room. The contact made a shiver run through my fingers and up my arm.

In that moment, I knew. I was glad that I was in Cascade Valley too.

By the time we said goodbye to two more sets of campers, I finally felt like I was getting the hang of my role as *camp counselor/social media marketer/crisis handler*. Every day was a whirlwind, and every day brought a new challenge for me to navigate. I woke up early every morning with a spring in my step and crashed into my bed like a log every night. There were plenty of volunteers and chaperones to handle the campsite, so I wasn't needed for overnight duty. I probably would have been useless baggage anyway. Never had I experienced such a deep, in-my-bones exhaustion. But it was the good kind of exhausted. The kind that only comes after a day of hard work, when you know you've accomplished something good.

I was quickly convinced that Caleb's summer camp was making a difference. By the time the parents returned to pick up their teens on Sunday, most of them were met with smiling faces. Each new group had been kept small enough to give our volunteer counselors and teachers the opportunity to connect with the teens on an individual level. They received one-on-one riding lessons, experienced plenty of fun, character-building games, and were given a hearty dose of encouragement and wisdom throughout the week.

When Lana had arrived to pick up Jax at the end of the first week, she'd stared at him with guarded eyes. "Hey, big guy. How did things go this week?"

Jax had walked past us, carrying his sleeping bag. "It was good." He'd tossed the response over his shoulder casually. His mom looked to me for clarification.

"Splendidly," I'd replied promptly. "Jax has natural instincts as a rider. As soon as he got some confidence under his belt, it was like he'd been riding forever."

"Oh...." A wave of relief had washed over her pretty face, but it had clouded quickly with another thought. "And how was his mood this week?"

"He seemed to enjoy himself for the most part," I smiled at her reassuringly. "Perhaps you can find a local stable for him to ride at back home?"

The toe of her tennis shoe had scuffed the earth. "I'm not sure I could afford that," she'd said, regret in her tone. "It's just Jax and I at home and I don't have a lot of extra money for riding lessons right now."

I nodded. "Let's stay in touch then. Maybe Jax can come back up on a weekend every now and then?"

The invitation had been extended by Caleb. We knew Jax and Lana lived in Bozeman. They could be at the ranch within a couple hours drive. We'd all agreed that more time on the ranch would do the young boy good.

"That's so kind of you to offer." Lana had turned to Jax eagerly. "Did you hear that? Maybe you can come back some weekends when you aren't with your dad?"

Jax had thrown a questioning glance in my direction. I replied with a nod and a smile. His eyes had lightened another shade, but he'd kept his cool façade in place. "Yeah, maybe. That could be cool. Can we just go now? See you, Ms. McCade. Thanks for all the help this week."

"I'll be in touch," Lana had said, shaking my hand as Jax climbed into the car. Her eyes drifted past me, and I'd watched as her cheeks had suddenly flushed. I'd turned to see Vincent walking in our direction. She lifted a hand to wave at him.

"Thanks for everything," Lana said as Vincent approached. "I really appreciate what you're doing here."

"This is my brother, Vincent. Vincent, this is Lana, Jax's mom."

Vincent shook her hand. His gaze had lingered on her, his smile shy, but warm and friendly. "It was great to have Jax with us this week. You're welcome to bring him back anytime."

"Thank you. So much. For everything." She'd hugged me before climbing into her car.

"You'd never guess from the hair and the clothes, but that boy could have a future as a great cowboy," Vincent said, his eyes lingering on the retreating vehicle. "I don't think he wanted to leave."

. . .

Mom had lingered in Florida for several weeks after her cruise ship redocked, visiting old friends, and soaking in the ocean breezes. She had also made the trip up to New York City for a visit with Demi. The time though had finally come for her to return home and she was due back four weeks after camp had begun. I was glad. I wanted to get her wise perspective on all the things happening in my life. The future was beginning to unfold before my eyes, and I wasn't sure if I had the courage to do what needed to be done.

One morning, I rose early and dressed in the dim light that was just beginning to peek through my window. Bypassing my now everyday uniform of worn-in jeans, t-shirts, and boots, I opted for a loose pair of tan linen pants and a white cotton eyelet blouse. Pulling my curly, gingered hair into a bun, I tried to smooth it out so that it would have at least the semblance of neatness that evening. Nervously, my stomach fluttered as I walked downstairs.

I wouldn't be going to camp today. Instead, I'd be driving by myself into the city to catch a flight back to Seattle. All at once, everything that I'd been praying for seemed to be coming to fruition. The senior director of a group of orphanages scattered across several countries in Europe had been on a fund-raising tour in the States. We'd already spoken several times and now she had requested an in-person interview with me during her stopover in Seattle. It was everything I'd been dreaming of and I was terrified.

I'd been on pins and needles since I'd applied for the position, but I couldn't understand why I woke the morning of my interview wishing that I didn't have to go. The woman was looking for a bilingual director with experience in marketing and PR campaigns, a role that I was more than qualified to assume. Everything was playing out just as I'd hoped, but it would have been a lie to pretend that I wasn't apprehensive.

"I'll just be gone for the night," I reminded my brothers as I grabbed a piece of hot, buttered toast from the plate on the table. "And then I'm bringing Amanda back with me for a visit. I expect you men to keep the house tidy while I'm gone. Especially you, Knox." I spread homemade apricot jam across the thick slice of toasted homemade bread. If my brothers thought it odd that I was going up to Seattle just to bring my friend back for a visit, they didn't question me.

Knox protested. "I'm not that messy."

"Your dirty boots traipsing across the house disprove that claim. I just want her to feel welcome and comfortable."

"We'll see to that," Knox replied cheerfully. "Amanda's pretty. I'll be glad to give her a tour of the valley."

"No, no, no," I shook the toast at him. "No funny business. My friend is off limits."

"But Caleb's our friend…." I heard Knox mutter under his breath sarcastically.

I blushed and glared at him, but I didn't respond. So far, we'd all done a great job of avoiding a conversation about that midnight kiss they'd caught us in the middle of. After my talk with Dean, the three of them seemed to have an unspoken agreement between each other to give Caleb and I space to figure out our relationship.

But what could I even say? I couldn't have asked for a better place to observe Caleb in his natural environment than the youth camp. There was a reason my heart seemed to leap when he was near. His calm, stern strength and masculinity softened around the kids. Even the boys who had swaggered into orientation day with a chip on their shoulders surrendered willingly to his leadership. Between Caleb and the therapeutic influence of the horses, the program was accomplishing its goals.

But that had hardly left time for us to do more than flirt subtly and text briefly before we fell asleep at night. With so many people milling about the ranch, there were few private moments available. But a few days ago, I had walked into the stables to return a bucket of brushes. Caleb had followed me into the tack room.

"Hey."

I'd turned to find him standing in the doorway of the small room, his frame filling up the entrance. His eyes had gleamed at me. My skin had warmed under his gaze. "Hey. Did you need something?"

"Just saw you walking in here and wanted to say hi," he'd replied. I still didn't know how to process what was happening between us.

It was confusing and intriguing and kept my insides tangled as I struggled to make sense of it all. And I felt so much guilt for keeping my plans a secret from him. I should have told him that first night on the ridge. *Where would I even begin now?*

"Here I am," I murmured, moving closer and turning my face up to his.

"Do you really have to leave next week?" he murmured.

"It's only overnight."

"I'm not sure that we can spare you." Caleb's index finger had brushed the outside of my arm. "Did I ever tell you that I'm really glad you told me how much my youth camp sucked and that you decided to take pity on me and fix it?"

Laughter had bubbled out of my chest at his words. "Stop it." I'd laid my palm against his chest and given him a little push. Caleb didn't even budge, but his hand flew up to capture mine. He had intertwined our fingers and held them against his shirt. "I never said your summer camp sucked," I continued. "It was just the marketing that needed a makeover. I only gave it the tiny bit of help it needed."

"Maybe I should let you give me a makeover too? Do you think you can fix all my flaws?"

I had pulled my head back then and pretended to look him over. "Nope, I don't think I can help you. You're beyond fixing at this point." *When did flirting with him become so natural? Just a couple of months ago I hated him. Everything feels so easy and right when I'm with him now.*

"Oh? That's what you really think?" Caleb had grinned. "Maybe what I really need is a kiss from you to turn this frog into a prince?"

"Is that why you came in here?" I'd dropped my gaze shyly.

"Maybe?"

"We're not supposed to be doing this here. Remember?"

"Let's call it a temporary case of amnesia."

"Well," I'd deliberated. "Maybe just one? Since I feel sorry for you."

"I'll take that."

It was without hesitation that I'd raised my face to meet his lips as he bent over me. Despite my confusion, these stolen moments thrilled me to my core. They were exhilarating and terrifying all at once. I wanted to run away, and I wanted more. Our fingers had intertwined. My free hand had slipped around Caleb's neck, pulling him down to me. At any second, one of the ranch hands could walk into the stables and catch us, but I didn't care. I was lost in the gentle pressure of his touch.

For that brief, stolen moment, Caleb had become my whole world. And he'd kissed me as if I was his.

When he had finally pulled away, Caleb rested his forehead gently on mine. His eyes were closed, his breath soft and tinged with the mint candies he kept in his pockets for the horses. "I know it was hard to let go of the opinion you had of me but thank you for taking the chance. We've been able to help so many kids this summer because of you."

My head shook. "I'm so sorry for misjudging you all that time. I wish I could take it back and do it all over."

"Do you think we've finally become friends?" Caleb's hand had cupped my cheek then. His thumb traced a slow, thoughtful circle around my lips. I stifled a shiver. His gaze was deep and intense and suddenly, it took my breath away.

"Maybe?" I'd whispered.

"Samantha, I want to tell you...." But instead of finishing the sentence, he'd swept down for another brief kiss that had left my head spinning and my knees shaking like a leaf.

Chapter Twenty

WHEN MY PLANE began to descend for a landing at the Seattle airport that afternoon, I peered through the window. The city that had once seemed like a magical emerald wonderland now seemed like an endless expanse of high-rises, condos, and tiny parks that couldn't begin to compare to the wide-open expanse of Cascade Valley.

I knew what had drawn me to city-life: excitement, opportunity, entertainment, shopping, and restaurants. I'd lived the country-life. I'd been a rancher's daughter. I'd worked in the hay field with my father. I'd mucked the stalls, cleaned the pastures, milked the cow, gathered the eggs, scrubbed the barn, and helped my mother with all the daily tasks that created the life we lived on the ranch. And it was a beautiful life.

But it seemed like a person could be anything she wanted to be in the city. It had been so easy to get caught up in the lure of modern culture when I'd turned eighteen and left home for the first time. Power, riches, and fame had never tempted me. I just wanted to follow a calling. I wanted a fulfilling career that I probably couldn't find in Cascade Valley, Montana.

There was only one place that I would find a man like Caleb though. There was only one serious, whiskey-eyed cowboy who made my heart pound faster every time he was near.

"All good things come from you, don't they, Lord? But what if there are too many good things to choose from? What do I do then?" I murmured the quiet words aloud and the woman next to me on the plane gave me a strange look. As the plane landed on the tarmac, I wondered if Caleb would miss me when I moved away or if Jenna would try to swoop in to fill the void.

"What have you done to yourself?" Amanda swept me into a hug that threatened to crush my bones when she found me in the airport. Her blond hair tickled my face as I hugged her back.

"What do you mean?" I glanced down at my ensemble nervously as I pulled myself from her arms. *I hadn't been gone from the city that long, had I? Surely fashion couldn't have changed that much in a few weeks? Could it?*

"Your hair, your skin, your eyes. You're positively glowing, Sammie. I've never seen you look so gorgeous. What are they feeding you out there?"

I laughed in instant relief. "Mostly freshly-laid eggs, sun-ripened berries picked from the vine, and lots of hand-churned butter and homemade cheese to be honest."

Amanda rolled her eyes and licked her lips. "Stop. You are making me drool. I fully expect to eat myself into a food coma this week."

"You're still coming back with me, right?

"Wild horses couldn't keep me away. I'm going to fall in love with a cowboy, move out to Cascade Valley, and become a country lass."

"I don't think you could make it in the country," I teased as we slid into a waiting ride share. "There aren't very many nail salons and indie coffee shops out there."

"Give me the right man and I certainly could make it." She gave me an exaggerated wink.

"Thanks for picking me up today, by the way."

"Of course. What are best friends for? Are you nervous? This is big."

"I'm very nervous," I admitted. I stared through the window as the driver merged into traffic.

"It's still what you want, right? Tell me you haven't changed your mind, Sammie."

"No, of course not."

"Good. Because this is your whole life ahead of you. Think of all you've worked for over the past few years. All the time you spent volunteering at that youth camp with your ridiculously handsome cowboy. What's his name again?"

"Caleb."

"Right, Caleb. He may be dreamy, but you deserve this chance to make your own dreams come true."

I nodded silently, feeling the pressure building in my chest. The feeling hadn't lifted by the time I walked into the restaurant that evening to meet the woman who would be interviewing me.

"Samantha." I recognized her from our calls. The elegant woman rose from the table and extended her hand to shake mine. Her voice had the soft, Spanish accent I immediately recognized from our phone calls. Luxurious dark hair hung down her back. She was petite and poised, and I immediately felt too tall and clumsy next to her. It was a relief when she suggested that we sit and order some dinner. "How good of you to come," she said. "And what a pleasure to meet you in person. I'm so glad that we could connect before I leave the States."

"The pleasure is mine, Sofia." I tried to calm my nervous energy as I settled across from her at the small table. I picked up my water glass and took a small sip to wet my dry throat.

"I feel like we've exchanged so many emails and spoken on the phone so many times that I know you already," Sofia said with a smile. I smiled back. "But I still have so many questions. Tell me more about yourself and why you want to move all the way to Europe to work in an orphanage."

I took a deep breath and uttered a silent prayer for help. Then I plunged into the conversation that would determine the fate of my future.

•   •   •

"It's so beautiful here," Amanda squealed, staring at the pastures and fields that lay scattered all around us. She'd been repeating the words at intervals since we'd left Bozeman and the land began to spread itself before us. The windows were down, and the mid-summer breeze blew through our hair. A grin lit up her face and sparkles danced in her eyes.

She looked so pretty and bright and happy that I wondered if letting her spend the week in the company of my brothers was the right decision. I hadn't been too worried about her suddenly falling in love with the country-life, but the delighted look on her face as she pointed out herds of cows and groves of trees hinted that I could be proven wrong.

"This is your property?" she asked as we turned onto the pine-lined driveway leading to my home. I nodded, but she kept chattering. "I cannot believe how beautiful everything is. You must be rich."

"Technically most of the ranch belongs to my mom. I only own a small stake in the operation. And we aren't rich by any means, but my dad did a good job building up our herd and it has paid off," I admitted. "Ranching is hard, costly work though. It's a good thing my brothers love the life so they can carry on his legacy."

She leaned forward as our farmhouse came into view. "Gosh, give me one of your good-looking brothers and a cute farmhouse and I might have to just move out here with you."

"It's not all flower-studded pastures and banjo-playing under the stars," I inserted quickly. "It's long, dirty, and tiring days. But I must admit that ranching and growing your own food really makes you feel like you've accomplished something."

"I can see why you are so tan and vibrant looking this summer. It's amazing out here."

I wasn't surprised to see that my brothers were home when we dragged Amanda's luggage through the front door. We didn't often have visitors. Especially not pretty, giggly ones like my friend.

"Oh, your house is just as cute as it can be. Well, hello there," she exclaimed as we walked into the kitchen.

Dean, Vincent, and Knox were stationed across the room. The smell of herbed vegetables and grilled meat wafted through the windows. I caught the distinctive scent of a gooseberry pie in the oven.

"Well, hello there back." Knox took the handle of her suitcase and wheeled it aside. "I'm Knox McCade."

"I remember you, Knox," Amanda laughed, her pretty white teeth flashing in a smile. She pointed to my older brothers. "And you're Vincent and you're Dean."

"It's a pleasure to see you again." Both men grinned at her, their eyes darting to Knox who stood staring boldly at Amanda as if he couldn't bring himself to drag his eyes away. I resisted the urge to roll my own eyes.

"What are you boys up to?" I motioned to the plates and dishes scattered across the countertops.

"We thought you ladies would like a late lunch after a long day of travel." Dean winked at me. "You're not a vegan or anything, are you, Amanda?"

"It depends on the week, Dean." She fluttered her eyelashes at him.

"I've got organic, grass-fed steaks on the grill. They'll melt in your mouth."

"In that case, I absolutely must try them."

I rolled my eyes and laughed. "So, my friend comes to visit and suddenly you three become chefs? Where has this effort been since I moved back home? I'd like someone to cook for me too."

"You're just our little sister," Knox teased. "We don't have to impress you."

Amanda plucked a slice of tomato from the cutting board where Knox was making a chopped salad. She popped it into her mouth and glanced at me, her smile saucy. "I could get used to this."

After lunch, we took our iced teas onto the porch to linger as the afternoon waned slowly into evening. "Gosh, your brothers are the cutest," Amanda said. "They can cook, run a ranch, ride horses, wrangle cattle, chop firewood. And I forgot how handsome they are too. None of them have girlfriends?"

"Dean and Knox have been dating two women from town. I'm not sure how serious they are about each other though. Vincent is so quiet that a woman is going to have to ask him out first." The sense of guilt that I always felt at the thought of leaving again spread through my chest. My family deserved more than being blindsided with an announcement that I was about to move across the Atlantic Ocean. Once I shared the news, was everything going to change between us?

My thoughts remained pensive throughout the rest of Amanda's stay. I couldn't shake the feeling that something bad was coming. I began to lay awake well into the night, wondering if God's promise that '*He would give us the desires of our heart*' also included so much doubt and apprehension? Shouldn't my decision and path be clearer if He was leading me into ministry overseas? Why was I so excited and scared at the same time?

Seeing Caleb again didn't ease my doubts at all. The day after we returned from Seattle, I pulled up in front of his farmhouse with Amanda in tow. My eyes did a quick scan across the grounds as we exited the truck. I spotted the man I was searching for almost immediately.

He was riding Beau, who had finally reached a stage in his training that he could safely be ridden in controlled environments. Caleb had been venturing out with him more and more. It had taken more than a little effort to tame the spirited horse. Shivers had run down my spine more than once as I'd watched Caleb work patiently in the arena with the colt. To my shock, a lifetime of equestrian knowledge had begun to set in again and I could see the potential Caleb was trying to coax out of him. But I'd discovered also that I had complete confidence that Caleb would turn Beau into the horse he was meant to become. Strangely, that's what Caleb's presence did to me. It made me feel safe and secure.

He was leading the current group of campers in a game of mock barrel racing, prairie stump style. Each rider was challenged to maneuver their horse around three small barrels placed at intervals across the yard. The rider who didn't bump the obstacles and completed the course in the shortest amount of time was declared the winner. The game had been a fun way for our campers to develop patience and communication with their assigned horses. Caleb had a knack for designing activities that were fun but that also pushed the boundaries of the riders and forced them to communicate with their horses.

My nerves fluttered a little as Amanda and I walked toward the group. When Caleb spotted us, I waved. The grin he flashed in my direction sent warm tingles rocketing up and down my limbs. Immediately, he nudged Beau forward. I flushed and turned to Amanda as he approached. "Amanda, this is Caleb Kane, the owner of this ranch. He's the one who launched the summer camp. Caleb, this is my friend from college, Amanda."

She gave me a look that I didn't have time to decipher before turning back to flash her exuberant smile at Caleb.

He tipped the brim of his hat toward her. "Pleased to meet you. Nice of you to visit." His eyes shifted between us.

"The pleasure's all mine." Amanda approached Beau boldly. "Is this handsome boy yours?" She stroked his muzzle.

"For now he is," Caleb replied.

"What are the chances that you have an extra one of these beauties around for me to ride?"

"The chances are good." He lifted his arm and waved in the direction of the stables. "Griff," Caleb called. "Saddle up Greta for Miss Amanda here, please." He glanced down at her. "I wouldn't have taken you for a rider."

"Oh, I love riding," she gushed. "It's been a while since I had the chance, but I took lots of dressage lessons as a teen."

Caleb nodded in my direction. "Ever since one of the mares took off running down the trail with Samantha and nearly bucked her right into the creek, I haven't been able to convince her to ride again."

The two of them exchanged a laugh. Amanda turned to me. "I would have thought you to be an excellent horsewoman, Sammie. Having grown up around all these cowboys…."

Her tone was teasing, but I couldn't help but feel a little offended. Amanda knew that I was afraid of horses. I nearly told Caleb to saddle up a horse for me too but stopped myself just in time. A short while later, Griff led Greta to her. She accepted the reins and stroked Greta's soft nose. With a quick, graceful movement, Amanda swung herself on Greta's back. I felt a flash of envy as she settled her small frame into the saddle.

"I haven't ridden Western in a while," she laughed. "Do you care if I join Caleb and the kids in their game?"

"Absolutely not. I have some work to finish up anyways. I'll be on the porch if you need me." I waved her off, plastering a pleasant smile across my face. Trust Amanda to zero in on Caleb.

She was quick to ask me about him the next time we were alone. "Ok, 'fess up. Why didn't you tell me that Caleb Kane is just about the nicest man on the planet? Besides your adorable brothers, of course? I thought you said he was an awful man."

"He can be nice when he wants to be." I skirted around the subject, avoiding her gaze.

"I'll bet. I thought you two were mortal enemies and that you were just using him to get the experience on your resume. Why do I constantly catch him looking at you like you're a ripe peach?"

I blushed and shook my head, my hair shaking wildly around my shoulders. "He most certainly does not look at me like that."

She sat on my bed and drew her legs up under her. "Oh, but he does, my dear. What have you been up to since you left Seattle? Is there something that I should know about?"

"Why would you even say that?" I wanted her to drop the topic, but Amanda pursued it with her usual relentlessness.

"There is something going on. I can see it written all over your face. You know I'm not going to stop until you tell me the truth. So, you might as well be honest."

I buried my face in my hands, feeling the heat spread into my fingers. "Ok, he kissed me. We've kissed. A few times now."

"What?" She bounced forward and pulled my hands away from my face, her tone rising in pitch.

"Be quiet," I pleaded. "I don't want my brothers to hear."

"You mean they don't know?"

"They caught us together one night, but we haven't really talked about it."

"I guess it would be rather weird if you did discuss it," she mused. "But what happened after he kissed you?"

He kissed me again. And several more times after that. And each time, it felt like the sun had burst through the clouds after a rainstorm. Aloud, I said, "Nothing can come of it anyway. I'm leaving. Remember?"

She shook her head at me. Her brow furrowed. "Europe? Or an epic love story with Caleb? That's almost an impossible choice. I sure do hope you know what you're doing."

I have no clue what I'm doing anymore. I stopped myself before I could admit out loud that I was more confused about the future than ever.

Amanda spent a few days in the valley and on her last day, we lingered in the sunshine, playing games with the kids and picking ripe berries from the forest just up the road. I had to admit that I was surprised at how quickly Amanda had adapted to the daily routine of our simple country life. She'd jumped in eagerly to help with chores, rounding up the chickens at dusk, even happily mucking out stalls for the goats and our milk cow. Her bright personality and Southern charm had also been a hit with the teens who were currently camping at the ranch.

Amanda made a natural camp counselor, and she didn't seem to mind a bit that most of our time together had been spent managing one chore or another. I had to admit, having a woman around who didn't glare at me as I often caught Jenna doing had been refreshing.

"Don't get me wrong. I love my life in Seattle," she had said a few times over the week. "But a girl could get used to this."

Now, I watched as she pulled her cell phone from her back pocket for the fifth time that afternoon. "You've been glued to that thing all day. Are you talking to someone special that I should know about?"

"Oh, you want me to spill all my secrets now?" she teased, glancing in Caleb's direction with raised eyebrows. "But if you must know, I just might have planned a little surprise for you."

"A surprise for me?"

"Yes. Because you are my dear, dear friend and the environment you, Caleb, and these volunteers have provided for these kids is truly amazing."

"Thank you," I replied. "But what has that got to do with a surprise?"

"Oh, you'll see," she said, looking over her shoulder toward the driveway. "Your surprise should be arriving any second now. And there he is."

She took off running up the drive, hands waving above her head, her long golden hair blowing behind her in the breeze. I shaded my eyes from the sun with my hand, peering at the car that was stirring up a trail of dust in its wake. The sedan had just turned off the road and was clearly a rental.

It wasn't until the car was within a few yards of me that I recognized the driver. "Jake," I shouted, running forward to greet him. Excitement and embarrassment immediately vied for first place in my brain. I was happy to see my friend, but after our last encounter, I had to admit that I was shocked to see him in Cascade Valley again so soon. "What are you doing here?"

Jake stepped from the car and extended his arms to me. Quickly, I moved forward to give him a hug. Amanda joined us and for the next few minutes, the space around us erupted into laughter, teasing, and good-natured jokes.

"So, what are you doing here?" I asked again when the flurry of greeting had simmered down.

"Amanda didn't tell you?" Jake replied. "She asked me to come back out to do a follow-up piece on the horse camp. She said that what you're doing here is so incredible that the rest of the country needs an update."

"You came all this way to write a follow-up piece?" I exclaimed in delighted surprise. Suddenly, I was overwhelmed with emotion. We moved away from his rental car and toward the head of the trail, where I could see a group of teens returning from a ride on the paths that led to the back of Caleb's property.

"I certainly did," Jake replied. "Sounds like you really worked wonders for this little place. I must admit that I had my doubts when I came out here the first time. I wondered if you were going to end up totally throwing away your opportunity to pad your resume this summer."

His lack of faith in the camp caught me by surprise. His lack of faith in me was an even greater surprise. But before I could turn back to him to protest, his arm flew up in greeting.

Jake waved as Caleb came into view. Caleb's horse danced through the tall grasses that blew in the steady breeze. He spurred the horse into a trot. As he grew closer, I watched his lips narrow under his beard. Caleb stared at Jake, a displeased expression across his face. Immediately, I wondered if he'd assumed that I'd invited Jake to the ranch again. I wished that I could tell him I was just as surprised to see my friend as he was.

The stern expression on Caleb's face had shifted into a neutral one by the time he dismounted. With long strides, he came forward and extended a welcoming hand. "I'm surprised to see you back in our valley so soon." The statement was for Jake, but Caleb dropped his gaze to me.

"My editor sent me out to do a follow-up piece for the paper. I hope you don't mind that I just showed up? Amanda wanted it to be a surprise for Samantha."

"Not at all," Caleb replied smoothly. The two men fell into stride together, quickly outpacing Amanda and I. Caleb's horse trailed behind them. "Happy to see you out here anytime."

"Your suitors meet again," Amanda whispered dramatically as we watched them. "Who will win the fair maiden's hand?" Her elbow dug into my side, and I flushed with embarrassment.

"Don't be ridiculous," I whispered back. Then louder, "I'll let Caleb show him around and answer questions. I'll be over there if you need me." I pointed to the far stable, where the recently returned riders were grooming their horses on the yard.

Later, when the sun had set, evening chores were done, and both campers and counselors were gathered around a fire to make smores, Jake dropped onto the stump next to mine. I smiled at him and handed him a large marshmallow from the bag. My brothers had joined us after dinner. They relaxed on camp chairs, legs outstretched, exchanging stories with Jake. Caleb sat across the fire from me, his head bent as he showed some of the boys camping with us this week how to tie a few fancy knots. They were glued to his every move.

I watched as his fingers deftly weaved a rope in and out. Laughter and boyish shouts filled the balmy night air.

I breathed deeply of the smoky scent of the fire and the roasting marshmallows, my brain filling with memories of childhood campfires. The night was still and deep, the soothing melody of crickets echoing in the grass. Coming home for the summer had given me more questions than answers, but I was glad that I was here.

Caleb had lingered in my vicinity most of the day. Every time I turned my head, he was in my line of sight. Jenna had been fluttering in my orbit too, drawn in by Jake's friendly banter. I knew that I had to talk to Caleb about Europe. The thought of having to walk away from our second chance at romance before we'd even seen where it could lead made me sick to my stomach. But the thought of leading him on made me even sicker.

I was lost in thought, nibbling a toasty marshmallow straight off the stick, when Jake tapped my arm. Amanda was seated on the log next to him. They were laughing about some memory of our adventures in Seattle, but I'd tuned them out a few minutes ago.

"We've made some good memories, haven't we?" He nudged my arm a second time.

I smiled in his direction, including Amanda in the expression. "Our group of friends certainly has had some great times."

Jake sighed dramatically. Out of the corner of my eye, I saw Caleb lift his head and glance at our little group. I cast him a small smile. "We really have. Life just hasn't been quite the same since we all grew up and got grownup jobs. Look at you, Samantha. The most grown up of us all. Taking a job and moving to Spain. You're really following your dreams."

Instantly, the night slowed to a screeching halt. Externally, everything began to move in slow motion. Internally, my mind raced as I processed what Jake had just said. My neck snapped up and my marshmallow stick dropped onto the dirt. I tried to speak, but the words fell out of my brain. Panic gathered in my throat. My hand flew up to cover my mouth and I cut my eyes toward my brothers, praying that they hadn't heard what Jake had just said.

By the astonished expressions written across their faces, his words had been heard loud and clear. Jenna made a noise that sounded like a cross between a cough and a snicker, but I was too busy staring at Caleb's face to glare at her. His eyes met mine in the rust-red glow of the leaping flames. His body had gone still, but his hands never stopped tying knots in the rope.

"Just don't forget about all your old friends when you're basking on the beach in the south of France next summer," Jake continued, smashing chocolate and marshmallow between two sweet crackers, oblivious to the bomb he'd just set off in the middle of our circle. The crackle of the fire and the contented chatter of sleepy teens were the only sounds once his voice fell silent.

"Samantha?" It was Vincent who spoke first. My heart dropped at the disappointment in his tone. "This is news. What is Jake talking about?"

My eyes dropped to the ground, waves of shame washing over me. I should have been honest long ago. I'd never intended for them to find out by accident.

"You mean she hasn't told you?" Jake looked from me to my brothers. "Samantha, I'm surprised. You should be proud of your accomplishment."

I wanted to glare at him, but I couldn't rustle up the anger. All I wanted to do was cry. I couldn't look at anyone but Caleb. I wished I could look away, but his unrelenting gaze held me firmly in place. Every second that passed was a dagger in my chest.

"Um, tell us what, Sammie?" Knox's voice urged me to speak. "What is Jake talking about?"

"Sorry if I wasn't supposed to say anything," Jake piped up, his voice full of sudden regret.

"I'm sorry, Sammie. I'm the one who told him." Amanda sounded stricken. "I didn't realize it was a secret."

I ignored my friends and tried to steady my voice. "I was going to tell you guys sooner, but I hadn't found the right time. I applied for a director's position at an orphanage in Spain. It's in Madrid actually and you know how much I've always wanted to travel through Europe. Anyways, I had an interview and…I was offered the position." My voice trailed off lamely.

"Wow, Samantha. That's really amazing." It was Jenna's voice that broke the heavy silence first.

Sofia had offered the position to me the same night that I'd interviewed over dinner. The offer had weighed heavily on me ever since. I'd wanted to announce it right away to my entire family, but I had been too nervous and too ecstatic. Everything was going so well. Our little corner of Cascade Valley was so peaceful. I was happy. And I hadn't wanted to break the spell.

I hoped that my family could understand that this was my calling. I was following my dream, just as our sister, Demi, had done. She'd left Cascade Valley soon after high school to pursue a modeling contract in New York. She was happy and successful now. This is what young women did. They went to college, they got a degree, they made plans, and they spread their wings to fly from the nest. But if this was what I was supposed to do, I wondered why I felt so sad about it.

"Samantha." Dean cleared his throat. His voice had deepened. "This is big news. Congratulations. You're going to take Madrid by storm."

Somehow, his kind words made my heart sink even lower. The tension around the campfire was so thick that I could have scooped it up like ice cream and deposited it on top of a big slice of humble pie. I knew that my brothers were disappointed that I'd kept this from them, but they were too gracious to make a big deal of it in front of my friends. I knew that they would wait to talk about it until Amanda and Jake were gone.

I looked at Caleb again, my eyes pleading with him to understand.

"You're leaving to take a new job?" Caleb shook his head, as if he was still trying to process the information.

"Yes. In a few weeks."

He stood abruptly, motioning to the boys who were busy practicing the knots that he'd showed them. "Night's over, boys. Head to the tents."

They protested but complied.

"That's going to be great for you. Congratulations," he said to me. Then he led the group toward the campsite where the tents had already been pitched. Everyone else took his cue and stood up, brushing off their pants and yawning.

"I'd better head back," Jake turned to me. "I always sleep so well in the country."

"Where are you staying?" I asked, barely registering his presence enough to form the question. My brain was too busy walking through the darkness with Caleb. I wondered what would happen if I ran after him and slipped my hand into his. Would he push it away?

"At the inn in town. I'm going to drive to your place in the morning to pick up Amanda. I'll give her a ride to the airport."

"Thanks for coming today." I didn't really mean the words. I would have meant them a half hour ago. Now, I was just sorry that I'd ever invited Jake to the ranch to write a story in the first place. When he reached for me, I gave him a half-hearted hug and wished that I had a time travel machine so that I could go back to the beginning of this summer and do it all over again.

Chapter Twenty-One

I KNEW IT wasn't a good sign that my brothers were still in the house when Amanda left the next morning. Instead of finishing up the morning's chores, they lingered as we waited for Jake. Politely, they helped with her luggage and shook Jake's hand when he arrived to pick her up. But the rental car had barely rumbled up the driveway when the three of them appeared in the living room.

I was at the window, watching Jake's sedan, wondering if I should have packed a bag and escaped to the city with them. Amanda had pulled me into a bone-crushing hug before she'd climbed into Jake's car.

"Everything's going to be ok," she'd whispered in my ear. "If you need a place to stay, my door is always open." And then she was gone, leaving me alone in my childhood home.

Sighing, I turned and faced my brothers. I had been awake all night, dreading the morning's light.

Dean motioned us back to the kitchen. "We've made some fresh coffee. Could we sit and have a talk, Samantha." My family usually only dropped their nicknames for me when it was serious.

"Of course." I marched past the three men. I kept my back straight, my shoulders squared, and my head held high. If they were going to make me talk about what had been revealed last night, I was going to make sure I kept my dignity. There was no way I was going to let them know that I was teetering on the brink of bursting into tears. Or that the guilt I felt was so heavy it was crushing my chest.

Life felt like it had overturned in the space of a few hours. If my brothers gave me any grief over my decision, I was ready to argue. I wished Caleb would argue with me. I wished he'd yell at me, tell me off, or otherwise say what was on his mind. I'd barely been able to get a response to my text messages and his calm, polite replies were driving me crazy.

ME: I want to talk about this. To explain.

CALEB: Is there anything to talk about though? If I know you, you've already made a decision. I'm happy for you.

CALEB: I need to get back to work.

I accepted the mug of coffee that Knox handed to me and clutched it, needing the heat seeping through the ceramic to warm my chilled hands. Sinking onto a chair, I leaned my elbows on the table, wondering if the headache creeping along my temples was going to turn into a full-blown migraine by the time this conversation was finished. Each of my brothers took a seat across the table from me, mugs of steaming black coffee in their own hands.

"So…." Vincent was the first to break the silence. I glanced up, surprised that Dean hadn't been appointed spokesperson for my judge and jury this morning. Somehow the fact that my most tender-hearted brother and his deep, gentle voice was the first to speak tore open my heart a little more. I sucked in a deep breath and exhaled sharply to regain control of my emotions.

"Samantha, help us to understand what's been going on this summer. Will you tell us more about the job in Europe?" Vincent continued.

I took another deep breath. "First of all, I want to say that I'm truly sorry the three of you found out like that last night. I don't believe either Jake or Amanda knew that I was waiting until the right time to tell you." I found myself choosing my words carefully, wanting to set myself up for the conversation the best I could.

"Why didn't you just tell us when you moved back home?" Knox interjected. "That would have made sense. This just looks like you've been sneaking around."

"Nothing was for sure." My voice rose an octave. "I didn't think that there was any point in making a big scene out of it if nothing ever materialized."

"But this is huge. We knew that there was a possibility of you moving out of state. This is Europe." Knox's voice rose and Dean quickly raised his hand. His tone was stern, but it was directed toward my youngest brother.

"Ok, let's not get worked up." He shifted into a gentler tone as he looked at me. "Obviously, we knew when you moved back home that it wouldn't be for forever. But we thought you would end up in New York with Demi or back in Seattle for work."

"We never expected you to run halfway across the world," Knox interrupted. Dean gave him a look and Knox fell silent.

"But we do want to make sure you're not making a rash decision. We love you and want what's best for you." My oldest brother stretched his hand across the table. I placed my hand on his palm. His fingers curled, swallowing up my smaller hand. "Surely you can find a job closer to home? There aren't any non-profit foundations you want to work at in the States?"

I shook my head, tears beginning to roll down my cheeks. Using my free hand, I reached up and dashed them away. "This is just something I need to do. Ever since my sophomore year when Dad talked about taking a trip to Europe as a family, I've dreamed about visiting. Do you remember him telling us that he'd visited as a teen with Grandma and Grandpa? It was a memory he wanted to pass onto us. And he never got the chance." My voice nearly failed on the last sentence.

A pained expression passed over Dean's face. "What happened to Dad was a tragedy. None of us have fully healed from the pain of losing him." He glanced at our brothers for confirmation. They both nodded solemnly. "But you don't have to chase Dad's dream. Living there is quite different than visiting."

I nodded, sniffling. "I know. But you don't understand what this means to me. All my life I've been the little sister. The annoying little sister who is always trying to keep up with her older siblings. Demi moved to New York. She's busy pursuing her dream. You three are obviously developing something big and important out here with your efforts to create a regenerative ranch. And then there's me. What do I have to offer the world?"

"You don't have to move halfway across the world to make a difference," Vincent's gentle words broke into my pause.

I flattened my hands on the worn table. So many meals had been eaten here, so many nights spent playing games or doing homework, so many memories made. The wood scratched softly against my skin. "No, I don't. But this is what I'm called to do. I've been so blessed with the life we have here. That's why I must go. There are children out there who need someone who cares. Spain is just the beginning of how much good I can do."

My brothers exchanged glances. Knox ran a hand through his hair in a frustrated gesture. Dean's lips tightened. Only Vincent met my gaze calmly. "The real question is simple. Is this what the Lord wants you to do?"

Even as I shook my head, a shiver of doubt raced through my chest. "Yes. I truly believe this is where He is leading me."

Vincent sat back and lifted his hands. "Then that's all there is to it. When do you leave?"

"In just a few weeks."

Collectively, they exhaled. "Well, then let's make the most of the time we have together, shall we?" Dean said for the three of them. "If this is what you want, we will support you."

"Like heck we will," Knox protested. Dean cut a sharp look over to him and with a quick shake of his head, Knox relented. "I mean, it's going to be tough letting you go, but I'll try my best."

Fresh tears sparked in my eyes. I reached across the table. They stretched out to grasp my hand. "Thank you. You have no idea what your support means to me." I tried to hold my emotions in check. The floodgates were going to be released when I was alone again.

Dean rubbed his fingers across the back of my hand. I could sense him preparing to say something else and I wanted to run away. I couldn't take any more emotional hits today.

"There is something else." It was Vincent who took the lead again. "We've tried to stay out of it, but this must be said. We don't really understand what's been going on between you and Caleb. You went from barely speaking to being unable to keep your eyes off each other. You do owe him an explanation for this."

"And an apology," Dean interjected. I felt my face flush.

"He knew all along that I wasn't planning to stay in Cascade Valley. I never lied to him about that," I protested.

"But you didn't tell him that you were planning to move to Europe." Dean shook his head.

I wasn't sure what the three of them were upset about the most. My move or the fact that they thought I'd led on their friend. And they were right. I'd let something begin with Caleb that should never have begun at all.

"We weren't even dating," I replied hotly. "I never said we were beginning a relationship. He said he liked me. I said I liked him. We agreed to get to know each other better and keep things casual."

"If he said he liked you," Knox barked. "That means that he has just been waiting for you to come around and realize how serious he is about you."

My eyes stung. "Thanks for making me feel worse." I pushed back my chair and stood abruptly. I turned and fled upstairs. My cheeks were stained with tears by the time I locked myself in my room.

When lunchtime rolled around, I had come to a decision. I came downstairs, wearing a comfortable dress and sneakers, wheeling my suitcase across the scarred wooden floor. All three of my brothers stopped what they were doing and froze at the sight of me.

"What's this?" Dean said.

I took a deep breath. "I know you'll say this is taking the easy way out, but I can't stay here. I can't go back to camp right now. I need a break. I need to get away. and I need to think. I'm going to visit Demi. I've been meaning to go up there. She'll want to see me before I move anyways and...."

I couldn't think of anything else to say. Everything felt like it was crashing around me all at once. I needed to think, to process what had happened. My sister and her tiny, cozy apartment in New York City felt like a safe place from the storm.

"But what about Mom? She'll be home tomorrow," Knox protested.

"I just can't stay."

"And what about the youth camp?"

I shook my head. "I can't go back there. Not if Caleb hates me now."

"I doubt he hates you," Dean said. "Have you spoken to him yet?"

"He just keeps saying that if this is what I want to do, that I should do it."

The three of them exchanged a look.

"I'll drive you to the airport," Vincent spoke, drying his hands on a dish towel. "Do you need to leave right away?"

I nodded, afraid to speak. "I'm on standby."

My eyes hurt and I didn't want to cry anymore. Knox and Dean came up to hug me. Their arms wrapped around me so tightly that it made up for some of the crushing disappointment that I knew they felt in my decisions.

"Take some time," Dean whispered in my ear. "We'll be here for you when you get back. It's going to be okay."

He felt a lot more confidence than I did.

• • •

Demi was overjoyed to see me. I'd forgotten how much I'd missed her smile until I saw her face light up at the sight of me. I fell into her arms the second I stepped out of the terminal. It had been a long journey, but her hug felt like a safe harbor from the storm I'd created around myself. Familiar, comforting, and safe.

"I turn my head and suddenly you are all grown up and spreading your wings." She breathed softly against my hair.

"And making a huge mess of things along the way," I moaned.

"Come home with me and I'll make butter noodles and we'll have a long chat."

Demi stretched her long legs along the sofa later. We were in her apartment, high above the never-ending rush of New York City. Night had fallen long ago, yet the ever-present twinkling lights of the cityscape never seemed to fade. "But why so many secrets? Why didn't you just tell us your plans right away? You know we will always support you."

"I guess I was just afraid that nothing would ever come of it or that you would all try to talk me out of it," I shrugged, setting my empty pasta bowl on the coffee table. Butter and parmesan dotted the bottom of the bowl. The simple dish was a comfort recipe my family had been making for many years.

I looked around the small room—kitchen, dining, and living room merged into one. The space bore my sister's elegant, effortless touch. I found myself envying her simple, minimalist approach to life. Demi didn't complicate everything. Demi didn't overthink every little action and word. She made decisions and good things just seemed to fall into place for her.

I'd come to New York to visit Demi last summer. After the confining space of my shared college apartment, her tiny, but pretty home had felt like a doorway to the excitement of the city that lay just beyond the threshold. It had been a magical summer, my first visit to such a grownup city as an adult. Yet, after weeks in Montana—under skies so clear that you could count the stars—I wondered how my sister could endure the constant noise.

"And Caleb. How in the world did that ever happen?" She shook her head incredulously, her dark silky hair brushing across her slim shoulders.

"I guess he grows on a person," I replied shyly. "Turned out, I had misjudged him. I'm surprised he ever spoke to me again after I accused him of negligence in front of the whole church. But he seems to like me despite my flaws."

The unspoken reminder of our father caused us both to fall silent for a long moment. I picked at a stray piece of fuzz on my sweatpants. "I like Caleb," I continued. "But we were just flirting over the summer. There couldn't possibly be anything long term between us."

Demi's stunning emerald eyes stared at me. A light smattering of freckles were scattered across her cheeks. An expression that I couldn't read crossed her face. "And why is that?"

"How could we ever be more than friends? Why would the Lord fulfill my dream of living in Europe, just to take it away by making me fall in love with a man whose life is rooted in the very location that I wanted to leave in the first place?"

"Are you falling in love with Caleb Kane?"

"No!" I protested, lifting my hands to cover the blush on my face. "I don't really know. But I can't deny that it would be easy to let those feelings grow."

Demi reached over and pried my hands away from my face. Her long, gentle fingers held onto mine, caressing the skin on the back of my hands softly.

"If there's one truth that I've learned over the past few years it is that our Heavenly Father is not a God of confusion. But I've also learned that while He will plant a vision and a calling in our hearts, His ways are not our ways. Train your heart to be open to His gentle persuasion. Remember to *Trust in the Lord with all your heart and lean not on your own understanding; in all your ways submit to Him and He will make your paths straight.*"

"Proverbs 3," I murmured instinctively, years of Sunday school lessons flooding my brain. "I feel like I'm wading through quicksand, Demi. There's pros and cons to every decision I make. How can I possibly know what the Lord wants of me when I just feel so bogged down and confused?"

"That's where trust and submission to His will come in. It takes practice, but if I know you, I know you'll dig and dig until you find the answers you're looking for."

I stared at our intertwined hands thoughtfully. The memory of Caleb's rough, calloused hand holding mine as we'd watched the sunset dip below the mountain peaks echoed in my mind. It hadn't taken long to discover that he was an enigma of a man. I didn't understand his quiet strength. It was the opposite of my fiery nature and desire to be heard. Caleb didn't let anyone run over him, yet he also forgave easily. He exuded masculine strength, yet I'd watched him care tenderly for a frail, elderly woman like she was his own grandmother. He was eternally polite, but I appreciated the way he often responded to my sharp tongue with a gruff reply of his own. Most of the time, I knew where I stood with him. I didn't have to guess. There weren't any games. Caleb was steady, and loyal, and true to his faith and his convictions. I liked that about him. More than liked. Respected.

It was time to admit, at least to myself, that I had a crush on a cowboy. Maybe it was even more than a crush. But was a budding romance enough to give up a lifetime of dreams? As I tossed and turned restlessly on Demi's couch later that night, I wondered if I would ever find the answer.

Chapter Twenty-Two

"SEÑORITA MCCADE?" THE lilting voice spoke softly at my side. I turned to smile at the small child standing next to my desk. Her lustrous eyes gazed at me solemnly.

"Yes, Alondra. What can I help you with?" I reached out and pulled her onto my lap. Smoothing the dark hair falling over her eyes, I hugged her tightly. The child was sweet and frail and precious, like the pretty lark she was named after. My heart ached to know that her parent's fatal accident a year ago had left her alone and in need of a new home.

I had been pleased to discover that the orphanage in Spain was cozy. Nothing like the cold, sterile institutions I'd read about as a child. There were plenty of children her age to play with. The staff were loving and kind. There was plenty of good, nourishing food to fill hungry bellies thanks to generous donors, but there was nothing like the love of a real mother and father to soothe the aching heart of a child. I just hoped that I could add back in a little of the affection that these children had missed since becoming orphans.

"Mateo doesn't want to play with me." Alondra's lower lip protruded, and I saw tears fill her eyes. "He told me to go away." A tear rolled down her soft cheek.

"Maybe Mateo is just having a hard day?" I spoke to her in Spanish, forever grateful that I'd become fluent in the language between high school and college. "Let's go talk to him and see if we can cheer him up." I set her on the tiled floor and took her hand in mine. Together we walked from the small office that I used toward the playroom.

A wide sliding glass door at the far end of the large room opened onto a pretty lawn. It was dotted with children's toys and activity centers. The house and property had been donated by a generous couple a few years after they'd lost their own son in a boating accident. Despite the fast approach of winter, the Spanish afternoon sun was still warm on our skin. Olive and fruit trees dotted the lawn.

A young woman on staff as a caretaker was standing in the yard. Catalina waved when she saw me appear in the doorway with Alondra. "I see she found you." She smiled and nodded at the two of us.

"Yes." I squeezed Alondra's hand. "We're looking for Mateo."

Catalina gestured toward the stone fence at the far end of the property. "He is playing by himself over there." We exchanged knowing glances.

Alondra and I found the small boy sitting by himself. He was leaning against the cold stone, knees drawn up to his chest. A miserable expression was painted across his face, and I ached at the sight of his sadness. He'd been left on the doorstep of the local nunnery as a mere days-old infant five years ago, moving around the system ever since. He had arrived at the orphanage shortly after I'd settled into the daily routine. I'd been working ever since he arrived to find him a permanent home.

Alondra and I knelt in the dirt next to the small boy. "Mind if we join you?" I asked.

He shrugged, his eyes never lifting from the ground. I reached out and grabbed a small, sturdy stick from the ground. I began to drag it across the dirt, tracing a pattern in the soft soil.

"What are you doing?" Alondra peered at my handiwork.

"I'm drawing a picture of someone special," I replied. "Sometimes when I'm lonely and sad, it helps me to draw a picture of someone who makes me happy. Why don't you try it?"

I found a stick for her and then picked up a second one. "Mateo, why don't you draw a picture too?"

"I have no one special to draw." His soulful eyes lifted briefly to my face, then dropped back down to the ground.

"Oh, surely you do," I said gently. "There are so many who love you, Mateo. Alondra and I, Señorita Catalina, and Señora Sofia. All the other children here at home too."

"This isn't my home."

"It's your home for now. Perhaps there will come a day when you go to a new home, but can you draw us a picture of something that makes you happy right now?"

Reluctantly, he took the extra stick from me. He held it like a pencil and began to scratch at the dirt. Alondra worked quietly and happily beside us. It was quiet for a few minutes in our little corner of the yard. Across the grass, Catalina played a game of catch with several of the other children. Their giggles echoed across the space. Absently, I went back to sketching in the soft ground, my mind tumbling over itself now that I had a quiet moment to think.

"Who is that?" Mateo's question broke into my thoughts, surprising me for a moment. He was watching me, his small face suddenly curious. I was glad to see the spark of light returning to his eyes. I looked down at the rough sketch I'd made in the dirt. A bearded face wearing a cowboy hat stared back at me.

"Someone special," I replied.

"Vaquero," Alondra giggled, pointing to the cowboy hat.

"Yes," I laughed. "Vaquero. Cowboy."

The little girl jumped up. She mimicked galloping across the yard, her arm raised and making a circular motion as she pretended to rope a cow's horns. Her antics drew a short laugh from Mateo.

"What did you draw?" I turned to him. He'd scratched a small house with trees and bushes and a dog running off to the side. A little boy and girl danced next to what I assumed was a creek.

"This would make me happy," he said simply, referencing my earlier request. Quickly, he passed his hand over the surface of the ground, erasing the sketch that he'd made. I laid my hand gently on his shoulder but didn't speak.

"Why don't you go play catch with the other children until dinner?" I suggested softly.

He nodded and the children ran across the yard together. On my way inside, I paused to watch. Many of the children laughed and played with abandon, lost in the throes of childhood games.

Several of them had special needs. A few were refugees who had been temporarily placed here until they could be reunited with a family member from their homeland.

Each child had experienced grief. But it was during these moments of joy that I found myself even more motivated to find them new, forever homes. I never wanted the look of happiness to leave their precious, sweet faces. I turned away, the emails that I still needed to write before dinner present in my mind. But Mateo's sadness ate at me as I worked.

Spain had turned out to be everything I'd ever hoped. I lived in a tiny, furnished apartment, shopped the markets every week, and spent every day in the company of children who deserved all the love I could ever give. I was content. I could see myself having a small, but happy life here in Spain. Yet, I couldn't help but acknowledge the sadness that still often stirred at my consciousness. At night, I often found myself scrolling through photos of my last summer at home, pausing to linger over the ones with Caleb in them. Sometimes, I let a few tears run down my cheeks before I forced myself to regain control of my emotions.

The last time I'd talked to Caleb in person had been shortly after my visit to Demi's in New York. My visit with my sister had lengthened from days into weeks. My mother had just returned to Cascade Valley and kept threatening to fly out to drag me back home. But I'd been stuck in a state of moping that I couldn't shake. I was afraid to return to the mess I'd made of everything.

Then one morning, almost two weeks before I left the States for good, I woke up and finally found the courage to set things right. I bought a plane ticket for Montana that day. When I landed a couple days later, my mother had been waiting outside the terminal for me. I fell into her arms, wishing that I could stay in her safe embrace forever.

True to my brothers' character, they'd welcomed me home with a gentle warmth. I'd spent the next three days wandering through the forest deeply in prayer. I'd wrestled with my future, tears rolling down my face. I still hadn't gone back to Caleb's ranch.

I joined my mother on the porch one particularly hot summer evening. She had motioned to the pitcher of iced tea on the table. We settled together on the swing to watch the sunset, occasionally talking but mostly just letting the soft silence fill the air. She knew everything that had happened since I'd moved home from college.

Mom had stayed up with me for two nights, baking cookies and preserving jam in the kitchen while we talked over everything. When Caleb's truck had rumbled down the driveway as the sun dipped behind the mountains, she rose.

"I'm going to give you two your space. I'll be upstairs if you need me." She'd leaned over to kiss my forehead.

I'd pushed the swing with one bare foot against the weathered porch planks. I hadn't moved as Caleb approached but watched as he'd settled onto the wicker chair near my seat. He'd removed his hat and set it on the table next to the chair. His brown eyes had reflected the auburn rays of the setting sun as he gazed onto the yard.

Caleb had been the first to break the silence. "Why, Samantha?"

I took a deep breath. "I didn't mean to hurt you."

"I'm sure you didn't. But in a way, you did deceive me."

"My omission of the truth was wrong." I tried to be brave as I met his gaze.

"Is this truly what you want? To leave your family, your friends, and the only country you've ever known. It feels like you are banishing yourself. Punishing yourself. Your father never had the chance to pursue this dream, so you feel like you must fulfill it for him."

He must have been talking to my brothers. The frankness of his speech startled me, but I hadn't expected anything less of Caleb. Frustrated energy radiated from his body. His fingers had clamped onto his knees. I could see the tension in his body as he held himself still.

"It isn't a punishment to follow a dream. And it has nothing to do with my father. I can serve so many people out there," I'd protested.

"You can serve people here."

"That is true," I'd admitted softly. "There are plenty of people in need in my own backyard. I'm not arguing that point. But I just feel like God has led me in this direction."

"You're willing to give up your community, your family, and the people who care about you?"

"I'm not giving them up. I'm just taking the love that's been given to me my entire life and trying to plant a seed with it somewhere else."

"And you're just planning to ignore the seeds that have been planted here?" A sudden bitterness had filled his voice. I knew he was referring to us. The fact that we'd gotten a second chance to pursue each other after I'd promised myself that I would always blame him for my dad's accident wasn't lost on me. Flirting with Caleb over the summer and learning to trust him again had finally brought me some of the closure I'd needed. But I didn't know yet if he was meant to be my forever.

"Maybe I'll change my mind," I said quietly. "My contract is for a year. I can reassess my plans after that."

"But what is there to reassess?" Caleb's voice had risen then. "Why bother if this is what you want?"

"It isn't all that I want," I'd replied, my own voice rising to echo Caleb's frustration. He stood abruptly and began to pace the porch in front of me. "I really like you, Caleb. Nothing has changed about that."

"Well, you know what?" He had thrown up his hands and nearly shouted the words. "I don't just like you, Samantha Mccade. I love you."

I'd sat in stunned silence for a long moment. The air had seemed to crackle between us. Then, I leaped to my feet, crossing the porch to plant myself in front of him. "What do you mean you love me?" I demanded.

A sad smile had appeared under his beard. He'd stared down at me, his eyes suddenly soft and filled with sorrow. "Four years ago, we stood at the lookout at my sister's wedding. I almost kissed you then. You had always been such a headstrong, wild-haired, stubborn girl, but suddenly you had become this beautiful young woman almost overnight. There may be seven years between us, but you've always challenged me in a way no other woman has. I was a fool to let you walk away after the accident. I should have pursued you. I should have gone after you."

I had shivered when his fingers brushed my hand, my heart over-flowing at his words. "I think it's always been you for me, Samantha. Life pulled us apart once. And somehow here we are again. If this is your ministry, I won't stand in your way. But my life, my business, and my calling are here. I want to follow you to Europe. I would follow you to the ends of the earth. But I think you need to go and find yourself first."

"And I'm not ready to live here forever," I'd whispered, moving closer to him.

I'd felt like I was stuck between two magnets, opposing forces pulling me both toward and away from the man standing in front of me. Lifting, I had twined my arms around his neck. Without hesitation, his hands had slid around my back, pulling me closer. Our breath had mingled in the heavy summer heat as Caleb leaned forward to rest his forehead against mine. I'd breathed in his scent of fresh hay and the mints he kept in his breast pocket for the horses. His firm body was steady against mine. We stood locked together as the evening faded into twilight.

When his head had dipped lower and he'd brushed his lips against mine, I had lifted onto my toes, longing to be closer to him. "Can I be honest?" I whispered. "I never expected to move home and fall so hard for you, Caleb. It's been the best surprise."

"And I expected you to be exactly how you are and you were still a surprise." He kissed away the tears slipping down my cheeks. "You're still wild and full of sass, with dreams bigger than the Montana sky and a heart that matches."

"We made a really good team this summer," I said.

"If you ever need a summer job, you know where to find me. And I'll be sure to write you a great letter of recommendation."

I'd rolled my eyes at his teasing words but had quickly grown serious. "Thank you for letting me be part of what you've created out here."

He'd only nodded, bending over me again. Our lips met eagerly. They'd brushed together, softly at first, then with an eagerness that had reflected our frustration. Heat radiated in my core. Tangling my fingers in his hair, I'd pulled him closer, chills racing up and down my spine. I should have let him go. But I couldn't. I'd wanted to imprint the moment into my memory.

My heart felt as if it had broken into pieces. Falling for Caleb would have been so easy, but destiny was leading us apart. "I'm so sorry," I'd sobbed against his lips.

His hands had cradled my face. "I just want you to be happy."

"What if I'm making a mistake?"

"It's all going to work out for good," he'd murmured in my ear. "The Lord will never steer you wrong when you place your trust in Him. Follow His calling. And if He wants to lead you home, He will."

I had wrapped my arms around him then and leaned against his chest as he held me, the night deepening softly as the moon rose in the sky.

Chapter Twenty-Three

I'D FOUND AN adoptive family for Mateo. I pushed away from my desk and leaned back in my chair.

They were the perfect family for him, a young couple from Barcelona who'd been married for several years. They'd been vetted thoroughly by our agency, had passed all their background checks, and were just waiting to be placed with a child. The catch? Initially, they'd requested an infant.

The challenge to adoption wasn't placing a newborn into a forever home. It was placing the other hundreds—if not thousands—of children who were quickly aging out of the preferred adoption age range.

Thanks to my networking efforts, I'd been able to place twenty older children from various orphanages around the country into their forever homes since I'd moved to Madrid in late-August. It was now just a few weeks away from Christmas.

I stared at the email I'd just received from Elena, the adoptive mother-to-be.

Tomás and I were just talking. Do you think the agency would approve us for a second child when we adopt Mateo? Built-in siblings. Is there another child who needs a home?

An overflow of emotion bubbled in my chest.

"Thank you, Lord," I murmured under my breath. He was proving to me day-by-day that when I placed my trust in Him, mountains were moved, and lives were changed. If they were willing, I'd recommend Alondra for adoption. She and Mateo were already like brother and sister. Seeing her find a forever home would make my heart burst at the seams.

Elena and Tomás were already scheduled to meet Mateo this week. I didn't plan to tell him the news until I saw how they reacted to each other. I'd make sure Alondra was present at the interview as well.

The week was shaping up to be a good one. Christmas was approaching. I'd already sent off boxes of presents for my family in the States. By this time of year, snow on our Montana mountains had already begun to fall. My brothers would be bringing the herd down from the range. The cattle would work their way through the bales of hay that my brothers had harvested in September as they weathered the long, snowy winter. The season had always been a magical time on the ranch. It was cold outdoors, but our home was always warm and cheerful. Winter in Spain promised to be beautiful, but lately, I had been admitting to myself that I missed home.

Sofia must have sensed my restlessness because she had been urging me to go home for the holidays. "Everyone should spend time with the people they love this time of year," she said, her lustrous eyes watching me closely. "And I think you need to see your family."

I'd waved away her suggestion, assuring her that I was content right where I was. But even I didn't know if I was telling the truth anymore. I kept telling myself that I was happy at the orphanage, but the ache in my heart said differently.

A notification popped onto my screen. With hasty fingers, I slid it open.

MOM: We'll be landing in fifteen minutes.

MOM: I can't wait to see your beautiful face, my precious daughter.

MOM: I hope Spain is ready for me!

The pilot must have just turned off the no cell phone sign. My mother's texts downloaded to me all at once. It hadn't taken her long to plan a visit and she was due to land at the airport any minute. Despite the eight-hour time difference, my family had tried to stay in touch over the past few months. I spoke to Demi often via Skype. My brothers usually communicated through text, checking in on me now and then. Mom face-timed me almost daily, but I couldn't wait to see her in person once again.

When I'd first arrived in Spain, life had been a whirlwind. My new role encompassed management of many day-to-day tasks within the orphanage, but it also required that I spend a great deal of time cultivating connections—with donors and other organizations, both in Europe and across the States. I had put the events of the summer firmly in the back of my mind, promising myself that I would process everything that had happened over the summer later when it wouldn't distract me from my duties.

Despite my efforts, my last conversation with Caleb was often on my mind. I had text him a few times when I first arrived in Spain. His answers were always polite and kind, but eventually, the frequency of our texts grew farther and farther apart. Now, it had been a couple of months since I had last spoken to him. He had done what he'd promised. He had let me go so that I could pursue my dream.

And I missed him. I missed the rasp of his voice and the way a smile would spread slowly across his lips as he tried to maintain his calm composure. I missed the way he challenged me to grow as a person…and the anticipation as he pulled me close to kiss me. I was restless without him just down the road. The empty space in my heart kept growing, but pray and think as I might, I wasn't sure what to do. And I was beginning to doubt that Caleb would hold onto his feelings for me forever. Maybe it was better if we both just let go.

But it wasn't until a little girl named Isabella had asked me where my children lived that I realized what I had done. "I don't have any children," I had replied to her, running my hand over her smooth black hair.

"Your marido?"

"No esposo," I answered. "I'm not married."

"You don't have a home either? No quieres una familia?" The little girl had stroked the back of my hand, her brows knit together with concern.

I'd bit back the tears that suddenly stung my eyes. Before me sat a child whose own family had been stripped away from her. And she was worried that I didn't have a home and family to call my own. She thought we had that in common.

The truth singed itself into my soul. No matter where the Lord would call me to serve, He'd blessed me with a family who loved me. My parents had built a marriage filled with love, respect, admiration, and trust. My siblings and I were the fruit of that foundation. Their example was the greatest gift that I could imagine, and I could no longer deny that it was a legacy I wanted for myself someday as well.

The problem was, I couldn't imagine the future anymore with anyone other than Caleb. And Cascade Valley felt farther away by the day.

. . .

"It's just a little snow, Sammie. You've driven in it a thousand times." My knuckles were white as I gripped the steering wheel and tried to talk myself through the flurries across the road. I leaned forward.

"You could have just let me drive," Demi spoke from the passenger seat. She looked unperturbed, despite my white-knuckled driving.

"I'm a big girl. I've got it," I said, my tone sharper than I intended. "It's just these flurries. They make it so hard to see the road." Tendrils of snow danced across the road like echoes of ghostly fingers. The highway had almost disappeared under the thin layer of white.

"We're almost there anyway. Caleb's driveway is just ahead."

My heart skipped a beat, and I couldn't help but peer ahead to catch a glimpse of the sign, even though we wouldn't be making a stop at the neighboring property. I wondered if Caleb had stayed home for Christmas or if he had traveled to join his parents and older sister. I had wanted to ask my brothers but hadn't had the courage.

My heart skipped a beat at the possibility of seeing him during my brief stay in Cascade Valley. I had so many things that I wanted to say to him before my return to Spain.

Demi and I were headed home to surprise Mom and the boys for Christmas. They were expecting her to arrive today. No one beside my sister knew that I was headed home.

Christmas. A holiday that I'd always loved but had often taken for granted as I'd grown up in my safe, country life.

It was Mom's visit that had pushed me to make the trip back home. I'd burst into tears when she stepped off the plane a few weeks ago.

"Don't cry, honey." Mom had held me close as I'd sobbed on her shoulder next to the airport terminal. "Is it that bad here?"

"No, it's wonderful," I had managed to squeak out between sobs. "The children, the orphanage, the progress I've made here. But I miss home. I miss all of you."

She squeezed me tighter. "We miss you too. Let's get my things and go home and have a good talk. You know, darling, I expected to be welcomed with Spanish wine and tapas. Not tears."

Her teasing tone had brought my laughter to the surface, and I'd looped my arm through hers as we headed for my tiny apartment. We stayed up all night talking, and by the first light of sunrise, my head had felt a hundred times clearer.

"How do I know if God is leading me in a different direction, Mom?" I'd asked her as we strolled the pretty streets after a few hours of rest.

"It's a hard question to answer," she replied. "But when you sense a peace in your spirit and an urging that you can't ignore, you'll know."

"Is it wrong if I change my mind about where I'm supposed to be?"

Her warm brown eyes glanced at me. "There are hurting people all over the world, Sammie. How do you know that you aren't supposed to be helping them closer to home?"

By the time Mom boarded the return flight for home, I'd made up my mind.

When I'd gone to Sofia to see what I could do, she nodded her head. "Sí, sí. I think you need to see your family, Samantha. The time away will do you good."

I hadn't argued but had immediately begun to look for a flight to the States. Demi had agreed eagerly to my plan. I had only been able to book a standby ticket and when I finally was called for a flight, it was a red eye to NYC. I landed the day before Christmas Eve and my sister immediately insisted on dragging me from store to store. We had even visited the salon and nail spa. I imagined that it was only because of her connections in the fashion industry that she was able to schedule so many appointments at the last minute.

"If you're going to show up unannounced, the least you can do is to be a showstopper."

I eyed her skeptically. During my months in Spain, my natural ginger-colored curls had gotten unrulier, and my freckles had intensified their takeover of my face. I'd taken to wearing a simple uniform of a linen dress and sneakers. My hair lived in a sensible bun, so tiny fingers couldn't yank the strands. I didn't wear makeup. My life in Spain, surrounded by children whose greatest wish was a home of their own, had simplified every one of my priorities and I was glad of it.

I was also glad that I had Demi with me as I tried on various outfits and consulted with the stylist over my hair. I'd embarked on the flight to Bozeman feeling like a new woman and ready to face the mess I'd left behind. The sense of courage and anticipation stayed with me until I approached the turn that would take us down the long driveway to our childhood home.

"Breathe," Demi reached over to lay her soft hand across my arm. "The boys are going to be overjoyed to see you."

I leaned into her touch, needing it to ground me and prepare me to see my brothers face-to-face for the first time in months. Though they had been nothing but supportive after our initial dis-agreement when Jake spilled the news about my new job, I still felt an awkwardness lingering between us.

The rented SUV rolled to a stop in front of our childhood home. The windows shone with a golden, welcoming glow. The eaves had been strung with colorful Christmas lights and I could see the shadowy outline of a Christmas tree in the front window.

It was home. And as I stepped from the car to grab my suitcase, I knew that there was no place I would rather be.

Chapter Twenty-Four

SHADOW'S SHARP, QUICK bark announced our arrival as we opened the door and let ourselves into the house. The border collie danced around us, his tail wagging fiercely. Warmth enveloped our chilled bodies as Demi and I stepped over the threshold. The scent of gingerbread and shortbread cookies filled the air. I inhaled the aroma of cinnamon, vanilla, and nutmeg as Dean strode hastily around the corner. The expression on his face was an instant battle of surprise and joy.

"Surprise," Demi shouted with a mischievous grin. She threw out her hands. "I brought you someone special for Christmas."

"What is this? What are you both doing here? Mom, Vinnie, Knox. Come see this." His long legs ate up the ground and two seconds later, Demi and I were enveloped in his arms. If I'd had any doubt of my welcome home, it was banished in that instant. He crushed us both in a bear hug and a second later, I felt the press of three other bodies against us. Arms were flung everywhere. Shouts of happiness and shock mingled in the air. I smelled my mother's signature floral perfume as she wrapped me in her arms.

"Hi Mom," I whispered against her hair. If she was surprised at my unexpected arrival, I couldn't tell. "It's so good to see you."

"It's so good to have you home," she whispered.

"It's so good to be home."

I was out of breath from the laughing, hugging, and shouting before the six of us untangled ourselves. Still talking and laughing, we moved together toward the kitchen, which had always been the natural heart of our home.

"Look at all of this," Demi exclaimed as she led the way into the warm fragrant room. "Christmas isn't until tomorrow. Right? Sammie, did we get the date wrong?"

I peered over her shoulder and stared in shock at our family kitchen. Food was everywhere. There were platters of turkey and roast beef, covered casserole dishes of mashed potatoes and stuffing, and at least a dozen cakes and pies and plates of cookies scattered across the kitchen surfaces.

"Um, are you guys planning to feed an army? Who cooked all of this?" I said, glancing back at my brothers. Mom clasped her hands together and beamed up at her sons.

Dean, Vincent, and Knox exchanged amused glances.

"Well, I guess we have a confession to make," Vincent said. "Do you remember us talking about Bear Creek Lodge during the summer?"

"Yes, vaguely?" I remembered that the fate of the old lodge had been a hot topic around town over the summer. Mr. and Mrs. Linton, the longtime owners of the ski lodge, were considering retirement. A large real estate corporation had stepped in with an offer to buy it. The sales price would have set the couple up for an easy retirement somewhere warm and tropical. However, the locals had been uneasy at the thought of a corporate firm of that size owning such a significant piece of Cascade Valley history. Bringing in an outside influence could have significantly changed the culture of the community. The hope had been that someone local would take over the lodge, but the last I had heard of the sale, no one had stepped up to claim it.

"Well," Knox shouted, interrupting before Vincent could continue. "We bought it. Just signed the papers yesterday. You are looking at the new owners."

"It's wonderful news, but now this family owns and has to operate a busy ski lodge," Mom interjected. She wagged a finger at her sons, shaking her head in disapproval. But I saw the pride in her eyes. "As if you aren't busy enough with the ranch already."

"Mom, we'll manage." Dean put an arm around her shoulders. "There are less chores during the winter and during the summer, we'll just hire someone to manage it for us. It was important that we keep the property local."

I shook my head, still struggling to comprehend the news. "Let me get this straight. You three are going to run a ski lodge? Doesn't the lodge have an event center too? Don't they host a ton of weddings and other occasions during the year? How are you realistically going to manage all of that with the ranch?"

"You don't seem to have much faith in us, Sammie." Vincent winked at me. He turned to grab one of the platters of turkey from the counter.

"I'm just failing to see how three cowboys are going to set up an elegant, mountain-side wedding. And who is all this food for? You could feed an army."

"Better go upstairs and get ready, ladies." Knox grabbed a platter and disappeared in Vincent's wake. "You arrived just in time for the festivities."

Mom turned to us. I realized then that she was wearing a soft, sparkly, pale pink dress that swirled around her ankles. It set off her dark brown hair and deep, lustrous eyes. A fancy pair of cowgirl boots peeked out from under the hem. "He's right. You girls had better run upstairs and change into something festive. It was last minute, but we decided to host a Christmas Eve party at the lodge tonight. We decided to go all out and invite the entire town."

Her eyes glowed and sparkled. I'd forgotten how much my mother loved a good party. She'd always been ready to throw on a pretty dress and cook up a storm for any occasion. The delicious-smelling food and elegant presentation made more sense now. "Go on. Go on. Doll yourselves up. We leave in fifteen minutes. You two made it just in time to help us set up the buffet."

She scooted us toward the stairs. Out of habit, Demi and I obeyed, grabbing our suitcases, and climbing the creaking wooden staircase to the room we had shared as girls. By the time I reached the top, my nerves were on edge. I felt my heartrate doubling, and I wondered if anyone would believe that I had come down with a sudden stomach bug.

"I don't think that I can do this, Demi," I gasped. "Mom said that they invited the whole town? I just came out here to spend Christmas with you all. What if he is there? I can't see…him. Not yet."

Demi looked at me, her expression sympathetic as she pulled a long-sleeved black dress from her suitcase. "I'm sorry. It's awkward but there is no way anyone is letting you get out of this one. You're just going to have to hold your head up high. Wear that forest-colored dress though. You look ravishing in it."

She flitted to the bathroom down the hall, leaving me to sink on the bed in misery. I would have crawled under the bedframe to hide for the rest of the night if Knox's voice hadn't called periodic time updates up the stairs.

"Ten minutes," he shouted.

The thought of being forced to go and not being dressed properly for the occasion spurred me to jump up and rummage through my suitcase for the dress that Demi had mentioned. It was new. I'd purchased it yesterday in the city, thinking that she was ridiculous for insisting that I buy a dress I would never have an occasion to wear. Now I was glad she had insisted that the forest green midi dress was just my color and style. The dress was cut with a fitted bodice, with long velvet sleeves, and a skirt that flared out at my hips. I added a pair of short-heeled cowgirl boots that were still lingering in the closet, gold earrings, and a quick run of the brush to smooth out my hair. Fortunately, I'd just gone in for a blow out yesterday.

When I stopped racing back and forth, I paused to look in the mirror above our old dresser. I didn't recognize the serious-eyed young woman staring back at me. Parts of her were me, but this woman looked too mature, poised, and confident. It was as if I had barely taken notice of myself the past few months and all that time, I'd been changing in so many ways. Suddenly I felt like I'd finally grown into my height and generous curves. The dress set off the lingering summer highlights in my ginger waves and the shade matched my green eyes just so. I was no ugly duckling-to-swan story, but even I had to admit that the dress was beautiful, and I felt beautiful in it. The feeling was a strange one.

"I guess it's now or never," I muttered to myself as Demi rushed back into the room.

The black, ankle-length dress skimmed my sister's slim frame. She was a couple of inches taller than me and looked every inch the elegant woman I had always longed to be. She stopped short when she caught sight of me. Her eyes widened and she grabbed my hand and urged me to spin in the middle of our room.

"Sis, you're stunning," she exclaimed. I blushed. Demi pulled me close and whispered in my ear. "If Caleb's jaw doesn't drop to the ground when you walk into the room, he's a foolish man."

"Did you know all of this was happening?" I asked her, gesturing to my new dress.

She shrugged. "It's been in the works for a while now. They wanted to surprise you with the news when we Skyped you on Christmas Day. I knew though that there was a possibility we'd be celebrating with a party at some point this week if the deal closed. I thought you would appreciate arriving prepared."

I wasn't sure how to feel as we proceeded downstairs together. "Am I the last to know everything in this family now?"

She glanced back up at me. "Well, you did move halfway around the world. Life moves forward at a rapid pace." She ended the statement with a wink, but it did nothing to soothe my quickly ruffled feelings.

My shoulders fell. "I guess you're right. I've been so preoccupied with moving and then my work. I've been so selfish."

She slid her arm around me as we stepped into the kitchen. Her red lips pressed against my temple. "Don't worry about it. We all go through seasons in life. The important thing is that you're here now and that we're all together. Trust the Lord with the rest of it. Ok?"

I pushed down the lump that suddenly rose in my throat. Now wasn't the moment to let my emotions get the better of me. I had made my choices in good faith, but now I needed to help make tonight the celebration that my family hoped it would be.

The snow had stopped falling by the time we donned coats and stepped outside, crushing my hope that we'd be snowed in and unable to drive to the lodge. The afternoon faded into early evening as we took the thirty-minute drive up the mountain. Our ranch was situated not far from the base of the hill, and I could see why my brothers had jumped on the opportunity to take on the project. As we approached the weathered two-story wooden cabin that served as both event hall and overnight lodge, I marveled at the glow that radiated into the twilight. The massive expanse of windows stretching all the way across the upper floor gave the lodge a striking façade. Golden light spilled over the balcony onto the snowy ground, lighting the surrounding forest.

I helped carry in the food, careful not to slip on an unseen patch of ice. My mother directed us to set each dish over the warmers on the buffet tables that had been arranged along a wall. Round tables covered in white tablecloths dotted the large great room. A fire roared in the old stone fireplace. Someone—my guess would have been Knox—had cut down the largest Christmas tree I'd ever seen and set it in front of the window. Lights twinkled from its branches and an old-fashioned popcorn strand and cranberry garland had been twined around the tree.

The scene was utterly and purely magical. The floor-to-ceiling windows spanned the entire length of the room, wrapping around the corner of the building. Even in the fading light, I could see over the pines and across the valley. The unique architecture had the effect of a massive treehouse, perched on top of the world. I understood why my brothers had been drawn to this place. It would be hard to see the charm lost through modernization. I was glad the lodge had new caretakers who cared about our valley's history.

The locals must have felt the same because I saw a line of bright headlights approaching as their vehicles wound their way up the mountain. Groups began to trickle in. I recognized almost everyone—shop owners from town, fellow ranchers from across the valley, and people from church—their faces bright and happy and welcoming as greetings were exchanged. It was a flurry of activity, a community event that accentuated the festive spirit of the season. But the energy in the lodge did nothing to calm my jumpy nerves as I waited fo the one person I hoped to see.

I felt his presence the instant that he entered the room.

I was chatting with the Pietra's about my hope to visit their home region of northern Italy the coming summer when my skin began to tingle. Lifting my head, I cast my gaze around the great room. Caleb's tall frame caught my eyes immediately. He stood more than a head and shoulders above the tiny, elderly woman clinging to his arm. He and Mrs. Jensen had just emerged at the top of the wide staircase that led to the second story great room.

It was just like him to make sure that she arrived safely. My heart melting at the thought of Caleb's thoughtfulness, I couldn't pull my eyes away from him. He spotted me a moment later. Our eyes met, drawn together like a magnet to metal.

We'd spent weeks together during the warm summer days, then months apart. We'd argued, then laughed, then argued again. Destiny seemed to have pulled us apart yet again.

But the trill that ran up and down my spine the moment I saw him again told me what I needed to know. I'd choose him, even if it meant reassessing what I thought I wanted for my life. Moving to Spain had been the right decision. But leaving this man behind had been a mistake.

I stepped forward, ready to cross the room to go to him. But then I saw Caleb's lips tighten, shifting to a straight line as he stared back at me. The shock at my presence was clear on his face. He hadn't expected to see me tonight. Squaring my shoulders and softening my face, I pleaded with him across the room.

Then I caught sight of the woman clinging to his other arm. An icy chill swept across my heart. I shivered just as Jenna caught my eye. The corners of her lips lifted in a smile. Her hand rose in a wave. The diamond in the ring on her left hand caught the glow of the fireplace and sparkled.

Dinner passed in a blur. When I wasn't on the verge of throwing up, I busied myself on the buffet, serving up fragrant, steaming plates of hot food. Everyone raved about the dinner my family had prepared. I couldn't imagine taking a single bite.

When I saw Caleb and Jenna enter the line for my table, I pretended that the plates needed a refill and hightailed it to the back of the kitchen. I didn't care if it was obvious that I was avoiding them. I wouldn't let myself break down. Not until I was safely on a plane back to Spain. Coming home had been the right thing to do, but my heart was going to end up shattering into a million pieces if I stayed too long.

Once again, it seemed that Cascade Valley was destined to bring me nothing but misery and heartache and loss.

Caleb and Jenna. Jenna and Caleb. I didn't know why I was even surprised. It was natural that they would fit together. She loved horses, loved the ranching life, and more importantly, loved the valley. I just wished that he had told me.

I lingered near the walk-in refrigerator. The room was cold, but I didn't want to rejoin the buffet line until I knew that they were safely through and headed to their table. I couldn't face them both.

I'd been a fool to think that I could waltz back into Cascade Valley and convince Caleb to listen to me. I'd hoped we would get the chance to talk, to clear the air between us. If we cared about each other, surely there was a way to make it work between us?

My mistake. Add it to the list of things I'd gotten wrong ever since I'd graduated and come back home. I couldn't even be angry. I'd let him go. I'd chosen everything but Caleb. And now he had chosen someone other than me.

My brain flicked with self-directed anger. I felt the fire ignite. If this was what Caleb had chosen, then so be it. I took a deep breath and squared my shoulders for the second time that evening. Spinning on my heel, I walked straight for the buffet line and resumed my post. Discretely, I glanced around the room. Dean, Caleb, Jenna, a blonde woman I had never seen before, and several others that I recognized from my brother's group of friends sat at a table on the opposite side of the room. I didn't let myself glance their way again. I may have come home for Christmas, but I wasn't sure that I belonged in this community anymore.

It was only when every guest had been served that I remembered the plates I'd left behind in the kitchen.

Knox passed me with two extra chairs tucked under his arms. I stopped him. "Is Jenna engaged? I see the ring on her finger." I blurted the words out without thinking.

He glanced at me, then over to her. "Yeah, she is. It just happened a couple of months ago, I believe." He started to say more, but Mom called to him to bring the chairs, so he hurried away. I felt as though a bucket of ice had been dumped all over my heart.

Shortly after dinner, the party was in full swing. The locals were taking full advantage of the opportunity to celebrate an impromptu Christmas Eve together. They laughed and talked. Someone cleared a space in the middle of the great room for a dance floor. Those who recognized me approached me with welcoming smiles, full of questions about my life in Europe. I'd been welcomed by everyone I knew. Except for Caleb and Jenna. They had kept their distance. I couldn't say that I blamed them. I'd be leaving soon and there was no point in dredging up the past.

We weren't friends. We weren't enemies. Caleb and I had disintegrated into nothing to each other. I watched Jenna's ring glitter every time it caught the light.

Children danced around the Christmas tree. Someone turned on the music. At some point, the snow had begun to fall again, and a light shower of snowflakes flickered in the glow from the lodge. Everyone was happy. Except for me. My heart ached too much to give myself over to the festive atmosphere.

I found myself fanning my face. The heat from the large rock fireplace was stifling, despite the size of the great room. I wanted a cool breeze across my face and a quiet place to let my feet rest for a moment. I slipped down the staircase toward the lower floor and the access to the outdoors. I'd recenter myself in the darkness of the mountaintop as the quiet snow fell all around me.

I slipped outside and crunched across the path toward the lookout ledge. At least the softly falling snow would shield me from sight of the lodge. The temperature had dropped, making me glad I'd grabbed my wool coat. I clutched it around me now. A deep sigh echoed from within my chest, my exhale frosty in the chilly air as a dozen thoughts swirled in my brain.

Well, Lord, I guess it's just you and me now. But how can I move forward with a joyful heart and no regrets when I'm so disappointed?

"You couldn't ask for a better place to celebrate Christmas Eve." The raspy tones of a familiar voice startled me from my reverie. Spinning on my heel, I watched Caleb approach from the shadows of the path. He stopped a few feet from me, snowflakes falling all around him. The moment felt like déjà vu, a memory of another night under the lofty night sky rising in my brain.

"Or a better night for a celebration," I replied, trying to hide my shock at the sight of him.

"I'm surprised to see you here," he said.

"My sister and I surprised my family just before the party." A sudden boldness washed over me. I lifted my chin. "And it looks like I owe you a congratulations too. I wish you all the happiness in the world, Caleb."

He tilted his head and took two steps closer. The distance between us closed until we were only a foot apart. I peered into his face. My heart ached with the hopeless longing that things could have been different. I'd come home with a heart full of hope. I'd be leaving with disappointment.

"And you?" He ignored my comment. "Are you happy? Is Europe everything you hoped it would be?"

"Yes and no," I admitted, determined to be honest. "I love my work. But tonight, with the entire town gathered to celebrate, it's hard not to miss everything I left behind."

Caleb's deep eyes stared down at me, their color lost in the darkness of the night. "It's good to see you back. How long are you in town?"

"For just a few days." I deliberated before continuing, but my curiosity got the better of me. "How did the last few weeks of summer camp go?"

"Things didn't run as smoothly without you here." Finally, I saw his lips turn up in the smile that I'd been waiting for. "You should stop by the ranch the day after Christmas. I would love to show you what we are planning for next year's camp. You were such a huge part of this year that I think you would like to see what we have planned for next season. If you're not too busy…."

I didn't know what to say. My mouth opened and closed until I finally panicked and stuttered out a *yes*.

"See you after Christmas then." Caleb turned away, then cast a look back at me over his shoulder. "You look beautiful in that dress, but wear something practical. Ok?"

I listened to the crunch of his footsteps as he strode up the path, back toward the sparkling sounds of laughter and music echoing from the lodge.

Chapter Twenty-Five

I HOPED AND prayed all through Christmas Day for a massive snowstorm to hit Cascade Valley, but to no avail. We woke up the day after Christmas to the sun shining and not a snow cloud in the sky. The dustings of snow we'd received earlier sat like piles of frosting on the frozen earth. It was a cold, but beautiful day.

While my family busied themselves around the kitchen and the barnyard, I slipped out and borrowed one of the trucks. I wasn't sure why I had neglected to mention my invitation to Caleb's ranch to my family, but the meeting seemed awkward enough without having to discuss it.

I planned to hold my head up high, congratulate Caleb and Jenna again, and try to maintain my dignity until I could hightail it out of there and return home.

The yard was quiet and empty when I arrived. The ranch hands would still be away celebrating with their own families. But I could see that the double doors of one of the stables stood open in the distance. All the horses had already been moved indoors for the winter season, leaving the pastures to rest until spring. They would be sheltered from the weather and during the worst of the snowstorms, could be exercised in the large arenas built into the centers of each stable.

I jumped from the truck and walked toward the open doorway, grateful that I'd worn old boots and an even older pair of jeans dug from the depths of my former closet. With layers underneath and a flannel coat, I hardly noticed the cold.

"Hello?" I called as I approached the stable.

"In here," Caleb's gruff voice replied from inside the building.

I stepped inside, my eyes taking a moment to adjust to the change in lighting. The familiar smell of horses and hay met my nose. A couple dozen curious equine faces peered over their stall doors at me.

Caleb stepped into the hallway, his right hand holding a pair of reins. He was dressed warmly in jeans and a thick wool coat. "Good, you're finally here. You remember Sandy, don't you?" The elegant mare behind him tossed her head. Caleb looked me up and down, his expression unreadable. "You'll probably want to wear gloves, so that your hands don't freeze. I think there's a pair your size in the tack room."

"Um…." I stepped forward. "I do remember Sandy, but what is happening here?" I looked around, waiting for Jenna to appear. But the stable appeared to hold only Caleb, myself, and two long rows of Arabians tucked safely into their stalls. I saw a second horse standing behind Caleb. He tossed his head, and I recognized Beau's spirited demeanor from the summer. "Is that colt safe to ride?" I eyed him skeptically.

"Beau's progressed marvelously in training," Caleb replied, casting a glance at the horse with a look of pride.

"Well, why are they saddled? What's going on here?" I demanded.

"We're just taking a little ride."

I stared at him. "Caleb, you do remember that I don't ride, correct?"

"Um, you do remember that you rode Sandy just this past summer, right?" he countered. Our eyes locked and I refused to be the first to blink and look away.

"And then I almost broke my ankle." I planted a fist on my hip and squared off at him.

"Well, maybe if you don't make her take off running, that won't happen today." He brushed off my sarcastic tone with a smirk. Then his face grew serious. He stepped closer to me. "Samantha, do you really think I'd ever let anything happen to you? I know you're not comfortable on horseback, but can you trust me today and just try?"

Suddenly, my heart was threatening to thud out of my chest. We were only a foot apart, our eyes locked. My lips parted and I took a deep breath. The sound of his voice as he'd said the words.... "But what about Jenna?"

"What about her?" Caleb stared at me.

"Won't she want to come along with us?"

"I don't know why she would." He maneuvered Sandy around and gestured for me to mount her. "We're not going far. I just want to show you something and it'll be easier if we just ride there. You're safe with me. I promise."

I could have argued. I could have planted my feet and refused to take Sandy's reins. Or I could choose to take my own fears by the reins and refuse to let my anxiety rule my decisions for once. I'd conquered so many of my fears surrounding the horses this past summer. Could I take the next step and ride again? It was the first time that I'd heard Caleb say my name in months. I knew that it couldn't mean anything, but when he spoke to me like that…. I decided to trust him now.

I moved forward, capturing Sandy's reins in my hand. My hand on the saddle horn, left foot in the stirrup, I lifted myself up and swung my free leg over her back before I could think too hard about what I was about to do. Riding just this once wouldn't kill me. And part of me wanted to show Caleb that I wasn't the same woman who had moved to Spain several months ago.

Caleb nodded his approval and quickly mounted his own horse. Without another word, he led us from the stable, stopping only to secure the doors before we moved down the path that led to the sloping hills behind the pastures. Even in winter, his land exuded a raw and delicate beauty. My breath was frosty in the clear winter air. I gripped Sandy's bridle, praying that I could stay calm. I was so focused on not doing anything to spook the horse that I didn't pay attention to the trail.

We rode for awhile on the snow-dusted path, then passed a large grove of pines and suddenly emerged in a wide, open meadow. A creek ran through the middle, its edges already frozen. I pulled in a sharp breath as I looked across the scene. I'd forgotten how beautiful the wilds of Montana were when they lay at rest. The golden grasses were drying, tinged with this week's snow. The frosty hills beyond the meadow rose toward the mountain peaks. The silvery green pines extended their protective boughs over the meadow, like mother hens herding their chicks.

"We're going to extend the summer camp next year." Caleb's voice broke the silence. "We thought this would be a good location for an immersive camping experience. Living off the land, foraging, cooking over a fire, connecting to nature again. It's far enough away from buildings and devices and distractions to make a difference."

"What a wonderful plan," I murmured. With a quick movement, Caleb dismounted. He approached me and held out his hand.

"Walk with me for a minute?"

Nodding, I swung to the ground and waited while he tied the horses to a log that had fallen near the path. Stepping carefully over the wet earth, I walked at his side as he led us a few paces toward the creek.

"Do you recognize this spot?"

I glanced at him. "No, I don't."

"Just up the creek there is exactly where you decided to back yourself right down the embankment and nearly break your ankle." His laughter rumbled into the soft stillness of the winter morning. "If you could have seen your face when you landed in the water. I felt bad, but your expression was priceless."

I peered toward the spot he indicated, recognition suddenly dawning. I felt a flush come over my cheeks at the memory of Caleb scooping me up from the water to carry me back to my horse. I'd never been so embarrassed in my life. I'd yelled at him and protested when he tried to help me. But that day was the day that something had finally shifted between us. I'd finally begun to let go of the resentment I had unfairly carried toward him. My heart constricted with longing for what could have been between us.

I turned away from him to hide my emotions. Now it was too late. Jenna may have been absent at the moment, but I felt her presence looming all around us. I'd returned to Cascade Valley with a lingering hope that if we just saw each other again, there could still be a chance that Caleb would want to work things out between us. But the sight of the ring on her finger had completely crushed that spark.

It was shocking to realize how differently I felt about him compared to less than a year ago. When I'd finally let forgiveness bloom in my heart, everything had changed. I'd found a second chance to rekindle what we had begun to explore long ago. Caleb and I were both strong and willful, but we were kind and passionate too. I knew that I wanted him to be happy. If that meant he found happiness with Jenna…. I walked a few steps forward, pretending to look at the view across the meadow.

I heard the soft fall of footsteps behind me. Then Caleb's warm fingers pressed into my shoulder. "Turn around, Sammie."

I lowered my head, hoping that I could hide the tears threatening to spill onto my cheeks at any second.

"Look at me." His voice rumbled again along my skin.

I couldn't bring myself to obey. Keeping my eyes lowered, I clenched my hands into fists at my sides, trying to control my emotions. He stood in front of me, mere inches separating us. I stared down at his snow dotted boots. Then I felt his finger slide under my chin. Gently, he pressed my face up to meet his gaze.

"Were you even planning to tell me that you were back in town?"

"Yes," I sniffed. "I wanted to talk to you. But then I saw…. You know what, it doesn't even matter. What matters to me is that you're happy, Caleb."

In one swift, fluid movement, Caleb's arms surrounded me. He yanked me forward, crushing my body against his. His arms wrapped around my waist, holding me closer than I'd ever been held before.

"That's the problem." His voice had become thick and graveled. "I'm not happy. I'm miserable. I thought that I could live without you. I thought that I could let you go if God was leading you away, but I can't."

Wildly, I shook my head. "You can't say that to me."

"And why can't I? Look me in the eyes and tell me that you're truly happy right now. That you feel complete."

"I'm not happy." My voice rose and I pushed feebly against his chest. "But that doesn't matter."

"And why not?" Caleb demanded.

I stared at him, my expression incredulous. "Because you're marrying another woman. I shouldn't even be here with you right now."

Shock crossed his face. "And who am I supposed to be marrying? The only woman I want to marry is you."

"Stop it," I shouted. "You're with Jenna. I saw the ring on her finger, Caleb. Now let me go. I'm going home." I pushed against his chest a second time, this time making a stronger effort to escape his arms. I struggled, but Caleb simply tightened his arms around my waist. Suddenly I realized that he was laughing. I stopped and stared at him.

"That's what you thought? Is that why you wouldn't speak to me last night? Jenna is engaged, but she isn't marrying me."

My jaw dropped. "But last night? The ring? You came to the party together."

"Because her fiancé is out of town and didn't want her driving up the mountain alone. I was picking up Mrs. Jensen anyways and asked Jenna if she wanted to catch a ride with me."

I watched his face, trying to discern if he was telling the truth. A sense of hope blossomed in my heart again. My hands came to rest on his shoulders.

Caleb bent his head. The warmth in his whiskey-colored eyes felt like a balm to my soul. "Samantha McCade, if I have to follow you all the way to Europe in order to fit into these wild dreams that God has given you, then I will. I've lived with you in my life, and I've lived without you. But it doesn't feel right to live without you forever. I know you have to finish out your contract." His voice was raw and earnest. "But I love you and I want to make you mine forever."

My hands slipped around his neck, pulling him down to me. We were inches apart and, in that instant, I knew without a shadow of a doubt that this was where I belonged. "I love you, Caleb. I do. I love you." Laughter bubbled from my chest as I repeated the words, the sound echoing across the meadow.

"Is there a way to make this work?" he said. "I want to walk by your side no matter what the future holds."

"I have another eight months in Spain to finish out my contract."

"I can wait."

"Say it again."

"Say what?"

"That you love me."

"I love you, Red." Caleb bent over me. His lips were only a breath away as he whispered the words. "Today, tomorrow, and forever."

"Well, you may love me now." My tone was playful as joy overtook me. "But I know for sure that I loved you first. Way back when I was just a freckle-faced, wild-eyed girl crushing on her brother's best friend."

He rolled his eyes and laughed like I'd known he would. I smiled and stretched to claim the kiss that had been in my dreams for months. Caleb dipped his head and our lips met in a dance that was sweeter than the sparrow-filled song of the valley on that quiet winter morning.

Epilogue

MY HEART FLUTTERED with anticipation as my eyes focused on the familiar black metal gate approaching in the distance. The rental car's sunroof was open and the late summer rays warmed my skin and hair. A soft breeze played across my face, and I smiled every time the diamond ring on my left hand caught the sunlight. The sweet scent of hay had accompanied me for the last few miles. I breathed deeply of the fresh country air. In the distance, the pines thickened as the mountain sloped upward toward the ski lodge. I'd probably find myself taking a drive up there before the end of the day.

I was home. The large suitcase in the back seat contained most of what I owned. Funny how life brings you full circle. I'd spent most of my teenage years and all of college wishing that I could fly the coop and explore the world beyond the confines of Cascade Valley. And I'd done it. I'd followed what I believed was my calling and landed in Spain for an entire year. The country and the people there had welcomed me with open arms. I'd fallen in love with the ministry that I felt God had called me to pursue. But now, new adventures called, and I was ready to embrace the future that my Heavenly Father had planned for me.

After a year, I'd ended my contract with the orphanage in Madrid. Over that time, I'd successfully helped to place many children into new forever homes. I had poured my soul into the work—fundraising, signing new donors, and creating new families. But as I had approached the year anniversary of my move to Spain, I knew that it was time to spread my wings once again and fly home for good. I was still connected to the network of organizations that I'd cultivated a relationship with during my time in Europe, but I was now planning to use my marketing skills to raise funds for a web of orphanages scattered across Europe and into Africa. There were so many needs to be met, and I prayed daily that God would give me the ability to serve Him and others well.

When I'd surprised my family for Christmas last year, a new plan had begun to work its way into my imagination. The day before I had been scheduled to fly back to Spain, I had pulled my brothers aside and presented an idea. If they would wait for me, I asked if they would consider allowing me to take on the job of event coordinator and marketing director for the ski lodge that they had just purchased.

Shock and confusion had flooded their faces at first. But when they realized that I was serious, the scene had burst into happy chaos as they eagerly accepted. In my spare time, I had been overseeing most of the events from Spain for the past eight months, working closely with Malia DeWitt to coordinate the details, but now I was headed home to fully take over my duties.

Reflecting on all the changes the last year had brought, I turned toward the heavy metal gate onto the tree-lined driveway, the familiar pristine white fence flashing by as I drove. Tingles ran through my fingers as I stopped the car. I stepped out and spent the next few minutes wandering the yard, scanning the pastures for a glimpse of the worn-in Stetson I knew so well. Finally, I peeked into one of the white stables, hoping that I would find my handsome, bearded cowboy there.

"Hi, Griff." Instead of Caleb, I spotted the older man just as he was exiting the tack room. I raised my hand to wave. Griff's face broke into an immediate and effusive smile under his gray handlebar mustache.

"Well, if it isn't the prettiest redhead this side of the Tetons," he shouted, striding toward me. "How are you, darlin'? Are you back where you belong for good?"

I accepted his hug. "I'm back," I admitted with a sudden flush of shyness. "Is Caleb around? I was hoping to find him here before I headed home."

"He's over at your folks this afternoon. Helping your brothers fix one of the tractors, I believe."

I glanced around the stable. My eye fell on the open tack room on the other side of the arena. "Would you mind if I saddled up a couple of the horses and took them for a ride?"

Griff's eyes twinkled. "Not at all. Everything around here… well, it's yours."

I flushed again. "Thanks, Griff. I'll see you soon." I called the last words over my shoulder as I walked toward the tack room.

Thirty minutes later, I walked Sandy and Beau through the stable doors and into the bright Montana sunshine. With a deep breath, I kept ahold of Sandy's reins and swung up into Beau's saddle. The fine-boned, lithe horse moved restlessly beneath me. Caleb had kept me updated on the colt's progress over the past eight months. The spirited young animal had become an excellent horse to ride. Caleb had decided that he was too special to sell, and I agreed. The breeze played with Beau's cream-colored mane. His head angled so that his dark, lustrous eye could keep an eye on me. It was the first time that I would be riding him, and I was alone. Yet I didn't feel any fear as I bent over his shoulders to whisper in his ear.

"Are you ready for this, boy?" I murmured to him. His ears swiveled back and forth as he listened carefully. With a light tap of my heels on his side, Beau moved forward. Her reins in my hand, Sandy kept pace contentedly at our side. We trotted down the driveway and when we reached the road, I took the left toward home. The open and empty road stretched before us.

It didn't take long for a new and exciting itch to begin to work its way down my spine. I looked over my shoulder, then swung back to check the road ahead. We were only a couple of miles from my family's ranch and there weren't any cars approaching in either direction.

"Let's do this, Beau." I lowered my body over his withers and tapped the colt's side again. I spurred him into a gallop. He didn't hesitate to leap forward, taking the road with graceful strides, his mane flowing backwards into my face. Good-naturedly, Sandy leaped with us, immediately breaking into her elegant run. The road flashed past, the horses' hooves striking sharply on the asphalt.

"Yes," I yelled, the exhilarating sensation overtaking me as the horses thundered toward home. A smile spread itself wide across my face. I welcomed the open road and the wind whipping through my hair. When I saw the driveway in the distance, I tugged gently on Beau's reins. "Ok, boy. You proved it. You sure can run."

Sandy followed Beau's lead and we slowed, turning into the driveway at a leisurely trot. I approached my childhood home, my heart swelling with happiness at the sight of it again. Instead of stopping at the house, I followed the road toward the hayfields, anticipation building as I peered ahead, searching for the one face I longed to see. I saw him first, his hat pushed back on his forehead as he hung over the engine block of the tractor.

"Try it now," I heard him call and the rumble of the tractor broke into the afternoon.

"Caleb," Dean yelled. I watched my brother's hand lift and point in my direction. Caleb turned, catching sight of me at once. He didn't hesitate, but started immediately for me, his long strides eating up the ground. I slid off Beau and leaned against the horse, feeling the power of his shoulders against me. He nuzzled my pocket, looking for treats, then turned and began to graze when he didn't find any.

I leapt forward when Caleb held out his arms to me. He swept me up, my feet lifting from the ground as he pulled me into a tight embrace. I nuzzled into his collarbone, breathing in his familiar scent, my arms wrapped around his neck.

He kissed my neck, his lips working their way up to my jaw. "What are you doing here? You weren't supposed to get in until Friday."

"I changed my flight last week." I murmured into his shirt. "I couldn't wait another day to see you."

"You should have told me. I would have driven to the airport to get you," he said.

I shook my head. "I wanted to surprise you. And I wanted the time to think."

"About me?"

I blushed. "Yes. About you. About us. About everything the next few years will bring us."

Slowly, Caleb lowered me until my shoes touched the ground again. He grinned at me. "So, the real question is, what are you doing with my horses?"

"Don't you mean our horses?" I cast a glance back at Beau. His white coat glistened in the sunlight.

Caleb nodded, his face still puzzled, clearly waiting for an answer.

I lowered my head, hiding the smile creeping across my face. "I brought the two of them along to ask my fiancé if he would like to take a ride with me?"

He eyed me. "Well, I would. But my fiancée doesn't ride horses. She's scared of them."

I nodded solemnly, leaning closer to him and lowering my voice to a whisper. "Well, I have a secret," I said. "For the past few months in Spain, I've been riding at one of the local stables. I've gotten pretty comfortable on the back of a horse again, but I wanted to surprise you."

"And why would you want to do that?" Caleb asked, his lips twitching under his dark beard.

I gazed at him earnestly, hoping that my eyes conveyed every emotion that I felt. "Because I want to be able to ride up to my husband on our wedding day on his favorite stallion. Wouldn't that be a grand entrance for a horse rancher's bride?" My fingers played with the soft hair at the nape of his neck.

"Very grand. About as grand as our exit will be, when I whisk you away on horseback as the sun sets over the valley that we'll call our home." Caleb's voice became a husky growl as he lowered his head to claim my lips in a dance that I hoped never came to an end.

Acknowledgements

This book would never have been written if it hadn't been for the goodness and grace of God. I've been creating stories since childhood. Yet for years, I struggled to find my voice in writing. I worked and I labored, and I have several nearly completed novels sitting in my drafts that may someday see the light of day. However, it wasn't until I sat with my Bible study one day and decided to finally surrender my pen and talents to be used for the glory of God that Song of the Valley was born.

This book and all the future books in the McCade Family Series are the outward expression of my love for my Lord and Savior, Jesus. Writing Song of the Valley was an incredibly personal endeavor to me. Through it, I worked through some of my own struggles and search for my calling just as Samantha did. I am eternally grateful to the Lord for trusting me with Samantha and Caleb's story. I hope that you find it as thought-provoking, uplifting, and heartwarming as I hoped it would be.

The story behind Caleb's ranch is a special one. Many years ago, my grandmother introduced me to one of her friends—a lovely woman named Sandy. Sandy raised Arabian horses on a beautiful, tree-lined ranch in Central California. I fell head over heels for the special breed. Though Sandy passed on several years ago, I hope that the elegant and spirited Arabians featured in this book are a worthy tribute to such a sweet soul.

Some say that writing is a lonely job. I've never found it so. The support and encouragement I've encountered along this journey has been more than I could have dreamed. My eternal gratitude goes to:

The bookish community which has been a never-ending supply of support and encouragement. An author is really nothing without readers and you are truly some of the best to be found. Who would have thought that a nose-in-her-book introvert like me would find a home in such good company?

To my beta reading and book promotional team who took the time to not only read my manuscript but to also give me such incredible feedback, thank you. Receiving your messages and talking about this book and these characters was pure joy. You are all such dear friends. To Tori, Charisa, Lindsey, Hailey, Natalia, Krystal, Adah, Ashley, Shannon, and Hannah—thank you for generously promoting my book, encouraging me every step of the way, sharing your ideas, and being just as excited about this story as I am.

To my dearest friend, Erica Dansereau—my fellow author, critique partner, sister-in-Christ, book lover, and wise advice-giver— thank you for sharing this exciting journey with me. Thank you for your amazing feedback, for generously reading (and re-reading) this book, for being excited about every novel idea I tell you about, and for always being a strong shoulder to lean upon.

To Gram, my fellow bookworm—I am so blessed to have you for a grandmother. It is because of you that I love the mountains, being outdoors, horses, gardening, dogs, cooking shows, and reading. Watching you take such joy in reading fiction has been a lifelong inspiration for me. I love you.

To Mom and Dad—it is to both of you that I owe a lifetime of thanks for not only gifting me with my first laptop, but also instilling in me a love for the Lord and a deep passion for reading and writing. Thank you for reading countless books aloud to me, Mom. I still remember afternoons spent reading our latest books out loud to each other with a fond heart. You encouraged my love for writing and this book may never have been written without your influence. And thank you both for giving me a strong foundation in the Word of God. I'm so grateful to you and love you both.

And lastly, to my best friend and husband, Joe—you are the inspiration for all the men I have and will ever write. In their character and personalities, I see snippets of you. Your humor, your strength, your wisdom and goodness, and the way you love unconditionally are present in them all. Thank you for being such a great muse. From the moment we met, I knew we were destined to be together. Your endless support as I wrote this book meant the world to me. My heart is yours forever.

Britt Howard has been crafting stories ever since she can remember. She works as a freelance editor for other indie authors and thought it was high time she published her own book. She lives in Idaho with her husband and her dog. This is her debut novel.

www.britthoward.com
www.instagram.com/britthowardauthor